ACCELERANT

Books by Ronie Kendig

Dead Reckoning

Discarded Heroes Series

Nightshade

Digitalis

Wolfsbane

Firethorn

A Breed Apart Series

Trinity

Talon

Beowulf

Quiet Professionals Series

Raptor 6

Hawk

Falcon

Operation Zulu: Redemption

Abiassa's Fire

Embers

Accelerant

The Tox Files

The Warrior's Seal

Conspiracy of Silence

ACCELERANT

ABIASSA'S FIRE

BOOK TWO

RONIE KENDIG

an imprint of
GILEAD PUBLISHING

Accelerant by Ronie Kendig
Published by Enclave, an imprint of Gilead Publishing, Wheaton, IL 60187
www.enclavepublishing.com

ISBN: 978-1-68370-048-7 (print)
ISBN: 978-1-68370-049-4 (eBook)

Accelerant
© 2016 by Ronie Kendig

This is a work of fiction. Names, characters, places, and incidents are products of the author's imagination or are used fictitiously. Any similarity to actual people, organizations, and/or events is purely coincidental.

Cover designed by Kirk DouPonce of DogEared Design
Interior production by Beth Shagene

Printed in the United States of America

For the last nearly dozen years, one person has read
every piece of drivel and genius (ha) I've written.
Stories that never made it past twelve pages.
Stories that made it to 200k words.
She's read them all. She has laughed with me,
sharpened me, and encouraged me. Always.
The truest of friends. In gratitude and appreciation,
I dedicate this second book of the Abiassa's Fire series
to *Shannon "Shanneo" McNear.*

Thank you.

A hundred-thousand times, THANK YOU!

THE PEOPLE
OF ABIASSA'S FIRE

House Celahar
Royal Family of the Nine Kingdoms
seat of power located at Fieri Keep in Zaethien, Seultrie

Zireli Celahar—(Zĭ-rel'-ee) king of the Nine Kingdoms; the "Fire King"

Adrroania Celahar—(Ăd-rō-ăn-ya) queen of the Nine Kingdoms

Kaelyria Celahar—(Kā'-leer-ee-uh) daughter of Zireli and Adrroania

Haegan Celahar—(Hā-gen) son of Zireli and Adrroania

Zaelero Celahar—(Zah-lĕr-ō) Haegan's forebear; first Celahar to become Fire King; fought the Mad Queen and restored the Nine to the ways of Abiassa

Asykth Family
Northlands seat of power at Nivar Hold in Ybienn

Thurig Asykth—(Thoo'-rig) King of the Northlands

Thurig Eriathiel—(Air-ee-uh-thee-el) Queen of the Northlands; wife to Thurig

Thurig as'Tili "Tili"—(Tĭl-ee) eldest son of Thurig

Thurig as'Relig "Relig"—(Rĕh'-lig) second eldest son of Thurig

Thurig as'Osmon "Osmon"—(Aws-man) youngest son of Thurig

Thurig Kiethiel "Thiel"—(Thē-ĕl) youngest and only daughter of Thurig; love interest of Haegan Celahar; one of four companions Haegan joined on the journey to the Great Falls

Klome—(Klōm) stable overseer

Langeria—(Lăn'-gehr-ee-uh) a territory in need of a strong alliance with Ybienn

Gaeord—(Gā-ord) as'Tili's manservant

Tarien—(Tahr'-ee-un) handmaiden

Colonel Aburas—(Ah-boor-ahs) second in command of the Nivari, the Asykthian guard

Baen's Crossing

Jarain—(jah-rān') mayor of Baen's Crossing

Eftu—(eff-too) high marshall of Baen's Crossing

Legier/Legier's Heart

Aeash—a servant

Aselan—(a-seh-lon) cacique of Legier's Heart

Bardin—(bar-den) member of the Legiera

Byrin—(by-rin) right hand of the cacique; brother to Teelh

Cacique—(ka-seek) the leader;

Carilla—(ka-rill-uh) worker in the cantina

Entwila—(en-twill-uh) one of three Ladies of the Heart

Hoeff—(hoff) giant who practices the herbal arts

Ingwait—(ing-wāt) matron of the Ladies of the Heart

Markoo—(mar-koo) member of the Legiera, quiet

Teelh—(teel-uh) member of the Legiera; brother to Byrin

Tnimre—(nim-ree) one of three Ladies of the Heart

Toeff—(toff) giant who works with the cacique

Wegna—(weg-nuh)—an Eilidan reader

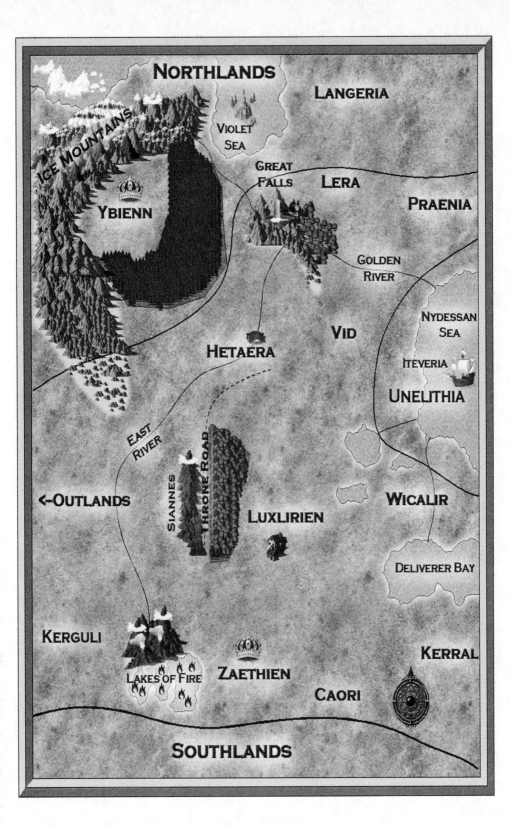

Our doubts are traitors,
and make us lose the good we oft might win,
by fearing to attempt.
— WILLIAM SHAKESPEARE

1

The bloody image of King Zireli fell away as Chima lifted into the ash-riddled air. Smoke and flames streaked into the skies, not only of their own violent will, but wielded at the hand of a master accelerant. Searching. Hunting for Haegan as he fled the hopeless battle that had cost his parents their lives. He squeezed his eyes shut against the devastation, his hands gripping the raqine's dense fur. But no distance or expanse could separate him from the visage of his father in death.

Zireli's son, heir of the Fire King, Haegan glanced back to the smoldering keep. In that heartbeat, he saw the Deliverers standing amid the ruin. Remembered as acid on his tongue the terror they had struck in him. And the furor as they forbade him from killing Poired.

Why? Why would Abiassa stay his hand? Deliverers were her justice embodied. All-powerful. All-knowing.

And they had forbidden him from slaying the beast who had ravaged the kingdoms. Terrorized the people. Murdered his father.

Everything in him wanted to turn back. What justice was there when Abiassa allowed evil to go unchecked? Had not the Council of Nine said Haegan was the Fierian, Her chosen warrior? Was it not his role to mete out her retribution?

He dug his knees into Chima's side, forcing her to angle to the left. To bring her around and head back to the keep.

White-hot fire shot through his wrist. Haegan screamed as the pain blazed across his arm. Glowing. Red. As if an ember itself had embedded itself in his forearm.

You are forbidden, Fierian. This is not yours to do. The Deliverer's reminder scorched his mind as its touch had his wrist.

A throttling-staccato angry purr rippled through Chima. Even with the wind tearing at his ears, Haegan heard her refusal. He turned his face to the sky and let loose a cry of anguish and frustration.

Chastised. Defeated. Humiliated. Haegan, prince of Zaethien and all the Nine, hunched forward over the sleek red neck of the raqine and stared down at the limp body of his sister slung in front of him.

Be well, sister, he thought as they glided away. Months had passed since she had first drawn him, unwitting, into her scheme. *What were you thinking, Kae? What madness seized you?*

Though anger tinged his thoughts, Haegan staved off the desire to blame her, even as behind them Zaethien burned, Zireli's Jujak army routed.

Grinda. Where was he? Where were the Valor Guard?

His heart seized at the thought. His father's own warriors, the fiercest among the armies of Zaethien. Their might would be needed to subdue this enemy. To bring justice to the deaths of the Fire King and his wife.

Mother.

Tears stung Haegan's eyes. But he dashed them away. No time or tear could be spared.

Boom!

The enormous noise drew his attention to what lay below. Trees . . . a dark cloud hung over them.

His heart hiccuped. "No," he whispered, the lone word caught on the icy breeze of the wind as he beheld the giant birds that rose from the forest. Not just a flock. Scores! Such that he could not count nor could he see beyond. Beneath them, flames pursued the frantic creatures.

Poired.

Though he could not hear the taunting laugh now, it filled him. Consumed him. Horror and awe stabbed ice into his spine at the sheer power of the display below, though he was no stranger to the incipient's abilities. On the bridge, with the king's body sprawled between them, Poired had even manipulated Haegan's own thoughts against him. And now—though Poired must be a mile away or more—pockets of fire erupted in once-quiet sections of the forest.

He was driving the birds after them.

Squawking, wings flapping in wild panic, the birds had no pattern. No destination save one: away.

Yet they were coming straight at him and Chima.

His heart raced, watching the sea of black harried wings snapping harder and harder.

A ball of heat blasted past him.

Haegan gave a shout.

Chima banked to the right, hard.

Digging his fingers into her fur, he held on for life and limb. Buried his sister's body between himself and the beast as his world tilted to the side. Nothing but a vast expanse of icy and ash-laden air existed between him and a brutal impact upon the hard earth.

Haegan gritted his teeth, feeling the pull of Primar's gravity against his limbs. They would fall to their deaths. End this battle for the Nine with a great splat upon the fields south of the Throne Road. Poired would win, killing all the Celahars within the span of one hour.

"Chiiiimmmaaa," Haegan ground out, his limbs aching from holding on.

Her body, undulating with power and agility, rippled beneath him. She leveled off, and he breathed a sigh of relief. He reached for a better hold to haul himself back into position.

Pain pierced his shoulder blade—a bird pecking at him. Haegan cried out. "Away with you!"

Another dove at him.

Haegan ducked, but was too late. A stab of the beak took a chunk of his cheek. "Augh!" He covered his head with one arm, not daring to loose his grip on Kaelyria, who lay unmoving, still.

A black blanket descended on him. Wretched birds squawked and flapped. Their wings snapped his own long blond curls in his face. He pressed his chest against his sister's back, only to feel claw and beak drilling into his spine.

Chima banked hard right. Haegan's legs swung around, dangling. Even as he hung off the raqine's side, Kaelyria barely stretched over the neck aright, Haegan noticed the birds were not merely attacking him. They were picking chunks off Chima's back.

Anger rose within him. She was a mighty raqine, breathed into existence by Abiassa Herself. Her kind had faded from the lands, save Chima, Zicri, and Ebose, his brother. It was his task to protect her.

But how?

Haegan could wield—but it was as effective and accurate as lobbing a cannon from within a cyclone. Neither could he predict what he would hit or how hard. But . . . there had to be something he could do.

A volley from Poired shot into the sky.

Six birds went limp, stunned or singed by the heat wake, and plummeted to the earth. Haegan frowned, watching over his shoulder as they fell to their deaths.

Arms trembling, he held on tight, though he tried not to injure the mighty beast. But with each tremor—both of chill and exhaustion—that twitched his muscles, Haegan felt his grip slipping. Fear washed through his body, threatening.

As he struggled to regain a solid seat atop the raqine, he noted his sister sliding. In the opposite direction. Kae! His heart beat faster. She had been so perfectly situated. Why must she start slipping now?

Even as he wondered, Haegan saw Chima's muscles ripple beneath Kaelyria's body.

"No!" Haegan shouted, his voice lost in the wind. "Chima, stop!"

But another twitch and Kaelyria slid free.

As if finally relieved of the burden and glad for it, Chima shook out her spine. Clinging by a fistful of fur, Haegan cried out. His feet dangled over the lands that were but a blur of greens fading to browns. "Augh!" His throat went dry. He swallowed "Chim—"

Haegan lost his grip. He dropped through the air, his only thought for Kaelyria. He swung around, his body tumbling.

A bird pelted him. Angrily pecked and squawked.

But then fell away.

Haegan saw her. Saw his sister—so far. She would hit long before he did. *"Chiiiimmaaaaa!"* he howled, terror gripping him tight.

Something large struck him in the back. He flipped up and over, momentarily flying upward. Until . . .

Oh no.

His body surrendered once more to the exertion of gravity's mighty claw. But when he tipped back toward the earth, he saw a miracle.

Chima dove, spiraling straight toward Kaelyria. She swept over the princess and glided up easily from the dive. When she sailed out in a graceful arc, Kaelyria was gone.

And still I fall. It would serve him just to die this day. When he had so miserably failed his mother. His father. When he had been stopped from killing the man responsible for so much death and destruction.

Haegan surrendered to the call of Death, unable to shake two thoughts: it would have been easier to have the Deliverer end his life on the bridge, and Chima had been right to shake him from her back. He had not deserved to fight with so noble a creature.

In the battle of Fieri Keep, he had done only one thing well: failed.

But then—a pair of black-as-night eyes locked onto him. With two mighty, thunderous flaps of her wings, Chima shot through the air like an arrow. Straight at him.

Thud!

Screaming tore at his ears. A din so consuming, he could not shift away from it. Needles peppered his face and hands. Painful. Numbing. Haegan pulled his head up—and saw nothing but a white-gray blanket. He blinked and groaned.

And immediately, he lifted.

He threw his hands to the side and grabbed on.

To fur.

He glanced around, his wits slowly clearing. Chima. Though he now knew where he was, there was something more. Something . . . What? He could not sort his thoughts. He shook his head.

She gave a low, chortling response, her wings locked as they glided miles over the lands. He flipped over and caught hold, only then realizing he could not feel his fingers. They were blue. Ice clung to the tufts of her fur.

Haegan noticed the sun had vanished. Blue skies had given way to blankets of gray etched in white. Where are we?

Haegan took in their surroundings. Compass points were impossible to determine in the thick blanket of white that covered the sky and terrain.

Storm.

He felt the word as much as thought it. Felt the fear. This wasn't just a passing storm. Like the one that had overtaken his life, this one was here to stay.

"Ch—Chima," Haegan spoke, his teeth chattering against the cold. Every twitch of his muscles hurt. Shivering hurt. Trembling hurt. It was too cold.

But his sister! Forget the pain—had Kaelyria died?

Grief tore at him like the sharp teeth of the wind. Seeking warmth as much as comfort, Haegan lay against Chima's warmed body. Patted her side. "Just get us to Asykth, Chima. Get us back to your home."

But even as he spoke, icy rain broke free from the clouds. Drenched him. Needled him. In moments, he could neither see nor hear. His own thoughts were a chaotic storm as well, tangling and tumbling over one another.

Chima pressed on, her wings flapping harder. Her shoulder muscles pumping fervently as the storm made flight difficult.

As he lay there, Haegan saw the icicles forming on the tips of Chima's feathery wings. Not for the first time did he wish he could wield with as much skill as his father. Warming Chima would be simple for a trained accelerant. But to him, Fierian, destroyer of worlds . . .

He curled his hand away from her fur. Should he try? Could he contain the Flames? *Abiassa, Chima struggles. I know you tasked her protection to me . . .*

But if he did not control it—he would burn her alive.

Kill himself in the process.

Yet, if he did not try . . . they would die regardless.

He stretched his hand toward her wing. Touched the cartilage support. Took a breath for courage. *Please, Abiassa.*

2

Afraid to blow them up—it would not be the first time lives had been lost because of his so-called gift—he hesitated. Ice became snow. The air itself seemed to be snow. So thick, Haegan could not see his own hand. He ducked, burying his face against his arm and her spine. He looked at his fingers, close to his face, as he thought to mutter words he had never been taught, yet that sat on his tongue, ready to usher him into his role as Fierian. A role he rejected. Wanted no part of.

But as he realized his heart was slowing because of the freezing conditions, he feared for Chima. Perhaps just a whisper, then. Eyes on his hand, Haegan parted his lips. *"Imnæh . . . wæit—"*

Though no glow erupted, heat wafted between his lips and knuckles. The beginning of embers. Haegan smiled. Pressed his hand to Chima's back and whispered—slowly—the words. Over and over.

Chima chortle-purred her appreciation.

Haegan slumped against her, focusing on her pleasure. On her warmth. With death pushed back and held at bay—for now—he could not shut out the painful truth of the situation—because of him, Seultrie had been taken. His father killed. Poired had won.

He sagged in defeat. His mind ran rampant through the last few months, terrorized by its own paths. Kaelyria's attempt to stave off the attack of the kingdom's enemy. Blazes, she had meant well, but she had unleashed a terrible burden upon him. One that had been at best unfair, and at worst painfully cruel.

Yet he could not fault her, could not lay at her slippered feet the whole of the blame. Would not. He'd lost her—Kaelyria was dead. That was his fault. Darker, more sinister forces were at work to destroy their family's legacy. To tear down the will and purpose of Abiassa across Primar.

And I am the Fierian, destroyer of the very worlds I seek to protect. Those which have been my home and my hope. His father and grandfather and countless ancestors had been tested in battle and proven mighty enough to rule as the Fire King. They fought against tyranny and many little Poireds through the years.

Now he was the one who would destroy all they fought to protect. All he had been raised to esteem.

An escape must exist. He must find it.

Without warning, Chima dropped altitude. Haegan fisted the fur at her neck, noticing the icy shards that cut into his hands. He winced but knew better than to release her, lest he fall to his death.

He squinted around. White sheets of frost and snow drenched his visual field. The sky blurred as snowflakes stuck to his eyelashes. His cheeks burned from the frigid temperature. Though he pried his hand free, his fingers forbade him from uncurling them. With a groan of pain, he focused on heating them.

Again, Chima descended. What had she seen? Were they at last coming up on Ybienn? The flight had consumed hours that felt more like years, for the fright and freeze that had eaten at his courage and strength.

Haegan stretched to the side, trying to see around Chima's broad skull. For a time he saw nothing, then looming gray shapes resolved about them. He strained forward—

A massive rock flew by.

Haegan jerked back, his heart thundering.

He glanced behind them, only to find the face of a mountain glaring back. He whipped around, startled. Disoriented. Where had Chima taken them?

Thwap. Thwap-thwap. Thwap.

Strange, but to his ears each flap of her powerful wings seemed louder than normal. And . . . multiplied, as if a half-dozen raqine beat the passage between the cliffs. Haegan frowned, glancing to the side, where naught but white greeted him. Echo? It sounded like—

Chima rattled. Banked hard right.

Haegan grabbed tight, his heart in his throat as she dropped several dozen feet. Tucked her wings.

His heart rapid-fired. What was she doing?

They angled left. His hips slid in that direction. Was it terrible of him to be glad he wasn't fighting to maintain his own seating when his sister had fallen? Vanished. His stomach revolted, churning at the thought. "Chima!" he shouted, angry. Vindictive.

She nosedived.

He tangled both hands in her fur, seizing any semblance of a grip. But she canted. His legs lifted up, his body inverted. A strangled cry scaled his throat. His back arced. Air whipped at him.

All at once, with a mighty snap of her wings, she stopped short.

Haegan sailed through the air. The weightlessness terrified him. Though he screamed, the roar of the wind suffocated sound. Terror snatched his ability to think. He fell through grayness and snow. Wind buffeted him. He tumbled over again, his blurring mind reaching for Kaelyria.

Thud!

Pain exploded through his temple. Breath yanked from his lungs. Fire scored his hands and elbow. Gray clapped to darkness and a halo of snow enveloped him.

Haegan blinked. Found himself staring up at the angry storm. Everything hurt.

Wait. Not true. Nothing. He felt absolutely nothing.

He pried himself off the ground, surprised that his hands dropped several inches before finding terra firma. Propped up, he grunted against the half-dozen aches that permeated his muscles. The excruciating pain of frozen fingers. The inability to shiver because he was too cold. Hunched beneath the pain, he glanced around. Saw nothing but grays and darker grays. Even his breath had gone so cold that it failed to plume before his face.

A warbling reached his ears. He jerked around, to the right.

Blazes! Chima towered over him, yet he felt not her warmth nor her presence. How long had he lain in the snow? The wind howled and chewed at his body like a frozen bone. Tensing as he pushed over onto all fours, he squeezed his eyes shut, consumed by the fire of frostbite and self-loathing. His people were fighting for their lives. His parents were dead. Kaelyria—

Haegan hung his head as he knelt on all fours. *Sister . . .*

Chima chortled again.

"Where have you deposited us?" he muttered, climbing to his feet. Aching, burning, fiery—*how could it feel like fire when he was frozen through?*—feet. He started toward her.

His foot hit something and he pitched forward. When he glanced down, his heart jerked. His sister lay in a heap. Blue. "Kae!" Heartsick, he brushed the snow from her face. Pulled her out of the drift. How? How had she gotten here?

A low, threatening rumble emanated from Chima.

Haegan glanced back at the raqine, confused by her growl. The storm had thickened, the drifts heavier still. She had gone from an ebony beast to gray in a few blinks.

Chima must have carried Kae—by some miracle not injuring her with those sharp claws—but the how was unimportant. He must find shelter from the blizzard or they would both die. And Kaelyria would go faster because she was asleep, her body cooler. Strange—so strange for her to be cold. For the warmth of her touch that had given him comfort for so many years to have vanished. "We need shelter!"

He stared stupidly at Chima, who stood with her head tilted as if listening. But not to him. He knew not why he had shouted. She could not speak back, even though she could sense his thoughts or feelings . . . or however the madness worked between a raqine and its bonded.

A keening noise went up from Chima. Through squinted eyes, he watched her rear on her hind quarters, shake her head back and forth, then snap out her wings. The force thrust him against the cleft.

She shot into the elements.

Haegan lunged forward. "No!" He twisted around, staring into the gray barrenness. "Chima!" She couldn't leave them. Not here

Sense me, he begged her silently. *Sense my terror. Come back!*

Only the howling wind answered.

Defeat pushed him around to stare again at his sister's still form. Hands on his head, he searched their surroundings, desperate. Though he could see little, it was enough to know they were stranded. A wall to his back. A sheer drop—how far he could not tell because the elements defied him—before him. His eye caught on a cluster of ragged shapes off to the right. Trees. It would be their only hope. He must make for it, though the mountain soared into the nothingness. Which meant the hike would be brutal. But perhaps . . . perhaps he could find a spot to bury them in forest litter. Leaves and brambles—anything! They must find warmth. He could push heat into hands, but without food or shelter, how long could he keep up the strength required? And heating this area . . . he looked up at the dangerous slope of the mountain where drifts had begun to crest over the rocky outcroppings above. Melting the wrong patch of snow here could start an avalanche.

Too risky. The trees, then.

With a plan in mind, he bent toward Kaelyria.

Snow flew at his face. Not from the sky, but from the ground.

Haegan drew back, surprised. Had he dropped something, disturbing the snow? Annoyance tugged at him as he reached once more toward his sister.

Poof! Thunk!

Wobbling from the impact, an arrow stuck up from the hard-packed earth, mere inches from Kae's shoulder and his hands. Haegan jerked around, scanning the monochromatic scene. He searched the trees, knowing the copse to be the best place to hide and shoot the unsuspecting. He saw no one. But someone had fired that arrow.

But why attack? Why venture into this storm? Was the arrow a warning? Or had they missed? The next one—

Haegan pushed to his feet, shoulders squared as the wind buffeted him. "I mean no harm," he shouted into the swirling air.

When no answer came, he slowly bent toward Kaelyria.

Tsing!

Thud!

A trail of fire licked his shoulder. "Augh!" Haegan clamped a hand over the spot and felt its warmth.

No. Not the warmth of his blood.

Warmth of the embers. The Flames. He clenched his fingers, which were rapidly and painfully thawing under the heat of his power, willing himself to control his anger. Anger had been his weakness. It seemed to amplify his inability to harness the Flames.

He spun and went to a knee beside his sister.

"Touch her not!"

At the command, Haegan yanked toward the voice. What he saw pushed him backward. A half-dozen men. Blurry but towering. Fierce. Shoulders broad. Leathers and furs wrapped their arms and faces. Barely visible, their eyes shone with the same determination glinting in his mind.

"Who are you? What do you want?" Haegan motioned to his sister. "We need shelter."

"Have ye any idea where ye be, thin-blood?" came another voice. To the left. Close.

Haegan stood, frozen through. Aching. Angry. "Though I may not be trained or a wildling, is it not obvious we're in the Ice Mountains?"

"A tongue on this one," another man chuckled.

"And a wicked choice in women. She looks scant ready for the weather."

"Aye. And him—he not be cloaked for Legier."

Legier. He'd heard that before, during the ear-numbing hours spent with his tutor, the aged accelerant, Sir Gwogh. But what had the Histories said of Legier?

"Ye've entered Eilidan lands, boy. To what end?"

Eilidan? Haegan searched the men surrounding him, unsure which had made the demand. "Sh—shelter. That is all. My raqine landed here of its own mistaken will."

"A raqine?" Laughter echoed across the cleft, and finally, Haegan found the eyes of the man who spoke.

He wore a brown-and-white spotted fur around his neck and mouth—which would explain why Haegan didn't know who had spoken at first. "Have ye too much ice in that brain?" His taunting laugh closed the distance that separated them. "Raqine are creatures of myth."

"Perhaps he is touched—bringing a lover to the clefts?" This voice belonged to another and his timbre seemed to bounce off the rock face.

"She is no lover—"

"Kidnapped then." A smaller man stepped forward, angling toward Kaelyria.

"Leave her!" Heat roiled around Haegan's fists, creating a *hiss* as snow melted away beneath him.

Wariness crowded out the mockery of the burly men around him. Haegan turned, slowly eyeing each so his threat was made known. So that they understood he would defend Kae to his own death.

"Who is the beauty, then?"

"Stole her from Ybienn, I bet."

"Nay," another countered. "Too pretty for Ybienn. She be Iteverian. Or a Southlander."

"Nothing good comes from the South." That voice came from behind.

Alarm ran through Haegan. He spun. Felt the eruption of heat in his hands.

"Still him!"

A black blur registered seconds before pain shot through his temple.

3

Warmth cocooned him. Drew him deeper into its embrace. He settled in, burrowed into the softness that whispered surrender. But something tugged at his awareness. A soft keening that demanded his attention. Demanded he surface from the darkness.

No. He wouldn't heed the demand. He pushed it away. Shouldered into the soft warmth.

But it hurt. His feet hurt. A moan sifted through his sleep, lifted him from the dregs of heavy slumber.

"He wakes," a deep voice rumbled.

Pain. Shards of pain stabbed his feet. Prickled his fingers.

No. Sleep. He wanted sleep. Rest. To forget.

So soft. So warm. So . . . quiet. Gone was the storm. Gone was the—

Storm.

"I thought ye said he was awake." The voice was authoritative.

"Aye. That be what Hoeff said. He comes. Then goes." The deep, rumbling voice sounded like the mountain itself. It dug into Haegan's mind and drew him farther out of the darkness.

"Find me when he's coherent."

Haegan forced his eyelids apart. There was a blur of movement to the side. It stopped. The shape grew in front of him. A man. Burly. Lightly bearded, his face slowly came into focus. Dark hair. Dark eyes. "I would have answers, thin-blood."

The room swam. Haegan moaned and toppled back into the darkness.

• • •

Thunder and pain snapped Haegan awake. Sitting up with a start, he froze in the darkness. Somber light from a dozen paces away provided the only illumination. He shifted. The dais on which he lay was strewn with pelts. Gorgeous, thick, and soft, they provided more warmth than he would've thought possible. Almost too much. When he nudged them aside, he noticed his hands. White and brown bandages wrapped his fingers and palms, tied off around his wrists. Had he hurt them?

And his clothes—leather trousers. A jerkin with long sleeves and a brown fur-trimmed collar. Fur boots as well. None were his. Who had dressed him? The thought sent a shiver through his body. Had they seen the mark on his back?

He looked around—rock everywhere. Except across the doorway. That held a gate of heavy wood and iron. He was a prisoner.

Kaelyria!

Haegan jerked around. "Kae?" His vision straining in the dim light, Haegan stood. His head throbbed—a painful reminder of the encounter on the cliff. He stumbled to the wall, bracing himself with bandaged hands.

Strange. No pain. His thoughts tumbled one upon the other. The gate. His hands. His sister.

His head was too heavy for this. He stared beyond his bandaged hands to the darkened passage outside his cell. A dull glow lurked beyond his prison, barely illuminating walls, ceilings, and floors hewn from cold rock.

A quick survey of the room revealed no windows. Just more of the same stone. Even the bed was but a carved platform. He must be underground.

As he took in his new situation, he sensed movement to his right. A shadow lurked. Eyes stared back at him. A mirror?

The form shifted. Haegan yelped. His heart jumped when the form took solid shape—a man! A very large man. Arms as thick as singewood, the stern man gave him a slow nod. And then he growled.

Haegan drew back, his jaw slack.

The mountain of a man inclined his head. With an awkward turn, he angled one shoulder down, gripped the iron gate, and though it seemed he did little more than twitch, the gate groaned open. The huge man ducked through and moved into the passage.

"Wait," Haegan called, reaching toward the emptiness as the gate slammed shut, imprisoning him again. "Why do you hold me here? Am I prisoner for intruding on Eilidan territory?"

The lumbering man stopped. He turned and came back; quiet reserve and strength shone in his eyes. Not normal eyes. Rather than round pupils, he had vertical slits. Sadness tugged at the man. How Haegan could detect that, he wasn't sure. But he did. The man growled again.

No, not a growl. He was talking! But the resonance was too deep, the echo filling the rocky room. Haegan could only gape.

"Ye will grow used to it," said another voice from behind the larger man. "Come." The second man, hands on a leather belt where a dagger lay strapped, stepped back and waited as the giant reopened the gate.

"He rest, Byrin," the mountain rumbled.

Disapproval rippled through Byrin's face. Of normal size, he seemed a warrior, a man of action.

"Ye are heard, Hoeff," Byrin said. His brown eyes met Haegan's gaze, and Haegan had the sudden feeling that those eyes had seen plenty. Those hands had done much. He was not to be trifled with. Byrin snapped his hand at Haegan. "Come."

Haegan swallowed, skating a glance between the two men. "Where?"

"To stand before the Legiera and answer the cacique."

Stilled at the word, an old word, one no longer used in the Nine but rife with tales from the Histories of those who'd taken to the Outlands, Haegan scrambled to make sense of it. *Cacique* was the title used among the Kerguli for their chieftain. How then was it that the title had come to the Ice Mountains?

Haegan took a tentative step forward, unsure what he was to answer for. He peered up at—*what was his name?*—Hoeff as he slid by. The burly man towered over him. His shoulders seemed to span the entire wall. Haegan shifted back, the urge great to shrink. He nearly laughed. There was no urge. Beneath this man, he *did* shrink. Everything seemed small.

A hand tightened around his right forearm.

Haegan flinched and snapped around.

"Ye have already defied Eilidan laws by trespassing on Legier. An act the cacique not be taking lightly." Warning sparked in Byrin's eyes. Though his tone held neither malice nor anger, he clearly was used to obedience. "Move."

Haegan lifted his jaw and surrendered his instinct to argue. To fight. To demand respect.

"Respect is earned, my prince. And often at a high price among those outside these shielded walls," Sir Gwogh had said repeatedly.

They stepped through the passage where darkness gaped. Haegan hesitated, but even as he did, Byrin reached into a small crevice in the wall and drew out what looked like a simple stone. He lifted it to the lone source of light embedded in the rock, and tapped it. A soft snick, then the small stone glowed.

"Mahjuk," Haegan whispered.

The soldier snorted. "Ignorant thin-blood." He hauled him down the passage and around a corner, light haloing them within walls.

"Where is Kaelyria? Why are you holding me here?" Haegan felt a tightness in his chest, not to mention the aching in his feet and legs. Though he moved, each step took a concerted effort. As if he himself had stone for legs now that he was belowground.

Without response, the soldier remained a half step ahead and continued. Wiry hair a shade or two darker than Haegan's rimmed a bearded face. A scar like a deep crevasse severed the beard along his jaw. Taller by an inch or two, Byrin had neither the brawn nor the breadth of the mountain of a man they'd just left.

Tired. Already Haegan's body rebelled against the exertion. What was wrong with him? His feet shuffled. Tangled.

Byrin tugged him onward, making Haegan stumble.

"I beg your mercy," Haegan murmured. "I'm unusually tired."

"Ye slept for three days. How much do ye need, thin-blood?"

Three days? The words pierced the haze that had enveloped him since waking and finding himself in this surreal, subterranean world. "Is rudeness a mark of the Eilidan as well?"

The man spun, the heel of his hand flying toward Haegan's face. It stopped a fraction shy of Haegan's nose. "Speak not of what ye not be knowing, thin-blood."

"Byrin," a voice snapped into the hollow passage.

The soldier's flaring nostrils bespoke his anger. "What?" His hot breath flowed strong against Haegan's cheek, as he looked to the newcomer.

"He waits," the other man said.

Byrin grabbed Haegan's tunic and jerked him forward.

Haegan stumbled into his thick chest.

"Be glad, thin-blood," Byrin hissed in his ear, "that our cacique wants ye alive."

Haegan righted himself, suddenly longing for the droning of an old accelerant, one he'd long grown tired of but endured for lack of any other companionship. He'd spent the last ten years shut away from the rest of his father's court, away from his parents as well. Beside his sister—"I would have answers."

With a thrust, Byrin tossed Haegan through an opening.

Haegan stopped cold, surprised not only at the dense crowd before him but the enormous hall they'd entered. Light stones hung in gleaming braces, throwing the light around the hall. The ceiling rose to a towering center, where a tiered candelabra dangled more light stones. Tapestries of whites, light grays, and ice-blues depicted various scenes—one a man on the mountain. Another a gathering of white-cloaked men in a hall.

No, not *a* hall—*this* hall.

Incredible. Especially the way the light stones played with the tapestry threads. Beautiful! Two men stepped from the throng and caught him by the arms. They drew him forward through the tangle of bodies.

"What is this?" Haegan demanded, his patience thin. "Release me at once!"

As if yielding to his will, both men pitched him forward—to the ground.

On his knees, Haegan slid across the stone—straight toward roaring flames. He was headed straight into a massive pit in the center of the great hall. Heat breathed against his face, hot and hungry.

With a yell, he threw himself backward, his bandaged hands working against him. His knees felt the scorch of the flames as he fought to escape the conflagration. Haegan scrabbled to a stop. Only as a breath shuddered through him did he see the figure among the flames.

Haegan's chest squeezed. Air caught in his throat as he stared up at the man, whose face glowed with the light of the flames. Sitting among it and yet not devoured? What was he? A Deliverer?

Byrin grabbed Haegan's collar, holding him in place like a wild dog. "The thin-blood, Cacique."

Haegan blinked. Only then realizing the cacique sat *behind* the flames. A great pit separated the leader from the men. Leathers and pelts covered the massive seat upon which he sat. Black hair, shot through with gray, curled and framed a stern face. A trim beard traced his jaw and lip. He wore a leather vest, well-oiled but also well used, tied in a crisscross over his chest and about his waist. His arms were bound in greaves, much like the Jujak and Valor Guard.

Haegan should stand. Halfway up, he met resistance. Hands clapped his shoulders, forbidding him from fully finding his feet, and pushed him back down.

"Why are ye on my mountain?" the cacique demanded.

Haegan recalled his countless lessons in diplomacy and propriety. "I believe I have the right to know the name of those who—"

"Ye have no rights here," the cacique growled. "Ye are in Eilidan lands and ye disgrace Legier with yer thin-blood presence."

Haegan started at the tone. "I beg your mercy—"

"Beg as ye like, but ye will not have it."

Surprise held him fast. Diplomacy had failed.

"Why are ye on my mountain?" the cacique repeated

A sharp poke in his back pushed Haegan forward as Byrin barked, "Caciques don't ask a third time, thin-blood."

Haegan swallowed, then looked at the man on the chair. "It was a mistake."

A resounding chorus of *oochak!* rang through the large hall, startling Haegan. He studied the gathered men. They might not wear the glittering finery of the Valor Guard or Jujak, but they were fierce and well muscled, their expressions and faces hardened by life in the mountains.

"Costly mistake," the cacique said. "Not many are willing to admit they entered Eilidan lands."

"It was not of my will, good sir," Haegan managed. "My raqine—"

A guffaw silenced his words. Rumbles of laughter filtered through the room—just as they had on the cleft when he'd mentioned Chima.

"Ye are young," the cacique said. "But not so young as to believe legends and myths. Some call us savages, but even my men"—he motioned to the burly group—"the Legiera know not to believe such fancy."

"Next he'll be tellin' us he's a prince."

"Nay," someone grumbled, "he be not that stupid."

A chill traced Haegan's spine. They mocked him, imprisoned him. Yet there was an edge in their expressions, waiting for him to give a reason to end his life. And he felt the probing glare of the cacique. "Clearly you would be rid of me as willingly as I would be of this"—he glanced around—"place."

The cacique's expression remained stony. His fingers flicked.

A shadow peeled from the wall. Another man as enormous as the mountain in Haegan's cell, except this one wore a dark gray tunic, stomped into the firelight.

"Ye'd think the youngling had never seen a Drigo."

Haegan's mouth went dry. "D—Drigo are myths."

"And yet ye believe in raqine." The cacique's words were as sharp and swift as a blade.

"In truth I have spoken, Cacique. 'Twas naught but a mistake to be on this mountain—"

"Aye, that is truth," the cacique muttered.

"How fair can a system be if such a simple truth is not heard and considered?"

"Then ye—a stranger and a child—would question our elders and laws?"

Haegan inclined his head. "Nay. But I would seek your mercy—"

"Which I have said ye will not have."

"Then to what end is this meeting?" Haegan held out his hands. "To determine my expulsion? My death?" Silence draped the cavernous meeting hall. Unnerving, unbending silence. Haegan shifted, his words echoing in his ears—*my death*. "You mean to kill me then."

Fist to his lips, the cacique squinted across the flames at Haegan. "Tell me, youngling, have ye no concern for the woman ye dumped on Legier?"

"I dumped no one. As for my concern—aye. I asked your man of her but he gave no answer." She was dead and they meant to taunt him. He would not give them fuel.

The cacique considered him. "Curious that ye argue but do not inquire after her health."

Health? Then . . . "She lives?" Hope ignited, taunting and cruel. When there was no response, Haegan took a tentative step, anxious for an answer. "I did not ask because I believed her dead. No one mentioned her and when I inquired of your man"—he nodded to Byrin—"I was ignored."

With stiff, powerful movements, the cacique stood and crossed the room, situating himself in a large, carved chair at the head of a table to Haegan's right. "What is yer name?"

Even as Haegan thought to turn toward the cacique, a sword slid into place against his neck, keeping him still. Why did he seek Haegan's name? Was it of importance?

A man, bent crooked, hurried to the cacique with a silver platter of food and set it on the table. Another delivered a goblet and poured steaming red liquid into it.

The mark—they'd seen it. No, he would expect more fear. Less mocking. Perhaps they had word from the Nine about the fugitive prince . . . He could not recall from his Histories what sort of alliance or non-alliance the Ice Mountains held with the Nine. Would the truth hinder him more?

More? They intend to kill you!

"Very well," the cacique said, his elbows on the table as he lifted a leg of meat as long as his arm. "Since ye lied to us about the circumstances of yer arrival, invaded our territory, and refused to speak and give witness to yer identity, ye will be my prisoner until better judgment finds ye."

"I am called Rigar."

With a glare, the cacique dropped the food. The platter clanked against wood. He shoved the chair back, an ominous groaning of wood on wood as he stood. Fire roared in his eyes as bright as the pit now behind him. "Ye think me a fool, thin-blood?" His sneer darkened his eyes to black. "Ye think because I live in the mountain, I have no skill? That I am ignorant—"

"N—no." Haegan stumbled back, but hands propped him in place. Refused him escape.

The cacique stalked toward him, his long white fur cloak swinging.

"Ye dare bark orders at me. Ye dare threaten my people when ye dump a dead girl at my door."

"Dead." Haegan couldn't breathe. Kaelyria— "But . . ." He had hoped the cacique's mention of her health meant she had survived. Questions assailed him. How far had she fallen before Chima caught her? Had she struck something? What if she'd hit her head when Chima landed? Or simply frozen through?

Frantic. Desperate. If she had died . . . then in truth, he was the only one left to save the Nine.

As Fierian.

No. No, he would find another way. He could not accept that mantle. He would not destroy. There had been too much destruction already. Still, the imperative remained—he must return. "I demand—"

Like a flash, the cacique was there, stabbed a palm at Haegan. Fury lit the leader's eyes. *"Demand?"* As palm met nose, Haegan's head snapped back. He crumpled.

Pain seared his neck and face. Warmth slid across his upper lip and down his chin. Haegan gathered his wits, reeling over the attack.

"Ye will not make demands of the Legiera, thin-blood!"

Haegan wiped the blood away, grinding his teeth. "I have done nothing to deserve this abuse or imprisonment. Release me and her body, so I may return to my home and give her a proper burial."

"Seems he might be too big for those pelts," someone grumbled.

"Ye hold no authority here, youngling." The cacique flicked a finger at Haegan. "Or would ye test my icehounds?"

A low growl climbed the walls and struck Haegan with a terrible chill. Icehounds. Haegan refused the incredible urge to search the hall for the vicious beasts.

Silvery-blue, the hounds slunk through the throng with teeth bared, snarling. They were beautiful. Terrifying.

"Toeff, return him to his cell," the cacique said.

What was to keep them from locking him away forever? "You can't do this!" As the enormous man again morphed out of the shadows—*how did he do that when he was so impossibly large?*—Haegan locked onto the leader. "Answer one question. Please."

Expectation hung in the room as the cacique waited, his demeanor no more accepting than before.

Haegan tempered his anger. "What have you done with her body?"

Brown eyes held his. "The dead are important to ye, then?"

"Not the dead. Her."

"Yer mate?"

Haegan gritted his jaw. Would a confession reveal too much? What harm would it be to answer? Nothing political could be gained.

The cacique, bearded and brawny, considered him for a moment with keen, probing eyes. "Remove him," he instructed the giant.

When Toeff moved in, Haegan started. "I must return to Asykth!" Rally the warriors. Talk with his mentor and seek the advice of those he trusted most. *And what of Thiel?*

The cacique was on his feet. "Ye are of Asykth?" That intense gaze once more tracing every inch of Haegan's body.

Haegan hesitated, sensing the challenge. Sensing the danger he'd stepped into. And remembering far too late how the men of the mountain and the Asykthians had long been in civil dispute. Their hatred for each other nearly as strong as his father's for Thurig the Formidable, King of Asykth.

Disgust replaced anger. "All the more reason to hold ye captive. Secure him."

4

Never had he seen such beauty and such danger. Aselan, cacique of the ice-dwelling Eilidan and protector of Legier, stood at the entrance to the chamber in which the healers had lain the woman. When they'd nestled her in the pelts, her skin had been as pale as the fur of the icehounds at his side.

Hoeff, twin to Toeff, tended the desperately ill woman. Despite Hoeff's enormous size, his actions were gentle and caring. It mirrored the soul of the giants, the heart to serve, heal, and aid. Mesmerizing how the giant's massive hand somehow seemed soft against the silkiness of her alabaster hair over the snow-colored pelts. White on white—camouflaged. Just as his battle pelts protected Aselan when he left the safety of the Legier's Heart.

Hoeff lifted a white linen packet from an etched alcove in the stone and laid the poultice, a salve most likely, on her throat. With almost a reverence, he drew the Caorian wolf pelt to her chin.

Now that she was properly covered, Aselan dared cross the threshold. When the Legiera lifted her from the snow, she'd looked old enough to have produced a long line of heirs. But now, with color seeping back into her face . . . she was young. Much younger than he—perhaps not more than twenty. To his nearly thirty, she was but a child. It would bode poorly for him as cacique if she died. The Council of Ladies would take it as a sign of his failing leadership.

"Will she live?" he finally asked.

Hoeff stopped. Skated a glance over his shoulder. With a sigh that sounded more like a groan, he lifted a shoulder. "She not breathe stench of Death now." He creaked around and stared down at her. Shook his head. "But healing will be long. Slow. If happen at all." Another shake.

Aselan had never seen Hoeff so disturbed. And neither had he seen the gifted healer unable to draw the bite of the mountain from a body. Asykthians scoffed at the idea that Drigo had other-worldly powers, but the Eilidan had seen them work miracles time and again. Though Toeff and Hoeff would be the first to say it was not *their* gifts, but what Abiassa allowed.

"Why slow?" *Was it the Lady Herself slowing this healing?*

"Hoeff not know." The healer reached his long arm to the medicinal table where ground herbs sat beside a shallow bowl. He dumped the mashed contents into a pot of water, steam rising from the spout. "Though she badly injured, most of what ail her—" Again, he shook his head, long tight locks waving. "Hoeff not find source."

"Keep looking. She must live." Warm, soft fur brushed his hand, and he rubbed Sikir's ears, grateful for the ever-present company of the hounds.

"Yes, Master."

Hesitation in Hoeff's words held Aselan at the door. "What concerns ye?"

"The source—Hoeff not think it . . . worldly."

"What else is there?"

"Master know." Hoeff lifted a small towel and dipped it into the poultice-laden water. He drew it up, steam swirling around his large hands, and wrung it. Gently, but without the consideration most men would provide, Hoeff brushed aside the girl's blonde locks and tugged aside the collar of her bodice.

Aselan turned away—but not before catching sight of the pendant resting in the hollow of her throat. *By the Flames!* He jerked his gaze down, his heart pounding. Sikir and Duamauri growled at his changed heart rate.

"Master?" Hoeff had seen the pendant, too. His large, bulging eyes came to Aselan's.

"How have ye not seen this before now?"

Hoeff shrugged. "The Ladies dress her, but Hoeff keep her covered, as required in the first few days."

The Ladies. "Say nothing to anyone. I must speak with the Legiera," Aselan said quickly. Like shifting icebergs, the pieces of the last two days were slipping and colliding. Holding her here—if it was *her*—would be cause for war.

"But she—"

"I know!"

"If they—"

"I *know*!" Aselan smoothed a hand over his beard, thinking. "I know, Hoeff." He fought off the panic that threatened to unseat the confidence he'd rebuilt over the last few years. Confidence that he could be a leader. But this—this *girl* could ruin everything! "Don't let anyone see her." He started for the passage, desperate to escape the daunting truth, desperate to wash his hands of this nightmare. Then he stopped. If she died . . . if she died under his care—"Can ye heal her?"

Hoeff gave a shrug, grief stricken. "Hoeff not know, Master." Tears welled in the giant's eyes. Not healing someone was akin to killing them in Drigo honor.

"Hiel-touck." Even muttering the oath did little to appease Aselan's panic. Striding through the passage, he felt that panic slip into anger. By the time he reached the fifth level, the heat of fury coursed through his veins. With the icehounds trotting in front of him and intent to sound the alarm, he rounded the last corner.

Ingwait stood there, her wrinkles all the more prominent with the head-to-toe gray garb. A simple braided silver circlet crested her forehead, where sprigs of hair sprung out defiantly. Head and neck bound in a white pelt, she held her hands before her. Confidence wreathed her.

It made sense now. *"Ye."*

She gave a slow nod.

"Ye knew and allowed me to shelter her here?"

"As the Drigo would tell ye, Abiassa brought her to the mountain."

"Abia—" Aselan's anger vaulted. "This wasn't the Lady. This was a raqine lost in the storm."

Ingwait's laugh rippled through the cavernous platform. Her green eyes sparked. "Have ye ever seen a raqine get lost?"

"Ye realize the war brought to us now?"

"A war for yer heart, Thurig As'Elan, one I have long told ye would come, even before Doskari chose ye."

At the mention of his late wife, he shouldered into her. "Those people—her people, the Southlanders—they will obliterate this mountain and all in it if they learn she is kept here. They are *accelerants*, Ingwait!" Through gritted teeth, he spoke with vehemence. "I will not allow my people to die because ye want to fulfill yer own prophecy."

"*My* prophecy?" Her voice went shrill. "Ye forget, Aselan, who put ye on the pelted throne and set ye as guardian over Legier."

"Cacique," a voice came from behind.

Aselan shifted to Byrin, who stood with his brother, Teelh. The two must have seen the rage in his expression; their eyes widened, Byrin asking without words what had happened. Teeth clenched, Aselan gave Ingwait one more glare before storming toward them. "Call the Legiera."

Immediately, Byrin turned to the void that gaped over the high platform, cupped his hands over his mouth and made a loud, long trilling noise. It echoed through the community, to every level and cave.

Aselan stormed to the warrior's hall and shoved through the double-hung doors. Even as he reached the pelt throne, he noted that his men were gathering. He swiped a hand over his mouth. Planted his hands on his leather belt and stared into the ever-roaring of the pit. Flames danced and popped, crackling like his nerves.

"We're here."

He faced the men, nodding as Teelh secured the doors with a heavy beam. "We have a problem that for now can go no farther than this room." He heaved a breath he did not want to breathe. Carried thoughts he'd rather gouge from his brain. "The girl is heir to the Fire Throne."

Dead silence gaped. Then complaints shot up. Faces blanched and anger quickly replaced surprise.

"And the Servant of the Lady knows," Byrin muttered.

More shouts and groans.

"That old woman knows everything."

"Kill the girl!"

"Is the boy her brother?"

"Can't be. The prince be paralyzed. Everyone be knowin' that."

"Brother or guardian, they mean naught but trouble for Legier's Heart."

"I say bury them both—nobody will be the wiser."

Disappointment pulled at Aselan. "*We* will be the wiser," he barked, his tone echoing the growling of Duamauri and Sikir. He paced the floor. "I called this meeting to determine our options. If word of their presence reaches the Fire King, we will be dead."

"Speaking of that fire-breathing dragon, how did he not stop the boy from stealing his daughter?"

"Yeh—he would've singed him alive."

"Unless the princess sneaked off with the boy. Is he her lover?"

"Send them down the mountain," Byrin finally said. "Send them down and make sure they find their way to Ybienn."

"Yer brain is frozen," Markoo muttered. "That storm is mighty angry. Tellers are saying we will be buried for another month as Legier rages."

Aselan lowered himself to the pelted throne. Seated on the edge, he bent forward and rested his elbows on his knees. He roughed his hands over his face and beard. Legier himself seemed set against them.

"Cacique." Teelh squared his shoulders. "I'll take them. Deliver them safely to Asykth. 'Tis our only hope to avoid war."

Aselan wasn't surprised. Teelh was one of his most loyal men and the best tracker, who could find his way out of a thousand forests blind. Which was exactly why Aselan couldn't allow him to go. "Too risky—if we lose ye—"

"Ye doubt me?"

Aselan snorted. "Nay." But then he sobered. "Nor do I doubt Legier's anger at this hour."

"Why? What have we done?"

"I know not, Teelh. I know not."

"If she be the heir to the Fire Throne and it be found we have her, there will be naught but fire and ashes left of us." Byrin stepped forward, his position as Aselan's second affording him the right to stand at his side. "We must send them down."

"Ye would risk yer own brother's life?" Aselan asked.

"Me own brother rather than the thousands of Eilidan within the Heart."

"Oochak," Teelh responded with the warrior chant.

Torment gripped Aselan. The storm would kill all three and nobody would know until first thaw. "I need another option."

"But—"

"If Teelh dies going down, the heir and that boy die, too. If that happens, we guarantee war." Aselan sighed and his gaze drifted, seemingly of its own accord, to the second table, where Markoo sat, stein in one hand and stone light in the other, staring at the table through a tightly knit brow.

"Markoo?" Aselan had long considered him as a brother, not simply because their ages were nearly well matched, but because Markoo held nothing back.

Long brown curls shielded grey-green eyes that lifted to meet Aselan's.

"Have ye thoughts?" Many times the younger man had presented scenarios that had been more . . . pacifist. And he had borne the brunt among the men, who called him weak and lacking. Still, Markoo sat resolute in his more peaceful thoughts. Aselan would not have him change.

A wary gaze took in the room as Markoo considered the men, his stein, then slowly came back to Aselan. So, he *did* have an option. One that would not carry well with the men.

"Ye have no fear to speak yer mind here," Aselan said, a true statement but also a remonstration against any who might mock or attempt to silence him.

Markoo wet his lips then swiped his thumb along the stein. "Befriend the boy."

Scoffs scraped the room.

"Quiet," Aselan warned. "Go on."

Metal scuffed wood as Markoo pushed the stein aside. "The storm forbids anyone into its bosom, even the Fire King. Befriend the boy while he must remain, find out who he is and why he's with the princess." He motioned to the hall. "We all saw he was unwilling to speak at certain times—yet willing to make demands where he had earlier been terrified." Markoo lifted his chin. "That lends that there are hidden truths, and perhaps things we can use to advantage."

"How?" Byrin barked.

"He sees himself as her protector."

"A failed one—she nearly died," Byrin growled.

"But still her protector." Markoo shrugged. "If we show our intentions are not to harm him or befoul her, as her protector, he can be a voice of reason when the storm lets up and they return to the Lowlanders. Perhaps even stay a rage by the Fire King. And speak truth to the Asykthians that we did no harm."

Well-spoken. Yet . . . "What if he's not her protector but her lover?"

"I assure you that is not the case."

That the boy dared enter and speak brought Aselan to his feet. He faced the side entrance where the boy now stood. "Ye tread dangerously, thin-blood, entering the Hall of the Legiera." Aselan's gaze slid to the giant behind the boy.

Burly Toeff shrugged, a slight movement barely discernible with the thick-skinned, short-necked build of the giants. "He would answer the question."

5

Thurig Kiethiel gripped the hilt of the sword in both hands, noting the way her slick palms loosened her grip, endangered her ability to spar. She ignored the bead of sweat that dropped into her eye. Hair clumped and matted to her face, she tried to slow her breathing. Focus on her goal—disarm her brother as'Tili, leader of her father's loyal guard, the Nivari.

A glint barreled at her.

Sucking in a breath, she parried. Stepped sideways, but not before feeling the sizzle of Tili's blade in the air. Steel clashed against steel, jarring up her arms and into her shoulders. She growled and shot daggers from her eyes at her brother. "Mother will have yer head if ye harm me."

"Then ye must be faster, dear sister." He gloated. Danced to the side, turned and drove his sword at her again, hard. "For I am to serve our brother at his wedding."

"Knock 'im in that curly head of 'is, Thiel!" Laertes shouted from the side. "Yer leagues faster than some knobby-kneed prince what's gots fancy boots and stockings of a girl."

The fury that spread over Tili's face gave her guilty pleasure. "Stockings." He lowered his chin and brow. "Ye would have a boy do yer fighting?" He straightened, shrugged—tipping his blade narrowly close to Laertes, who gave a shout and jumped back. "But then, maybe girls aren't meant to—"

Thiel lunged.

And Tili was there, sharp and focused as a raqine in battle. The blades shrieked as he drew his along hers until he managed to work her sweaty grip against her. Her sword clanked to the floor and slid across the marble.

Only as she stared in disbelief at her retreating weapon did she feel the sting of his blade against her cheek. She touched a finger to it and drew it back. Bloody. She gaped angrily at him.

"Be it my fault that ye are easily distracted and overcome?"

She slapped the sweaty hair from her eyes and growled. "Give me a horse and I will pound ye into the ground!"

"A steed? What, would ye have dreads and ride half-clothed as well?"

Anger stamped through her. He mocked Cadeif, the warrior who had interdicted and saved her life when she was but fourteen, claimed her among his people to protect her. "Had ye met an Ematahri in battle, ye would not be so fast to mock them."

"I mock nothing, dear sister." Tili sauntered over to her weapon and used the tip of his blade to hoist it from the floor, tossing it up and catching the hilt. "I have great respect for the savages."

"Those *savages* saved my life! Taught me how to fight from a horse."

"That is well—in the Outlands or in their forests." He extended her sword over his arm to her. "But here, where winter is more brutal than those warriors?" He shrugged. "Horses are not always an option, Kiethiel."

She grabbed her sword, noting that the others—still-silent Praegur, and Tokar—watched from the side, their sparring partners enthralled with the spat. "Then what? Winter will defeat me as well? I am not capable enough to live among the Nivari?"

Confidence, which held him sure and bold, slid away. A mask of confusion and surprise gave chase. "Nay, sister." He motioned around, holding out his arms. "That is why we train. Nivari are strong fighters. With blade, with dagger, with hand. It must be this way so we may war on whatever terrain the battle arises."

Cadeif had pushed her hard to fight from bareback. To not be on the ground, which was weak. But where was he now? And Haegan?

"Then perhaps I no longer belong here." She pivoted, the petulance of her words pushing her from the training room. What madness had driven her to such foolishness? She had better sense than that!

"Thiel."

At Tili's call, she tucked her head and hurried down the long hall with its great height and chandeliers, unwilling to be cajoled. Patronized.

"Thiel, wait!"

She pivoted, slipping through a side passage, praying she was quick enough to evade her brother. She broke into a run, sprinting past the servants and narrow corridors that ran along the nooks and crannies of Nivar Hold. Passages she had used as a child to escape her embroidery and other futile "women's" work. She would have had a sword, even then!

A brown door caught her attention. Hesitating, she glanced at the floor. Noticed no glow from the other side. She dashed inside the room, quickly secured the door and rushed across the floor to the chair facing the great pit. She dropped against the thick fabric and pulled her knees to her chest. Curled there, with no fire in the massive fireplace, she quickly noticed the chill of the great library. Hugging her knees did nothing to chase away the shivers, but she drew them tighter still when she heard the handle creak. She sucked in a breath and stilled her breathing.

Light spilled across the wall-to-wall books. The illumination seemed to reach toward her. She cringed, resisting the urge to shield herself from the light. But it swept around the chair, casting a shadow on the wall.

Then vanished. The latch secured.

With a sigh of relief, she relaxed, her temple against the wing of the great chair. The cooler air here aggravated the cut on her cheek. She touched it, found the blood had clotted and closed the wound. He may have given her a scar. Father would tan his hide for that. Haegan . . .

She almost laughed. Haegan would've had one of those light-exploding moments and wiped out the entire room.

A pang shot through her chest. She missed him. Worried for him. He had left five days ago and there had been no word. What if Poired captured him? How she longed for answers. And a fire.

Breathing against her fingers lessened the ache of the lower temperature, but still cold tremored through her limbs. She gritted her teeth against it, wondering if it was cold wherever Haegan was.

"There is no word of that among the spies," her father had said when she implored him to send a search party to rescue him. But there had been something in his eyes that stopped her from probing for more answers.

Which left her—Thiel's teeth chattered—believing Haegan lost in some barren wasteland. Injured. Probably fighting off wolves and wilderbeasts.

Or dead.

He could be dead.

He is the Fierian, Kiethiel. His purpose is not yet fulfilled, so he cannot be dead.

Then where was he?

She would not forget the kiss. He had been talking and purposeful on the night of her gala, when without warning he bent and kissed her. So tender. So wonderful. She blushed at the thought, grateful for the solitude and darkness to hide such an unwarrior-like act.

But she loved him. Her brother had guessed as much when she cried like a fool the night Haegan was told of his identity and the prophecy. She cried because she saw the hurt and fear in his eyes. It was not difficult to recognize them since they mirrored her own. And she hated herself for it. She would be stronger for him. She must be.

A cozy warmth wrapped around her, seducing her into a near sleep.

Warm. So very warm.

Thiel frowned. Lifted her hand and curled her fingers. No ache. How . . . ? She glanced to the side.

Moonslight caught a crystal votive and reflected a face.

With a yelp, Thiel lurched from the chair, right foot back, ready to fight.

Amber glowed against the fire pit. "Mercy, Kiethiel."

Mouth dry, she breathed his name, "Drracien." Shaking off the alarm served to anger her. She slapped his shoulder. "Blazes, ye gave me the fright!"

He held out his hands, placating. "I hope—"

"Did ye follow me? What do ye want?"

He smirked. "Forgive me, my lady, but"—he motioned to the chair—"I believe I was here first."

She looked to the pair of high wing-backed chairs. Truth. When she entered, she had been intent on escape and not inspected her surroundings. *Great way to get killed.*

"You seemed to need the quiet solitude. I said nothing for fear of intruding."

"Or chasing me away."

Drracien inclined his head, black hair dipping over his dark eyes. He had never been subtle about his attraction to her. In truth, to all females.

"Ye . . ." Another glimpse at the chair she'd been in. "Ye warmed me."

He pursed his lips and offered a shrug. "You seemed cold." He splayed his fingers and pushed them toward the ceiling.

"No!" She caught his hand. "Please. If ye light it, the others . . ."

That smirk was back. "But, my lady, we are alone in the dark."

Heat fanned through her cheeks. "No," she said, looking toward the main door that led to the residence hall. "We're not. There are many in the house this dark eve." She reached for the brass handle.

"You are worried about him."

Thiel hesitated before the beveled glass. "If ye intend to cajole me—"

"Only to reassure you."

"I know." She huffed. "He's the Fierian. He has to be alive."

"Yes . . ."

Thiel frowned and faced him, noticing a hesitation. "What?"

Drracien swallowed and flashed his palms out with a shake of his head. "It might sound crazy, but I can feel him." He stared at his hands. "The Flames he stole from the others, from me . . . I can feel it, but the full strength is out of reach."

Anger bit through her resolve to leave. "Stole from ye?"

"At the Falls." Drracien shrugged. "I can't explain what happened when he jumped in, but I was . . . lessened. I believe every accelerant experienced it."

"What madness do ye speak of?"

"It makes sense, for him to have such extraordinary power, for his purpose, there is only one accelerant needed."

"But many are needed to fight Poired." A streak of panic lit through Thiel. "Are ye saying—"

"No." He walked to the fireplace where a small blaze now glowed against the stones. "I don't know." He rubbed his forehead. "It's why I was here, trying to think through it. If Gwogh had but stayed to answer our questions, if I still had access to the libraries of the Citadel, I could search out the answers. Determine what's happening. How Haegan's rise to power—"

"Rise to power?" Thiel's voice pitched, echoing in the library that consisted mostly of glass and books.

Drracien gaped at her as if she'd stepped from the Great Falls again.

"Of course." It made sense. Haegan *had* to rise to power. How else would he bring about the prophecy of razing the lands and cleansing it of Poired and his army? It just sounded so strange. Yet . . . he was a prince. "'Tis just . . ."

"So hard to get used to, isn't it? To you, he's the bumbling boy who nearly got us killed a half-dozen times."

She glanced at her hands, the green stone of Nivar tangled in her family's ring. It captured the light from the pit. "He was only supposed to step into the waters and heal his sister. Go home. Live happily ever after." She pried her gaze from the ring and looked at Drracien.

Flames danced and popped, light and shadows playing over his handsome face. He was an enigma. Quietly rebellious. Fiercely loyal. Their relationship had started with threats and animosity. Now he seemed content here. "He believed in ye, right from the beginning. Why have ye not gone after him?"

Something roiled through Drracien's expression as he held his hands toward the pit, savoring the heat. But then he laughed. "Step outside and I would explain."

She glanced at the darkened window. The weather had steadily worsened in the days since Haegan's departure, the brief respite from winter now ended in a swirling snowstorm.

"In earnest, ye can sense him?" She swallowed, afraid to hope. When he didn't answer, she stared up into his dark eyes. A strange nausea swirled through her that she could not sort.

"In earnest."

A shuddering breath rippled through her. Not from the chill in the library. But from relief. "Then he lives."

6

"I am Haegan, son of Zireli, king of Zaethien and the Nine Kingdoms, supreme commander of the Nine armies." He stood with strength he did not feel, inwardly or outwardly. "The woman who died on the cliff was my sister, Kaelyria, heir to the Fire Throne and the Nine."

The men before him exchanged slow, meaningful glances and made Haegan shift, all too aware that he stood alone in this world now. None of his family remained.

"Ye have brought a heap of trouble on me and mine, coming here with the princess." The cacique walked a wide berth around the fire, his face etched in anger. "Ye bring war to us."

The words seared Haegan's heart and conscience. "I . . . I tried to save her. I meant to return to—"

"Tell me why I should not throw ye out into the storm, let ye fight yer way back to yer double-minded weaklings."

Haegan had no doubt the cacique would make good on his threat. "Because I can testify that my sister's death was no fault of yours," Haegan said, grateful once more for the mental sparring Sir Gwogh had engaged him in many times. He sighed, allowing his shoulders to slump just a little. "In truth, my death would pass quietly in the rage of this storm. There will be no retribution. For there is no one to wage it."

The cacique hesitated—his icehounds came up—then glanced to the man on his right. He faced Haegan. "Speak plainly."

Haegan swallowed. Shoved back the cruel images from the mouth of

Fieri Keep. "The Fire King is dead. As is the queen. I am the last of the Celahars."

Surprise and shock rippled through the enormous room. The men grouped up, muttering. One shouted, "He means to entrap ye, trick ye into believing this, then he'll bring the Jujak to the Ice Mountain."

"Nay, I have conjured no trap," Haegan asserted, sending out a firm, reassuring look. "If the Jujak come, it will be but for a singular purpose—to capture me." He tried to steady his ramming heart.

"The Legiera would have yer story, Prince." The cacique lowered himself to his pelt throne and leaned back, the icehounds reclining at his feet. "Start with how ye're no longer paralyzed."

At least they had not killed him yet, but Haegan wondered at the wisdom of sharing so openly among people his father had nearly considered enemies. *Abiassa, guide me . . .*

But he began. "Poired Dyrth and the armies of Sirdar encroached on our lands, threatening our people, overtaking our neighbors. Fear was rampant and many believed Seultrie would fall. Though my father-king traveled with his Valor Guard and the Jujak to stave off the enemy's advance, we were losing. In an act of desperation, my sister made a pact with an accelerant to transfer her gifting to me."

"Are we supposed to believe this?" Byrin groused from a chair to the right of the great throne.

"Let us hear him out," the cacique said, holding up a hand. "But I warn ye, thin-blood, already yer story reeks of rot."

"I speak only the truth," Haegan said, but he felt the issued warning. "What my sister did not know is that the accelerant was disgraced, removed from the Brotherhood. What his motives were, I know not, nor did she. Through him she effected a transference, a long-forbidden act of exchanging gifts. My sister knew this would heal me but she did not know the cost—her own health and strength. She lay in Seultrie, paralyzed in my place, while I was forced to flee the keep, the Fire King's wrath against me great."

"The Celahars destroying their own house," someone chuckled. "A fabler couldn't weave a tale so great!"

Haegan cringed at the taunt. His family had unwittingly destroyed themselves, and the truth of it pained him. When they only sought to protect what Abiassa had bestowed. Did he not owe his father's memory some defense? But what was he to say? What could he do?

"Prince?"

Haegan blinked away the burning and the thoughts. "I beg your mercy. It has been . . . hard."

"Mayhap he needs time in the crèche with the younglings."

Sobered, Haegan straightened his shoulders. "I fled to the Great Falls for the Reckoning. Kaelyria told me it would heal us both, restoring all back to former states, but me to full healing. Having been paralyzed, hidden from friend and foe, I took the bait. Greedily."

"I bet ye did."

Guilt hung like a lead stole around his neck. As he came to the part at the Falls, he faltered. If he explained what happened, it would reveal him as the Fierian. What would they do to him? Throw him out regardless? He could not blame them if they did.

"So ye journeyed to the Falls."

"Aye. I did."

"And ye were healed."

"Of a sort. Only, I learned from my aged tutor, who tracked me down, that Kaelyria had not told me the full truth of her endeavor."

Aselan tilted his head to the side, stroking his beard. "And what was that?"

"That she would never recover. The transference, it is true, healed me. But it robbed my sister of her strength—"

"Ye said that already, thin-blood," Byrin groused.

"—and her gifts." Haegan held his peace.

"Gifts." The cacique stilled. "She lost her ability to wield the Flames?"

Was he so cruel as to ask the question when his sister was dead? Anger turned bitter on his tongue. "Her death has made that question irrelevant, I would think." His words came out harder than he'd intended.

The cacique twitched. "Ye said the Fire King is dead."

Haegan managed a small nod.

"Ye saw him die." Aselan was on his feet, head angling from one side to the other as he closed in on Haegan. "Yet ye said ye were returning to the *Asykthians*."

Haegan nodded. "I . . . I was injured at the Falls. One of the companions I made in the weeks leading up to that event turned out to be the daughter of Thurig the Formidable."

The cacique stilled. Stared at Haegan. Hard. "Daughter?"

"She had been . . . on a journey. But when I was injured, we were close enough to her father's home that she delivered me there to recover." Haegan left out the part about how the Falls had devastated his body because it was the ignition point of becoming the Fierian, the destroyer of all this world knew. And he should probably leave out that Thiel rescued him on a raqine. That he and Thiel had a mutual attraction. That he'd kissed her before spiriting back home to try to save his father. That his every thought these last few days was of getting back to her.

"She took ye to Nivar Hold?" Doubt hovered in the cacique's words.

"Aye. While I recovered there, word came that Poired had lain siege to Seultrie. I left at once to help my family."

"What could ye, an injured boy, do to help? And how did ye reach Seultrie?"

"As I said, I rode a raqine."

"A raqine."

"They are real," Haegan bit out.

Snickers skittered through the hall.

"And how did ye intend to help?"

Haegan looked at his bandaged hands. Thought of how his anger had driven him southward, how he was ill-prepared to face the powerful Dyrth. How the Deliverers had stopped him from killing the madman. It had been foolhardy to think he could stop him. Humiliating.

"Think not to withhold answers from us, thin-blood."

Haegan considered Byrin, his burly size. A threat lay within his words, as if he were daring Haegan to lie. What did they know? Could they know he was the Fierian? If they'd seen the mark on his back . . . What would they do if they knew?

"I see so much in yer eyes, young prince. So much ye hide. So much ye protect." The cacique stood over him—and yet he didn't. They were eye to eye, the same height, but somehow the cacique had a much larger presence. "My concern is the danger ye bring. Yer very presence threatens my people."

Haegan swallowed. "It is . . ." He ached to release the burden. But would it mean his death? If he died, then Seultrie would have no one to lead her. The Nine would be undefended. "I did all that I knew to do." He had already failed once. What else could he do?

Aselan's eyes narrowed. "No." He shook his head. "There was more than that behind yer eyes." The cacique stepped back, nodded to Toeff. "Return him to his cave."

• • •

"It makes no sense. All we know of the prince—crippled and without gifts. Yet, here be this boy who can stand and wield. How? Ye believe the thin-blood?" Byrin muttered at Aselan's side as they watched Toeff escort the prince from the hall.

Shoulders slumped, head down, Haegan did not have the arrogant bearing expected of a spoiled prince. But the son of Zireli lived with shame, so he wouldn't be wrapped up in himself. But his tale . . . "I know not." Something was missing. Something important. "Once the storm eases, we send Teelh out to verify the Fire King's death. See what news he can find."

"But we saw on the cliff the boy can wield."

"Aye." Aselan bobbed his head. "But my concern is how he has it and the kind he has. Let us hope he didn't figure out the purpose of the grass."

"If he removes it, there's no telling"—Byrin shuddered—"the danger."

"Aye." He sighed. "I'm going to check on the princess."

"When will ye tell him she lives?"

"When I am convinced the Eilidan are safe." He clasped Byrin's fore-arm and patted his shoulder.

"Oh. Verified this morning—Chima is in the nest."

"I thought as much." Aselan almost smiled as he made his way to the lower levels, where the stones were warmer and the passages quieter, where healers worked their gifts and Eilidan were healed. The halls were hushed, the caves even more so as he trudged to the far end. Amber light glowed outside the door, the wood propped open.

Hoeff always insisted on it when tending a female.

Aselan stopped at the opening and greeted the Drigo healer. "Ye are acknowledged, Hoeff."

Head large and eyes seemingly larger, Hoeff nodded. "Thank you, Master."

Covered by a half-dozen Caorian pelts, the princess lay on the dais, her face glowing beneath a sheen of perspiration. But the stone lights sat along the lower edge of the dais. For warmth. Aselan frowned. Why would she need warmth? Most patients needed cooling bladders during illness. "Why the stone lights, Hoeff?"

"She very cold. Hoeff notice if he keep her warm—much more than Eilidan—she better."

"Thin-blood," Aselan muttered at her.

The Ladies had clearly tended her again. Her silky white hair now lay in a braided halo that rimmed her forehead. Pelts tucked around her slight frame teased the edge of her chin. Color seeped into her cheeks.

"Then she improves?"

"Hoeff think so. But slow." He moaned and gave a disappointed shake of his head. "It make no sense to Hoeff. Poultice not work."

"Have ye used yer gifts?"

"Of course, Master. Hoeff use night and day—the poultices."

Aselan touched his arm. "No, friend, yer *gifts*."

Eyes widened. "Forbidden."

And it had been with good cause—Drigo healing on a human was like trying to drink from a waterfall. Most Drigo were unable to reduce their potency to be effective for human patients. "For Eilidan." He nodded to the princess. "But she is Seultrian."

"But she still Abiassa's child. Hoeff cannot harm her."

"She is not simply a child of Abiassa, Hoeff. She is a wielder of the Flames."

Hoeff's hard intake of breath was startling. He shifted. "No." Stared down at his patient, her hands. "She wield?"

"Try."

Hoeff frantically shook his head and stepped back, hands clasped together. "No. No, Master. Hoeff not hurt anyone. *She* will call me home. Hoeff will return to the Dark Halls."

Aselan touched his arm.

"Do not make me, Master."

"Peace." Though Aselan knew a single word from him would be taken as a command by the Drigo, for they existed but to serve, Aselan would not abuse that. "I will not ask it." Though he wanted to. He wanted answers. Wanted to weigh the princess's rendering of the events at Seultrie against her brother's. He wanted to see her eyes.

"Master, Hoeff must leave for replenishment."

Aselan nodded and moved aside to allow him to exit. "She is well to rest alone?"

"Yes, Master." Hoeff shuffled down the long passage, which darkened and lit in response to his movement.

Aselan glanced at the ailing princess again, something holding him there. A small moan drifted from the dais. Was she well? In pain? He returned to the cave and studied her, assessed her. She didn't move. When she moaned again, he stared down the passage. He should not be alone with her, and he did not have the skills to aid her. Perhaps he should call Hoeff back.

Softly, she moaned again, her delicate brows knit.

Aselan started toward the dais, then thought better of it. Once more, he glanced down the passage, seeking Hoeff. The stone hall lay empty, the warm glow of stone lights his only company. He moved to the dais and frowned down at her, then eased onto the healer's stool.

Motionless. Her lips relaxed. Her eyes closed, peaceful.

Had his mind conjured the noises? "Princess?"

Still nothing. No sound. No movement.

He glanced at the stone lights, thinking how Hoeff said the ambient warmth was helping her heal. Yet her brother said she'd lost her ability to wield. Perhaps the warmth of the stone lights was a comfort, a balm? He shifted one stone light closer to her face. If he could talk to her. Ask her—

Blue eyes stared back at him.

Aselan started. His heart tripped into his rib cage.

Drowsy and seemingly unfocused, her pale eyes drifted back beneath the cover of her eyelids.

"Princess," Aselan called her back from the dregs of sleep. "Princess, can ye hear me?"

A small grunt. She shifted her head. Her lips parted and she swallowed, her brow knitting. Her eyes fluttered again. She breathed heavily, as if it took every effort to wake herself.

"Wa—" She went still again. Eyes closed.

"Princess?"

"Water," she murmured, unmoving.

Though he should not be alone with her, Aselan went to the tending table and lifted the ceramic pitcher. Blocking his path, Sikir lay stretched along the wall, head propped back against it, not fully surrendering to sleep. Aselan stepped around the hound to pour water into the tin cup then knelt at the dais. "Here, Princess."

Her eyes opened again. She locked onto him quickly this time.

"Water," he held it up for her view, then to her lips. He cupped a hand behind her neck and lifted her, so she could sip the liquid, then set the tin to her rosy lips. "Drink."

She rallied and leaned into the water, her manipulations clumsy from the illness and long sleep. Her hand came from under the pelt and braced the back of his. The difference in their coloring—hers so pale and soft, his dark and calloused—struck him. His large, hers delicate. His cold, carrying the ice of the mountain that had been his home these last ten years, and hers holding the warmth of the pelts and stone lights. "Easy," he muttered as she drank.

Like an ice dagger it hit him. Aselan saw her hand. Stilled. Haegan had said she was paralyzed. Her ice blue eyes came to his as she shrank back against the pillows. He slipped his hand free, ignoring the silkiness of her hair. The warmth of her neck.

She wet her lips and swallowed, her features weary. "Thank you."

Duamauri came to her bed and sniffed.

The princess's eyes widened.

He should ask how she could move. Or perhaps her brother had lied? "Ye—"

But exhaustion dragged her quickly into that ragged sleep. Aselan set aside the cup and pushed himself back onto the healer's stool. Why would the prince lie to them?

7

"*Come down and enjoy the fire.*" *The taunting laugh of Poired Dyrth sifted through the thick smoke and ash as he stood on the overlook of the Lakes of Fire and stared up into the castle.*

Hungry, angry flames danced over the fields, leaving them blackened and sizzling. A barren path that reached toward the keep. A spark shot across the distance. Latched onto the wall. Crawled up . . . up.

Smoke filled his nostrils. "No." Haegan watched from his bed, powerless. He was alone, paralyzed, the keep abandoned. If the fire reached the chamber, he would die.

With each lunge, stones gave way, dropping hundreds of feet to the earth. Piece by piece, the fortress surrendered to the flames, their sharp claws digging into the stone. Ragged teeth chewing through mortar.

He searched the chamber for help but only saw the dangers—curtains that kept the cold out would also keep the smoke in. The hand-carved bed with its posters would become a funeral pyre. "Help!"

"There is no help for the worthless," Poired shouted, his laughter echoing, as if he had two voices. As if he could be in two places at once. "Are you worthy, Fierian, to face me?"

Haegan shook his head, sweat dripping and burning his eyes. Each drop became a spark. He jolted. Jumped. Tried to get away, but the heat made his body pour sweat. A loud groaning pulled his gaze to the walls. The center bowed and collapsed in defeat.

"Fight me, Fierian! Are you afraid? Afraid you will be as your father, weak and a disgrace to the one you serve?"

"You cannot even name Her," came his father's shout.

"Why would I? She is but a figment, a spark of hot wind."

At the sound of his father's voice, Haegan scrambled, suddenly able to move. The burning floor singed his hands and knees as he searched through the clouds of smoke. "Father! Father, where are you?" But the roar ate not only mortar and rock but his words as well. "Father!"

"Prince of Seultrie, waste not your breath on the dead."

"He's not dead!"

"He is! I snuffed out his pitiful life," Poired shouted as he walked through flame and smoke to stand over Haegan. His shoulders were unnaturally large. His hand massive as waves of heat roiled over his frame.

"No! I will not—"

Laughter punched through the firestorm. "You?" He took a step forward, his boot pounding against the crumbling floor that alone prevented Haegan from falling to his death. Another step. "You think you have the power?" Another.

The floor canted. Poired, caring not for the danger he caused, screwed his lips tight, drew his hand to his side, fingers gnarled as if he held an orb, then thrust them forward. "A gift, Prince!"

Daggers of heat and lightning shot out.

Haegan shouted and threw up his arm, ready to fight. Duel as King Thurig had taught him.

Blue tendrils of light—intense, white-hot fire—snaked around his wrists. Coiled. Constricted. Sizzled. Dug into Haegan's flesh with a searing bite.

"Augh!" Haegan pitched himself back. Anger sprang through his chest. He hopped to his feet. He flung out a volley of white-hot fire, but this time, it was swallowed, not by fire or smoke. But by Poired's cruel, insidious laughter.

"Yes!" Poired shouted with a laugh. "Yes! Feed me your anger. Taste it, Princeling."

Gritting his teeth, Haegan crossed hands over his chest. Stomped his feet out, shoulder-width apart.

"Haegan!" a shout snapped through the void.

Startled, confused, Haegan glanced around, but he saw only a curtain of fire.

"You are weak just like your father!"

"Haegan, no!" came that voice again. "Haegan—please, listen."

"You will not distract me with the taunts. I will destroy you, Poired!"

"Haegan. Son!"

The word resonated like a brass gong in his head. Haegan stumbled. The stone floor beneath him shifted. Wobbled. He flung out his hands to catch his balance, and he saw his father standing to the side. Reaching to him. "Father!"

Flames stabbed through the mortar in the floor. Giant stones fell away. Feeling the greedy pull of gravity, Haegan threw himself back. Now a great black chasm separated them. His father teetered on a lone shard that stood precariously. Defiantly.

"Father," he breathed. Gauged the distance.

Just as the words were spoken, the shard holding his father shuddered. His father's eyes went wide. The tower fell. His father faded long into the dark crevasse of death. "Haaeeggaannn!"

"No!" Haegan lunged upright. His own shout echoed in his ears as he sought his bearings with a frantic desperation. Cold. Perilously cold. Stone.

Ice Mountain.

Breaths came in heaving clumps as he stared around the semi-darkened room, the only light emanating from the passage. Tangled in his sweaty tunic, he fought the pelts. Shoved them aside as a gargled cry climbed his throat. *Father!* He threw his legs over the side of the dais and bent forward, gripping his head in his hands. Heart ramming louder than drums, he labored through another few breaths.

That dream . . .

"Father," he whispered. His father was dead. Seultrie taken. And there was nothing he could do. Grief wrapped him tight, suffocating.

Snatches, glimpses of the nightmare sparked at him. Poired's laugh—would that torment exist to his last breath? Would he never escape it?

And mother—she hadn't even been in the dream.

Kaelyria. Why wasn't she in the dream either? He'd failed her the most. By the Flames, he'd tried. Fough with desperation and earnestness. And the Deliverers had stopped him. He fought them, as well. And they punished him.

The wake of a fiery heat rose in him. He pressed his bandaged hands to his eyes, as if he could push away the images. Was it better that he sat captive in the mountains, unable to do more damage? Now, Grinda and the other generals could lead the way a true army should be led.

Like an icy bath, Haegan had a sudden, sharp awareness he was not alone. He lifted his head and jerked.

No more than twelve cycles, a petite girl stood before him. Her hands were clasped in front, and her earthy brown eyes sparkled with pleasure. In traditional Eilidan garb of a long tunic and leather cloak to ward off the cold, she also wore leather trousers, secured with shin guards that bled into boots.

His gaze hit the iron gate, securely locked. How had he not heard her enter?

"Replenishment," she said, her voice soft as she motioned to a cup and bowl on a serving table.

"Who are you?" It did not matter, in truth. She was a servant. "How did you get in here?"

"The same way ye got in here," she said, a hint of laughter in her words.

Even children mocked him. Haegan looked away.

The dream . . . He remembered Poired's attack bolts coiling around his wrist. He turned his hand over and glanced at the bandages that still covered them. He'd been told it was best for them to remain on.

But why? He felt no pain.

"Some wounds cannot be seen."

At the girl's words, Haegan glared at her. Didn't she have work to do? Somewhere better to be than here, annoying him? "Shouldn't you be . . . cooking or something?"

"Oh, that's not for me to do."

Her words pinged across his mind, an echo of the Deliverer's on the bridge. And still she remained, staring. "Am I holding you back?"

"Of a sort." Her smile glowed. In fact, all of her seemed to glow. As if she enjoyed the irritation she created.

"What is your purpose?"

"Ye." She gave him a look as if to say her purpose was obvious, that he must have slugs for brains.

His gaze hit the food tray. "You want me to eat what you've served, so you can leave?"

"I want ye to take what I served so ye can be replenished."

With a huff, Haegan stood and went to the table, the torment of the nightmare howling through his mind still. He stared at the tray, disappointed with the offerings. A chunk of bread. A small bowl of some brown broth with specks of gray and orange. Beside them, tin cup of something . . . gray.

"Sometimes, despite the purpose or benefit, what is laid before us is less appetizing than the feast we'd imagined."

"Truer words were never spoken." Haegan lifted the bread, but suddenly had no appetite. "I think I'll just rest."

"Afraid not."

Haegan spun around, surprised to find the cacique there, the giant behind him and the heavy gate open. "I would talk to you."

Amusement skittered across the cacique's face. "Of what?"

Haegan turned away with a long sigh, his mind stuck in the crumbling tower. The raging inferno. His father's shouts. It meant but one thing—there was no king on the Fire Throne. His people were leaderless. "I must leave the mountain."

The cacique laughed. "Ask again when ye can say it like ye mean it."

"Sir, you mistake me. I—"

"Come," the cacique said, angling to the side and heading back down the passage, the hounds rushing ahead of him. Always on point. The giant took his position again, and the girl . . . she must have slipped out.

Haegan hesitated. "Sir—"

The cacique turned back. "I am Aselan. And ye said ye wanted to talk." He bobbed his head down the passage.

Annoyance battled his desperate need to do something. But what? His father was already dead. Poired had taken Seultrie. "Why must my hands be bandaged?"

"Legier's bite," Aselan said as they took to stairs hewn through the mountain and passages so narrow, Haegan's shoulders scraped several times. "Happens to those who play in the snow too long."

"You speak of frostbite?"

"Aye," Aselan said with a chuckle.

"But my fingers—"

"I have no answer for that, youngling. Damage to yer palms was moderate, but how ye did not lose fingers . . ." He shrugged and led him down a wider passage. At the end, he motioned him into a room.

Haegan stepped in, surprised at how it opened, allowing him to breathe a little easier. Several curtained bays waited, a few of them occupied with sleeping patients.

"Hoeff," Aselan called as he approached the broad-shouldered man.

Haegan hesitated, only then recognizing the oversized man, this one the mirror of his guard. "Two?"

"Twins," Aselan acknowledged. "Rare among the Drigo."

"Prince as'Tili called them Unauri, as did King Thurig."

With a snort, Aselan guided him onto a dais, raised higher than his bed in the cave they'd placed him in. "The Asykthians use terms that make them feel better and smarter. Unauri—'men grown too tall,' they say. But Drigo all the same."

It explained much. Even as he accepted the words, a thought intruded. "Sir, I must beg to leave at once."

"Why is that, Haegan of Seultrie?"

"I must return to Ybienn. The Valor Guard are waiting for my return."

"To what end?" The cacique stood with his arms folded again. Was it to make himself look larger, more intimidating the way a cat does, or the way a dog's hackles raise? "Ye said yer father is dead, that Dyrth took Seultrie. What are ye to do?"

Haegan's agitation grew as the giant drew up a stool beside him with a tent-like contraption, which had a tiny slit that he slid Haegan's hand through.

"Often, Legier's bite is upsetting to see. Hoeff uses the scaffolding to hide his work. What ye cannot see does not sicken ye."

"But there is no pain," Haegan restated his earlier thought.

"Because Hoeff is a masterful healer." Aselan arched an eyebrow. "That is his gift from Abiassa. Now—why are ye so anxious to leave the Heart?"

Haegan jerked his hand back. "I *must* return to lead the battle."

The cacique started, but then laughed. "Ye?" He wiped the corner of his eye. "Youngling, ye could not even anticipate my men on the mountain. How are ye to defeat one as powerful as Dyrth?"

Haegan glanced at his unbound hand. His uninjured hand. "There's no mark."

8

Would the prince ever come out with it? The truth. That he could wield? It was a story worth hearing, Aselan was certain. For it was said the prince was crippled, yet he was not. That he had no gifts, but he did.

And now, his parents were dead and his sister—healing, somewhat. But without the sangeen herb that somehow quieted the ability of the accelerant to draw on the embers, Legier's Heart stood at risk. "The healing is not complete."

Haegan held up his hand. "Not a single mark." He turned it over.

"Germs do not need to be seen to cause damage." Aselan nodded, a knot forming in his gut. "Please—allow Hoeff to finish his ministrations."

"But I'm fine."

"Did ye know that to a Drigo, not fully healing a patient is akin to murdering them?" When the boy looked askance at the giant, Aselan pressed on. "Ye would not put that guilt on such a gentle soul as Hoeff, would ye?"

Haegan surrendered his hand.

Once his hands and wielding were secured again, Aselan guided him back to his holding cell. Sikir ambled up for an ear rub and Aselan obliged, his eyes on Haegan's back. The more he watched this young prince, the more certain he became that there were things far greater than wielding he concealed. "What secrets are ye holding, Prince Haegan?"

The muscles in Haegan's neck contracted as he swallowed. "Secrets?"

Shaking his head, Aselan almost smiled behind the prince's back. The boy had a lot to learn about lying. "We all hold them, but yers hang as stone lights around yer neck, both weighting ye and revealing ye." They entered the temporary cave where Toeff waited. "Ye are acknowledged, Toeff."

When the Drigo returned to his seat, Haegan remained standing.

"I would have the truth, since ye are among my people."

"But they aren't your people, are they?"

Aselan arched an eyebrow.

Haegan knocked his hands, the bandages clearly awkward and annoying. "When you're crippled for ten years and nobody wants to acknowledge you exist, and you have the great honor of an aged accelerant as your guardian and tutor . . ."

"Sigils and Histories."

"Until my eyes bled." Haegan gave a soft snort. "I noticed the Ybiennese sigil on your ring."

Stroking Sikir, Aselan wished he'd discarded the piece long ago. He was not interested in playing games. "Ye said they are not my people, but ye are wrong. The Heart has been my home for more than ten cycles. I am their cacique."

"Would you trust them before your blood?"

Aselan lowered his head. "My blood betrayed me," he said, his words tinged with the pain of that memory, though he tried to hide it. "So, yes, Prince." He nodded. "Before my blood."

"Does your family know you're alive?"

Aselan rubbed Sikir's velvety ear. "Ye ask that as if it would make a difference." He shook his head. "They know, Prince. They've always known."

The prince paled.

"Ye were abandoned to a tower by yer blood, yet ye are surprised at my answers."

Haegan lowered his curly-haired head. "It is true. I was left there. My father rarely visited."

"Yet there is fondness in yer words." Aselan squinted, wondering. Were these lies? Had the prince lied his way into the Heart?

"When I returned to Seultrie—"

"On a raqine," Aselan injected, not willing to pass up the chance to taunt the boy.

Haegan's lips pressed together. "Aye." His gaze hopped around. "I had a confrontation with my father."

Aselan had had a few of those with his own father.

"He blamed me."

"For?"

"The Transference. He believed I was angry over his negligence, accused me of stealing her gifts."

"Yet ye are fond of him?"

Haegan swallowed and looked away.

"Ah," Aselan shook a finger at him. "There is that secret ye hide."

Haegan went still.

On his feet, Aselan stared down at him. "Shelter and food ye will have, but not much else till ye reveal what ye withhold. Something is missing, something ye are ashamed of, or some criminal act ye committed." He moved to the door. "Until I am certain my people are safe, ye will remain here."

Haegan punched to his feet, eyes ablaze. "I *must* return to Asykth." Desperation clung to him like the sweat that rimmed his face when Aselan had found him earlier, staring at the empty serving table.

"Nobody goes out in the blizzard. I will not risk one of my men escorting ye down—"

"Then blindfold me," Haegan pleaded. "Just let me go. Throw me out and let me find my own way."

Sikir and Duamauri stood. Hackles rising, they growled at the prince, and he shrank from them.

Aselan stepped out and secured the iron gate over the cave. "Even I am not as cruel as that." He turned and nodded to the giant. "Ye are acknowledged, Toeff. Be sure he remains rested and fed—and within this cave."

"Of course, Master."

Aselan patted his shoulder, then headed down the passage and descended to the lower levels. The mouthwatering aroma of stew and flour cakes rose from the refectory, but he could not shake the conversation with Haegan. More accurately, he couldn't shed the image of his father, shaking his fist at Aselan. Thundering his order for him to fulfill his duty as heir to Nivar Hold. That his loyalty should be to his blood, not a woman and a savage tribe.

His mother . . . she'd dared not defy his father, but she had sent him letters. Reported Thiel's ordeal. Then her absence, upon which he'd had the Legiera scouring the spine for her. His mother had a strength not many understood. But he still wished she had stood up to his father. Nobody had.

In truth, what could be said? They had all turned their backs on him, and the doors to Nivar Hold forever closed as he walked into the Ice Mountains with Doskari.

"Master?"

When Duamauri whimpered, Aselan blinked, startled to find himself standing at the door to the princess's shelter and Hoeff behind him. He ignored the embarrassment and faced the giant. Why had he come here? "How does she fare?"

Hoeff smiled. "Better." He motioned into the room. "Marsel stew good for her."

Aselan eased aside as the healer trudged past, taking up the entire doorway with his large frame and a steaming bowl. "Stew?" He entered behind the giant. "She's well enough?"

Hoeff set the bowl down and shifted aside.

Aselan's heart jammed into his throat as ice blue eyes met his. Princess Kaelyria sat propped up, resting against the stone wall beneath a pile of white-gray pelts. Her hair hung in a loose plait across her shoulder. She offered him a slight smile, then looked down.

"I—I beg yer mercy." What was he doing here? *It is yer duty to be here. To verify her well-being.* "I see Hoeff speaks truth—"

"Hoeff always speak truth," the giant said, hurt drenching his words.

"Of course, Hoeff. Ye are acknowledged." Aselan shook off the near-laugh as he refocused on the princess. "Ye are sitting up." Concern sped through him. The prince had lied to them then? "I was told ye were paralyzed."

"When I left my home, I was. But now . . ." She seemed pleased. With herself or the healer, he couldn't tell. "It is wonderful and surprising. I have no explanation."

"To be sure." Why was there a chokehold on his throat? "I'm glad to see ye better."

The princess tilted her head. "That may be a stretch of the truth, sir,

but I do improve." She looked to the giant. "Thanks to the gentle ministrations of this kind healer."

Duamauri trotted to her dais.

As his large hound approached, sniffing loudly, the princess went
white. "I've never seen one so . . . so close."

"He is the male of the pair—and quite obstinate."

Without warning, Duamauri leapt up onto the pelts and curled up
at—*on*—the princess's feet.

She pulled in a gasp.

"*Tsst*," Aselan gave the *down* signal to the icehound using his teeth.

Duamauri's ears swiveled and he turned bored, white eyes to him.
Ignored the command. Stunned, Aselan flicked his finger, pointing the
hound to his side. With a disgruntled groan, Duamauri lumbered off the
dais. He shook his spine as if shaking off the insult of being told to get
down.

The princess laughed. "I daresay he's annoyed."

"He is not the only one. I beg yer mercy. He's not normally so rude."
He should leave. Talk with Byrin and Teelh about sending Haegan away.
Sending them both away. "If ye'll excuse me—"

"Aselan."

He stilled.

"Might I ask . . ."

"Of course, Princess."

Expectant eyes came to his. "What of my brother?"

9

"It has been six days. Surely ye do not still deign to tell me nothing is wrong." Thiel crossed her arms as she stared down her brother, who sat at a knobby wood table in the kitchens.

Tili tossed down his fork. "Blazes, girl! Can ye not let one wink pass without yer lovesick fretting?"

Thiel popped him on the back of the head.

Her brother came up like a geyser, caught her hand, and twisted her around.

She ducked beneath his arm and counter-twisted.

Tili flipped her grip. Pinned her against the wall.

She growled her defeat.

He grinned, stepped back, and wiped the corner of his mouth where a bit of gravy from the roast streaked his almost clean-shaven jaw.

"Something is wrong," she insisted.

"And with the blizzard, we can do naught." He returned to the bench at the table and lifted his spoon. "Perhaps ye should go back to stitching."

"I'll stitch yer eyes shut in yer sleep!"

He snorted. "Please—do me the favor. Atelaria is coming."

"Ye jest!"

"Nay, though I wish I were. Father said they are coming down from the Violet Sea for the wedding."

Atelaria was her age and had beauty in spades. The last time they visited, Father nearly skewered Tili for not taking an interest in his cousin.

"They say she has the beauty of Abiassa," Thiel taunted.

"Ye be touched in the head. To take as my bride one who is of family blood 'tis foul and . . ."

"Proper? Expected?"

His lip curled as he stared over his roast. "Boring."

"Be not worried, brother. She has no interest in ye, besides. Last she was here—"

"Mind yerself." He stabbed his spoon at her then scooped some meat into his mouth and chewed. "She goes after one of my men, I'll string her up meself."

"Jealous?"

With a cough, he thumped his chest. "Jealousy has naught to do with it. My concern is with Poired turning that blood-gaze northward. We need all the men we have and more." He shook his head, black curls swaying. "I will not have the Nivari distracted by wiles." But then he grinned. "But 'twill be good to have her here."

Thiel frowned. "What, a change of heart?"

"Nay, means ye'll be out of me hair in the training yard."

This time, Thiel pushed his head into his food and took off running. His roar caught up with her as she skidded around the first corner. She grabbed the wall and propelled herself down the hall. Breathless and lighthearted, she slowed to a trot. It was good to be home again. It was good to be—

Feet pounded behind her.

Tili bore down on her. "Ye thin-blood lover!"

She launched forward, but then stopped short as she saw two men enter a room behind their father. Tili plowed into her but caught her shoulders, seeing the same thing.

"Who are they?" she breathed.

"Elders," Tili muttered, his voice low. "Stay here."

Stay? What was she, a dog? She grabbed his arm. "I'm just as much the king's heir—"

He pressed a finger to her lips. "And ye've been gone the last few years. Things have changed."

"What things?"

"Not yer mouth, that much is sure."

She smacked him. "Who are they?"

"Inele Larrow and Faus Sharton." He stepped in front of her, forcing her behind him. "Ambassadors to the Nine."

"Haegan!"

"No," Tili muttered. "They wouldn't care about him. This . . . this is worse."

"How? Why would ye say that? What do ye mean worse? How do ye even know?"

Tili jerked around. "Quiet," he hissed. "Whatever has brought them here in this storm . . ." He shook his head. "Wait here, Thiel."

"I—"

"Wait," he said, his voice a growl. He turned and strode to their father's receiving room.

Hands fisted, lips taut, Thiel sneaked along the thick rug that lined the marble hall. She slipped around the gilded table with flowers, brought in from the greenhouses. Tiptoeing beneath the massive oil painting of her grandfather, whose stern gaze had always given her chills, she ignored the reprimand he seemed to be giving. If her father caught her, he'd become Grandpapa reborn.

Voices rattled against the wood. Tili had left the door open. Whether baiting her or affording her a means to listen, she wasn't sure. He still owed her for the face full of roast.

Words rose and fell. Not necessarily an argument, but not far from it either. She leaned out, peering through the slit. Her brother stood tall, handsome beside their father. The two made an imposing presence. Tili's expression went severe, and he exchanged a glance with Father.

"My little spy," came a soft voice.

Thiel gave a start and turned. "M—"

Her mother's finger to her lips silenced her. She gave a nod and peered in through the same crack Thiel had used.

"Ye are sure?" her father demanded.

"There is no doubt," one of the ambassadors said, his voice grave. "I heard the report firsthand from a dying Jujak. While defending his queen and children, Zireli was brutally murdered by Poired. The Celahars are lost."

10

"You look ridiculous."

"As much as you, dear brother."

Trale Kath stretched his neck, hating the way the stiff collar poked into the soft skin under his chin, and at the same time noting that he could make good use of the stiffness in a strike. "At least I'm not wearing ribbons and have half my flesh on display."

A blade pressed to his throat in a flash. "Distracted you, didn't it?"

"Murder me and the Infantessa will be sadly put out," he said, bending over the rail as she pinned him.

Astadia grunted and swung around, the fabric of her skirts billowing like the waves crashing against the cliff some fifty feet below. Mist spray carried on a warm breeze. Glittery goli birds, wings tucked against their long bodies, dived down and vanished beneath the foamy wake of the sea. A small inlet cradled the deep blue waters, with jagged rocks stretching up the northern lip of the tear-shaped bay.

"He promised us we'd be free."

The warm balustrade was made of white marble, gold streaking through it with random elegance and glinting beneath the sun in a display unlike anything Trale had encountered before. Pressing his palm against it, he peered at the waters, where the tide drifted away from the rocky cliff and sailed out to sea. It'd journey long until it traced the coastline of the Yaopthui and slid into the Catatori Ocean and freedom.

Astadia whipped around to him, her russet hair rippling in loose waves as she moved. "We did things—things I never would've done. To be free."

Unlike his sister, whose desperation for freedom sometimes blinded her, Trale had never once believed Poired's promise of liberation. What Trale saw behind those sick, empty eyes was more of what existed around the mouth of Sirdar—pain. Death. He had never been good enough, no matter how hard he'd tried. Protecting Astadia had been his attempt at atonement. *A foolish hope,* he guessed. *It is good to serve the Infantessa this way.* Maybe he could redeem himself after all.

"How can you not be angry?" She flung out her arms and motioned to the sea, then to the cliffs and trees.

"What good will that do?" Trale muttered.

"Every good! Rail against his brutality with me. Tell me it's wrong—that we should be free." Her face glowed bright with intensity but also the defeat that consumed their lives. His sister was beautiful and deadly. Trained by his own hand and skills. Borne of necessity. For survival. "I can't do this anymore, Trale." Her words were but wisps in the salty mist that curled loose strands of hair around her face. She sagged against the balustrade. "It eats at me."

Trale touched her shoulder. "Courage, Astadia. Look around you—we stand on the balcony of the Infantessa herself!" *It is an honor to be here.*

"I care not one whit about a spoiled girl's pretty view."

"As you should not." The stiff voice came sharp and firm from behind them.

Astadia glanced over Trale's shoulder, blue-green eyes widening and her golden skin whiter than the surrounding rock. Trale slid his eyes shut, cursing himself for not guiding her to a calmer state before she did exactly what she'd done. She knew better than to give over to idle talk where walls had ears.

"Bow," Trale hissed as he pivoted, stealing a fleeting glance at the Infantessa as he went to a knee. "Your Highness."

"Your Highness," the deep voice boomed across the receiving hall. "At your request, the Kaths, Astadia and Trale, present themselves to you."

Silence gaped, the hard floor digging into Trale's knees. A crick in his back needled him. No doubt the Infantessa sought to ensure they both felt the full awkwardness of Astadia's sharp words.

"Rise, heirs of Kath."

Trale nearly laughed as he pushed to his feet. Heirs of Kath? Who was

Kath? They'd both been dumped in a tavern named *Kath* on the night of a quickly quelled uprising against Sirdar.

In keeping with Iteverian customs, Trale kept his gaze down. He had no doubt of the pain her guards would inflict across his shoulders and back should he dare look. But in that stolen glimpse, he'd seen her. She could not be any older than they—a mere twenty cycles—yet she ruled a vast kingdom.

Her pale blue gown dusted the gleaming marble floor and matched the color of the clear sky beyond the balcony. A white scarf of sorts wreathed her head and neck, pleating down into the bodice of her gown. Atop a stiff headdress of gold brocade, the shape of a crescent moon was rimmed in gold cord and accented with pearls. Pale blue sheer material ran the length of both arms, held in place by a ring on the middle finger of each hand.

"Ask them: Sirdar's right hand sent you, did he not?" she said, her words meant for her steward, the question for Trale and Astadia.

Irritation skimmed through Trale as he waited for the steward to repeat the words, for only then could he respond. And not to the Infantessa. But to the steward. "Infantessa Shavaussia wills that you answer: Sirdar's right hand sent you to me, did he not?"

"Please tell the Infantessa that Sirdar's right hand did summon us to Iteveria." Blazes, he hated formality!

"Ask them, Roberts, if they know to what end they are in my presence."

"The Infantessa would have you respond: Do you know to what end you are in her presence?"

"We have—" Trale bit down. Swallowed. "Please tell the Infantessa we are here to do as she commands." Surely the Infantessa did not think they would name openly that they were being sent to kill someone. A person unnamed. Who must remain so until the Infantessa spoke it.

Trale curled his hand into a fist, hearing the slightest of huffs from Astadia. His patience had been long and honed compared to her short-fused temper. She had little tolerance for useless things and people.

Whispers skated back and forth.

Trale dared his gaze to the edge of her blue gown. The skirts adjusted slightly, indicating she might not be looking at them, but at her steward.

His gaze skimmed up a little more to the bodice richly adorned with pearls, tiny crystals, and more gold threads. The white fabric around her neck maintained her modesty. Her chin—a golden brown, rounded slightly with youthfulness. Womanhood had not yet fully claimed her. She was well-formed, her bodice proved that, but the maturity of age had not refined her facial features. Yet . . . maturity beyond her years rimmed her brown eyes. Depths of knowledge, grief unimaginable—so much dwelt in those orbs that reminded him of the forest of Ankdoar. Yes, her eyes—

Eyes?

Trale blinked at his stupidity. At the same instant, a blow to the back of his knees sent him to the marble floor.

Astadia cried out.

Fingers against the cold stone and gaze rightly corrected, he braced himself. Anticipated his sister's move. Caught her wrist before she could fly into action. "No," he said, a grimace tightening his words and grip. He peered up at her with sidelong glance. "No. My fault." The backs of his legs ached. So did his pride.

"Gaze upon the Infantessa again and you will feel more than the sentry's staff against your legs," Steward Roberts said as his booted feet slid into Trale's visual range. "Are we understood?"

"Painfully." Trale divided his thoughts between self-annoyance and this whole façade. But it drove home how the Infantessa had gained her reputation as a coldhearted ruler. One who demanded obeisance and fealty. Total subjugation or death.

Trale had seen plenty of death. Had delivered death. He did not want to become it.

Or perhaps he already had.

11

Awareness plucked Haegan from a fitful sleep. He stared down the length of his legs and shifted them. Still able to move. His gaze hit the heavy door. Still a prisoner.

He felt her before he saw her and jerked upright.

The servant girl stood at the table again, this time working over a small tray. She lifted a piece of cake and smiled at him. "I have a treat for ye." Her hair was woven into a braid unlike any he'd seen before. Complicated. Yet . . . delicate. Thick. Wrapped around her shoulder, it hung to her waist. She wasn't particularly beautiful—not like Thiel—but neither was she ugly. Kindness. Was that what compelled him to silence this time?

She came, extended the slice of cake toward his mouth.

Awkwardly, Haegan started to reach for it, only to remember his hands were bandaged.

She lifted her eyebrows. "Now ye see why I assist." With care, she tucked the piece between his lips. "Sometimes, having help is exactly what we need, even though our pride insists we do it on our own."

Haegan chewed slowly, surprised at its sweetness. But there was another flavor to it. A sweetness that wasn't . . . sweet. That made no sense.

She brushed her hands together as she returned to the tray.

He swallowed. "Who are you?"

"I thought it obvious." She held out her hands. "I'm a servant."

"No, your name. What is your name?" He hadn't really wanted her name, but she'd made him feel foolish, and he sought to deflect that feeling.

She tilted her head. "Ye may call me Aaesh." Now she came with a tin cup.

"I can do that on my own."

"Yes," she said, her brows lightly knotted, "but must ye?"

"I beg your mercy."

At this she smiled. "Very well." But she still held the cup for him.

Haegan gave up and took a swig, then swallowed. "You said I can call you Aaesh, so is it not your real name?"

"Not the whole of it."

"What is?"

"Aaeshwaeith Adoaniel'afirema."

Haegan stared, not remotely willing to attempt repeating that. "You're not from Legier."

"It is where I am." Her earthy gaze never wavered. "And ye are not from Legier, Haegan of Seultrie."

Something whispered through the room. A breeze. No—not a breeze. Something strange. Tickling his ears and the back of his throat. His hands—they felt weird. "No. No, I'm not. Thought the locked door might give that away."

"Are ye so easily restrained?"

Haegan blinked. Who was this child that she spoke like an adult? And so boldly? "You must know how to undo the locks, so you could free me."

"And what would that teach ye?"

"That you're kind."

"And that ye're weak."

Pride dented, Haegan drew up. "Did you not just say that sometimes having help is exactly what we need?"

"There is wisdom in discerning those times."

"Now I'm a fool? What do you know of me? Do they not teach manners where you come from?"

She smirked. "Manners, yes. And courage as well as loyalty. And not to ask others to do what ye must do for yerself." Her words were unusually accurate, piercing the soft spot of the last week.

"What have they told you? I suppose they say I'm a coward."

"Nay, Haegan, those are yer own words."

His chest burned. His hands. "Do you not have friends you want to play with?" Anything to get her out of here. Out of his head.

"I have six friends, and they are always ready when I am." She smiled. "But I am looking for a new friend."

Haegan snorted. "Sorry. I would not waste your time."

"Why would it be a waste of my time?"

Worrying a loose thread of the bandage, Haegan fell silent. Coward. She'd nailed him on that one. Seultrie was without a king. Her people . . . lost. The Nine floundering.

They needed a king.

"And here ye lie," Aaesh said softly, pulling his gaze to hers. "Sometimes, our most likely ally is the unlikely ally."

"I don't understand."

Voices in the passage drew his attention seconds before the iron gate swung inward. The Drigo and Aselan entered.

"Dress, Prince." Aselan tossed clean clothes at him.

"You are releasing me?"

"Nay, the storm still rages. No one leaves the Heart. Get dressed." He pointed to a small divider that afford a modicum of privacy.

"I must return, Cacique. You know this." Haegan stepped behind the tightly stretched leather screen and changed. "I am the only living heir of Zireli. It is my duty, my *obligation* to do whatever it takes to wipe out the scourge that is Poired Dyrth." Would he never shake the images of that cackling devourer of accelerants? Shrugging the tunic into a more comfortable position, he stepped from behind the divider. "Please release me so I may—"

Aselan swept his foot out from under him and at the same time grabbed his throat, slamming Haegan down and pinning him to the dais.

Air punched from Haegan's lungs. He gaped up in shock at the cacique.

"Ye cannot see me coming, ye cannot see yer enemy coming. Tell me, how will ye stop Poired, thin-blood?"

Pawing with bandaged hands at the cacique's strangling grip, Haegan choked out, "I will bring war to him."

Brown eyes narrowed beneath a fringe of black hair. "Think ye not that yer father did exactly that?" Aselan sighed then released Haegan and stared down at him. "What do ye know, what can ye do, Prince, that yer father did not?"

Humiliated, Haegan pried himself off the dais.

Aselan stood before him now. "Ye have what, seventeen, eighteen cycles?"

"Eighteen." Just. He'd not celebrated the day of his birth because he'd been running for his life.

"Zireli was forty-three when he perished. Nearly twenty-three of those years spent as Fire King."

Haegan would never forget . . . his tormenting dreams would not grant him the freedom to do so.

"He spent ten years learning in the Citadel before being taken under the wing of the grand marshal for final training." Aselan crossed his arms. "Only two men have trained with the grand marshal in the last decade— yer father and Thurig. Do ye not know yer Histories, Prince? I thought ye had an aged and wise guardian looking after ye."

"He was a pestering annoyance, but, yes, Gwogh was wise."

"Gwogh." Aselan's gaze widened, then he nodded. "Think back to the first Celahar to take the Fire King's throne."

"Baen, who became Zaelero the Second."

"How many children did Zaelero have?"

"But one—"

"Nay nay nay," Aselan growled, his icehounds slumping on the ground in apparent boredom. "Just like a Celahar . . ." he muttered before turning back to Haegan. "Three. There were *three* children born to him by Nydessa: Ybienn, Hetaera, and—"

"Zaethien."

"Why is it, Prince, that ye recall only yer ancestor?"

This . . . no, it didn't make sense. "I studied what was in the Histories."

"Bah!" With a quick wave to Toeff, Aselan sighed and exited the room, his icehounds trotting after him.

Haegan stepped forward cautiously, but the cacique had already stormed out of sight.

A blast of hot breath skated down his neck, ruffling his tunic. "Toeff think you should hurry," the giant grumbled.

Scurrying behind the hounds, Haegan banked left as he had seen the cacique do seconds earlier. But when he got there, he found a six-point juncture. All possible routes stood dark and barren.

"Quickly, Prince," Aselan's voice boomed from the left.

Two openings. He squinted into one and caught a faint glimmer of light. Haegan ventured in, his shoulders tightening at the darkness. Never mind the cold that chewed his bones. How could they live with the damp, dark, and cold?

He would trade it all in a heartbeat for the Lakes of Fire. To feel the heat against his face again. Summer breezes that cleared his sinuses. Unlike the relentless cold here that—without Hoeff's teas—would make it difficult to breathe, let alone think.

And the darkness! "I cannot see," he called into the passage. "I . . . cannot see," he repeated, his voice falling to a whisper. "And I'm alone." He glanced back, but there was only a dot of light at the far end.

Weight pressed against his chest. Constricted his throat. Hating the confined space, he closed his eyes. Huffed through his nose. *Breathe. Just breathe. Don't think about it. You're fine—in the tower overlooking all of Seultrie.*

Which burned to the ground.

The tower . . . crumbling . . . crumbling. His father's shout!

Being chased from the only home he knew. Holding his father as he died. Carrying Kae to her death. Alone. Defeated. Nothing he could do. Now he would suffocate on the frigid anger of Abiassa.

"Find a—good, ye used yer head. Hurry. Bring the stone light ye touched."

Haegan snapped his eyes open, the area around him illuminated. Stone light? He hadn't touched—Haegan looked at his hands. It was not a stone light providing him direction, but him. Heat wakes warbled around his hands, flames dancing gently.

"Prince! I have duties. Hurry."

He swallowed, seeing now that the bandages had fallen to the ground as ash. Amid them, unburned, a green plant of some kind. *I did not think there existed enough heat in these cursed passages to draw out.*

His gaze again hit the plant. He could wield now. No pain. No marks.

The plant. Haegan seized that truth then stalked with fierce intent toward Aselan's voice. Stormed out of the passage.

Aselan turned his head—and snapped fully around, a blade in hand.

"You knew," Haegan growled. "You knew about me. The bandages—my hands were not injured."

The icehounds growled, slinking forward, heads down. Teeth bared.

Dagger to the side, no doubt more than able to use it, Aselan held out a staying hand, first to the hounds, then to Haegan. "Easy, Prince. It was necessary. Accelerants do not enter the Heart—are not allowed to—because not only would ye draw heat, ye would sap our very air. 'Twould suffocate everyone here."

"The leaves—"

"Sangeen." Aselan shook his head. "They've worked before." Another shake, brown eyes wide. "I know not how ye were able to burn them off. Those leaves should have numbed yer ability to draw on the embers. It was not meant as harm against ye, but as protection for my people."

"Do you know what I am?"

The blade in Aselan's knife glinted as the cacique tightened his grip. His gaze never left Haegan's. "A guess. The marks—Hoeff panicked when he saw them. It's why he suggested the sangeen."

And they didn't try to kill him. *Sometimes our most likely ally is the most unlikely ally.* Aaesh's childlike words pushed Haegan like a dog nudging his hand, calling for his attention. Haegan stemmed his fury but let the embers roil around his fingertips in emphasis. "I have no desire to hurt anyone, but I must leave."

"I swear to ye, doing so would risk yer life. 'Tis no jest, Prince. The blizzard is especially cruel. At first tempering, Teelh will escort ye down."

"How are you able to gauge the weather from down here?"

"A cavern—there's a way to see the skies from there."

"Take me to it."

"No."

Anger spurted. Light erupted.

Aselan shoved out a hand. "Wait!"

"There is no trust between us, Cacique. You have held me hostage behind iron bars, with herbs to dull my abilities, with a guardian who

could crush my skull like a fly and a pert girl who brings me stale bread."
Haegan felt the heat plumes and leaned into them, savoring the warmth.

"I would show ye something, Prince Haegan. Something that might change yer mind about singeing me." Aselan straightened and stood tall. "Despite the circumstances, despite the attempts to protect my people, no harm was intended."

"The herb you placed on my hand—"

"Drigo medicine with no lasting effects" He shrugged. "It has worked on others."

"You've had accelerants—"

"Two, more than three cycles past. They saw how their gifts affected the Heart and asked for it."

"Willingly?" Haegan's voice pitched.

"Aye."

"Then why did you bind mine without permission and deceive me?"

"As ye said, there is no trust between us. Not yet. Do ye forget the clearing? Yer hands glowed. I saw yer intent to wield against my men." Aselan's eyes were earnest, his tone even. "Had ye struck the mountain, an avalanche would have buried us—and perhaps even parts of Ybienn outside the wall." Aselan pointed to a staircase that spiraled out across a cavern. "Come. Let me show ye."

It would be but a simple act for the cacique to pitch Haegan over the iron rail to his death hundreds of feet below, where darkness concealed the depths. Though he hesitated, Aselan did not. He strode up the narrow ramp to the stone steps and moved ahead of Haegan by several feet.

Trust.

12

They rounded a stone wall, squeezed beneath an arch, and stepped into a great room. Simple but large. A long table straddled it, affording space for little else but the half-dozen chairs snugged beneath it. Aselan walked to the other side. A narrow, pencil-legged table pressed against the far wall.

Haegan reticently entered. "Why did you bring me here?"

Whistling, Aselan waited as the hounds left the room. Then he pointed to a tapestry hanging over the great fire pit.

Haegan's gaze rose to the piece, fluttering beneath a stiff breeze that circled down from the vents. Stitched resplendently, though time had taken its toll on the fibers and vibrancy, it still resonated with incredible artistry and craftsmanship. Three kings stood there, arms folded—just as Aselan stood now. Circlets crowned two of the figures who flanked the middle king. Recognition sparked through Haegan. "Zaethien."

Aselan nodded. "The First."

Haegan's heart thumped a little harder—if that was Zaethien, then the other two . . . Had Aselan been right that Zaelero sired three children, not just the one? Haegan's gaze skipped to the figure on Zaethien's left, surprised to see it was not a man, but a woman. More strident was the fact that the man on Zaethien's right bore an uncanny resemblance to the man standing before Haegan. "You favor him."

"That would be because he is my forebear, Ybienn."

Haegan started.

"That would make us cousins, would it not?" Aselan asked. "But in truth, it goes deeper. I am Thurig As'Elan, firstborn of Thurig the Formidable."

Haegan stared, suddenly seeing the resemblance. Not just between Aselan and the prince in the tapestry, but between Aselan and the king who had given Haegan a crash course in wielding. The bearing and powerful presence had handed down well from father to son.

"But I am also *not* his son." Aselan lowered his gaze for the first time and eased into a chair. "At least, not by his account."

"He disowned you? But Thurig was more a father to me than my own."

Pain, sharp and swift, flashed through Aselan's expression, but then he looked down again. "It does not surprise me." Leader of hundreds, if not thousands. Powerful. Mighty. Feared. Yet he too knew the ache of abandonment.

But the tapestry—why had this been hidden from Haegan, from the Nine? What did it matter that there were three children of Zaelero versus the one, the only heir within—"The Histories only record one heir from Zaelero."

Aselan pointed to the tapestry. "The ladder—use it and climb up there."

Haegan frowned.

"Must ye fear me at every suggestion?" Aselan growled as he shoved back the chair and went to the wooden and iron ladder that hung from a track hidden behind the tapestry. Using his dagger, he disturbed the tapestry and craned his head back, looking beneath the hem.

Noisy and grating, the ladder scraped to the side. Aselan gave it a shove, then climbed the seven steps, head and shoulders disappearing behind the blue tapestry.

Something poked out beneath it, then Aselan descended, a large bound volume in hand. He flung it onto the table so that it slid across the surface, spinning to a stop in front of Haegan. Even with the lettering upside down, Haegan could make out the crowned tri-tipped flame of House Celahar. Bold gold lettering scrawled over the leather cover. Histories.

Haegan looked to Aselan. "By what means have you come by this?" He reached out, tentatively touching the binding. The edges dipped in gold. With care, he eased open the cover. "The ancient language," he said, studying the elegant lettering and cantillation marks. He could not help recall the meeting in Nivar Hold with the Council of Nine. How they'd cornered him. Saddled him with the great weight of his purpose in life. A cruel purpose. One that relegated him to Destroyer.

His fingertips touched the words, trailed the lettering. Illumination flared beneath his fingers. Haegan drew in a sharp breath and jerked back.

In a flash, Aselan stood at his side. "What did ye do?"

Feeling like a scolded child, he pulled his hand away. "Nothing."

"I trust ye with a rare copy of the Histories, and ye attempt to burn it?"

"No!" Haegan cried. "In earnest, I merely touched it." But had he been angry when touching it? "My anger . . ." He curled his fingers into a fist. "I beg your mercy. It was not intentional. When my anger flares—it flares."

"Accelerants are trained from the very beginning to control the embers."

"I have no formal training, not like my father," he admitted. Then glanced at the cacique. "Your father tried . . . he tried to teach me." Haegan sighed and looked down at the Histories.

"It seems my father has become more free with his secrets in his old age."

"But you know he can wield."

Aselan looked away. "Aye, and the truth of it divided us. His lies, as well as the choice of whom I bound with."

Haegan frowned.

"I chose a Legieran woman, the daughter of the last cacique. By binding with her, I gave up rights to the Ybiennese throne."

"And your father—"

"Said if I left, I could never return."

"But you chose her."

"No," Aselan said, his expression weighted with old grief and yet softened by memory. "She chose me."

Haegan said nothing, sensing something deep and almost sacred beneath the three simple words. All at once, he saw Aselan as more than a foreign chief, an antagonist, a barrier to his will. He saw a man, a widower, Thiel's brother made orphan by their father's rage.

After a moment, Aselan lifted his shoulders in a shrug, breaking the spell. "And I loved her."

"Was there no compromise to be made?"

Aselan sighed. "My father pursued the party I traveled with back to the Heart. Slaughtered a dozen Legiera in his anger against me. The Nivari sent smoke bombs down the few vents they were aware of. Not the most important—those we protect heavily—but enough that lives were lost."

Haegan stood rigid, disbelieving. "That is not the man I met in Nivar, the one who helped me learn to wield."

Sorrow darkened Aselan's eyes. "It is the man I knew."

Stunned, Haegan thought of how his own father had pursued him. "My father sent his Jujak after me."

Aselan sighed heavily. After a few moments of pained, awkward silence, he motioned to the book. "Can ye read it?"

"It is the ancient tongue," Haegan mumbled, shaking his head and remembering how ancient words had fallen off his tongue a few times. "I cannot . . ."

And yet, even as he slid a finger above the text, the words seemed to bend to understanding in his mind. "I . . ." He frowned. How was this possible? He leaned closer. "I don't understand . . ." But he did. The words somehow translated in his mind.

"What?"

"I—I can't—I don't know the ancient tongue, but somehow, the words are making sense."

Angling the book aside, Aselan scanned the thin pages. Flipped several more and came to a page with an illuminated painting that matched the tapestry over the door. He traced the lettering down to a line. "Here—read this."

More than a little unsettled at the things Abiassa did with him, Haegan forced his gaze to the page, knowing now the reason his old tutor had bored him with letters and Histories was that he'd known . . . Gwogh had known all along what Haegan was.

But that could not be. Haegan had no giftings as he lay in that bed.

The book. Words. ". . . and after the great war when Abiassa and her Deliv—" The word caught in his throat as he recalled the burning being standing between him and Poired.

"Much to take in, is it not?"

"'Tis . . . familiar."

"Read on."

Haegan skipped the word. " . . . protected and aided Zaelero, delivering into his hands all the lands west of the Catatori, She bestowed upon him the love of a woman and the blessing of three heirs, Zaethien, Ybienn, and Hetaera, all powerfully gifted with the Flames to protect Her lands."

Haegan stopped, frowned. "This . . . this isn't right."

"Because ye don't believe it?"

"I *read* the Histories." Had all but memorized them in the hours and years spent with little else. "I know them. These—it should read: 'rewarded Zaelero with the love of a woman and the blessing of their offspring, Zaethien, ruler of the Nine, powerfully gifted—'"

"Aye." Aselan scanned Haegan's face. "That is what ye were taught."

"That is what all the Nine are taught." A craggy voice crawled through the room.

Haegan stepped back, startled. Uncertain.

The tapestry above the door shifted.

He gave a shout.

Aselan steadied him as the tapestry drew aside. A heavily robed shape lowered down the ladder, still talking. "Remove truth from the Histories, Parchments, and Legacies, and what is known as truth changes." The bent shape touched the floor and her feet scratched against the stone as she turned. "Does it not?"

"Ye are not to be among the people, Wegna."

"Then ye should not bring them to my library." Wiry white hair stuck out from a black cap that framed a face kindly touched by the years. From beneath an overcloak, she produced another book, partly wrapped in cloth. Smaller, but just as old. She handed it to Haegan, eyes alight.

Haegan shot Aselan a furtive glance.

"She's old and strange, but—that trust ye spoke of in the passage? She has all mine. Even if the truth is cruel, she will give it to ye."

"Truth is neither cruel nor kind. Mankind is."

"See?" Aselan shrugged.

With reluctance, Haegan accepted the bound volume.

Wegna nodded eagerly, pointing to it with apparent glee. "Yes, yes! I knew it."

Haegan frowned again and met Aselan's confused expression.

Patting Aselan on the chest, Wegna bounced on her toes. "I told ye, did I not? I told ye that he would come." She clapped. "Here, of all places—just beyond the Cold One's Tooth. In Legier's Heart!" Tears ran down her face as she looked to the ceiling. "Thank ye, Lady, for giving me this great honor to guide yer Fierian."

13

He would drive his dagger through his own neck to end this insipid charade.

"The Infantessa Shavaussia would have you follow her."

Trale dared to lift his gaze—but just enough to see the Infantessa's skirt sweeping away. He darted a look to his sister.

Murder glowered in her blue-green eyes.

He sighed and gave her a cockeyed nod that said, what choice did they have? None.

They trailed the Infantessa and her steward out of the receiving room, down a short hall, and through a set of dark wood doors. They stepped into a great glassed-in hall—a solarium.

Heat and humidity immediately pressed their clothes against their skin. Trale felt it more difficult to breathe even as a bead of water slipped down his forehead. He flicked it away, searching the room for the duo.

Astadia gave a grunt, her lip curled as she hefted a suddenly damp skirt. "Madness," she hissed, turning around, searching for their escorts.

With a thud that rang through the room, but also dropped silent all too quickly, the doors behind them shut.

His sister sucked in a breath. Went as still as a doe. "Trap," she mouthed.

A flicker of blue caught his eye through a thick tangle of trees and vines that climbed stone pillars carved from the very face of the cliff the palace had been cut into. He touched Astadia's arm and nodded toward a trellised walkway enmeshed in vines and more flowers. They moved forward slowly, Trale wishing they had not been disarmed before entering the receiving quarters. But they did not need blades to kill.

Trale slowed his heart. Trained his ears to listen. Honed his olfactory senses to take in everything. He'd always had an unusual ability to detect scents. But here, with strange mists and incredible humidity, scents were muddled. And yet . . . stronger.

But it was getting harder to hear.

Astadia flicked him a scowl, apparently noticing the rising din that wasn't voices or music. "Water," he whispered as they stepped through a final arch.

The Infantessa stood beneath a glass wall that broke the path of the waterfall, the Nydessan waters crashing and splitting right and left into the pool below. She was alone, hands clasped before her, blue skirts splotched to a darker blue where water had splashed them. Her face glistened.

Trale yanked his gaze away, but no blow came.

"Come." Her voice sounded distant, but he knew it was the roar of the falls. "Closer!"

Gaze down, Trale moved toward her, wondering where her mouth-piece, Steward Roberts, had gone. Whatever she would ask them, she clearly did not want it to come back to her. He understood. She was powerful. Some might think her weak for not ending her enemies at her own hand, but not Trale. A strong person knew how to delegate.

"Please." The Infantessa's voice strained against the din. "I would have your gazes as we talk."

Did she jest? Or perhaps a test—daring him to look at her and get whacked across the skull. Even as he considered her words, her dress fluttered closer. She stood before Astadia, and her small fingers touched his sister's arm.

"Please."

Trale slanted a look at his sister, who did the same to him. Together, they dragged their gazes to the Infantessa.

"Yes, please—we have little time." She shifted even nearer until he felt the brush of her skirts against his leg. "The falls will conceal our conversation," she said, her voice soft yet. "As you can imagine, there are ears everywhere here."

Trale couldn't hide his surprise or concern. Especially at the fact that there were no guards visible. Did she trust them? *It is an honor to be with her.*

"Do you know why you were brought here?"

Trale frowned. "As you command, Infantessa." His gaze dipped to her small waist, but not before he scanned the vegetation around her. Where were the guards?

Her eyes sought his again, rich and deep and kind. "Are we any of us true masters of our hearts or destinies, Mr. Kath? Surely you are not naïve enough to believe we control our futures?"

Mr. Kath? He nearly snorted. Were he master of his destiny, he would forbid anyone such formality. "Control is an illusion."

"Trale," Astadia hissed a remonstrative whisper at him, her expression severe.

"Nay," Infantessa Shavaussia said, her small hands again touching Astadia. "He speaks his mind."

Aye, he did that. Before this powerful queen of the eastern seas more than he had anywhere else. Being home, among his people—though they had been forbidden from visiting anyone they knew—it infused Trale with uncharacteristic recklessness.

I would risk it all to have her favor.

"It pleases me." Her words, soft and nearly lost in the roar of the falls overhead, encircled his mind, drew his eyes to hers. She was waiting for his gaze once more, an expectant smile on her full lips. Color pinked her cheeks. "He chose well, Trale Kath."

His mind rebounded from her eyes to her words and back. "He?"

"Poired." She dipped her head, the pearls in the fabric hooded crown swaying. "He will summon you here and deliver an order to kill the Celahar heir."

"The princess?" Astadia asked.

Shavaussia laughed. "Oh mercy, no. She might have been Zireli's heir, but she's dead. No, dear. He's after her brother—"

"Prince Haegan?" Astadia's face lost its color as she stepped back. "He is our target?"

"You know him, then? You've met the prince?" The Infantessa homed in on Astadia's reaction and response. Like a bird of prey ready to strike a wounded animal along a path. She seemed too interested.

Trale cursed inwardly. They had met the prince at the Falls, but mentioning that would bring them great pain at the hand of the Dark One who held their chains. Which was worse—serving beauty or dying in darkness?

He interposed himself between them. "What would you have us do, Infantessa?" He lowered his own gaze in hopes of distracting her again by his close proximity.

She took a tiny step back, teetered on the heels of her expensive shoes and seemed to fall.

Trale caught her, a hand around her waist.

She gasped.

Had he hurt her? He met her eyes, the color of Iteverian wood, a deep brown yet golden, too. They searched his face, and he felt a cold buzzing at the back of his mind. In his arm, she was smaller than he'd thought. Much smaller than Astadia. A tiny waist. And that bitter scent—of kizzy spice, used in pies and breads—the hint of it hung in the mist that haloed her head. Crown.

Crown!

She could have you seared within an inch of your life! "Mercy," Trale whispered, stepping away and feeling Astadia's firm touch against his spine when he'd backed into her.

The Infantessa smoothed her hands down her blue gown.

Nervous.

Trale searched her gaze again, confused.

She refused his gaze, looking to the side instead. "You must bring the prince here."

"Alive? Or dead?"

Her eyes widened and snapped back to his. "Alive, of course. What good is he dead?"

Trale bit back the retort, knowing she was still the ruler of the East and the Nydessan Sea. He dared not speak his mind to her. But what good was the prince *alive* here?

"Do you intend to kill him here? An exhibition of your power?"

The Infantessa seemed to cool at Astadia's pursuit of an explanation. "What purpose he serves is my concern, assassin. Bring him to Iteveria if you want to live."

"How—"

"I care not how." The Infantessa straightened. Her chin jutted.

"Infantessa, is there a problem?"

Trale instinctively stepped back and looked to the right, where the steward appeared out of the mists.

"It would seem these assassins deem themselves fit to question my will."

Trale shook off the confusing signals and realized what he'd mistaken for attraction was her plying his will. Using his own weakness against him.

"Bringing him here alive—" Astadia took a step toward the Infantessa.

In that split second, he realized her mistake. He reached for his sister as a half-dozen guards coalesced from the vegetation, blades drawn. "Easy."

The Infantessa Shavaussia paused at the entrance to the solarium. Her cool expression raked over Astadia. "Perhaps Poired chose poorly."

"Don't—"

Trale hooked Astadia's arm. Stepped in front of her and met the cold-hearted Infantessa's gaze. "Because you command us," he said, the words painful and, in truth, the only acceptable response. Poired would have Astadia beaten if he heard of her outspokenness.

Something flickered in the Infantessa's gaze as she swirled out of sight amidst a heavy protection detail.

Alone with Astadia and the mighty roar of the falls, Trale wondered . . . What purpose did the Infantessa have in bringing Prince Haegan here? Had she found out what Trale had discerned, what he'd heard whispered through the encampment around the Great Falls?

He heard the crack at the same time he felt his sister's smack on the back of his head. He caught her wrist then released it just as quick.

"What is wrong with you, you dull-witted, brainwashed male?"

Trale scowled.

His sister fluttered her hands and touched his chest. Leaned into him. Made her voice sickeningly sweet. "Oh, Trale, you're so powerful—"

He shoved her away. "Leave off."

"In truth, are you so idiotic not to see her exploiting your weakness, as every Iteverian assassin is trained to do?"

"I have no weakness."

"You are a man! That you have sight makes you weak when a woman is present."

A repetitive noise silenced them both. They both angled their ears toward the sound, listening. Two heartbeats later, a storm of black moved through the halls of the Infantessa's home.

Poired.

Trale felt as much as saw his sister's defiance swell once more as the black and red cloak slapped hard against Poired's legs. He stomped toward them, fire blazing in his eyes. Orange flames glowed around his hands. Heat wakes warbled around him.

Trale's stomach clenched, and his lunch threatened to reappear. Though he thought to grab Astadia's arm and drag her to her knees, he had no need to worry, for his sister had already sunk to the ground, her surge of rebellion short-lived in the face of Poired's wrath.

"You would defy the will of Sirdar?"

At the same time Poired shouted, Astadia flipped backward. The wake of heat proved so hot that chills pimpled Trale's flesh. He fisted his hands, knowing if he moved, if he attempted to defend his sister, it would go worse for her.

Thud!

She slammed against something.

Instinct pushed Trale up.

But Poired, skilled and preternaturally powerful, shoved him back to his knees with a singeing blow, even as he focused his anger on Astadia. Her screams bounced against the glass that protected them from the waterfall.

Stay, Trale commanded himself. Fisted his hands. It'd be over sooner. She would have a better chance of living if he remained silent and still.

"Think you the dog should be the master?"

"No—OOOOO!"

Breathing grew harder with each shout. Trale ground his teeth. Forced breaths through his nostrils.

I will kill him.

Astadia's shout grew into a sob.

I will kill him and bury pieces of him in the four corners.

Even as the thought took root, the anger and hatred burning deep,

Trale felt a tingling around his throat. It tightened. Constricted. He gasped, searching for a clear breath, only to realize Poired was wielding against him. He clawed at his throat.

His body lifted. Up . . . his knees unfolded. Trale focused on trying to breathe as he was hoisted off his toes by an invisible force. Swung around. Slammed against the wall. The pounding of the falls thudded against his shoulders and head. He groped for air, his lungs aching.

"What did she say?"

Trale flashed desperate eyes at Poired, who stood below him. He'd grown so powerful he didn't even have to hold his hands toward them as he wielded. He simply . . . willed it.

"Why did she bring you here?"

He suspected. The Infantessa said Poired wanted Haegan dead. She defied him in wanting the prince here in her palace. But surely she wanted to kill Haegan herself. Was there so great a difference where he died?

Trale's temples pounded.

Something in him refused to betray the Infantessa. But he knew Poired could sear his brain to dust. The edges of his vision began to cloud.

"*What* did she want?" the Dark One raged.

"To be alone with my brother," Astadia said, her words heaving, voice cracking. Her breath came unevenly, but she pulled straight. "They were attracted to each other."

Confusion flickered through Poired's blazing eyes.

"It was disgusting," Astadia said, a curl in her voice.

The constriction lessened—but only a fraction. Realizing Poired bought Astadia's lie, Trale averted his gaze to further the deception. Make this incipient believe it.

"Are you so weak beneath her Inflaming that you cannot see the hag beneath the glamour?" Teeth bared, the Dark One growled. Threw Trale across the room.

He skidded over the slick floor and slammed into a thorny bush. Tiny little daggers pierced his back and side. He cried out.

"Find Haegan Celahar." He spat on the ground. "Find him and kill him, or I will boil both of you from the inside out."

14

Panic ruptured the thin veil of hope Haegan held that he might escape this subterranean prison and find Thurig. He stepped back, his heart in his throat. He looked from the crooked old woman to the cacique. "Fierian? I—"

"He does not accept what Abiassa has gifted him with," Wegna said, craning her neck.

"Gifted?" Haegan's pitched word bounced off the slanted ceiling. "I am to lay siege to the lands, scorch the life from them, decimate crops and—"

"Ye are to *free* the lands!"

Haegan snorted and shook his head, looking down at the book Wegna had handed him.

"The trust She has placed in ye is enormous, Princeling." Eyes as violet as the northern seas peered up at him, glittering. Excitement sparked, then faded. And it was as oppressive and startling as if his face had been covered by a thick blanket.

Wegna lowered her gaze. Shifted around, took a few steps, then started to glance back at Haegan—but stopped. "Hide from her and ye invite the Destroyers to yer door."

Aselan straightened and unfolded his arms, his mouth turned down.

Haegan felt the alarm echo in his own mind. "Destroyers? You mean Deliverers?"

Wegna's curled fingers wrapped around the ladder. She hung her head again. "Think ye there are only Deliverers? Ye smell of them, of their glory. And the longer ye are without their presence, the easier the Destroyers will find ye."

"She speaks madness." But Aselan's expression was fierce,

Haegan recalled his words that Wegna had never spoken an untruth. Panic drilled through him. He didn't even know . . . "Wh—what are Destroyers?"

The old woman released the ladder, her shoulders hunched more than before. With her head bowed, it all but disappeared behind her crooked shoulders. "The embodiment of darkness."

"You jest!" Haegan refused to believe it.

"For there to be good, there must be evil. For there to be light, there must also be darkness." She turned to him, her eyes more clear than he'd seen them before. "For there to be Abiassa's bringers of justice, there must be their counterparts, those who chose to follow Ederac."

"Ed—what?"

After exchanging a look with Wegna, Aselan frowned. "Ye have not heard of Ederac? Gwogh failed ye miserably!"

"Gwogh!" Her eyes widened. "He was yer guardian?"

"He watched over me, paralyzed as I was. Taught me the Histories and Legacies, the Parchments—"

"How long did he serve ye?"

"Serve?" Haegan snickered. "He was my tutor."

Wegna wagged her hand dismissively, the parchment-thin skin exposing her blue veins. "At what age did he come to ye?"

Haegan struggled to recall. "My—my mother brought him to Seultrie when I was five or six. When I fell to the poison, she asked him to be my tutor."

"Yes yes." Wegna grew animated, turning her gaze around as she looked up at the ceiling. It seemed as if she saw beyond stone and wood. "Yes," she breathed, hissing the last letter. "It all makes sense now."

Haegan blinked. Sense? *Nothing* had made sense since he'd walked into this library. "I beg your mercy, but there has been little clarity since my sister consulted with an incipient for a Transference."

She gasped. "Transf—" Her eyes bulged. "This . . . tell me! What happened?"

"I . . . " Haegan frowned. "She and this incipient—"

"No, after! How? How are ye here, if the transference—"

"I fled the castle. My father blamed me for what happened to Kaelyria, sent the Jujak after me."

"But yer gifts?"

Haegan frowned. "I had none before the Falls."

"Yes yes yes," she said, laughing. "The outpouring of Her healing love—it ruptured the thin veil of man's attempt to harness Her power in yer life." She slapped her palms together. "That is what I felt. That is when something in me awoke."

Haegan swallowed. Refused to look at Aselan. Or the book.

"You *are* the Fierian," Wegna said as she moved back to the ladder. "And Gwogh knew . . . Oh, yes, that mad, brilliant man, he knew. It is why he poisoned ye."

15

Aselan saw the blow land, saw something in the boy break loose even as he denied Wegna's words.

"No, you misunderstand. Gwogh *healed* me—as well as he could. My mother said whatever had been slipped into my food at the feast nearly killed me. From that moment on, I had no use of my body. Only my mind, and Gwogh was there to sharpen it. He stayed at my side with his inane ramblings."

"Mm," she said, hesitated at the ladder, though she held it in place. "It is a nice yarn spun to conceal the truth."

Aselan felt tremors running through the prince's life, splitting it apart. He also noticed the change in the boy's posture and the knot between his brows. He'd need to be ready.

"What are you saying?" Haegan demanded, tossing the book onto the table.

Aselan took a step toward Wegna, fearing she may need his protection.

"Forgive me, Fierian," she said, her voice all contrition. "I sense yer pain." She sighed. "Yer loyalty to Gwogh is great. And . . . it is my earnest hope and prayer that ye would once more gain that despite his poisoning ye."

"Gwogh did not poison me! That was the work of Poired's agents."

"Aye," she said. "There may be truth to those words."

Haegan shook his head. "In one instant, you accuse Gwogh. In another, you say it was Poired's—"

"A man does not have to be wholly—or even partly—divested to the Dark One to do his work for him."

"Your words are but a muddle of years and too much time spent alone with books, I fear."

"Give care," Aselan said, "where ye accuse and demean. She is a respected teller, and one whose counsel I weigh carefully."

"Aye," Wegna spoke up. "I have spent time with books, but not Histories or Legacies, as ye have presumed, Fierian," she said, her voice much softer. Subdued. It annoyed Aselan, for he had not seen the Reader so melancholy. "But with the texts written by Her hand."

Haegan hesitated at that.

Wegna pointed to the table. "Aselan, would ye lift the book?"

His pulse skipped a beat. "Nay." He'd seen two accelerants who'd visited Legier touch it and immediately need Hoeff's healing touch.

"Please." She nodded, her face a wall of determination. "He will not understand if ye do not."

Aselan glowered at the thin-blood. Stalked to the table. "Watch closely, Princeling. What I do"—he huffed—"I do not for ye." He fisted his hands, clenching tight. Then reached out. He steadied his breathing. Waiting. Anticipation made his hand twitch. He clenched it again, then shook it out.

Haegan snorted.

Anger churned through Aselan. He grabbed the book.

White-blue flames shot out, blinding. Searing. "Augh!" Aselan snatched back his hand, shaking it and ignoring the pimpling of his flesh in reaction to the scalding.

Haegan started and leaped back. "Wh—I—Are you well?"

Aselan tucked his chin and stared through his brow at the princeling, holding his aching hand close to his chest.

"But—but I held it."

"Pick it up," Aselan said, nodding to the side where the book lay on the table. He waited as the prince rounded the room and reached over the Caorian wood. Even having known the prince already held it once without repercussion did not stop Aselan's gut from tightening as the boy lifted it.

Bouncing his shoulders, Haegan looked at them. "I don't understand."

"The Hand has written it. The Fierian must wield it."

Haegan frowned. "How can I when I can't even control the embers? I can only wield when I'm angry."

"Ah, that is because of missteps," Wegna said. "The poison, the Falls." She sighed and looked at Haegan. "She must have known these things, so we must trust that ye will be able to open the *Kinidd*."

"The what?"

She pointed to the book in his hands. "Her Words to ye. Only ye, Fierian, will be able to read it."

"Let's just hope you don't scorch the pages." The thin-blood had eighteen cycles, yet he knew not how to wield, had never heard of Ederac, and the fate of the world rested in his hands. Hands that could singe the world into oblivion. Aselan had never been one to cling to the faith of the accelerants or the belief in Abiassa as one of the Creator's Heirs, but it was hard to ignore, hard to reject, when he watched this thin-blood hold the sacred book that had scorched the hands of a half-dozen before him.

Though Wegna scampered back up to her hidden room, Aselan did not move or speak. Haegan had much to work through. And it almost seemed as if that part of the prince had shut down.

"It's glowing," Haegan muttered.

Aselan started. Stepped closer to the book with iron interlocked triangles embedded in the hide. "It's just the stone lights."

Haegan nodded. Weight crowded the young man's features, his eyes tracing the symbol over and over . . . lost in some thought.

"Are ye well?"

Haegan snorted. "Nay." He rubbed his forehead. "Nor have I been these last months." Grief etched its wretched marks on his face, tugged against his shoulders. "She has taken everything from me—my parents, my sister . . ."

Aselan considered the prince. "Ye loved them much?"

Haegan blinked and met his gaze. "My father . . . we came to an understanding in the end. My mother was attentive but distant, treading a fine line between my father's disapproval and her own heart." Turning the book over and examining the spine, Haegan sighed.

"And yer sister?"

The thin-blood smiled. "A heart of gold and a will of steel. There was never a day she did not visit me, bring me news of the Nine—and not the news Gwogh fed me of alliances and skirmishes. She let me know of people, her friends. She had fallen in love with a Jujak, though we both knew Father would forbid it because she had been promised to Jedric."

"Jedric?" Aselan raised his eyebrows, surprised. "I've heard his father's lands have been left untouched in the siege."

Haegan considered him, the pale blue eyes discerning. "How? He's between Caori and Seultrie—both are taken."

"That is the question."

"You accuse of him of collusion?"

"I accuse no one. I state the facts," he said, motioning them out of the library and once more into the dank passage.

A smile tugged at the corners of Haegan's mouth. "You would have done well in the Nine." He breathed a sigh. "Kaelyria was a master at negotiations. Quick witted."

"Ye were close?"

"Quite. She never gave me an inch, but she always gave me her time."

Their conversation was edging too close to dangerous. Aselan guided him back through the passage to the cave cell.

Toeff rose from his station outside the prince's cave.

"Ye are acknowledged, Toeff." Aselan stepped aside for Haegan to enter the cell. As the prince did, his annoyance at being a captive evident, Aselan waited for Toeff to secure the gate. "I will speak to my men about lifting yer restrictions." He nodded to Haegan's hands. "Keep those cool."

He turned to Toeff and showed him his own hand. "I have need of yer brother's healing. Where is he?"

Toeff's large, bulging eyes flicked to Haegan, then back. "Tending, master."

With the princess, then. Aselan headed down to the quarters where the prince's sister was tended. Thoughts, jumbled and tangled, tossed through his mind as he hustled down the steps, deeper into Legier's Heart.

"Cacique!"

Aselan hesitated on the landing, gazing up a couple of levels.

Teelh bent over the rail. "Legier's rage recedes."

The storm was slowing. His men would be glad to see the light of day and feel fresh air on their faces. It also meant with Teelh's help, Haegan would leave soon. 'Twould be madness to go out anytime within the next few days, as the deep snow would hide crevasses. But Teelh knew Legier and the Cold One's Tooth better than anyone.

"Good news, eh? We can be rid of the thin-blood!"

"Indeed," Aselan managed. "I'll be in the hall shortly." With a quick wave, he continued his course. When he gained the juncture to the section where Hoeff tended Seultrie's heir, Aselan slowed. Leaned against the wall, a stone light poking his shoulder. He cared not. The easing of the storm changed things. The prince would leave. The princess would want to leave as well, he was sure. Neither knew the other was still alive. Had he been wrong to withhold that from the two heirs? She was not yet able to travel, surely. Would the prince leave without her?

"You are well, master?"

Aselan pushed off the wall and smoothed a hand over his beard as he met Hoeff's gaze. "Much thought, my friend." He held out his injured hand. "I could use yer ministrations."

Hoeff shuffled backward. "Here, Hoeff have extra."

Aselan followed the giant into the side room of the princess's chamber. She'd been accommodated in a multi-room suit to afford privacy for her needs and so there could be no remonstration or accusation of maltreatment at his hands.

He kept his eyes to himself as he stood at the table that Hoeff bent over, his large hands moving nimbly from bottle to cup to mortar and pestle. When Hoeff shifted to face him, he fully blocked the room. Aselan relaxed a little as the giant cupped his wrist and lifted the poultice.

Hoeff grunted. *"Kinidd."* His brown eyes came to Aselan's. "You touch *Kinidd?*"

Focusing on the ministrations allowed Aselan to avoid the accusing eyes. He winced at the cool poultice that drew out the fire and infection of the burn.

"Only *Riætyr* touch," Hoeff rumbled.

"'Twas but a mistake," Aselan said as the giant wrapped a length of bandage around his palm. "Wegna . . . I was helping her."

"Hoeff say not listen her again."

Aselan smiled, flexing his fingers and noticing that already it felt better. He lowered his voice, counting on Hoeff's uncanny hearing to pick up his words. "Can she travel?"

Wide brown eyes came to his. Hoeff gave a very slow, lumbering shake of his head.

Why was Aselan so relieved at that answer? Yet he could not keep the Fierian here any longer. He wanted the boy out of the Heart, away from the people. He was unpredictable and naïve. Dangerous. But his sister . . . His gaze strayed to the side, toward her dais, which Hoeff gratefully blocked from view. He should know better.

Hoeff moved to clean his station. And a pair of ice-blue eyes held Aselan's.

His heart caught, frozen still beneath her gaze. Would his heart hesitate every time he saw her? She lay stretched out on the bed, pillows propped behind her torso and holding her slightly upright. Enough that she could see around the room with ease. Her white-blond hair, the sides braided, lay wrapped around the crown of her head.

Crown.

As the rightful heir to the throne left vacant by the Fire King's death, she should be wearing a crown. Aselan snapped out of admiring her.

"Playing with fire?" she asked, a smile toying at her pink lips.

Fire? Had she detected his skipped heartbeat? But when she looked at his hands, he cleared his throat. "Helping our aged Reader."

"Reader? Burning your hand helped a reader?"

He recalled how her brother warned the princess was quick-witted. "And how do ye fare this morning?"

"I was well until your healer told me I probably would not heal any further." Path etched her words, though she tried to hide it.

Aselan looked to Hoeff, who had planted himself on his chair in the corner, unusually burdened.

"I am not sure which of us was more distressed at the news," she said around a fake smile.

"Drigo are extremely empathetic."

She nodded, gaze down. "My wounds," Kaelyria spoke into the stillness, "are not of this world, he says."

Curiosity gripped Aselan, but he reminded himself these were things he should not already know. She seemed so sad, and he searched for something to cheer her. Instead, guilt tugged at him for concealing her brother from her. Haegan had said they were close. She could probably use the comfort of family.

"I made a deal with an incipient, and . . ." She smoothed the animal pelt around her. "It seems I will live with my decision for the rest of my years." Her eyes glossed, but she sniffed and pushed a smile into her face. "I will not dwell on the darkness that threatens, but rather on the light."

"Light?"

"Yes," she said, again running her hand over the fur. "Before I . . . came here, I could move only my head. Nothing below my jaw. The joy of feeding myself"—she hefted a cordi fruit from the bowl beside her—"is exquisite."

"Are ye always of an optimistic nature, my lady?"

Kaelyria bit into the fruit, catching the juice running down her chin. She slurped the juice and laughed.

Aselan offered her a towel.

"Optimistic?" Her delicate eyebrow arched. "Hardly. But if this is to be my lot, I will not have it in darkness." Though she took another bite, she had fallen prey to some thought that left her beleaguered. "I would, however, have a word with you, Cacique Aselan."

He inclined his head and tucked his hands behind his back.

"What word of my brother?" She sighed. "Is he dead? No one will speak of him. I know he brought me here, and it's been a week."

"So ye know where ye are?"

Hesitation clung to her. Setting aside the fruit, she leaned back against the pillows. "No, not with certainty." She wiped her hands on the towel. "Am I to remain crippled *and* ignorant then?"

Surprise coiled around him at her forwardness. "Nay." He dragged a chair over. "But I must have answers before there can be any for ye."

"Why? Have I injured anyone? Am I a threat—without use of my legs and without guards?"

"What do ye know of Poired and his armies?"

"That they have taken the only home I've ever known. That they have burned most of Seultrie, and her neighbors, to the ground. That refugees are flooding Hetaera and northward to avoid his scourge."

"And the Fire King?"

She jerked her gaze away, but just as quick, lifted her chin. Defiance creased her eyes. "Poired murdered my father before my very eyes."

"And the queen"—hesitation held him for a second—"yer mother?"

Her nostrils flared. "Dead." Eyes shone with unshed tears again, but she refused grief its power.

"And if yer brother is also dead—"

A tear wrestled her composure and broke free. She swiped it away. "*I am heir to Seultrie's throne.*"

Aselan's heart chugged to a stop.

"But regardless of whether Haegan is alive or dead, I cannot take the Fire Throne. It is not mine to take now."

"Why?"

She swallowed. "I have lost my gifts." Lifted her hands. "I cannot sit upon the Fire Throne if the Flames have left me."

"Left ye . . ."

Her lips pressed together, whitening the edges of her mouth. "I sacrificed the Flames in a vain, foolish attempt to save the Nine." Another tear. Then another. "And it was all for naught. They are dead. My whole family is dead. And Poired has the Fire Throne."

16

Trees. He wanted to see trees. Not the scorched skeletons of the forest left standing in the wake of Poired's army. Longing stirred for the thick-fingered branches and their leaves that offered protection from the sun. Feathery fronds that fragranced valleys.

Instead, only ash and smoke filled his nostrils. With few supplies but more than enough determination to break free of the scorched lands, Trale jogged a steady clip northwest. It was freeing, rushing through the country, listening to the rhythm of the lands. The wind in his face, its roar against his ears.

He ran.

And ran.

"Trale," Astadia called from behind.

Too soon. He wasn't ready to stop. "Nightfall."

"I cannot wait that long to rest. Please." With that, he heard her break the rhythm. Slow to a stop beside a mostly dried-up river. The lands had sucked hard from that wellspring, leaving it but a streak of muck.

For a heartbeat, he considered leaving her. Not stopping. But the thought startled him. He would never leave her. What was wrong with him? No matter how strong the urge to get away from Poired's stench, he had a pact with Astadia.

Trale circled back to where Astadia squatted, drawing water into the filter can. She then held it over her waterskin, the water morphing from brown to a moderately clear liquid, thanks to the membrane that held back impurities.

"We need to get moving," Trale said.

"We haven't stopped moving in six hours," Astadia growled. "What are you running from?"

Inflaming. But just as quick, the thought vanished from his mind. "We have a mission." Swiping a hand under his nose, he pivoted and walked to a small overlook. He crouched there to scan the plain.

"Yes, but if we continue at that pace for the next week, we'll be dead." Astadia retreated to a small patch of brown grass. "They'll have to drag our carcasses into Ybienn."

He huffed. Just had to get out of here.

"Is it Poired or the Infantessa you flee?"

"Both," Trale said, still feeling the ring of fire around his neck after Poired nearly suffocated him. But that was nothing compared to the humiliation of succumbing to Inflaming. Was that what really happened? It was the only logical explanation, though he detested the truth of it— that he had really succumbed. "But her . . ." He shook his head. "She wasn't telling us everything."

"Of course she isn't telling us everything!" Astadia pitched a small pouch of dried fruit at him. It landed with a soft thump at his boot. "I don't like her. Pretentious and too much frippery."

"You're jealous of her frippery." Astadia had always yearned for nicer things when they were bouncing around orphanages as children. When they set out on their own, she gave up hope of nice things, especially once Poired collared them.

"I want none of her frippery if it is at the cost of living with that Destroyer looking over my shoulder." Astadia's words were true and fierce. "She only told us to bring Haegan back. But he wants the prince dead. How do we satisfy both?"

He'd wondered that many times since leaving Iteveria.

"Maybe she wants him alive, so she can kill him herself?"

Trale pivoted in his boots, still crouched as he looked at his sister. "What if she wants him *alive*."

"Right—that's what I said, so she could kill him."

"No," Trale said. "Alive-alive."

"Where's the purpose in that?" She hopped to her knees. "Besides— you tell me how we're supposed to smuggle that prince halfway across the

Nine without getting ourselves killed? If Poired gets wind that we have him—we're all dead." She pointed the tip of her dagger at him. "That is the real reason—she wants *us* dead."

"That doesn't make sense."

"Nothing makes sense!"

• • •

LEGIER'S HEART, NORTHLANDS

Aselan strode to the pelt throne, his mind lingering on another throne of pelts—the dais upon which the princess reclined. Her soft words. Her pale blue eyes. He walked behind the fire, raging and soaring, throwing its smoke up to the tiny hole some hundred feet above them. He stopped, gazing over the fire to the men.

Sitting, he motioned for them to take their seats around the tables. "Toeff, bar the door."

As the giant complied, Aselan turned his attention to the matters plaguing him. "Teelh tells me Legier's rage has quieted." He nodded to the burly man, who rose to his feet.

"Aye, Cacique. It has." Teelh hooked his thumbs in the belt that secured his pelt tunic. "The winds are strong and the snow still falls, but I've trekked in worse."

"When could he set out?"

"At first light," Teelh said. "It'd take us the full day to make it down, but I can have him to Nivar Hold before the gate is shut."

Aselan nodded and fixed Teelh with a narrowed gaze. "Think ye the thin-blood can handle the journey?"

"I'll carry him if the need be," Teelh growled. "The longer he remains in the Heart, the more chance we have of invasion or war with the Nine."

A series of ayes rippled through the hall. The hounds snarled, as if agreeing.

"There is a complication."

The men quieted, their eyes on him.

"Two, actually." He drew in a deep breath and let it out. "Byrin, Teelh, and Bardin—ye saw him wield on the ledge."

"Aye," the three agreed.

"I took him to Wegna."

Only the flames moved and popped.

"She believes him to be the Fierian."

Stunned silence evaporated as shouts went up, demands to throw him out into the wild and let him fend for himself. For them to cut the breath from his lungs now before he had chance to start his destruction with the Eilidan.

"Ye would set yer hand against Abiassa?" Aselan spoke loudly, demanding their attention again.

"Were we to believe in Her—"

"Yet ye believe in Her prophecies, enough to slit the throat of an orphaned prince?"

Silence fell, heavy with anger and disapproval. Aselan let it stretch as he turned his gaze from man to man.

"Ye spoke of two problems," Byrin said at last, his voice stiff.

"Aye—his sister is the heir to the throne. I have not told the princess her brother yet lives."

"Why?"

"To gather information, discern if his truth was her truth."

"Send them both down with Teelh."

"Master," Toeff's deep voice vibrated in the large room.

Surprise tugged at Aselan that the giant would speak. He had never interrupted their proceedings. "Ye would speak?"

"Aye, Toeff know Hoeff say princess cannot move. Fragile."

"I care not," Caprit snapped. "They are trouble. Send them out."

"Where is yer honor?" Aselan demanded. "Ye would send a paralyzed woman into Legier's rage. If she died—"

"It'd be her own fault for straying onto the Tooth."

"Nay," Byrin said. "Teelh is an able tracker, but having to carry someone down—"

"We would not make it before nightfall," Teelh said. "We'd freeze to death."

Aselan rose to his feet. The icehounds leapt up and circled around him, one on each side. The Legiera fell silent. "I've heard yer concerns, yer complaints. It is decided—Teelh will set out at first light"—*Abiassa, let this be right*—"with the prince. They'll travel to Ybienn, where Teelh will be given shelter for the night, as is the custom of the Ybiennese. He'll return at first chance." He dare not show an ounce of hesitation. "The princess will remain here until she is recovered enough to travel."

"And who will make that decision?" Caprit asked.

"Hoeff will, since he has tended her and will tell no untruth." Aselan stood. "It is settled. It is said."

The men grumbled in unison, *"Oochak!"*

17

"Thin-blood. Come with me."

Haegan pushed slowly from the hard dais, eyeing the cacique through the iron gate. Toeff opened the barrier, and Haegan stepped out. "Is something wrong?"

But Aselan was already rounding the corner at the end of the passage. Haegan hurried to catch up, frustrated with the cacique's inattention. What if Haegan got lost in the labyrinth of passages? Hustling down a flight of iron steps, he found Aselan wasn't waiting. *Blazes.*

Haegan threw himself after him.

As they hit the third level and Aselan banked left, past the cantina, he threw over his shoulder, "The blizzard weakens."

Haegan's heart jerked. "I can leave?"

"Teelh prepares supplies as we speak." Around one corner. Down another flight. "In the morn, ye will break yer fast and venture into the storm."

"But I thought—"

"Legier still rages, but with Teelh's guidance, ye will make it. Ye'll obey his instructions without argument unless ye wish to die."

"Is that a threat?"

"Nay, Prince. 'Tis a promise of what ye'll face when ye leave the protection of the Heart." Aselan's stride slowed—no doubt deliberately.

Had he not been attentive, Haegan would have collided with the Eilidan leader. Instead, he fell back a step.

They had reached a small landing, and for the first time, Aselan hesitated in his headlong progress. His gaze flicked from one shadow to another, then he turned to face Haegan.

"Are you well?" Haegan asked.

Brown eyes sparked and snapped to his. "Ye have asked me every rise about the storm," Aselan said, his voice low and intense. "But there is something lacking in yer questions, Prince."

A quick gust of air from somewhere blew Haegan's shaggy curls into his face. He scowled, feeling a challenge from the leader. "What would that be, Cacique?"

"Earnestness." Aselan's eyes narrowed with meaning. "Ye speak of yer great desire and the urgency with which ye must return. To war against Poired."

"I do—I must."

Aselan pointed to Haegan's hands. "When we spoke with Wegna, ye said ye can only muster the embers when ye're angry."

Wetting his lips gave Haegan time to draw his courage together. "Not only," he muttered. "But . . . mostly. Or it would be correctly said, when I am angry, it consumes me."

"And yet—yet we are all alive."

Haegan frowned.

"Had ye set yer will on leaving and we impeded ye, would ye not have singed us all, whether ye willed it or not? I know not yer true reasons, Prince, but the fury of war grows not in yer heart. Ye have not left because ye do not want to face what awaits ye."

"My desires are irrelevant. I must return—it is my duty as the last remaining heir of Zireli. I"—he tried to breathe but his chest tightened—"must." The last word came out as mere whisper.

"There be no conviction in those words."

Haegan hesitated, then slumped back against the rail, letting it poke into his side. Pain was a solid reminder that he could walk. He could talk. It must be the hand of Abiassa that had so changed his course. How could he stay here when the storm raged—not in the pure snow that claimed this mountain, but in pure evil?

"You speak truth." Haegan sagged. "I have seen enough destruction and death." His breath shuddered through his lungs. "I do not want to be the cause of more. I do not want it. I will not be the Fierian."

Aselan said nothing for such a long time that Haegan looked up. The cacique was gazing out over the iron platform, watching his people bustle about their daily business on all six levels. Yet somehow Haegan knew he listened.

"I . . . I am alone, Aselan. I'm not even sure what I fight for—there is nothing left." A pair of brown eyes glittered in his memory, but Thiel seemed distant. Perhaps even lost to him. He must plot his own course. Away from Ybienn, where she had set her heart. "I have nothing to fight for." He snorted. "As you so ably pointed out, I don't even know *how* to fight."

Aselan gave a firm nod, and it seemed as if he had decided something. "Let's go."

"Where?"

"Patience, Prince."

Up another level, then down. Soon Aselan held out a hand as if staying one of his icehounds. "Wait here." He disappeared around a corner.

Haegan shifted to the side to see past the junction where four rooms split off the end of the passage. Inside one, Aselan stood with his hands on his belt. He nodded to someone, then stepped out of view. A moment later, a large shape filled the door. "Toeff?" Haegan's mind sputtered. "B—but I just left you."

"Hoeff, not Toeff. Toeff guardian. Hoeff healer." The giant trudged past him in slow, fluid movements.

Voices came from the room, soft and low, drawing Haegan closer. He eased around, stretching his neck to see into the room.

A weight clamped against his shoulder.

Haegan pitched forward, his heart thudding.

"Master tell Prince wait."

Duly chided, Haegan acknowledged the giant and eased away from the door. "Of course, of course."

"Stay," Hoeff growled. The giant turned and headed down the passage, apparently expecting Haegan to comply. As if Haegan were one of the icehounds the cacique owned. But Haegan wasn't a dog, wild or otherwise.

He slipped closer, again craning his neck to peer inside the room.

Aselan knelt on one knee at a heavily pelted dais. Taking in the room proved fairly simple, though the cave had ample space with a small foyer, a couple of chairs, and then an alcove containing the dais-bed. A tapestry covered the wall. And, no doubt, protected the room against the cold. Had Haegan been so looked after, he might not have this perpetual chill shivering through his limbs.

"Haegan?"

A blast of heat shot through him at that voice. He froze. Then looked to Aselan, who came to his feet with a fierce glare. Then he shifted back, revealing Kaelyria lying amid the mound of pelts.

Groomed and smiling, she held out her arm to him. "Brother!"

Six strides carried him across the space. He dropped onto the dais next to her. With a gargled laugh, she threw her arms around his neck. Hugged him tight.

Haegan held her, savoring the warmth of her, but confusion tangled his mind. "You . . . you're alive," he murmured into her thick blonde braids. "They told me you were dead." Then he recalled what Gwogh said. "And you can move."

"As you can see," she said, leaning back and staring into his eyes. "I am very much alive, and the Drigo healer has improved my . . . situation." Pain flicked across her face. Her smile faltered.

"You're alive." His mind could not wrap around it. He smiled at her. Shook his head. "It is too much . . ." He breathed a half-laugh, half-sob. "I thought I had lost you. That you'd died."

Her delicate brow rippled, but she kept her hold on him, her fingers pressing against his back and shoulder. "We are here, together."

He tugged her closer.

She wobbled. "Careful," she managed, her voice wavering.

"Easy with her, Prince," Aselan said from the corner.

Haegan punched to his feet. "I need not your help. Besides, you lied to me—"

Aselan rushed forward.

"—told me she was dead!" Haegan thought it an attack. He thrust out his hand, heat warbling around his fingers.

"Haegan!" Kaelyria shrieked as Aselan's arms encircled her shoulders with care. Her palm out to Haegan, she shook her head as the cacique supported her.

Haegan took a step back, realizing the cacique had stopped Kaelyria from tumbling off the dais. His heart clenched as he watched Aselan settle her back carefully, talking quietly, then draw a pelt around her waist.

"Ye are well?" Aselan asked.

"Yes. I thank you," Kaelyria said and her eyes lingered a mite too long on the Eilidan leader, who also lingered in his touch.

Humiliation crowded Haegan, shame that the cacique knew more of his sister than he did. Anger rose. "You lied to me."

"Nay." The cacique stood, his lips flat beneath his beard. "I have never lied to ye." He breathed out heavily. "But I did allow yer own belief to remain in place until I could discern what threat ye both presented. For that, I beg yer mercy."

Embarrassment mingled with indignation and confusion. What had transpired between his sister and this mountain man? He hated that Aselan had kept her from him. That he had been so much a concern and threat.

"Haegan," Kaelyria said, motioning him close again. "Come, brother. Comfort me as I did for you all those years."

He lowered himself to her side, glad when Aselan moved back. "I went to the Falls as you said." Gwogh had implied that Kaelyria had lied to him. Now he saw the truth of the old accelerant's words. "You said it would set everything right."

She touched his cheek. "I said the words I knew you would hear, Haegan." Tears welled in her eyes, and her lips twisted in an apparent fight against the wellspring of grief. She shook her head. "I did not mean . . ."

"You singewood," he teased, though the words were raw and the pain real. He marveled that their roles were reversed. So many years she had visited him, encouraged him in that lonely tower. Day after day at his side, tauntingly calling him singewood to lighten stiff conversations. "Why? Why did you do it?"

"It had to be done."

"At this cost?"

"Especially," she said, her eyes fierce. "I could not allow him to grow more powerful with my gift and Father's. And that was his intent."

Haegan leaned down and hugged her. "I will always be here for you, Kae." He pressed his lips to her forehead.

"I beg yer mercy, Prince," Aselan's voice intruded, "but I believe ye cannot keep that promise. Ye must tell her."

Kaelyria's brow knotted. Her cheeks rosied as she looked from Aselan to Haegan. "Tell me what?"

His eyes traced the layers of pelts across her lap, seeking an escape from the truth. Anything not to have to look into his sister's eyes and tell her his future. What he would cause.

"Haegan?" With a gentle touch, she lifted his jaw until their eyes met. The last few months washed away and once again, she was simply his sister. "What ails you?"

"Everything," he admitted miserably. When he was a little boy and scraped his knee, he would fall into her arms. But as the years melted away and Gwogh's influence grew stronger, so did Haegan's will. Yet, he sat here, longing to be that boy again. To cry away his anger. Because the other option was frightening, dangerous. He thought of the Ematahri he'd inadvertently killed. The way Drracien had been afraid of him.

"Remember what you saw at the Falls." Gwogh's urgent words during his recovery in Ybienn spiraled out of the dark chasm that held most of his memory from the Falls. He recalled jumping from the cliff. He recalled seeing Gwogh trying to stop him. Then his own anger. And then . . . nothing. Until he woke up, staring at Thiel.

What had he forgotten? Gwogh said he'd seen something. How did Gwogh know he'd seen something when Haegan himself could not recall it?

"What has happened?" Concerned etched Kaelyria's eyes.

Where was he to start? So much had passed since they parted ways in Seultrie. And there were pieces of him still angry that she had thrown him into this peril through the Transference. But therein lay folly, blaming her for something Abiassa called him to do.

"Haegan." Insistent and tinged with panic, she cocked her head. "Speak well and true, brother, for we have no secrets, and we are in no position for falsehoods."

"The Transference . . ." He wrestled with the tumult of words, truths, perils, and prophecies that tumbled through his mind. Gwogh's words when Haegan insisted he couldn't wield: *"that simply is not true."*

"It changed me."

She frowned.

He could play this ruse no more nor bear the pain of it. "They say I am the Fierian."

Eyes widening, she fell back against the pelts, all joy and vigor gone from her. "The F—" Her face twisted in pain. "You?" She shook her head, her gaze drifting momentarily to the cacique who stood guard. "No." Again, she sat forward and touched his arm. "You cannot wield. 'Tis impossible to be the Fierian without the embers and abiatasso. And in truth, you do not want that, Haegan. It's . . . the Fierian is a scourge."

"I can," he whispered. "I can wield—you gave me yours."

"No." She scowled. "That's not possible. Cilicien said my gifts would be but stored within you, but without the abiatasso, which is there at birth, you could not wield."

"I fear we both know the character of ka'Dur."

She deflated. "Aye. A wretched creature. I ignored my own judgment out of desperation." Glittering pale blue eyes took him in, searched him. "You can wield. Truly?"

"You needn't sound so surprised—I am not a complete singewood, as you insisted for so many years."

Pain creased her forehead. "I beg your mercy. It was a cruel taunt by a miserable, spoiled sister. And not an ounce true." She sighed. "Then you will do it, be the Fierian?"

"'Do it' implies will and choice. I have neither." He sighed.

"But Seultrie—"

"Aye." Truth burdened his shoulders with guilt and responsibility.

"I cannot go back, brother."

"Of course, not now." He gave her a reassuring nod. "But when you're recovered enough."

Grief carved painful lines in her pretty face. "I am dead." Her voice tremored. "You know how cruel they are to the invalid."

"Aye," he said, his chest tightening. "Well aware."

"And at a time like this, with Poired raging—" Kae's lower lip trembled. "They need a strong ruler, Haegan. I cannot go back. I will not."

He saw her resolve. Separating brick and mortar was been easier than separating his sister from a decision once set.

"You know what must be done, Haegan, especially now that you can wield."

Haegan frowned.

"He has spoken often of returning to defend Seultrie," came the cacique's rough voice.

Kaelyria nodded, smiling. "It is right, Haegan." Tears made her eyes seem large. "I was never meant to rule."

"You are the heir."

"Only because the succession was changed when you were poisoned."

Gwogh. Haegan tasted the bitter truth of that statement.

"They already believe me dead. Better to let them think so. You cannot argue it."

"I can. My mind is keen enough, but I am no warrior. I would be a king who cannot fight in a country engulfed by war." He glanced at the cacique. "Even he showed me I am ill qualified."

"Then he can train you."

Haegan stilled. Felt the cacique do the same.

"He's to leave on the morrow." Aselan sounded terse. Decided.

Kaelyria looked at Aselan and seemed to share a silent dialogue with the cacique before slowly turning back to Haegan. "Must you?"

His heart thudded against the question. "The realm is without leadership. Our people—"

"So you *have* thought about taking the throne."

"I thought you dead. There was no one else."

She studied him, and he had the sense she saw straight into his insecurities. "Does Kiliv Grinda live?"

The question took him aback. Was she suggesting he cede the throne to his father's top general? "To my knowledge, he still lives." He glanced at Aselan, who shrugged. No news had penetrated the storm.

"Then borrow a week or two. If winter rampages here in the North, as Aselan has told me, the cold will have settled at least as far south as the Siannes. With our father dead, Poired has probably encamped in Zaethien or Luxlirien until the thaw. You know Grinda—as long as he draws breath, he will hold the Jujak together. They will be waiting when you return."

Aselan cleared his throat. "She's right, Princeling." His voice betrayed a grudging admiration that made Haegan uncomfortable for multiple reasons. "No general worth his salt would attempt the Siannes in winter unless he had no other choice."

"Stay," Kae said. "Learn what you can from Aselan, so you are better prepared to fight." Her hand covered his. "It will give us more time as well, before you head off."

Haegan didn't like this subtle alliance between his sister and the cacique. "We should go to Ybienn together. Maybe craft a way to carry you—"

"No!" a roar erupted behind them. Though it vibrated the beams, the voice was not angry. Hoeff stepped toward them. "The princess not go. She rest. Heal."

Haegan twisted toward the cacique.

"Hoeff has complete authority over the healing caves and patients. He does not like when we go against his instructions, not that I would."

"But you are Cacique."

"And he is Drigo. Have ye tried to cross a Drigo?" There was mirth in his voice. The cacique stepped into the room a little farther. "It has been but six days since ye arrived here. The princess was on the verge of death. Ye yerself believed her dead."

"But if we carry her—"

"That ye speak such reveals yer ignorance of Legier and the Cold One's Tooth. Both would shred a person not used to the heights or rigors of navigating the spines." The cacique shook his head, arms crossed. "No, for the sake of peace and the well-being of my people, the princess will not leave the Heart."

"And you will train my brother," Kaelyria said, no question in her words.

Aselan gritted his teeth. Then nodded. "I will train him."

18

Would that Thiel could claw out of her skin, free herself from this useless, idle nonsense. But she was a Thurig. Daughter of King Thurig and Queen Eriathiel. As such, it was required that she give welcome to the Earl and Countess of Langeria and their daughter, Lady Peani, pledged to marry Thiel's brother Relig.

With her parents and three brothers, she stood on the platform of the great hall, surrounded by a sea of nobility who'd ventured out on this icy winter day.

A trumpet sounded. The official pronouncement that the Langerian contingent had entered the courtyard. An anticipatory murmur rippled through the crowd. Expectant faces looked to her father, who stood proudly in his full-dress uniform. Relig shifted nervously beside him, ready for his bride-to-be to make her appearance.

The large, carved doors swung inward. Silence dropped. The herald stepped in, squared his shoulders and announced, "The Earl and Countess of Langeria and the Lady Peani Ibirel."

Among the party were at least a dozen Langerians, led into the parting sea of bodies by the earl and countess. Behind her parents, Peani walked resplendent in a peach gown that made her dark skin glow. Her small tiara, nestled amid coils and braids, sparkled as she and her parents bowed low before the king.

"Yaorid, Lumira, welcome to Ybienn," King Thurig's voice boomed across the Grand Ballroom.

The earl stepped back and held a hand toward his daughter, who waited, cheeks flushed, for the official welcome. "King Thurig, it is an honor to present to you and your son, in hopeful respect of his continued agreement to take as his bound, my daughter, Peani Clarentia Ibirel."

Ever graceful and elegant, Peani tucked her right leg behind her left and gave a low bow. Only when the girl ducked out of view did Thiel see the three behind her. Members of the Violet Sea Watch, no doubt, by their severe uniforms designed for protection against the bitter elements but also to strike fear into the hearts of their enemies, the Rekken. Skin weathered dark from years on the water. Black hair from the long line of Langerians. The Watchman in the middle stood tall and stared boldly at Thiel.

Heat shot through her. Haegan would singe the blood from the impertinent man. She pushed her attention and annoyance to Relig, who seemed to have frozen in his spot as he waited for their father to turn to him. Only then could Relig accept Peani, though the formal ceremony would not take place for a fortnight.

Finally, her father stepped aside and looked to Relig, who released the breath he'd been holding and moved regally down the three steps to the main floor.

The earl extended Peani's hand toward Relig, who clapped his feet together and gave a curt nod to Yaorid. "With the favor of the Lady, I accept yer daughter and from this moment forward bind my heart and life to hers, if she will have me."

Peani rose, her cheeks positively crimson. "It is my honor, Prince Relig—and my pleasure."

Pleasure? Peani had added to the formal wording. Thiel looked to her mother, who was smiling at Relig as he led Peani up onto the dais, a symbolic gesture of her leaving her family and joining theirs. The pair faced the crowds.

"Celebrate with us," the king announced, "as House Nivar is joined to Ibirel of Langeria."

As the nobles queued up to offer their congratulations to the couple, Thiel could not help the jealousy digging hard into her heart. Had Haegan remained—would that be them? Instead, she stood here, cocooned in silk and satin, *celebrating*. Haegan could be in dire need of help. Dying somewhere awful. Or already dead.

"He will return, sister," came Tili's deep whisper at her ear.

Thiel glanced over her shoulder to where her brother stood, his broad chest slashed with the imperial sash, which identified him as the crown prince. "Then why has he not come?"

"Because he's a thin-blood and unable to tell time," Tili muttered good-naturedly.

But what if it was more? What if—

"His purpose is not fulfilled, so he must yet live."

At his matter-of-fact words, she looked into her brother's eyes. Siphoned strength she'd lost. Courage that had waned. "I pray ye are right."

"Rarely am I wrong." He straightened, his gaze drawn to something. Thiel turned and was surprised to find the Watchman before her, his eyes—appropriately—on her brother.

The broad-shouldered Watchman bowed curtly. "Yer Highness." His fist crossed his chest and thudded against a leathered badge. "I am Yedriseth of Haroessa."

Surprise coiled through Thiel—Haroessa. One of the four noble houses of Langeria, known for their might and hardiness.

Tili edged forward, extending his arm. "Well met, Yedriseth. I recall the demonstration of the Watch two years past. Ye won the match."

Yedriseth inclined his head as he clasped forearms with her brother. "Sadly, that was my brother." He straightened, his jaw angular and seemingly carved out of stone. As he released her brother, he slid his gaze to Thiel, an obvious hint that he wanted an introduction.

"Ah." Tili chuckled, his hand coming to the small of her back. "Sir Yedriseth, allow me to introduce my sister, Kiethiel, only daughter of Thurig the Formidable."

Yes, dear brother, please remind him of our father's formidability.

Yedriseth bowed. "Princess, it is an honor."

As propriety demanded, Thiel acknowledged him with a tip of her head. "I thank ye, sir." But catering to this nobleman wasn't in her blood.

"Will ye remain for the entirety of the festivities?" Tili asked, saving her from an awkward silence.

Yedriseth nodded. "My unit is assigned to the earl's protection. We will escort him back to Langeria once the binding is complete."

Tili angled his head. "Is the threat from the Rekken so great now, that the earl needs a military escort?"

Yedriseth's expression hardened. "Greater with every rise of the moons."

Moons. "Not the sun?" Thiel asked.

"Aye," Yedriseth said with a smile, apparently pleased she had joined their discussion. "The Rekken prefer nocturnal attacks."

"Cruel," Thiel muttered.

"And lethal, Princess. They give no care to innocents or damages. They are intent on one thing: war."

A familiar face bobbed through the crowd, snatching Thiel's attention and focus. "If ye will excuse me," she whispered, hurrying off the stage and weaving through the crowds toward Drracien. Though she lost sight of him a couple of times, she eventually homed in on the accelerant.

"Tell me it is not true." Thiel gripped Drracien's hand tight. "I beg ye."

The brooding accelerant gave her a surprised look. "I would say whatever you wanted to have you throw yourself at me like this."

Thiel rolled aside her irritation and his words, focused solely on one thing. "It is said the Fire King and Queen Adrroania are dead." She squeezed his hand again. "There are rumors Haegan is as well, that he could not have survived Poired's attack."

Drracien lifted a shoulder. "What am I to say? I was not there."

"Ye said ye could sense him—the embers."

"I did," he said with a nod.

Hope squirmed through her fears. "And still? Ye can still sense it . . . *him?*"

After a light shake of his head, he shrugged again. "I haven't given it much thought. I—"

"Swear to me that he is still alive."

Drracien's dark brow rippled and he drew back.

She could not endure not knowing any longer. She must have the truth of Haegan's situation. "Do it—swear!"

"He is honor bound only to Abiassa," came Tili's quiet but reprimanding voice as he joined them, his posture stiff. Disapproving.

Drracien lowered his gaze . . . to their hands. Only then did Thiel fully understand her brother's disapproval and Drracien's suddenly sweaty brow. She was holding his hands. In public. Before Abiassa and everyone. Thiel withdrew her touch and straightened.

"Yer oath is to Abiassa alone, is it not, Accelerant?" Tili's gaze roved the all-too-attentive crowds, but his words were laden with warning.

"It is," Drracien said quietly. "The Guidings forbid us from swearing oaths beyond that."

Thiel bristled. "Tili, ye know well I only meant—"

"Peace, dear sister." He situated himself between her and Drracien, still watching the people. "The reports—"

"Were vague."

Tili's gaze darkened as he scowled at her. "The Fire King *is* dead."

"Aye." The grievous loss did not belong solely to the Nine but to all of Primar. And served to lessen Thiel's grief a fraction. "But there is no proof Haegan died as well." She nodded to Drracien. "Our friend here has said he could sense the presence of Haegan's embers."

Tili's eyebrows rose. "This is true?"

"Of course it's true," Thiel hissed. "What? Am I liar now?"

"Ye are a woman concerned about the man she has thrown herself at," Tili said with a chuckle.

"Would that be me or Haegan?" Petulant, unrepentant Drracien never knew when to stop.

"I threw myself at no man!"

"Good eve, accelerant," Tili said, pulling Thiel from the shadows. As they walked, he angled toward her. "Ye shamed yourself—"

"Drracien is merely a friend."

"I meant with yer treatment of Sir Yedriseth."

"Yedriseth?" she squeaked. "He sought—"

"Respect. Ye gave him none."

Thiel lowered her head. "Ye know well he sought more than that. He had *intentions*."

"Every eligible male in the realm has intentions toward ye because ye are daughter of the king." He huffed. "No matter yer own tied-up affections, ye *must* act with grace."

"I will not be pandered to and flirted with just to further a kingdom."

"What of Haegan?"

Thiel stilled. Frowned at him. "What do ye mean?"

"Assuming he is alive, he is to be the Fire King, yes?"

A trap lay within that question and she dared not answer.

"And think ye that ye are ready to be his queen? Think pandering and flirtations will cease merely because ye wear a different crown? Whether with Father or Haegan, many will seek yer favor because ye influence men of power."

Thiel turned to him, surprised. Her brother might have mischief and cheek, but he was a shrewd leader already. "What of ye?"

He frowned. "I am yer brother. I need not yer favor. And yer wiles influence far too much as is decent."

She punched his shoulder playfully. "I meant that ye are a man of influence, Tili, so what will it take for yer head to be turned by a girl?"

He grunted, his expression dark and serious. "Much."

• • •

"Hands up!"

Fists raised to either side of his face, Haegan stood in front of Aselan, who had shed his pelts and leather tunic for a lighter, linen one. For the safety of the men and the people of the Heart, Haegan wore the bandages and the sangeen leaves, lest he become angry during the training and inadvertently lash out.

"Up," Aselan growled, adjusting Haegan's right hand a little higher. "Protect yer face and neck."

Haegan nodded, sweat trickling down his temples and chest. Six or seven Legiera stood by, ready to assist with his training, and all too willing. Already his arms ached from holding them up.

"Feet!" Byrin shouted from the side, his large, pelted foot sweeping Haegan's out from under him. "Light on the feet."

It was hard to relax when his thighs were burning and trembling. But he clambered upright again and forced himself to comply. To learn.

Aselan slid side to side, bouncing as if on air. "Stay light. Ready. Relaxed."

Haegan's gaze drifted to the cacique's feet as he nodded.

Thwak!

Pain thudded against his jaw, the reed in Byrin's hand flashing away even as Haegan tasted blood and stumbled.

"Yer hands were down," Aselan said.

Frustrated he could not keep his hands up—*how many times had Byrin struck his jaw?*—Haegan grunted. Wobbled back into place.

"Feet. Stay on the balls of yer feet."

Huffing, Haegan pulled himself back into place. Reminded himself he'd asked for the training.

Almost immediately, Aselan's punch came at him.

Haegan snapped his wrist, blocking the strike with his forearm. Which was bruised and aching. But he blocked.

"Good," Aselan said—even as he struck again.

Haegan blocked with his left. Then his right. Right again.

"Feet." The reed cracked against his shin again.

Haegan grunted. His legs collapsed.

Aselan lowered his hands. Stepped back. Not a drip of sweat on his tunic. "Take some water, thin-blood. Ye need it."

His long hair plastered to his face and dripping sweat like a trickling creek, Haegan moved to the table where a pitcher of water waited. Palms on the wood, he lowered himself—with a series of groans and grunts—to the bench. His arm trembled when he lifted the pitcher. He gulped several cups between panted breaths. Wiped his brow using his tunic, which seemed more like a wet dishrag than clothing.

"The ring!"

"Oochak!" muttered several Legiera, who grouped up.

Watching the men form a circle in the middle of the room, Haegan frowned. That did not look good.

"Come, thin-blood." Byrin was grinning far too much.

One of the more scrawny men emerged from a small room with a handful of reeds. He handed them out to the Legiera.

"Prince," Aselan said, pointing with the reed to the center of the ring.

Exhaustion riddling his bones, Haegan climbed to his feet and shuffled to the perimeter.

Hand on Haegan's back, Aselan guided him into the center. "This be where ye learn to go light on yer feet."

After a furtive look around the group of mountain men, Haegan knew this would not end well. Or soon enough.

"Keep moving," Aselan said, even as a stick slapped his right calf. It stung and he hopped to the side.

"Eyes out, hands up," Aselan ordered even as another strike nailed his shin.

He'd go to bed welted this night. The strikes weren't hard enough to break skin, but they were enough to serve as punishment for not being light or quick enough on his feet.

"Dance, thin-blood," Teelh taunted.

A particularly well-placed blow buckled Haegan's knees.

"Hold," Aselan said as Haegan went to the ground.

Panting, groping for a breath that did not hurt, he braced himself on the cold stone floor. Then pushed up.

"Ye asked for training," Byrin chuckled.

"Aye." Haegan drew a ragged breath. "But not a flogging."

"In a fight, there is little difference," Teelh said.

Aselan motioned with the reed for Haegan to stand. And despite the agony roiling through Haegan's limbs and body, he saw in Aselan's face something he had not anticipated—respect. There was no gloating. No demoralizing pleasure in beating Haegan. Each of these men had been in this ring at one time. They had endured. They had fought. They had learned.

So would he. Swallowing hard, Haegan came up. And the dance began again.

• • •

LEGIER'S HEART, NORTHLANDS

Clacks and shouts rose from the training yard. On the settee in the yellow sitting room, Thiel dug her fingernails into her palm as she sat poised, back straight, chin lifted. Hands resting in her lap, she smiled. At least, she thought she did. Her face had gone numb hours ago.

Mother chatted with Lady Lumira and Peani. Silks. Flowers. Ribbons. Attendants. Sleighs. Everything for the wedding and celebration ball afterward. The family dinner. The nobility event in the great hall. The ceremony beneath the Tri-Tipped Flame and arch. Every detail attended to, laughed over.

And I merely want a sword. Cadeif had trained her to always have a blade ready. It would explain the cold steel strapped to her thigh even now. Her gaze drifted to where it lay, hidden beneath the satin and brocade gown.

A particularly loud clack jarred Thiel. She twitched, the urge great to rush to the window and see who was sparring. Her gaze drifted to the windows. Was it Tokar? He had been livid with the way Tili had challenged and pushed him. Or perhaps Praegur, who had become especially adept at swordplay. Even Laertes was never far behind the others, though half their size. The Nivari had taken a liking to the lad, adopting him like an unofficial mascot.

"Kiethiel?"

At her mother's prompt, Thiel blinked. "Mm?" She turned to discover the other three ladies watching her. No—worse. They were waiting. For an answer. To what?

Awkward silence was broken by taunting laughs.

Her mother straightened more. "I'm sure yer invitation, Peani, to have Kiethiel stand out fer the wedding was a shock."

Stand out? The wedding—binding. "Of course," Thiel whispered, shoving breathlessness into her words, then a silly laugh that made even her cringe as she worked to cover her blunder. "That is normally reserved for family."

Peani blushed prettily, looking between the mothers in a way that told Thiel the point had already been made. "Aye, but as I have no sister . . ."

"It is an honor," Thiel's mother said, her words firm.

Right. Honor. But strange. To stand out. "Whatever ye would wish," Thiel conceded.

"In earnest?" Peani asked. "It would mean a great deal."

Clack. Augh! Shouts vied for her attention. A particularly raucous shout plucked at her attention. That sounded like her brother.

Answer. Answer Peani. "Then—then it is decided."

"Marvelous." Her mother's stern expression lurked behind a thin veil as she rose and rang the bell for a servant. "Since that that's settled, let us be going. Mistress Raechter will never grant mercy if we keep her waiting. She's so eager to meet ye, Peani."

As the others rose to don their coats, Thiel slipped over to the window. As she had suspected, Tili sparred with Tokar. But a surprise addition to the training yard was Relig. He might be a decent fighter, but he preferred books and diplomacy.

"Never did I dream I could marry one so handsome."

Thiel resisted the urge to roll her eyes at Peani's declaration. Instead, she turned and smiled, searching her face for falsity. For evidence that the thing more attractive to Peani was not her brother's "handsomeness" but his position as second in line to the throne of Ybienn and the Northlands. But she saw utter devotion in the girl's eyes. "Ye truly love him."

Blue-green orbs widened. "Of course." With that Peani swirled and returned to their mothers and Atelaria. Back in the yard, she saw Laertes skirting the perimeter, fending off an attack by a Nivari. The men had been kind to her young friend, and she was glad to have him in a safe place. To allow him to be reared with respect and mentors strong in mind and body.

Puffs of smoke shot up through the trees to the right. Thiel glanced there, realizing Drracien and her father must be training together. Haegan should be there as well. Learning how to harness what was within him.

"Shall we?"

Thiel turned back and saw the queen's guards waiting at the doors with the men of the Watch. Including Yedriseth. His expression smoothed as he looked at her, and he gave a slight nod.

Altogether, they made a sizeable group as they headed out to the home of Councilman Raechter, whose wife had invited the women of the hold to a private gathering. Even as the sleighs pulled into the grand estate on the outskirts of Ybienn, the number of other sleighs and coaches warned that this was no small assembly.

An hour later, immersed in ribbons, perfumes, and gossip, Thiel rubbed at her temple.

"Fare ye well, Princess?" Sir Yedriseth asked, making one of his many rounds through the parlors, which were half the size of Nivar Hold's, but still quite elegant, with mirrors and gilt trim.

"Aye," she said with sigh, lowering her arm and stretching her spine.

"Ye stand on the perimeter and not with the ladies."

"Am I under yer protection now?" she asked, lifting an eyebrow at his boldness.

"A wise guardian is aware of more than his charge."

"True enough," she said, watching as the councilman wandered past a particular group of young ladies for the fourth time. She supposed it was because of her mother that he was even present at a ladies' party. The queen stood across the room, a cup of tea balanced on its saucer in one hand. Her gaze, too, was on the councilman, and judging from the disapproving look, Thiel suspected her mother found his presence more an impropriety than an honor.

"Yer host seems fond of the ladies."

Thiel hesitated, but refused to play into his hand. It annoyed her in one respect that Yedriseth had come from Langeria and already noticed a weakness in a Ybiennese leader—the man seemed to stray easily from his wife. Find comfort with younger women. Or girls, in this case.

"One would wonder, Sir Yedriseth, why ye are within and not guarding outside as the Nivari do."

"The Nivari are not outside," he countered.

Another truth. They remained quietly in the shadows, bordering the interior but unobtrusive. It was her way of trying to hint—

"Of course, yer intention was to put me in my place, I suppose."

If her point was taken, why did he remain beside her? She gave him a sidelong glance.

He smirked. "Well put, Princess." With a curt bow of his head, he backed up and returned to his duties.

"Isn't he dreamy?" came the giggling voice of her cousin, Atelaria. "What did he say to you?"

"Nothing of value." Thiel's gaze once more hit the councilman, who was eyeing eighteen-year-old Seraecene, daughter of another council member. Wouldn't that put things to riot. She'd have to mention this to her mother.

"I think he favors you," Atelaria said with a sigh. "Why do they all favor you?"

"Because I could not care less if they do." She smiled at her cousin. "Ye should care less, Atelaria. Then they'll be falling over ye."

"You toy with me," Atelaria pouted.

Thiel laughed. "It was cruel of me to do so. I beg yer mercy."

Atelaria nodded, victorious. "I would ask one favor, cousin." She had well maneuvered that situation into her own favor. "Introduce me to your friend."

"Which friend?"

"The handsome one—Tokar."

• • •

He stood there on the other side, out of reach, separated from Haegan by a chasm of roaring fire. Bruised. Bloodied. Blackened by fire and death.

"Father!"

Footsteps—strangely loud in his ears—crept from the shadows. His heart raced, watching as the deeper darkness crawled toward his father, who stood, oblivious to the threat and danger. "Father—move! Go! Run!"

But his father stayed. Stood. Stared.

"No."

A form came at Haegan. A strange coldness enveloped him. A vice cuffed his throat.

In a heartbeat, Haegan's eyes shot open. Reality wrestled with the fog of sleep. Warned him of danger. He blinked. A dream?

No!

A figure towered over him. Hooded. Strangling him!

Haegan gripped the forearms with still-bandaged hands, choking. He thrashed, flooded with panic and dread.

"Ye are dead, thin-blood. *Dead.*"

The hands fell away and the man removed the hood. Byrin's salted hair lay askew as he looked down at Haegan with a mixture of disappointment and something else. Pity? He backed up as the cacique stepped into the room.

Aselan stood over him. "Ye must learn to fight from the ground. Being pinned is the surest way to end up dead." He turned and started for the door. "Get up. Dress. Meet us in the hall."

Rubbing his throat and shaking off the terror of being choked—now he understood why Aselan had insisted he wear the sangeen to bed—Haegan peeled himself from the pelts. Agony tore at every muscle and sinew, reminding him of the last eight days of torture. Training.

Legs slung over the bed, he sat for a moment. Let the weight of sleep drain away. Who did he jest? This wasn't merely sleep. It was utter exhaustion. But even in his dreams, he'd detected the threat. His subconscious had heard Byrin entering. But the dreams—the terrors had stymied his ability to sort fact from fiction. He must conquer these dreams. He *must* be rid of them.

Dressed and dragged to the hall, Haegan stood before the Legiera. There was not a piece of his body or mind that did not sag beneath the weariness.

"It is in these days—where exhaustion threatens to overrule—that ye must fight harder. Lose to the exhaustion, consider yer life forfeit."

Haegan nodded. Knew it to be truth. But would that he could just sleep . . . for another day.

Without warning, his leg kicked up and his head flew backward. By the time the pain in his skull registered, he lay on the floor. Aselan had laid him out flat. Groaning, he cringed. Closed his eyes.

"One of the most dangerous positions is to be on the ground, beneath yer attacker."

Pain bled through every pore of his body, but he forced his eyes open.

Aselan knelt at his side now. "If ye are pinned, ye want to be unpinned. Flip the tactic." He planted his hands on Haegan's throat and gripped firmly. "How do ye get free?"

Haegan gripped Aselan's arms.

"Aye—but do not push up. Pull apart."

Haegan tried. Couldn't. His arms were too tired.

Aselan pointed to his own throat. "Grip me." Once Haegan held Aselan by the throat, the cacique showed him a maneuver. "Grip the wrists and pull outward. Even if yer attacker is five times larger, ye pull on one arm. Anything to break the grip, so ye can breathe. Like so." He showed Haegan the move. "Once ye've done that, slide yer fist through the opening in the arms, straight through and push the hard part of yer wrist and forearm into their neck." Even as he spoke, he did the move.

Pressure against the side of Haegan's throat forced him to turn away.

"Once ye have leverage, keep going until ye can either get free or flip the positions." Aselan patted his own chest. "Do it."

Gripping Aselan's strong forearms, Haegan struggled to be stronger.

"C'mon, thin-blood. I'm killin' ye."

Haegan gritted his teeth. Pried.

"Do one arm, then."

Shifting the tactic, Haegan used both hands on one wrist and managed to shift the pressure.

"Aye, now fast—through the arms with yer fist and arm."

Haegan punched his fist through the gap and planted his forearm against Aselan's neck.

"Push, twig, push!"

With a meaty grunt, he pushed. And Aselan was forced aside.

Exultant, Haegan sagged. But Aselan began again. And again, until Haegan wanted to cry. He had nothing left.

But at that point, Byrin stepped in. Or rather—he dropped in. Right on top of Haegan. Forearm and bicep squeezing Haegan's neck.

"Twist the lower half of yer torso out from under him."

Haegan struggled.

"Do it! Scoot hard. No matter how absurd it might feel."

With trembling limbs, Haegan struggled out from beneath the thick-chested Byrin.

Hours—*or was it days?*—went by. Haegan grew more exhausted. Less capable of thinking, he slowly realized his movements were growing clumsy yet automatic. By the time he sat on his dais that night, numb from head to toe, he could no longer count the hours they'd spent training. Everything hurt. At least, he was sure it would if he could feel anything.

"Are you well?"

He looked up, startled to find Kaelyria in a wheeled chair in the doorway. The sight of her brought a smile to his lips. "I'm alive," he said wearily. He gestured to the chair. "That's a clever contraption."

"Someone—a Drigo—named Coeff made it for me." She shrugged, then frowned, looking at him more closely. "You are covered in bruises."

"Aye." Even breathing felt like it took spectacular effort. But he'd seen the disappointment in Aselan's expression when they'd broken for the day. "I'm slow."

"You always were." The teasing in her voice had always been there.

Haegan snorted. "I've laid in a bed for ten years and now I am tasked with being Abiassa's champion—and yet, I cannot defeat even one of these Legiera."

"Must you defeat them?" She rolled farther into the room and spun around so her chair was against the wall, facing the door, but she laid her hand on his.

"No, I must live. And that is what he is teaching me. But he is twice the man I am with ten times the strength and agility." Haegan sagged beneath the realization. "I have never been enough, sister. And I fear I never will be."

"You are called by Abiassa not because you are the mightiest or the strongest, but because you are willing."

Aaesh entered with a tray of replenishment

Haegan frowned at her. "I'm not willing."

Aaesh arched her eyebrow. "No? Who is training, nearly killing himself to be better, stronger?"

Haegan sighed. "I am training because Seultrie needs a strong leader."

"Seultrie has fallen, brother. You speak of a battle that has already been lost." Kaelyria squeezed his hand.

Aaesh stood before him, hands clasped. "Yer sister speaks well. The battle is not for the city or even the Nine. It is for the world. It is with Sirdar's agent, Poired. It is within ye, born out of yer abiatasso."

"Even that training is incomplete."

Kaelyria frowned at him. "What training?"

"Wielding," he said to the side. "You had years of training with Father and the Citadel. I've had none, save what King Thurig provided at Gwogh's behest—"

"Thurig?" Kaelyria jolted.

"Aye, I spent time in Nivar Hold before what happened in Seultrie. What good it did me—" Haegan shrugged. "I have little control over it."

"Do ye think the Lady so foolish?" Amusement bled through Aaesh's words. "She can grant ye the abiatasso and fill it with Her fire, but She cannot guide ye?" She motioned around the cave. "Or place ye where ye can learn?"

Haegan frowned at Aaesh. "The confrontation with Poired is coming. There is no time to learn."

"Learn what?" Kaelyria asked.

Truth? Was his sister deaf? Did she not hear their conversation? "Wielding! Fighting."

"Yer anger seizes ye now, does it?"

Haegan frowned at the bold servant.

"Remember what Thurig told ye of yer anger and wielding?"

How could she possibly know what Thurig had said? He'd warned Haegan that he clung so tightly to his anger over injustices that he became volatile.

"What if it were more than that?" Aaesh said. "What if yer anger was not merely yer own?"

Now, Haegan scowled. "What right have you—"

"Haegan!" Kaelyria shook his shoulder.

Haegan grimaced, her tight hold crushing against the bruises from training. He grunted and pulled away, giving her a searing look. "That hurts!"

"Mercy—you just frightened me." She looked to the servant girl, then back to him. "Are you well?"

Haegan's gaze hit Aaesh, who gave him a strange, ethereal smile then left the room.

"Better now," he said with a shaky laugh. The impertinence of the servant. He would need to speak with Aselan. "I am not used to the way of the Eilidan."

Kaelyria drew back, blinking. "I . . . neither am I. But—are you well, brother?"

He rubbed his forehead. "Tired, I suppose."

Her expression said she did not believe him but would not argue. And he was glad. "I will leave you to rest then."

"Good," he said, managing a smile. "As I have no doubt Aselan will be dragging my bruised body from the pelts long before I am ready."

• • •

NIVAR HOLD, YBIENN

The fortnight before the wedding was supposed to be one of parties and extravagances. In truth, it was a week of introducing Peani to the greater families of Ybienn so they could fawn over her.

Thiel did not begrudge the beauty the attention. But she was loath to spend one more minute playing the king's daughter when she should be doing something to find Haegan. Anything.

A few days after the gathering at the Raechter estate, Thiel accompanied the other ladies to the nearby monastery, which was said to have been built long ago by Draorian, one of Baen's Six. Loitering by a window overlooking the broad lawn, Thiel spotted children playing crux, a game involving a bat and a net suspended between two poles. Amused, she glanced back to her mother and the others, who were enthralled by the conductor's explanation of the paintings adorning the walls, then she sneaked out the door. Hurried across the snow-crusted lawn.

A feathered ball popped into the air, one of the more spry lads sending it in the wrong direction—straight toward Thiel—instead of the net. She let the ball drop so it didn't sting her palms, then retrieved it.

"'ere, Miss." The boy holding his hands up for the ball could be no older than Laertes. "Give 'er a throw. Ye can do it."

Cheeky twig. Thiel pitched the ball at the net, making it cleanly through the formed hole.

The boys gaped, then looked at her.

"She's on my team," said a smaller boy, earning him a broad grin from Thiel.

"She cannot play. She's too old," the pitcher said.

"Don't ye know," Thiel teased, "'tis not proper to tell a lady she's old."

After a short debate, it was decided she could play. But only outfield. As they told her where to stand, Thiel saw a blur of gold move along the hedgerow. She frowned, distracted momentarily when the feathered ball popped into the air once more. The pitcher snagged it just as Thiel again spotted the gold uniform. A Watchman?

Curiosity drew her to the row of hedges. She peered around the corner and its long path, and discovered the notable Yedriseth. Shoulders drawn back, he towered over another man, his posture screaming confrontation. But their tones—despite only being twenty paces away—were low. Angry.

The other man was shorter, rounder. Hair rimming his head like half a bread ring filled with spiced meats. There was something familiar . . .

"Miss?"

Thiel flinched. Looked over her shoulder. She raised a hand, then glanced back to Yedriseth, who had locked onto her now. "I thought I saw the ball go this way."

"It's right here," the pitcher declared.

"My foolishness," she said, hurrying back to the lads. She positioned herself so she wasn't facing the hedgerow, but would be able to see when Yedriseth emerged and who he was speaking to so animatedly.

She clapped as the boys made another netter. What was taking Yedriseth so long? He'd seen her, hadn't he?

The ball went airborne—and she caught it this time. Tossed it back to the pitcher.

"Yesterday I saw ye in the training yard with Prince as'Tili. Now I find ye are inclined to athletics as well?"

Heat shot through Thiel's spine as she realized Yedriseth stood behind her. But how? Where had he come from? "Four brothers." And an Ematahri warrior-sponsor.

"Four?"

She could not believe she'd made that mistake when the change had happened so long ago. "One is no longer among us."

"Ah, by the Flames, I am sorry. But they have a sister to be proud of, one so unafraid of adventure and willing to lift a sword. Were ye my sister, I would be proud."

Thiel glanced up at him, surprised at the compliment but more annoyed than pleased. Despite her irritation, she would not set him straight. Her brothers had not groomed the fighter in her. That had been Cadeif. And the training had served her well in protecting Haegan—well, as best she could.

"Do all women train with the Nivari?" His gaze was soft, admiring. "Or just the princess?"

The door to the gallery opened and her mother and the other ladies spilled out. The queen's eyes found Thiel at once.

"Ah, I have been missed," she muttered, glad to avoid his query. "If ye will pardon me, Sir—"

"It is my duty to return ye to the queen and countess." He offered his arm, and though everything within her demanded she refuse him, there was no legitimate reason for the slight.

Thiel rested her hand on his arm, and they started across the lawn. The queen watched, her expression stiff.

"The queen does not appear to be in good spirits."

"She has a daughter she cannot tame," Thiel said, before she thought better of it.

"On the sea, a woman like ye would be the honor of her sect." His words were quiet, and he said no more as he delivered her to the other ladies. With many thanks to the conductor, they loaded into the sleigh. On the way back to Nivar Hold, the Watchmen and Nivari trotting alongside the sleighs, Atelaria whispered anxiously, wanting word of what Yedriseth had said to her.

Had he promised to love her always?

Had he asked about Atelaria?

Why must Thiel always win the good men?

There was only one good man Thiel held a romantic interest in. And he had yet to return to Nivar. But as the coach bounced and trounced back, her mother's gaze more than once lanced Thiel. A reprimand was coming; she could feel it.

When they arrived at the hold, Thiel set out for her own room at once, but her mother's request to speak privately thwarted her escape. Thiel closed her eyes. "I know ye would reprimand me—"

"Reprimand?" Mama gave a soft snort, then went to her armoire and opened it. She drew something out then came to Thiel with it.

"What is this?"

"Ye are to write down everything ye saw today, and at the Raechters."

"Why?"

Her mother's eyes were not harsh, but they were also not yielding. "Because ye are told to."

"Write down what I saw?"

"Every detail, no matter how small."

"I am tired. I hate writing. I want—"

"Ye will do it every day, Kiethiel. And each morning, bring it to me."

Exasperation wound through Thiel. First she must attend every silly event with Peani and the wedding party. Now, she had to write them down, as well? Was she to carve out her eyes, it would be less painful!

• • •

Though snow covered the rear lawn of Nivar Hold, a massive fire roared in the pit. Around it, Thiel sat with Praegur, Tokar, Laertes, and Drracien, drinking warmed cordi juice.

"That brother of yours is likely to kill me—by running me into the ground," Tokar grumbled, shaking his head. He stretched his arm, grimacing.

"If he runs ye hard, then he sees hope in ye," Thiel said.

"Which is more than we can say." Drracien teased a tiny flame from the fire and balanced it on his finger, staring into it as if it held answers he sought.

Tokar grunted. "You're just jealous."

The accelerant pinched the flame out of existence. "Of being knocked in the head with a training sword? Of being beaten to a pulp trying to learn close combat?" Drracien scoffed, rolling his fingers as he turned over his hand. A brilliant blue flame danced on his palm. "I do not need brutality to render my enemies ineffective or dead."

"That's what the weaklings say when they can't master the sword."

In a heartbeat, Drracien flicked the flame at Tokar.

It grabbed onto his tunic. A dull orange now, it spread in a quickly widening circle, the flame eating through the fabric. Tokar threw himself up with a shout. Patted his chest.

Drracien laughed so hard the rest joined in.

With a stomp, Tokar lunged forward.

"This seems the livelier party," came a new voice.

Thiel recognized it. And ignored its owner.

"No party," Tokar muttered. "Just good friends enjoying the fire."

"Mind if we join ye?" Yedriseth came around, the firelight flickering against his handsome face as he and his three Watchmen motioned to the stone benches.

Though Thiel felt Drracien's gaze, she said nothing. Did not look at him. Must Yedriseth pace her? She did not want his attention. She did not want his sidelong glances.

"Any word of Prince Haegan?" Drracien asked.

This time, she looked at the accelerant. "Not yet. But word will come."

"You speak of the Fire King's son?" Yedriseth asked as he sat with his elbows on his knees.

"Ye know another Haegan?" Thiel asked, her words more sharp than she probably should've allowed.

"I am certain he is not the only boy of that name in the Nine," Yedriseth countered. "Ye are sure he is alive?"

"Yes." Thiel shot Drracien a look, willing him to agree.

He complied. "It is very likely."

"Ye know this how?"

She nodded to him. "Drracien is an accelerant."

"In earnest?" Yedriseth seemed to consider him more seriously now. "I thought Thurig banned all accelerants. And especially after what happened in Hetaera."

"What happened?" Tokar asked, his words challenging. Agitated. Thiel tried to quiet him with a glare, but he had never succumbed to her plyings before.

"A high marshal was murdered by one of his own," Yedriseth said.

"And what?" Tokar chuckled. "You think our friend is a murderer because he's an accelerant?"

Yedriseth lifted his hands. "I spoke no such words."

"The Fire King is an accelerant as well. Is he a suspect in your book, too?"

"The Fire King is dead," Yedriseth said.

"Haegan is an accelerant," Thiel said. "Is he also suspect?"

Yedriseth seemed to deflate. "I beg yer mercy, Princess. I did not intend a confrontation."

Mayhap, but he did it so well. She saw a shadow move inside the house. "If ye will excuse me . . ." She hurried away from the group, feeling her skin crawl, her annoyance rise.

"Princess."

Thiel clenched her eyes. Kept going. Searched for the shadow. Had it been Tili?

"Princess Kiethiel, please wait."

With a huff, Thiel stopped. Turned.

"I beg yer mercy. I meant no offense out there. I only wanted conversation and company."

"I should free ye, Sir Yedriseth, of any misconceptions."

His dark features were rimmed with confusion now. "My lady?"

"While I appreciate yer interest, please be aware that I will in no way return yer affections. My heart is wholly committed to Prince Haegan, and that will not change." She let out a shaky breath, relieved to have put the truth out there quite plainly, so he would beg off.

Sir Yedriseth gaped.

Had she been too harsh?

Then he laughed.

Thiel frowned.

"I beg yer mercy, Princess, but . . . ye are mistaken."

She scowled.

He looked down, rubbing his forehead, as if embarrassed. "In this, ye are right—I have sought yer audience and attention. But it is not for the reason ye presume." He swiped a finger over his lip. "I am ashamed to admit it, but I had hoped to befriend ye so I could have an introduction to Prince Haegan."

This time, she gaped. "Haegan?"

"Aye." He smiled again, nervously.

"How—why?"

"He is to be the Fierian, yes? I . . . would give him my sword."

• • •

LEGIER'S HEART, NORTHLANDS

Trust. He'd put his training in Aselan's hands, and indirectly, his very life. Which was why he'd allowed the Legiera to blindfold him and lead him through passages until the increasingly chilly air raised the hairs on the back of his neck and his ears popped.

It'd been three weeks of training. The bruises were an ugly yellow, and though Haegan had learned much and the techniques were coming more easily to him, he was far from a warrior. But Aselan had not given up on him, nor had he ridiculed or taunted him. The only thing Aselan had done was push Haegan. Farther and harder than Haegan thought he could endure.

"No talking from this point onward," Aselan said quietly.

Haegan nodded as Byrin and Teelh guided him up over some sort of stair or ledge.

"Easy," Aselan said. "Three steps down."

Haegan made it, toeing the stone. A strange warmth filtered out to him as the path they walked leveled out. With it came an odd smell. Earthy. Musty.

A cool hand cupped his arm, which told him the men who had guided him weren't holding him any longer. This hand was cold. Not warm as theirs had become.

"Okay, thin-blood," Aselan whispered, his voice barely audible. "Remember what I taught ye. Count to five, then remove yer blindfold. Once ye hear the bell"—what bell?—"ye will have ten *very* short seconds to get free." Something was laid around his shoulders, and Aselan adjusted it.

Ten seconds? To get free? But he wasn't bound. What would happen after the ten seconds? Was he standing on a cliff's edge? But again—what danger could present itself? They were in the Heart.

"I—"

"Shh." Aselan laid a hand on his shoulder. "Ten seconds after the bell." He patted his back.

Suddenly, darkness whooshed in. Loneliness. Ten heartbeats—each one reminded him of a year he'd been in that tower. Alone as he was now. Chilled. As he was there, lacking the Flames. Five seconds had passed, so he removed the blindfold, only to find a dark room.

A bone-vibrating gong rattled the air around him.

Bell! Haegan started counting, suddenly aware that time had slowed to a painful cadence.

One . . .

He strained to see in the darkened area. Blinked rapidly, aware another second had fallen away.

Mounds surrounded him. Black. Some were small, no bigger than his knee. The rest were at least shoulder height. He moved, his feet light, his thoughts racing.

Three.

But then . . . then the mounds started moving.

Heart jacked into this throat, Haegan froze.

A rumble trilled through the cavernous space. Light seeped through a crack in the ceiling. No, not a crack—a gaping hole far overhead. And the mounds—they were shifting. Morphing.

Four.

By the Flames! They weren't mounds. Raqines! Dozens. Curled in for the winter's slumber. *Never wake a wintering raqine.*

Haegan trembled.

A rock crunched beneath his foot.

Thwap!

A large raqine snapped around.

Haegan ducked. Dropped his gaze but skated a look through the area, searching for the exit. He spotted the three stone steps they'd led him down. A narrow—very narrow opening—to safety.

But even as he realized that, even as another second fell away, Haegan realized the ground beneath him was not gritty or hard. It wasn't rock or silt.

Fur.

His brain buzzed.

Fear spiraled through him with the adrenaline speeding in his veins.

More rumbles. Another *thwap*.

Then a rush of wind with a firm slap. Wings. That's what Chima's wings sounded like.

"They're waking, thin-blood. Hurry if ye want to live!"

A growl trembled through the nest of raqines, a meaty roar that seemed to draw the rest of the great beasts from their long nap. Haegan stayed low, using the larger size of the raqine to shield him as he bounced on his toes from one spot to the next.

Another thirty paces to the steps.

How many seconds? Haegan faltered, realizing he'd stopped counting. He tripped. A blast of heat rushed over his shoulders.

"Augh!" Haegan glanced back, stunned to find a raqine stalking him.

The beast was nearly twice the size of Chima. How had it grown so large? Teeth bared. Its hackles rose.

Haegan edged backward. Knew if he stopped moving, he'd be their first meal of spring.

"Haegan—out of time!"

He pushed himself. But at the same instant, the raqine crouched. Muscles rippled.

Haegan shouted—but it was lost amid the chortling, primal scream he knew well. Chima seemed to fall out of the air. She landed and spun, rocks and dirt spraying Haegan as she faced off with the other raqine. Both roaring and snapping.

"Now!" Aselan ordered.

With a lunge, Haegan threw himself through the narrow opening.

Hands pulled him back. In shock, he watched as the much larger raqine and Chima rolled in the dirt. They both came up with a disgusted snort. The larger one roar-chortled at her, as if reprimanding Chima for the move, then shook out his pelt and returned to the others.

Chima shook out her fur twice, looked over her shoulder—startling Haegan with fire-red eyes—and sent a chortle his way.

"Chima." He took a step forward.

"Nay," Byrin said, holding him back. "She not be yer pet, thin-blood."

Haegan frowned.

"She protected ye because ye are bonded, but she still be a raqine. And that be their den. Ye don' enter the den, especially so near the end of the wintering."

Haegan nodded. Swallowed. Shook off the shock, the terror. "And ye put me in there?"

Aselan nearly smiled. "We knew yer raqine would protect ye."

Disbelief rattled through him. "I didn't know there were so many."

"Now ye see why we stay in the mountain."

"For their protection, or for yours?"

"Both." Aselan smiled. "Come, we must talk."

Back in the great hall, a feast was served. Haegan sat with Aselan, surprised that the cacique allowed him a seat of prestige.

"Teelh will take ye down the mountain in the morning."

Haegan stilled, a thick leg of meat in hand. "Tomorrow?" His stomach clenched as he glanced around at the men. He had not thought he'd regret leaving this place, but the men had trained him. It'd created a bond he hadn't realized existed until now. "So soon?"

Byrin guffawed and slapped him on the back. "Look, the thin-blood has a taste for the cold after all."

That he did not. But for the friendship, the kinship—yes.

"Ye are to take the Fire Throne, and Poired is poised to overrun Luxlirien. Ye must go."

Haegan nodded. Aselan was right.

"The task before ye is not one I envy, Haegan. But know ye will always have friends in the Heart."

"And my sister?"

Aselan hesitated.

"How long will you allow her to remain?"

The cacique seemed to let out a breath. "As long as it pleases her."

"She may not choose to leave."

Aselan said nothing.

"I would ask, Cacique Aselan, that you pledge to protect her. I would not want to have to return to judge you for mistreating her."

Aselan smirked. "On my oath as a Legieran."

"Oochak!"

"Good. I thank you." Haegan nodded, sensing a great relief. A rightness, for the first time in many days. "Oh—and one thing. I would recommend you relieve Aaesh from her duties. She does not know how to hold her tongue."

Aselan frowned. "Who?"

"The servant girl. The one who brought my replenishment and clean clothes."

With another frown, Aselan gave a nervous chuckle. "Ye jest. No woman has tended ye—it would violate our laws. Toeff alone has brought ye food and clothes, and there is none here by that name."

"No," Haegan laughed. "You toy with my mind."

"I think ye do that well yerself, my friend." Aselan laughed and excused himself from the table. "Eat up and rest up. The morrow comes early."

...

NIVAR HOLD, YBIENN

"Yield!"

Applause rippled through the sandy training yard where Tili had pinned another Nivari in a mock battle. The setting sun cast long shadows over the arena, with darkness soon to put an end to the demonstrations that were part of the final festivities before the evening's feast and tomorrow's wedding.

Thiel watched as her brother rose from his mock victim and clasped forearms before turning and bowing to the king and the crowd. From the side of the yard, Relig smiled at Peani, who sat with the nobles on the platform.

"My king," Tili spoke loudly to break the din of the crowds. "As champion of this event, I have one request."

Her father chuckled. "Name it, champion."

Tili gave a cock-eyed nod. "I would challenge the Princess Kiethiel for one final demonstration."

Surprise tumbled through Thiel's chest. She peeked at their father, then back to Tili. Would they allow it? Would Mama? She dared not look.

"An unusual request," her father said, his expression neutral.

"For an unusual event." Tili stepped toward the platform, gesturing widely to the spectators. "I would have the crowds witness that even our women are strong. That the Lady Peani has chosen well the family with which she will rule."

Her father glanced to his right, to her mother, the queen—who had drilled Thiel on attire and court politics and ladylike manners until her ears bled. She would never let this stand.

Then her mother turned her gaze to Thiel, and a tiny smile slid over her lips, as if they shared a private joke. The look in her eyes—Thiel couldn't breathe.

Pride.

Queen Eriathiel nodded.

Thurig stood and faced Thiel. "A challenge has been set, my daughter . . ."

Thiel rose as well, and her smile felt it might split her cheeks. "A surprise to be sure, Father, for I did not think my brother would have himself bested in front of Abiassa and everyone."

At her absurb threat, the crowd's nervousness was broken by laughter.

Her father guffawed and took her hand, leading her to the stairs, where, releasing him, Thiel descended onto the training yard. Makule and Tokar were there. At once, they began strapping a protective leather vest onto her torso.

"Does he intend to humiliate me?" she asked as Makule laced up greaves on her arms.

"I know not—there is only this: Tili is never one to go easy."

"And I have the childhood scars to prove it." She grinned.

"Chin up, then. Watch his eyes."

"We both know that does not work with Tili."

"Aye," Makule said as he handed her a sparring sword. He winked and bumped her shoulder with the side of his fist. "Glad to see ye have yer wits about ye."

Duly protected, and suddenly feeling ridiculous, she strode out into the yard with the soft crunch of sand padding her steps and the shouts of the crowd hiding the drumming of her heart. "What game is this, brother?" she asked as they stood together.

His brown eyes glinted with no mischief. "No game. Ye are a worthy fighter, Thiel." Her brother was handsome. And arrogant. And the best man she knew—save Haegan.

Surprise tugged at her, then her eyes narrowed. "Ye mean to distract me."

"I mean to show that my sister is a fighter." He took her hand, turned to the crowd, and held it up. Then bowed. When he faced her again, he released her hand. "As I taught ye." He paused, then gave a slight smile. "Nay, as the Ematahri taught ye."

More surprise. Her brother had spoken little of her time with the fierce woodland fighters, so to hear him encourage her now . . . Thiel stepped back with her right foot and let her arms hang loosely at her side, sword gripped firmly. *Relax, Etelide.* She drew in a breath and let it out slowly.

The sparring bell rang.

Thiel remained as she was, watching her brother, who crouched a little lower and began to circle her, his sword in front of him. Not tense, but also not relaxed. He was ready.

He grinned.

Distraction.

She turned, waiting. Felt her pulse knock up a level under the crowd's scrutiny. It was normal for him to feint right then lunge left.

And he did. She crossed her arms before her, bringing the sparring sword up and expertly blocking his strike as she swept away and to the side.

The crowds cheered at her agility in deflecting his attack.

Tili grinned again.

Heart thundering, Thiel stood ready. But she felt the spike of adrenaline. The fear that she'd humiliate herself.

Tili dove in again, this time left. She swung around, dipping low with both hands on the hilt and drove the weapon up. *Clack!* A deflection. He slammed down, but again, she blocked. Then struck. He blocked.

Though only three clacks of their swords, it felt like a dozen.

"Let your enemy tire himself," Cadeif had always instructed. But she'd never been good at *waiting* to get stabbed.

Thiel rushed in.

Her brother circled his sword around hers. Her wrists twisted and she knew if she didn't counter, he'd disarm. Thiel ducked and rotated, coming up and shoving herself away. Panting, she drew back her right leg and arm. Ready. Or at least, looking like it.

The crowd was shouting. Behind Tili, she saw their father come to his feet. He gripped the rail that separated them. "Father will skin ye alive if ye harm me," she taunted.

"Then ye had best fight well, or I will hold his anger against ye."

And he was diving in again. Swords clacked. The vibrations numbed her fingers. Tili was fast, she knew, and this was not his most ardent pace. He was going easy on her. And somehow, that annoyed Thiel. "Ye are slow, brother."

His eyebrow arched. "I thought ye'd never notice."

And like lightning, he was all feints and strikes. In a blink, she felt the blow of his wooden sword against her backside.

Laughter rippled through the crowds, and heat through her face. She turned, nostrils flaring. He would pay for that.

"Aye," he said with too much pleasure in his voice and eyes. "There be the sister I know."

In a series of parries and thrusts, he was whirling her around the yard in a complicated dance of swords and maneuvers. She stayed with him, holding her own. Focused merely on watching his eyes and movements. Ignoring the shouts of the crowds. The cheers. The verbal winces.

With a feint to the left, then back to the right, she clapped her sword against Tili's side. He grunted, but just as quick—when she had taken a second to gloat in making contact—he caught the back of her left knee. She stumbled, nearly going down. The crowd gasped, but Thiel rolled through it. Steadied herself.

They were both breathing harder now—puffs of steam marked each exhale—and a bead of sweat tickled down her spine.

She swung up, determined to catch him off-guard. But she should have known better than to think she could outwit her brother in his arena. With a splicing move, he drove her arms up. Caught her wrist. Whipped her around and pulled her tight against his chest.

Thiel gasped as the blunt force of his leathered chest knocked the breath from her. Then she slumped against him. His sword pressed into her throat before she could blink.

"Well fought, sister," he said. "But I fear—"

Bells pealed through the city, an angry shout rising above the exuberance of the crowd. Even before the sound registered in her mind as the alarm, Tili had nudged her toward the stands. "Get inside," he said, casting away the wooden training sword. "To arms!" All around them, the crowd erupted into a frenzy of action as people scrambled away from the arena and Jujak stormed to the armory.

"What is it?"

"*Inside*," he hissed, already moving toward their father. Without stopping, Tili gestured to the Queen's Guard. "Get the women into the hold!"

Tokar met him at the base of the stairs leading to the platform. When Tili saw him, he pointed to Thiel. "Get her in the house!"

She would not be relegated to the house for all the citrines in the Nine.

"Go," Thiel said to Tokar, but when he stalled, she nodded. "I am well able to get to the house on my own. Go."

He didn't need another encouragement. She waited a few seconds, watching her father's expression go hard as he stormed down the steps of the platform. A few feet away, the Nivari traded sparring swords for steel, handing Tili his weapons and a shield. A heartbeat later, still buckling sword belts, the men rushed toward the gates. Thiel seized the chaos of the moment to slip away from the women being herded back into the hold and give chase.

Nivar's gate had been secured with the darkness that had fallen sometime during Thiel's contest, but through the press of Nivari and the remnant of Haegan's Jujak, she saw the foot gate opening. Shouts went up, but, unable to make out the words, Thiel struggled closer to the source of the commotion. Jostling and pushing, she stumbled and fell against someone.

Captain Makule glanced over his shoulder then scowled. "Nay, Princess, ye'll stay back. We know not who has come upon us unannounced."

Frustration coated her. She tried a line she hadn't voiced in years. "I am the princess—"

"Aye, and King Thurig will have my head if any harm comes to ye."

"And what will he say . . ." Dark shapes swarmed behind Makule, torchlight lapping over them. Three men. One was Tili.

Whispers drifted on the cold wind, and one word: "Eilidan."

"Savages."

"Traitors."

Thiel's heart caught in her throat. "Eilidan never leave the mountain." Why would they come down? The storms had stopped, but it would be treacherous still. And more than that—Eilidan never came to Nivar.

Makule pushed forward, muttering something about not letting a savage into the hold. The soldiers gave away to their captain, and Thiel fell in behind him.

"Makule, with me," Tili barked as the captain reached the edge of the crowd.

"Aye, sir," Makule said.

Thiel stepped to the perimeter, eyeing the curious forms draped in pelts. Ice clung to the fur-coverings. Head, hands, legs, feet. She could not even be sure they were men under the multiple layers protecting them. Their shoulders sagged; it probably hurt to walk.

What would be so urgent the Eilidan would leave Legier?

"Kiethiel."

She started, snapping her eyes to her brother, expecting a reprimand for not being in the hold. There was anger in his expression, but instead of a chiding, he handed her a parchment. "To our father. At once."

The opaque seal of the Eilidan cacique glared back at her. As'Elan! She snatched the letter and turned to sprint to the house. But the crowds were too thick. The spectators too curious. She pushed hard through them, then broke right, racing past the blacksmith and around the side of the raqine den and the stable yard.

Thiel burst in through the servant's entrance, remembering the day she'd landed on Chima with an unconscious, near-death Haegan. Up to the second level, nearly knocking over poor Atai.

"Give care, Princess!"

"Mercy!" She used the banister to haul herself up the last few steps. "Father!" Her voice shot down the long hall. She stopped, uncertain where he would have gone from the training yard. She'd thought he'd gone with Tili.

"Kiethiel."

Behind her. She skidded to a stop and pivoted. Saw him coming from the receiving room. "Father!" She waved the parchment.

Still wearing his official overcloak, he grimly accepted the missive and turned back into the receiving room. A fire roared in the pit, warming her even as she entered.

He broke the seal.

"What is it, Father?"

His gaze scanned the words. He hadn't moved.

She eased up behind him, straining to see over his shoulder. "Father?"

He started. Tossed the parchment into the flames. "Leave, Thiel. I must receive our visitors."

"Who are they?"

His brown eyes could not hide the truth from her. "Eilidan," he said. "The cacique's best tracker, Teelh. He seeks shelter for the night."

Cacique. "As'Elan." Though the question of her brother's welfare burned on her tongue, she dared not unleash it. Father's eyes warned her not to. "Will ye grant it?" She could ask Teelh how her brother fared.

"Law of Alaemantu demands it," he snapped. "I could do no less."

"Father," Tili's voice broke in as he entered. "Teelh of the Eilidan is here." He stood at the door, hands behind his back, gaze strictly on their father.

"Allow him in." When Tili turned to leave, Father nodded to Thiel. "Out the side passage with ye. Hurry."

"Why would they come? And in winter? It makes no sense."

"Thiel," her father said. "Go now."

"King Thurig, I present Teelh of the Eilidan."

Halfway out the side door, Thiel angled and saw Teelh enter. Alone. But there . . . there had been another with him outside. Two men in pelts had come through the gate. "Where was the other?"

"This is a most unusual situation, Teelh," her father growled as Thiel made her retreat. "Our lands have long been forbidden to the Eilidan."

"Aye."

"Ye know the penalty for invading." The hard words stalled Thiel in the side passage, her attention irrevocably drawn back to the room where the burly tracker stood, now without his pelts.

"'Tis no invasion, King Thurig, I assure ye."

Tili strode toward the side passage, blocking Thiel's ability to watch and listen. He gave her a chiding look before pulling the door closed. Frustration pushed her down the hall. Past the sitting room, where the glow of a fire provided more light than the torches.

Metal clattered against china.

She stopped. "Mother?" Thiel slipped into the room, nudging the door open farther.

A white shadow rose like a storm from a chair. The other Eilidan, still wrapped in pelts. Ice and snow clung to the fur, sparkling where it had begun to melt. But then the eyes—the eyes came to her. Thiel's heart vaulted up into her throat. "Haegan."

Pale blue eyes stared back. "Kiethiel."

Tears burned her eyes. She wanted to throw herself at him, but something about his manner, the tension radiating through his bearing, kept her in place. "They said ye were dead . . ."

His smile faltered. He shrugged. "I fled . . . Poired chased me from Seultrie. I could not save my father. Nor my mother." He shuddered through a breath. Then straightened. Then he seemed to shrug off the weight of that memory. "But Kaelyria is alive."

"Yer sister?" Relief rushed through Thiel. "That is good news, Haegan. I am very happy—"

"She's injured and paralyzed, but alive." His jaw muscle flexed.

Only then did she think of what he must've seen. What he'd done. She took a step forward, her hand reaching for him as if of its own will. Pain. So much pain in those blue eyes. And hooded in exhaustion. "Sit," she said, indicating the large chair. A steaming bowl of stew sat on a small table beside it. "Eat." She scooted the table closer, then drew the pull cord for the servants.

A moment later, Atai appeared. "Yes, my lady?"

"More wood for the fire. Have Gaord bring some of Tili's clothes."

"N—no," Haegan said around a shiver. "I must speak with Thurig first."

"Ye'll catch a death-cold if ye remain in those wet clothes." Thiel lifted her chin and nodded to Atai. "Firewood and clothes."

Haegan's gaze drifted back to the fire, his hands idle in his lap. "It is strange to be here . . ." He lifted a shoulder and shivered again. "Things were so different . . . before."

The distance between them had grown larger than she'd imagined. "How—how are ye?"

"Tired." A small smile played on his lips. "The trip was long and the mountain cold." He shuddered as if his body were confirming his words. "So very cold. I am not used to freezing with each breath."

She smiled. "Ye are far from home." The words weren't meant to remind him of anything, but to merely point to the distance from the Lakes of Fire. But Thiel saw her words had the former effect. "Ye were in the mountain this whole time?"

Haegan nodded. "Chima delivered me there. Would go nowhere else."

Thiel sniffed. "They nest in the mountains during the winter. She knew the storm was coming, most likely."

"Aye, Aselan said as much."

Thiel started. "Aselan."

His gaze came to hers. And he was different. Somehow.

"Blazes," came the awe-infused voice of Laertes. He darted across the carpet. "We heard you was back, but 'twas too much t' believe."

Praegur and Tokar entered quieter, slower. Haegan looked at them, but then dropped back against the chair, his misery evident.

"The soldiers said you come down da Cold One's Toof' wif the savage."

"He's Eilidan," Haegan muttered. "They're . . . good people."

His words did her good, somehow.

"Prince Haegan," Tili's stern voice snapped through the room, drawing their attention to the door where he stood. "The king would speak to ye."

Haegan lumbered to his feet. When Thiel stepped up to him, to aid him, he nudged her away.

Hurt splashed through her.

Haegan hesitated, his gaze on her. "I—"

"Prince," Tili barked.

Haegan, shoulders weighted beneath the pelts and blankets and so much more, strode out of the room as if to meet an executioner.

19

"Is it true? Yer father is dead?"

Exhaustion and defeat tugged at his limbs from the long journey and weeks of training, but Haegan refused to show himself weak. "He is."

"And yer mother, sister?"

"My mother is also dead at Poired's hand. My sister"—he breathed, relieved to offer a more positive report—"remains with the Eilidan. She has recovered some strength but is still partially paralyzed."

"Ye left yer sister with those savages?" Relig's lip curled.

"I saw no savages," Haegan said. "But yes—for her own health, she had to remain."

"Why did ye come down with Teelh? Why not wait until yer sister was well enough to travel?"

Haegan frowned. "Because my people are without a leader."

Tili coughed.

Relig scowled.

Thurig merely stared.

Their doubt in him drenched the room. Drawing his spine straighter, Haegan looked from one to another. "I am neither Eilidan nor Nivari. Neither am I a Jujak, but I am a Celahar, and my forebears have been on the Fire Throne for generations," he growled.

Thurig eyed Haegan's hand. "Careful."

Recoiling from the admonishment and his own disbelief that he'd let the embers roil so quickly, Haegan breathed deeply. "I beg your mercy. Exhaustion wears down my restraint."

Thurig eyed him, and, to Haegan's surprise, there was no anger in the king's face. "Tili, see him to his room."

"Aye, Father."

"Haegan, on the morrow, we will talk. Be prepared to give a full account of what happened in Seultrie, how ye lost one of my raqine, and your association with the Eilidan."

"Chima is not lost," Haegan countered. "She is wintering in the Heart."

Thurig's bushy eyebrows rose. "Very well."

Haegan gave a nod, too weary to object. As he followed Tili down the hall, he felt an ache worm through his arm. He grimaced, remembering all too well the Deliverer who'd afflicted him.

Once in the green room, Haegan was glad to find a fire already chasing away the cold. Tili walked to the wardrobe and opened the doors. "Clothes. Gaord will be here soon to draw the bath. Food will be sent up." He lit the torch in the wall brace, then gripped the door handle.

"That is it? No inquiries?"

"We of Nivar are not savages. When ye are rested, then we will bring interrogations." He nodded, suddenly so much and yet nothing like his brother in the mountains. "Rest well tonight, Princeling."

The hour spent changing, bathing, and eating sapped what little strength Haegan had left. He climbed beneath the thick blankets and felt the claws of greedy sleep drag him beneath its power.

Fire leapt around him. Taunting laughter echoed through the vast space—Legier's Heart! Despite the stone walls, fire consumed it. Children screamed. Smoke coiled around his face, choking. Haegan coughed, squinting against the ash scraping against his eyes.

"Haegan!"

He turned, the sound of his father's voice so clear and distinct. How was his father in the mountain? Had Poired tracked them here?

"Haegan, help me!"

Fear and alarm shot through him. Haegan held a hand up to shield his eyes, searching. "Father?" He shouldn't sound so uncertain, but it made little sense that his father would be here. Regardless, Haegan knew one thing above all else—he must find him. He surged forward.

Flames shot at him. The tips of the flames were like talons, piercing his clothes. Tiny little droplets of blood appeared on his white tunic.

"Haegan, go! Get out of here."

"No," Haegan screamed. "I am coming, Father!"

"No, you must stay out of his reach."

Darkness hid his father's voice and form, but Haegan braved the flames still. He must do this. Must not let Poired claim his father. The Fire King. The only one who could defeat the evil invading the land. Haegan had tried. He'd tried and failed. Now, his father was trapped in this burning blackness.

A figure of fire coalesced before Haegan. Crowned with a white-hot crown, the figure roared in laughter. "Think you to defeat me, Fierian?" Hollow and coarse, the laughter rippled across Haegan like heat waves, rustling his hair from his face. Searing his flesh.

A scream rent the air. The crowned figure stared at Haegan as he stood over something. Haegan strained to see past the flames and smoke.

His father, beard wisping with smoke and burning off, his hair drenched in sweat and blood, reached out from the flames to him. "Haaeegggaannn!"

Crowned in flames, the fiery figure smiled at Haegan, his sick pleasure at inflicting pain on Haegan's father apparent.

Anger pulsed through him. "I will stop you!" He lunged forward.

In a blink, the fiery man was there. Right in front of him. He drove that fire-blade through his shoulder.

"Augh!" Haegan dropped to his knees, holding his throbbing, bleeding arm. "Father!"

"Haegan, help me," his father cried.

But the figure stood over the Fire King again. Lifted that fire-blade with both hands, its tip poised over his father's heart.

To the right and left Deliverers appeared.

"Stop him!" Haegan shouted. "My father—save my father!"

But the Deliverers stood unmoving. Unseeing.

Desperation clogged Haegan's thoughts. Anger volleyed up.

The fire-blade rose a fraction higher.

"No!" Haegan shouted.

With that demented laugh, the monster drove the blade down.

"Noooo!" Haegan threw out his hands, blinding, white-hot light exploding through them. In the space of a heartbeat, he realized the terror he'd *inflicted. The horrible truth: he had not only vanquished the fiery-creature. He'd murdered his own father. A lone circlet, the one his father wore during common days, glowed hot as it rattled against the stone.*

He lifted the singeing metal, but it slipped down his arm. Morphed into a cuff. A gold cuff, flames dancing around it. But then—his father's head appeared in his hand.

Haegan gave a shout and tried to fling off the cuff.

But it stuck to him. To his flesh. To the very fiber of his being.

He threw himself backward. "No!"

Thud!

"Haegan!"

Light flooded in, a shape rushing toward him. Haegan cried out and shielded himself, ready to be attacked.

But the hint of roses coiled around his mind.

"Haegan." Cool air swirled as the figure dropped to the floor beside him. "Calm yerself. The Flames . . ." Soft, silky material brushed his hand. "Haegan, are ye well?"

He blinked, his surroundings coming into slow focus. Room. A bedroom. His room in Fieri Keep.

No. The bed curtains were wrong. The post carvings too . . . Raqines circled them.

Nivar. Nivar Hold.

"Haegan." Thiel's cold hands cupped his face. "Look at me, tunnel rat."

Haegan hooked his hand over her arm, breathing deeply of her scent. Relief was sweet and gentle. "Thiel."

"Aye, 'tis me." She squatted closer. "Are ye well? Ye're burning up!"

"I'm well," he muttered, tugging her closer, unwilling to let her go. "Bad dream is all." He had forgotten how soft she was.

The hall lamps bathed her round face in an amber glow, making her olive complexion that much more warm. A newly healed scar ran across her cheek. He reached toward it. "Who harmed you?"

"'Twas a training accident," she said and drew in a shaky breath. She tucked her chin.

A fire surged within him, deep and true. She'd pulled him out of the tunnels. Led him from Seultrie. Got him to the Falls. Brought him to Ybienn after the tragedy. Time and time again—"You . . . you save me."

She shifted, curling in closer. "I've missed ye." Her lips twisted. Tears glossed her eyes, bright with the hall light. "I was afraid ye'd died."

He touched his forehead to hers. "I think She intends for me to live for a long while yet, much to my chagrin."

"Do not jest," Thiel whispered. "And do not leave me again or I will end ye myself!" Strong and a fighter, Kiethiel had won the hearts of warriors and chiefs. She'd bested so many. And she wanted him close by. Tough but beautiful. A hard façade but a soft heart. And soft lips.

Haegan captured her mouth with his. Slipped his hand around the back of her neck and drew her nearer, deepening the kiss. She sedated the storm in him. Made him want to fight and be strong, the best of all men.

Her arms coiled around his neck, and he held her close, savoring her sweetness. Her softness.

"I love ye," she murmured, resting in his arms.

Voices came from the hall.

Thiel extricated herself with a blush. "Company."

Haegan came to his feet and held a hand to her as light exploded through the room. Tokar, Laertes, and Praegur were there. Along with a man Haegan did not recognize. Thiel stiffened.

A thrum at the back of Haegan's head buzzed through him.

"We heard a crash and came t' see if you was burning down the place again," Laertes said with an easy smile.

"Only in my dreams," Haegan admitted as he nodded to the others. Praegur came and stood beside him, resting a hand on his shoulder. Solidarity.

"She told me you would return," Praegur said.

"Aye. She seems bent on Her way. It is good to hear your voice, friend." He looked to the stranger again. "Have we met?"

"Ah," Thiel said, shifting closer to Haegan. "This is Sir Yedriseth, a Langerian Watchman. He came with Peani for the wedding."

"It's been what's mad and crazy, all jumbled with females and frippery," Laertes said. "I'll be glad when it's ov'a."

"It is an honor to meet ye, Prince Haegan," the newcomer said as he bowed formally.

Yedriseth. Haegan wasn't as familiar with the Northlands' ruling class, but something about the man made Haegan draw Thiel close and the embers even closer.

"We should let ye rest," she muttered.

"I hear the king plans to interrogate you tomorrow," Tokar said.

"Aye," Haegan said. "There is a lot to discuss."

Tokar extended his hand. "Then I will let you rest."

Haegan clasped arms and thanked his friend. Laertes grabbed a cordi from the fruit bowl before saying his good-nights.

The newcomer seemed most reticent to leave, but under Praegur's subtle insistence, they left together.

"I will let ye—"

"Please." Haegan tightened his hold on Thiel. "Stay. Talk to me."

"Can't sleep?"

"I do not want to." Not after those terrors.

"Ye seem . . . changed."

Haegan dragged a hand over burning eyes. "I feel I have lived two lifetimes in the last month." He stoked the fire then dropped heavily onto a small sofa. "Nothing prepares you to watch someone so brutally murder your parents."

"I cannot imagine."

Haegan shook his head, roughing his hands over his hair. "I wish I couldn't."

"Ye were gone a month nearly—"

"The storm shut us in, and Aselan didn't know if he could trust me, so he kept me imprisoned."

"Imprisoned? My brother kept ye imprisoned?"

Haegan nodded. "Honestly? I was glad. I realized I didn't want to come down. I didn't want to face what was coming."

"But ye did," she said, hurt in her eyes once more. "What made ye finally come back?"

"Your brother," he said with a smile. "Honor. My people without a leader."

"A more romantic answer would have been, to see the one ye love."

He smiled and scooted closer, tucking an arm around her. "You are the air that fills my lungs, makes it possible for me to endure."

"Then ye've accepted being the Fierian."

Anger churned. "No."

"How can ye fight what She—"

"Shh," Haegan said, pulling her against himself, resting her head on his chest. "Just sit with me. Let us . . . be."

The comfort of her, the warmth, cocooned Haegan. Drew him into a deep, peaceful sleep.

There came a subtle change in the air around him. A familiar one. That drew him from the dregs of unconsciousness. Warned him of danger.

Hands wrapped around his throat. More training. Aselan again, teaching him yet another lesson.

But Haegan's eyes snapped open. He lay staring up at a dark, unfamiliar face. His heart vaulted into his throat. Breathing became impossible.

Haegan thrashed, but the man was strong. His hands like steel.

Pull!

Haegan jerked the hand.

The man shifted.

Enough for Haegan to throw a punch through the opening. Ram his forearm against the man's neck. Force him away. With a shout, Haegan got his legs up and shoved with his feet.

The man stumbled. Haegan fell off the sofa, his mind pinging. Where was Thiel? Who was this madman? Am I dreaming?

With a snarl, the man charged him with a blade.

Haegan dove backward. Bumped a table. A lamp crashed to the floor, and one answer came to him: it was the newcomer. The one Thiel had introduced. Yedriseth.

"What do you want?"

Yedriseth sneered. "Ye, dead, Fierian!" He lunged, and Haegan drew on everything Aselan had taught him. He spun away, tried to counter with a punch to Yedriseth's ribs. But it wasn't enough. Three weeks weren't enough. Steel seared along his jaw. "Augh!"

Anger, hot and bubbling, rose through his veins.

Yedriseth's eyes widened.

Haegan clawed his hand and drew on the embers.

Grabbing Haegan's wrist, Yedriseth wrapped his arm around Haegan's, pulled him in. Thrust the blade toward Haegan's stomach.

"Bi'mwæi!" The words were on his tongue and searing the air in an instant.

Howling, the newcomer stumbled backward, cradling his knife-wielding hand to his chest. The blade and flesh had melded together. Fury and agony boiled in the man's eyes. With flared nostrils and tightened lips, he dove at Haegan.

Shouts came at the door.

Lifting his right leg, Haegan pitched forward. Stomped his foot and thrust his hands toward his attacker.

A blast shot forward. Focused. Direct. Plowed into the man.

Yedriseth collapsed to the ground, a hole the size of a cup sizzling through his chest.

"Haegan!"

"Seize him!"

The room flooded with Nivari. Tili and Relig. Praegur and Tokar. Thiel rushed around him, sucking in a hard breath. "Ye're bleeding!"

Haegan blinked, watching as Tili and Relig assessed the man on the floor.

"What happened here?" came the king's booming voice.

"Haegan, ye're going white," someone said.

With his hearing growing hollow, Haegan stumbled. Looked at the face but felt no recognition. He stumbled again.

"On the bed," Tili said, coming to his feet, pushing Haegan back.

He plopped onto the feathered mattress, staring down at the legs of the Langerian. "I . . . I killed him."

"What happened?" Tili asked.

"He attacked—I woke up to him choking me." A shuddering breath. "I managed to fight him off, then he had the blade. Tr—tried to kill me."

"And the hole in his chest?"

"He was about to drive it into my gut. I—I wielded."

• • •

Nine stitches to seal the cut bestowed on him by Yedriseth. One stitch for each kingdom. The coincidence did not escape Haegan. Was this Her way of mocking him? Or tormenting him? The next morning, face tight with healing scabs and swollen flesh around the threads, Haegan was not surprised to find Graem Grinda and Lieutenant Mallius stalking into the room.

"Our prince. We only just received word."

"I told them not to worry," Haegan said. "The attacker was alone."

"They've taken the other Watchmen into custody."

Haegan nodded. It made sense, though he doubted any of the others had been involved.

"King Thurig has asked the Langerians to attend him this morning," Grinda said.

"Aye, but you owe them nothing. They should be here, begging your mercy," Mallius groused.

With a lifted hand, Haegan said, "Leave it. There will be fighting enough when we return to the Nine." They went down to the meeting room, the door ajar and voices drifting out. Concern over canceling the wedding on the day of the event reached Haegan.

The Southlands were burning and the Northlands were celebrating—a wedding, but a celebration all the same. It rankled.

"Please. Haegan." King Thurig waved him into the room.

Inside, he found also the earl and countess of Langiera—neither would meet his gaze. Queen Eriathiel came to him with a sympathetic look. "My dear boy—I beg yer mercy. On the night of yer return . . ."

"Thank you for your concern." He lifted a hand toward his jaw and throat, but did not touch the site. "It will heal."

Tili and Relig were there as well, the elder eyeing the ugly gash. "Ye would fit in with my men, now. Not so pretty and long in the lash."

Haegan smiled, but felt the tug of the threads in his chin.

The earl stood. "Prince Haegan, I would like to offer a formal apology. I have sent one of my guard back to Langeria to question his family. We are quite confounded—he is of noble blood. Langerians do not promote violence."

Haegan inclined his head but said nothing.

"He attacked ye because ye are the Fierian?" Thurig asked.

"He stated as much," Haegan said.

"With the ideas many hold about the Fierian, I am not surprised—not that I condone or sanction the attack," Thurig said.

"Of course not," Haegan agreed. "It was an awakening for me."

"How so?"

"It makes sense that I am not the only one to despise the thing I am to become." Haegan sighed. "And as such, I must inform you that I will be leaving."

Thurig scowled, his thick brows angry. "Leaving?"

"Seultrie must be represented, and it's imperative I see to that."

"But ye have no army."

"There is an army," Haegan said, glancing to the two Jujak with him. "Where, I know not. But I will find the remnant. I must. My father would have done as much."

"Aye." Thurig stroked his beard. "Then the wedding should be delayed."

Haegan lowered his gaze. "I would not interrupt your celebrations. Please do continue."

The Langerians looked between him and Thurig, hopeful.

"In earnest. The snow has not receded enough for me to travel yet, but as soon as it does, I will depart." He nodded. "If you would excuse us." There was no legitimate reason, other than Haegan had grown tired. Of talking. Of explaining. Of thinking of what was to come.

"Of course—but Haegan, we must still talk about yer time in the mountain."

Haegan nodded, then bowed and left, the two Jujak trailing on his flanks. Where he was going, he didn't know. He just needed to breathe. He found himself standing on the balcony overlooking Nivar Hold. Amazing how the snow could make a place look peaceful when danger and threats lurked everywhere.

With a long sigh, he looked to Graem. "I would meet with the Jujak. Talk. Plan."

"Aye, sire."

"Princeling."

Haegan shifted toward the familiar voice and smiled. "Drracien."

"If I didn't know better, I'd say you were trying to steal my 'rogue' moniker." He nodded to the scar.

"Couldn't let you have all the fun." Haegan turned back to the expanse that spread before him. To the right, the training yard, but ahead, beyond the main gate, Ybienn stretched out in curling streets and undulating hills. Falling snow blurred the villages to blues, purples, and browns. Buildings huddled beneath the majesty of Legier and the Cold One's Tooth.

"Were you truly in the mountain with the Eilidan?" Drracien asked.

"Aye. Chima deposited us on a ledge there. My sister and me." Haegan drew a hand over the stone balustrade and sighed. "She is ill, and it was not possible for her travel down the mountain with me."

"And why did you return?"

"To lead the people of Seultrie—they need someone."

"What of Poired?" Drracien snorted. "I thought you were going to banish him to the Lakes of Fire."

Guilt coiled around Haegan.

"That's what you intended, was it not?" A note of injury had crept into the accelerant's voice. "That's why you raced out of here on that raqine, leaving all of us behind. Not asking for help. Not seeking any."

"Have you a point, Drracien?" Haegan started back into the house. "My mood is as foul as the weather on Legier."

A volley of heat struck between Haegan's shoulders, pitching him forward. He caught himself and spun back, frowning. "Did you just spark me?"

"You need training."

"And what? You're going to train me?"

Drracien held his palms out to the side. "I've been training accelerants for the last several years." He rotated his arm and wrist. Stared at his fingers, which he moved in a wave. Heat slid over each finger, then under the next, then over.

The idea was sound, but Haegan's mood . . . his agitation over recent events put him off. "I would not risk my temper this day."

"You have not the luxury of picking days, Haegan. He's out there. He defeated you once. And badly from the way you favor that wrist."

Stilled by the words, Haegan had not even realized he gave attention to the pervasive ache. "It was not . . . Poired."

"Come," Drracien said, clapping him on the shoulder. "We'll go to the sparring hall, and you can tell me."

There was nothing better to do. And to his surprise, the guards did not follow them past the stairs that led down into the sparring hall on the first level. Haegan felt relief at that. He stretched his neck as they entered a long, empty hall. At the far end, he saw stacked rows of sparring gear.

Gear that would do no good against his explosive gift.

Drracien cleared an area, then went to the far wall and retrieved two jav-rods before returning to Haegan.

"Your wrist, you said it wasn't Poired." Drracien laid the jav-rods down and gathered two lengths of rope. "Who then?"

"A Deliverer."

Drracien stilled, his face pale. "You jest."

Haegan ground his teeth and looked at the rope. "What's that for?"

"You'll see." He thrust his chin toward Haegan. "I'd remove the tunic."

"It's freezing!"

Drracien gave a cockeyed shake of his head. "Not for long." He slipped out of his own tunic, tossed it to the side, then lifted a jav-rod.

Reluctantly, Haegan complied. He removed his tunic, balled it up and pitched it in the corner.

"Blazes!" Drracien hissed. "Your back—the mark!"

"What?" Haegan asked, looking over his shoulder but unable to see anything.

"It's . . . changed." Drracien walked around him.

The marred mess had been there since he was saved from certain death near the Great Falls. He'd jumped after Thiel, who'd slipped off a rock and fallen a terrible distance. Then later, when held captive by the Jujak, the Ignatieri had come. "High Marshal Adomath said I was marked by Abiassa."

"It has to be Her," Drracien said. "When I first saw it, it looked as if you'd been bruised, but there was even then a semblance of meaning to it somehow." He came in front of Haegan. "But now it's almost a full symbol."

"Like what?"

"The Fire Triangle—but double. It's—" Drracien snapped his mouth shut.

Haegan scowled. "What?"

Drracien shook his head, his expression different. "It's what we teach first-years. The elements of fire: air, heat, and fuel." He pushed his dark hair from his eyes.

"Why would that be on my back?"

Drracien shook his head, then a flicker of something flashed through his eyes. "Perhaps . . . perhaps you are the embodiment of it."

"You make my head hurt." Haegan nodded to the jav-rod. "Going to run me through?"

Drracien smirked. "Arms out. Palms up."

Pushing aside his irritation, the questions about the marks on his back, the one on his soul, Haegan complied.

With care, Drracien adjusted his arms so they were spread wide, palms still up, then he laid the rod across it. "First rule of wielding—master your body."

"My body?" Haegan scowled. "Or the rod?"

"As of this instant, they are the same." Drracien stepped back. "Do not allow the rod to drop. No matter what. And you cannot hold it any other way."

Haegan straightened. "You jest."

"Not this time."

"I need help focusing my wielding—"

"For someone who was laid up in a bed for ten years, you aren't very patient," Drracien said.

"As you said—Poired is out there, burning cities, murdering Seultrians and anyone in his way. I do not have time to—"

"You're right." Drracien lifted his rod and with an arcing swoop, brought it to bear on Haegan's.

The rod vibrated through his arms. Bounced against his palms. And the right side fell, then the left. It clattered against the marble floor.

"Rushing into the fray with no skill but a gut full of anger worked really well protecting your family, didn't it?" Drracien drew back his hand, fingers curled away and his palm pushed out. "Tell me—where is your father?"

Shamed, Haegan looked away.

"And your mother? You have no need of lessons, so tell me—"

"I will tell you that Poired took pleasure in killing my parents. He would have killed Kaelyria as well, had my mother not protected her."

Haegan's heart thundered. "And just when I had the advantage and could have killed Poired, Deliverers stopped me. They appeared between me and that evil creature. Told me it was not mine to kill him. But I would not be sated. I would not yield. I had him. I could have ended all this." Haegan bounced his hand. "In my palm, the purest, most violent light I'd ever seen bloomed. And I struck out—But the Deliverers did not aid me. They *stopped* me—"

"Haegan," Drracien said, his voice calm, "focus."

"Not only did they stop me," he said, breathing around the anger and searing cold pain that filled his lungs, "but they punished me."

"Focus."

He held up his forearm. "*Punished* me." He slapped his chest. "For trying to stop this madness. For trying to return peace to the Nine."

"Haegan!" Drracien's voice snapped through the din in Haegan's head. He blinked.

Drracien nodded to his hand.

Only then did he notice the white flames dancing around his hands. "Why give me this ability if I cannot use it against him?"

"I know not, but you must learn to draw on that fire without anger."

"Why?"

"Because anger controls you. The Flames must be wielded from within, with the righteous judgment of Abiassa." Drracien produced a beautiful flame on his hand. "It's the first guiding."

"Drracien, I have not years to learn how to do this." Frustration pushed him to the bench that lined the wall. "Poired has taken Seultrie, killed the Fire King." Disbelief choked him. "I never thought . . . my father was so strong. How did he not stop him?"

"The Kindling."

Haegan looked up at his friend. Every hundred years at the Great Falls it was said the hand of Abiassa touched the waters at first light, providing healing to all who entered at that appointed time, kindling healing and hope.

"When you went into that water, it sapped my gifts. Since you left to return to Seultrie, I've spent every waking hour wielding the Flames." Drracien squatted in front of him. "All this time and I still am not back to full strength. Likely, your father experienced the same weakening."

The words seared, drilling right through the last of his strength. The dreams—the terrors. The reality—watching his father murdered so violently. And . . . if Drracien's words were true, had Haegan by default murdered his own father? "I didn't steal your gifts!"

"I dare not accuse you, Fierian." He smirked. "Come. We must teach you to draw on the embers without anger. Lest you begin your destruction in this very hold."

20

Celebration bells rang through the city, signaling the formal binding of Prince Relig to Peani of Langeria. Thiel stood on the balcony overlooking the courtyard, small city, and villages beyond, watching her brother wave to the people, who cheered him loudly. Peani was a vision in her white gown and veil, a crown of Nivar now nestled in her dark curls.

Thiel squeezed her fingers, smile frozen on her lips. The ache for it to be her and Haegan renewed. She stole a look into the house, searching the hall for him, but he was not there. As if he should dog her steps like a lovesick boy.

"Amazing, that Prince Haegan said to go on with the wedding," Atelaria said. "He was nearly *killed*!"

"He would not have a grand celebration stopped on his account," Thiel said. He was a better man than most.

"I just can't believe Yedriseth did that." Atelaria whispered, the crowds still cheering, her brother still fawning over his new bride. As he should.

Thiel did not want to remember. Did not want to think about the angry cut across Haegan's jaw. How she'd seen things in her encounters with the Watchman—things she should have pursued to understanding. "This is poor conversation."

Her mother turned and gave a subtle nod, apparently approving Thiel's ending the chatter about the attempted murder.

Atelaria straightened. "Of course."

Tili shared a laugh with their father and the earl, then his gaze hit Thiel. A flash of concern winked through his expression. Thiel shifted around to move to the other side of the balcony, but her cousin caught her arm.

"You have yet to make good on your promise, you know. Will you make the introductions?"

"To Haegan?"

Atelaria blushed. "No, to Tokar."

The scowl could not be stopped. But then, perhaps her dithering cousin would be a good fit for Tokar.

It was not soon enough that the family turned back into the house. After a brief respite in the family room for Peani to refresh herself, they joined the crowds in the great hall for the dinner feast. At every table, guests had been placed with care, alternating male and female. At the head table, Thiel found herself between Peani's father and Tili. Two longer tables jutted from theirs and extended the length of the great hall. Within sight but not close enough to talk, Haegan sat awkwardly between the two daughters of Councilman Holdermann. One, plump with her first child, was nodding off amid the chatter. The other's incessant giggles and the way she insisted on touching Haegan's sleeve grated on Thiel's nerves.

"Remember," Tili muttered to her quietly, "flirtations and pandering."

"She does not have to be so obvious," Thiel growled.

A man's arm slid between Haegan and the girl, delivering a plate of food. Something tripped in Thiel's mind. The man served, set down a goblet for the girl. Thiel glanced at the servant, willing him to move aside so she could see Haegan.

The servant stepped around Haegan's chair and slid a goblet—

Wait.

Thiel's heart skipped a beat. His hair. *Half a ring of meat pie.* Another beat lost. She grabbed her brother's arm. "That man."

Tili stilled, his gaze following hers. "What of him?"

"He was with Yedriseth the other day. Arguing in the hedges of the churchyard." She watched as he lifted a plate from the tray and removed its cover. The only one that had a violet laid across the meat. "Tili—the food."

Her brother was already sliding up. He walked swiftly, giving a signal to two of his men. He whispered something to the Nivari even as he continued toward Haegan.

"Princeling," Tili said as he bent forward. "I would have a word with ye."

Haegan frowned, glancing at Thiel, who raised a cup to her mouth—more to hide her nerves than to quench thirst. She nodded, and Haegan rose to follow Tili out of the hall.

One Nivari lifted the food and goblet, while the other hooked the rotund man's arm with a free hand and guided him out of the hall as well.

Thiel breathed a little easier. Looked at her own food, untouched before her, then slid a glance to her parents, who acknowledged her but then carried on so as not to create alarm. The air swirled beside her and she turned to Tili.

Only it wasn't her brother. "Haegan." She searched where he had once sat and found her brother flirting unabashedly with the councilman's daughter, who ate up the attention. Thiel almost felt sorry for the girl. There was as much substance to her brother's intentions as there was to water.

"Seems the food tastes better up here," Haegan said. His eyes were bright against his green coat and sash of nobility. A plain circlet was a surprising addition to his attire. He glanced down at himself and shrugged. "I am unsure where the clothes came from. They were in the wardrobe when I arrived back."

Mama. Her mother never overlooked the smallest detail.

But the cut on his face seemed to stiffen his speech and manner. It was hard to look at, hard to think that just a little lower and the attack would have been a murder.

"Drracien suggested it makes me look the rogue. Does it?"

She was staring. "Entirely."

Though he smiled, it didn't make it to his eyes. Would he always carry the fear of someone trying to take his life? "How did you know about the server?"

Thiel lifted her glass of water, but then thought better. "I spied him arguing with Yedriseth a week past. I knew not who he was—but when I saw him serving just then, saw the flower on yer plate . . ."

Haegan sighed, staring at the soup that had been placed there by a Nivari. "I find I have no appetite."

"Nor I," she admitted. "But there are at least five more courses."

Haegan sniffed a smile.

They ate little through the meal and talked even less, though she tried to draw him out. "Are ye worried much, for yer safety?"

His eyes widened. "For my safety?" He straightened in his chair. "Nay, I worry for Zaethien and Seultrie. For the Nine." Weight pressed against his brow, darkening his eyes. "We sit here—feasting, celebrating—when my people are fighting for their lives."

Thiel swallowed and withdrew, realizing the folly. Experiencing his guilt. Why could they not have met before the wars? Or after—once it was all settled and lives returned to normal.

"I beg your mercy, Kiethiel," he whispered. "I promised myself I would not spoil this evening."

A bell rang, silencing the hall. Her father and mother rose, as did Relig and Peani, along with the duke and duchess. A herald invited the guests to the ballroom for dancing. And due to formality, Thiel was once more drawn from Haegan.

• • •

Haegan stood on the cobbled patio beyond the ballroom, where music and laughter carried into the cool night. Two attempts on his life in the span of twenty-four hours. And there would be more. Relentlessly so. He ran his fingers into his hair—and caught the circlet. He removed it, staring down at the simple gold band. A gift from Queen Eriathiel. Gone were the glitter and gems of his life. Gone the fine things. Now, he had pain and war.

"My prince." Captain Graem Grinda strode toward him with Lieutenant Mallius and two other Jujak. Strange, considering their history, how comforting their presence was, a brotherhood borne of citizenship. "It is not wise for you to be alone, not after two attacks."

"Aye." And yet, Haegan was alone. "I beg your mercy, Captain. I just needed air." He held the circlet awkwardly, thought to toss it aside, but that would be disrespectful. Instead he turned his attention to the two Jujak whose names he did not know. "I would have your names, friends."

A lanky one with a freshly shorn head bowed. "Major Astante, sire."

"Lieutenant Lanct," the other, shorter but thick as an ox, said.

"Thank you. I appreciate your loyalty to Abiassa at this dark hour." Haegan looked to Graem. "What news is there?"

"Reports have come in at last. Two weeks ago, Poired laid siege to Luxlirien."

Haegan's mind staggered at the thought of the Nine losing Luxlirien as well. "Has he taken it?"

"If he has not, he will soon," the captain said with a grim shrug. "According to the reports, after Zaethien, my father gathered what he could and retreated to defend Luxlirien. But, truth be told, too many of our army fled, unnerved by what they saw at the keep. One report did mention that General Negaer and his Pathfinders were reining in as many as they could outside Hetaera.

Eyeing the bench, Haegan lowered himself to it and set aside the circlet, its metal clattering against the stone. It was so much more bleak than he'd imagined. And he had imagined plenty, having faced the desecrator himself in Seultrie.

"Many are quartered at Hetaera," Mallius put in, "and it is likely that many more arrive each day. But word is scarce coming from the Nine. We are up here . . ."

"Aye," Haegan muttered, understanding all too well the helplessness they felt. Yet at the same time, the quiet and peace of Ybienn gave them relief. Respite. Guilty, though it was. He studied each of the men around him. Came to his feet. "We will discuss this again on the morrow. Make plans to return."

Graem gave him a relieved nod. "It will be as you command." But then he hesitated. "Are you ready, my prince?"

He wasn't. Not in the slightest. But it was his task. "I must return."

Mallius, Astante, and Lanct bowed, then moved across the lawn, but Grinda's gaze skidded to the side.

Thiel slid from the shadows. Hurt wrenched her features into a knot. "Ye're leaving?"

Grinda bowed, then removed himself—but only to a respectable distance.

Haegan sighed. "I must. There is no leader for the Nine."

"There is an entire army—"

"Scattered. Retreating. In disarray. Even from my bed, I knew my father to be what united the Nine." Haegan stretched his jaw, feeling the tug of the stitches, and shook his head. "I am not half the man my father was, but I must do what I can. I must listen to the blood boiling in my veins."

Thiel glided closer. "Haegan, ye're the Fierian. If ye go—"

"I am a Celahar first." And if it were up to him, nothing else. "That is an answer I must bring to what rages in the south. I cannot stay here, playing to sympathies and—"

"What of me?"

Deflating, Haegan gently cupped her bare shoulders. Thumbed her silky soft skin. "Would that I could stay here forever with you, Thiel, but you would not ask this of your father, or even your brother. You would not ask them to ignore their people. Do not ask it of me. I beg you."

Because his will was weak. His desire even more so. He wanted no war. He'd expected no title or crown.

"Do ye not love me?"

Agony tore at him. "I—"

"No." Thiel covered his mouth for a moment. "Forget I asked." She tucked her chin with a regretful sigh.

Haegan kissed the top of her head.

Her fingers curled tight into his coat. "When do ye leave?"

"Soon." As soon as he had a plan. As soon as supplies were ready.

21

Tili stood on the platform overlooking the training yard. With the wedding two days past, he had his men doing double drills, especially the new batch of recruits just in from the villages. Below, they worked in the muddy yard to hone their hand-to-hand skills. He would have them versed in all forms of combat, not just the sword.

"They grumble," Aburas said, his voice a near growl as he leaned on the wooden rail, watching. He indicated with a nod the seventeen-year-old Kerralian who'd come in with Gwogh and the others. "He's the worst of the lot."

Tokar, who said he was abandoned young and knew not which clan he belonged to, had been mouthy and petulant from the start. He'd also treated Kiethiel with disrespect on multiple occasions and disobeyed Tili's direct order to get her safely into the house the night Haegan arrived.

"Put him with Etan."

Aburas grinned greedily. "Aye, sir."

In contrast to Tokar, Praegur, the dark-skinned boy, had said nothing in the weeks he'd been within Nivar Hold, but he seemed stout and steadfast. "What of the Kergulian?"

"Strong fighter. Loyal." Aburas nodded his approval. "More years and training on him, I'd wager he could take the Claw."

Interesting. Both that Aburas saw the potential in the Kergulian, and the mere thought of a Kergulian ranking among Nivar's best fighters. And Tili had well noted Praegur's protective loyalty to a certain prince.

He'd been distressed and angry when Prince Haegan hopped on Chima and left without talking to them. Or taking them.

"If the prince is back," Aburas said, "then the reports are true."

"Aye."

"The Fire King dead," Aburas muttered and rubbed the back of his thick neck. "Never thought I'd see that. Seultrie is without a leader."

"Nay," Tili said. "Their leader is here."

"The prince?" Aburas laughed. "The boy can't find his own—"

"He is the only heir able to take the throne, and it will be his unless he is challenged. Seek the Lady that Haegan rises to the task. Ybienn and her allies need a strong leader in the Nine. The Lady forbid Poired should turn his gaze northward."

Sobered, Aburas nodded. "Aye. We'll need an ally at our back if the Rekken come down across the Violet Sea and try to break southward."

"And we must not let that happen. If they break the forest . . ." He could not imagine what would happen. Chaos. Bloodshed. The world looked dark and bleak from his vantage.

At Aburas's beckoning, Major Etan climbed the platform and saluted.

Aburas returned the salute. "The commander would have ye take the Kerralian, teach him some humility."

Etan nodded to the yard. "Looks like he could use some discipline now."

With a wave of his hand, Tokar turned away from Naudus. He muttered something Tili could not hear, but his posture, his defiance of Lieutenant Naudus's command to get moving, pulled Tili to the stairs. He hopped over the rail and dropped the six feet to the field. After landing with a soft thump, he headed for the petulant thin-blood.

"Ye're not done sparring until I say ye're done," Naudus growled. "Back with yer detachment."

"We're tired," Tokar said. "We've been here since morning and haven't had even a crust of bread."

"Bread is earned. Sleep is earned."

"Look, I'm not even supposed to be here."

Tili came up on the Kerralian, noting the stares. The way the yard fell silent. The way Praegur lowered his gaze and took a step away from his friend. He threw a punch into the man's gut.

Tokar bent forward with a rush of breath.

Tili punched him again. Swiped his feet out from under him.

Tokar dropped to the dirt hard with a hefty *oof*. He cupped a hand over his bleeding nose as he peeled himself off the ground.

Breathing hard through his anger, Tili circled him. "Ye said ye've been here all morning, aye?"

Back on his feet, the kid looked stunned. Angry. "Yes."

"Then how was I able to level ye so fast?"

"You snuck up on me."

"No!" Tili growled. "Had ye an awareness of yer surroundings, ye would have noticed." He pointed to the circle closing in on them. "Everyone in this yard saw me coming but ye."

Tokar's face reddened.

"Ye want to eat?" Tili gave a cockeyed nod. "Ye can eat when ye land a punch."

"A punch . . ." Tokar frowned. "On you?"

"Ye've trained all morning." Tili rolled his neck. "Surely ye know how to punch someone by now. Naudus is the finest fighter."

Gaze skimming the crowd, Tokar no doubt noticed the gleam in Naudus's eyes. "I don't want to fight you."

"He's afraid," someone shouted.

Tili let the accusation hang in the crisp air.

"I'm not a soldier—"

"Color him yellow," another recruit taunted.

Tokar reddened more. He lunged.

Predictable. Tili caught the boy's fist. Twisted it behind and up, pitching him to the muddy ground.

Laughter sailed on the cool wind, carrying taunts and mocking. Weaklings. Thin-bloods are weak-bloods.

Tokar came to his feet, anger dug hard and fast into his brow. He put one leg back and hands up. Sparring stance.

At least he'd learned that much. Tili stood sideways, watching him, ready. A lot was going on behind those brown eyes. Working out scenarios. Thinking through attacks and defensive positioning.

He threw a jab.

Tili slapped it away, eliciting a chorus of "*Ohhhs*" from the men. But

Tokar hadn't followed through with another move. Testing. The boy was testing Tili, evaluating how he'd respond. Good.

Another jab. This time, followed closely with a right cross.

Tili ducked and blocked. Shifted to the side, and with his hand modeling a knife, he stabbed at Tokar's side.

Another *oof*, but the boy stayed in the game. He bounced away but quickly retaliated. A punch. A jab. A cross. A hook. Another punch. "Good." One right after another, with Tili blocking every one. "Good—but how am I blocking ye?"

"You're a blazing commander."

Tili slapped a knife-hand strike to Tili's throat. Hit it just enough to make the boy drop and gasp, but not enough to crush his windpipe. With a sigh, Tili backed up. "Get him some water." He planted his hands on his hips, staring down at the boy. "Get some food. Find me at the first bell."

Tili looked around at the circle of recruits, allowing his voice to carry. "The enemy outside those walls will not care if ye are not a soldier. Poired is murdering innocents and conscripting all males from boys to grandfathers. Think he will care what training ye've had?"

Tili's eyes found Tokar, and he lowered his voice. "If ye are to tend the Fierian, ye will need to know how to fight."

22

"Yes, yes, yes!"

Haegan tried not to let Drracien's enthusiasm bloat his head. It was little, what he'd done. Harnessing a flame and nudging it along the rope Drracien had secured between two posts. The flame danced over the line —without consuming the rope.

With a huff, Haegan turned away, suddenly impatient with the lessons. His mind was filled with concerns and questions. "What news of Sir Gwogh? When did he leave?"

"No news," Drracien said, coiling the rope and returning it to a hook in the wall. "He left shortly after you flew out on that raqine." At Haegan's side, he considered him. "What do you want with him? Last I knew you weren't exactly pleased with him."

"Nor am I now." He wanted answers. A confrontation. Justice. But it would do no good to reveal what he'd learned from Wegna about Gwogh. Was it true? Possible, even, that Gwogh had poisoned him? If he could just recall that fateful dinner when he'd fallen to the poison. A celebration, wasn't it?

Or perhaps . . .

He rubbed his forehead. "Why do I recall what I wish to forget and forget what I wish to recall?"

Drracien laughed. "Because you are singewood."

"Aye, my sister often said the same. But," Haegan hesitated, "I need to remember something from my childhood."

The merry mood fell away from Drracien. "I hear you." He nodded. "I would remember my father."

"You don't know your father?"

Drracien shook his head. "Neither his name nor his face, save that my mother always complained I had his eyes and look."

"Then pale and ugly?"

Apparently without thought, Drracien shoved out a heat wave. It rushed Haegan, but just as quick, it was doused.

Surprise fastened Drracien to the floor. "That's a fourth-level tactic," he said, with a mixture of surprise and awe. "How do you know how to do that?"

Haegan lifted a shoulder. He could not explain how he even had the ability to wield when all his life he'd been told he couldn't. Although, Gwogh had told him in front of the Council of Nine that "simply wasn't so."

They went out to the courtyard between the training yard and kitchens to wash their hands at the trough.

"What's it like?"

Scrubbing his hands, Haegan looked to the accelerant. "What?"

"Being a prince."

Haegan snorted and scrubbed harder. "'Tis no secret that my life has been less than ideal, especially for a prince."

"But they respect you."

Haegan met his friend's eyes and saw that Drracien indicated a group huddled just inside the eating area of the kitchen. The staff watched him over their steaming bowls and mugs. "Respect?" He slapped his hands in the air, then gathered heat to dry them. "Nay, they do not respect me. They *fear* me."

Drracien grinned. "What is the difference?"

"Even you know the answer."

After getting some food from the cook, they slipped onto now-empty benches, the staff having quickly vanished to the halls and their work. Haegan dug in, glad for the sustenance.

"I am sorry about your father," Drracien spoke into the relative quiet.

Haegan paused with his spoon lifted, hating the images that crackled through his mind. "Me, too." But he still had the reconciliation that had happened before his father's death. It was a gift. A bittersweet one. They'd stood in the high tower, and he'd realized they were not so different after all.

"You're forgiving of a man who, in your own words, paid you no mind." Drracien tore a chunk of bread and dipped into the broth of the stew.

"Before he died, he told me he used to come to my room every night as I slept." Haegan had so yearned for his father's attention, his approval. "He said he could not face me because he had failed me."

"He blamed himself?"

"Aye." And in those last hours, he'd had the approbation he craved. "He was so surprised—and proud—when he saw me wield. I could live in that memory for years." The pride . . . yes, the pride. "He was my father. And in the end . . . things changed."

"He saw you wield against Poired?"

"No, against him—my father." Haegan stared at the chunks of meat and vegetables in the bowl. "And then . . . I failed. Poired knew anger would be my undoing. Right from the beginning." He scooped up a spoonful of stew and shoved it into his mouth before he could be expected to say more.

Having pushed his bowl away, Drracien leaned forward and set both elbows on the table. "We teach first-years to manage that. Anger is the easiest fuel to manipulate for those with advanced training."

Haegan slid his gaze to his friend. "Advanced training."

With a lift of his shoulder, Drracien thumbed his jaw. "It makes sense, right, that Poired has had training."

Haegan had never put much thought into how the Dark One had gotten to where he was. It had not seemed important, considering the swath of destruction he was wreaking across the Nine. Now he realized the advantage that might lie in understanding his foe more fully.

Drracien spoke his thoughts for him. "I'd like to know who trained him. Grand Marshal Dromadric and High Marshal Aloing trained some of the fiercest accelerants."

"Including my father."

"Aye. And Thurig. And maybe your sister?"

"Mayhap." *Everyone but me. Again, I fail the kingdom.*

Movement down the passage lifted Haegan's gaze to the flickering shadows. A shape took form—his heart thudded. Thiel. She met his stare, then entered a room. An invitation to follow. Their time was short, so he would not miss a single chance.

"Give care"—Drracien's words followed him down the passage—"her brothers have enjoyed beating Tokar to a pulp in the training yard. Think not that they would give you better treatment, if you are caught with her alone."

Haegan shrugged off the warning. There would be no harm, no indiscretion. He slowed as he approached the doorway, listening for voices. When met with only silence, he peered around the jamb.

Thiel stood in front of the fire pit, staring down at the flames. When he moved to stand beside her, she took his hand, still saying nothing.

"Thiel, I'm sorry about the other night. I—"

She shook her head and squeezed his hand, stopping him. "Nay, I am the one who should be sorry. I shouldn't have said what I did—tried to keep ye here. 'Twas wrong." She took a breath and turned to face him fully. "I want to go with ye to the Nine."

Haegan frowned, reaching to tuck a tendril of hair behind her ear, noting how long it had grown since they'd first met "I do not think it wise."

"Aye, ye and most in this house, but the choice is mine."

"Is it?" Haegan asked, thinking of the reaction from her father if she left the safety of Ybienn for bloodshed and war. "And I do not want it for you."

Thiel drew back. Scowled. "How can ye say such a cruel thing?"

"Because I want you to live—to do well. To have a long life."

"But I am yer champion. Abiassa crossed our paths, ye cannot deny it."

"I deny nothing. But, Thiel . . ."

"I can see that yer words are as heavy and weighted as yer heart." She squinted at him. "Ye're . . . frightened."

Shame pushed his gaze down. Reality brought it back to her face. None who faced Poired lived. And the Deliverers would not allow him to kill the hand of darkness. Could he let her stand beside him? Fall beside him?

"Haegan, ye're the Fierian."

"I don't want that. I don't want to *be* that." He gritted his teeth. "All my life I just wanted people to accept me. To let me into their lives and thoughts. Now . . ."

Thiel brushed his hair from his face and touched his cheek. "Ye are the Chosen. Abiassa chose ye to wield the Flames and restore Primar—"

"Restore?" He turned away and stalked to the corner. "Raze is what the prophecies say. That the lands will be destroyed. People will die because of me—no, not simply because of me, but *by* me. By my hand!"

"But after death comes new life."

"I cannot see the good." Rubbing his temple did nothing to rub the truth from his mind. "I will return to the Nine as heir to the throne."

"And ignore what She has called ye to?"

Haegan said nothing. It sounded absurd put like that.

"To what?" An edge snapped into her voice.

Haegan saw the disapproval he'd expected, and it hurt. Cut deep. "Nothing."

"Haegan," she said, her words tinged in remonstration, "ye are many things, but a coward is not one of them."

He loved how her brogue had deepened since she'd returned to her family. But why did she feel as a stranger to him now? "And you know so much about me?"

"Now ye cower behind a sharp tongue? Is that to be yer best defense, tunnel rat?"

He frowned at her. He should not be surprised—she was a strong woman. A leader. A fighter. 'Twas why he'd grown attached to her, to her strength. Even without him, she would do well. Mayhap even better.

Death lay ahead if she came with him. He must say good-bye now. "You are right," he said with a curt bow. "I have no defense. Good day, Kiethiel."

23

The morning after Haegan's falling out with Thiel, a month almost to the day after witnessing his king's death, General Kiliv Grinda arrived at Nivar Hold.

Flanked by Graem and Mallius, Haegan made his way to the second-level library where the general waited. Haegan's limbs ached—as did his heart. His limbs from the pervasive chill in the air. His heart for the iciness of Thiel's response to the earlier encounter. For the knowledge of his own imminent departure. For the plight of his people and the news he knew Grinda must bring.

Haegan tugged the heavy cloak tight around his shoulders as they entered, sunlight streaming through the bay of windows and silhouetting a very familiar frame. In spite of the situation, something in Haegan lifted at the sight of the man who had treated him with more fatherly affection than his own father, the king. "General Grinda."

"My prince," General Grinda said, unmistakable relief in his greeting. His eyes flicked to Graem and he nodded before they returned to Haegan, taking in the gash on Haegan's jaw. "Looks like you couldn't wait to get into the fight."

Haegan fingered the wound gently. "Yes, it would seem someone felt I lingered too long in the peace of the Northlands."

"It will not happen again, sir," the younger Grinda said. "I've assigned myself and Mallius to the prince's personal guard, among others I trust."

"Aye. He's in good hands." The general nodded, but a heaviness weighted his face.

"Are you well, general?" Haegan asked.

With a grimace, Grinda indicated the chairs nearby. "We should talk." He motioned to the door as another man entered. "I've asked Commander Thurig to join us."

Haegan shifted, surprised. Uncertain. Especially when he saw Tili's dark expression.

"My father would have been here, but there was a meeting of the parliament he could not miss," Tili said with a curt nod.

"Of course," Haegan said as he motioned to the seats. "Please."

Grinda moved to a settee and lowered himself to it. Barrel-chested and thick bearded, he looked awkward perched there. "Seultrie and the Nine need a leader."

Haegan felt the swirl of dread in his gut. Unlike every other man in this room, he was not qualified to lead an army. "Aye."

Grinda wasn't one to back down. "I ordered the remaining Jujak to regroup outside Hetaera. Once I receive word they are encamped, I and the Valor Guard will join them—as your escort." His gray eyes fixed on Haegan. "I've called for the Council of Nine and the Elders to meet you at Hetaera. You will stand before them in the Contending, my prince."

Swallowing, realizing he would be tested—as all fire kings were—Haegan nodded.

Tili frowned at him. "Ye don't seem surprised."

Haegan's blue eyes turned to Tili. "I had hope that my sister would be returned and restored, but her giftings are gone." His shoulders seemed to sag as he shook his head. "The Fire throne must be secured by one with the ability to wield. She cannot wield. Therefore, by blood, it falls to me."

"There is logic to that, but no passion," Tili said.

He sounded so much like his older brother, but Haegan said nothing, grateful when the general spoke up.

"You must ride south with me when the Jujak are assembled," Grinda said.

Haegan sighed. "Aye."

Footsteps—heavy and many—pounded in the hall, bringing all the men to their feet. Tili held up a hand then moved to the door. "I'm sure 'tis nothing. Wait here."

Two Nivari trotted up to the commander and they talked quietly. Tili nodded to them, then returned to the library.

Tili's expression pulled Haegan forward. "What is it?"

"Word out of Baen's Crossing—Sirdarians."

Grinda stilled. Scowled. "Sirdarians?"

"Naught but a handful of scouts, but, aye," Tili said. "'Tis not good."

Haegan jerked visibly. "This far north—why?"

Tili considered him. "Ye said when ye flew away with yer sister, he chased ye."

"Aye, shot fire volleys for leagues—much farther than I thought possible." Haegan shoved his hair from his face. "You think they hunt me?"

"Without a doubt," Grinda said. "If that Watchman knew you were the Fierian, it is safe to assume word has spread. And you faced the Dark One, so he tasted your power. He will not stop till he has taken your gifts and you are dead."

Haegan felt sick.

"Aye," Grinda said. He looked at Haegan. "We must go at once to Baen's Crossing." When Haegan nodded, he started for the stairs, his intensity drawing the rest of them along behind him. "I will rally the Jujak here at Ybienn."

"The Nivari will saddle up and meet ye on the southern plain." Tili started for the door. Then glanced at Haegan. "Ye lost our raqine—"

"She flew off."

"—can I trust ye with a destrier?" Tili smiled, his taunt evident.

"I could no more restrain Chima than you," Haegan said. "What a destrier might do, I cannot say."

"Ye just have to stay on long enough to defeat Poired."

"Oh, is that all?"

Defeat Poired . . .

Why did the battle already feel lost?

24

Haegan stood at the wardrobe, stricken. *I am but a boy still learning to find his legs.* How was he to fight an impossible warlord? An impossible war? His own father with decades of training and experience had fallen dead in minutes against Poired.

Of course, that could be the fault of his feckless son, who had somehow lessened him, as Drracien explained, in the Kindling.

Was that it? Was he to die and be a sacrifice? *Why did You choose me? I have no idea what I'm doing.*

Which meant he would fail. And die. Just like his father. With another expulsion of breath, Haegan turned back to the wardrobe. He could not even pack his clothes, let alone confront a raiding party.

"Your shoulders are weighted with worry."

Haegan stilled at the deep voice resonating through the room. He slowly pivoted, his brow knitting together as he met his friend's dark eyes. "You speak."

Praegur held fast to his place just inside the door. "She grants it only when there is something to say, and to none but you." He indicated to the wardrobe. "May I serve you?"

Haegan blinked. "Serve me?"

Three long strides carried the Kergulian across the wood floor to the wardrobe. He drew out two pairs of pants and a clean shirt. As he folded the items and placed them in a satchel, Haegan could only stare.

"How long have you been able to speak?"

"Since your return. And it is a relief to hear it after these many weeks," he said, intent on his mission.

"Does it not drive you mad?"

Praegur smirked. "It was difficult to adjust to." He shrugged. "But She has a purpose in all this, and I trust Her."

Trust. Was that it then—he didn't trust?

"Sire."

Haegan cringed. "Do not call me that."

"I must. You are my king."

"Nay—I am not. Not yet."

"You are blood-born of Zireli and the only heir able to assume the throne. And it is clear, that as Fierian, you—"

"No!"

An eruption of light and fire streaked across the room, narrowly missing Praegur's shoulder and stopping him cold.

Haegan froze. "Praegur," he choked. "I beg your mercy." The words all tumbled out on top of each other. Ashamed and frustrated, he turned away. "I cannot even wield without error. How am I to lead a realm?"

"Sire."

Haegan slowly brought his gaze to his friend.

Concern knotted Praegur's prominent brow. "You must not entertain those thoughts. As a Celahar, you are committed to Her ways, yes?"

Haegan swallowed. "Of course." All his ancestors had dedicated their lives and children to Her, to serve.

"Then you cannot question what She does with your life. It is but for you to obey."

"You sound like Gwogh," Haegan said as he donned a winter cloak.

"He is a wise man, so I thank you." Praegur secured the buckles of the satchel and gave a slight bow. "Ready, sire."

"I would prefer you use my name in private."

Praegur hesitated. "Perhaps someday, my lord. When you are accustomed to being called 'sire.'"

They made their way down the stairs and found Tili, Relig, and Osmon attired in coats and boots. King Thurig stood with them, the entourage watching as Haegan approached.

Thurig's keen eyes assessed him. "My sons have told me of the attack

on Baen's Crossing. Ye have my sympathy, as well as the full support of
the Nivari, should ye need them." He nodded to the prince. "They will
accompany ye to the border and wait there for word from ye."

Haegan's insides quaked. "I thank you . . ." He did not even use the
name or title, for his addled mind could not sort the appropriate one to
use.

"Fierian," Tili said as he took a step back, clearing a path to the door.
"We have mounts ready for ye."

"I will need one for my advisor," Haegan said, nodding to the his
dark-skinned friend.

Tili stayed in stride. "Of course."

"Where is Grinda?" Haegan asked as they headed into the chilly day.

"Waiting in the stable yard with the Jujak." Tili donned a steel helmet
that framed his face, crowning his eyes and nose and mouth. "My men
are on the south plain, ready when ye are."

Tili and Osmon, dressed in battle armor but also in the raiment that
marked them as Thurig's sons—the ornamental mantles over their mail,
as well as the green paint that traced the T-shaped cutout of their helms.
Long green cloaks fluttered on the cold wind as they launched up onto
their mounts with an effortlessness Haegan envied.

"My king," Grinda's voice boomed.

"General," Haegan said, turning toward the commander of the
Seultrian armies—and stopping short. "I would ask that you not use that
title with me yet."

"You are my king, whether you wear the crown or not." Grinda held
up the Fire King's dark red mantle and cloak that changed color—from
orange to gold to white—with the intensity of Flames being wielded.
Clasped in his right hand was the gold circlet carved with flames. Not
the simple one he'd borrowed from the Thurigs and worn at the wedding.
The Fire King's.

"Nay." Haegan started for the reins of the destrier Praegur held.

"Sire, you are—"

"I am not crowned nor have I won the Contending. I have no right
to wear those."

"As Zireli's son, it is not only your birthright but your duty!"

"I can't."

"You *will*," Grinda growled, stomping forward, the mantle and circle held with respect. "Think not for one spark that this is about you, boy. This is about Seultrie. It is about Abiassa. It is about an evil so dark and so great people forget to breathe. You are blood-born of Zaelero and Zireli." Trembling with barely controlled passion, he shoved the piece against Haegan's chest. "Put it on and embrace what you must—for your people. *My* people. Think the Jujak will follow a boy, whimpering in his leathers, when they face the Desecrator reborn?"

The scalding lecture seared away Haegan's petulance. Heart thundering, Haegan felt more the boy who'd lain in a bed listening to Grinda's spectacular tales of conquest. "I am . . . ill prepared, Grinda."

The general cocked his head. "A man who takes this without considering the costs is not worthy of it."

"Really," Tokar said as he stepped forward. "You need to get your head out of your own problems."

"Give care how you address your king," Grinda's voice growled through the yard. "I will not grant another warning."

Haegan faced him. Nodded and removed the winter cloak. Grinda helped him into the ornamental mantle, then lifted the circlet. "Nay," Haegan muttered. "Not the Fire King's. I'll wear the plain circlet of a Zaethien prince. Until the Contending."

Grinda grinned. Lifted something from a satchel. "I thought you might." He handed the plain gold band over.

With a snort, Haegan allowed the general to set it on his head.

"Sire," Praegur said, then nodded over Haegan's shoulder.

He turned and found Thiel lingering on the fringes, and he went to her.

Thiel looked at the fire king's crown as Grinda returned it to a box. "Ye can no more fight or delay who ye were born to be than a raqine can change its wings." She smiled, taking in the circlet on his head. "Prince today, but king soon enough."

The weight of it crushed him, suffocating him with images of his father wearing it. Of the way it caught the sunlight. The way it made people sit up and take notice. His father had been strong. Powerful.

Thiel's eyes glowed as her gaze slid from the gold to his eyes. She smiled. He felt it all the way to his toes, reveling in the way she looked at him. "I would say come back to me, but this is not yer home."

"I must stay alive before I can consider life after or invite the one I love to share it with me."

Thiel's chin quavered with emotion.

"An' t' fink," came Laertes's awe-filled voice, "him what can't remember how he ended up in da tunnels will be him what commands da armies."

"We ride," Grinda's voice boomed.

Haegan took the reins from Praegur and climbed onto his horse. Outside the stable, he slowed the animal, glancing at the dozen Jujak in full attire, their uniforms as sharp and intimidating in their own right as Tili's had been.

A shout went up, the salute of the Jujak as he rode past, their helms dipping in honor.

He wasn't sure whether he or they had the bigger adjustment. They made their way through town, the townsfolk pausing to notice them, some stopping their business altogether and staring. For a moment, Haegan forgot the circlet sitting atop his head, pushing his blond curls into his face.

They met up with Tili's hundred on the southern plain, and together, they made the six-hour trek beyond the Black Forest to the border. The lands here were rugged and hilly, a remnant of turbulence stretching between the Ice Mountains and the lesser mounts leading to the Great Falls.

"We'll camp here," Tili announced to Aburas, then guided his mount over to Haegan. "Follow me."

Haegan jabbed his heels against the horse's flanks and hurried behind him up an incline. Tili slid to the ground, and Haegan did the same, matching the Nivari commander's large, powerful strides up a steep slope. Behind a bramble of brush and trees, they crouched and peered through the vegetation.

"The Valley of Draorin."

Beyond the open field that ran nearly a league, Haegan started at what spread out before him. Six massive statues lined a road that led to a thriving city. "Who are they?"

"Baen's Deliverers."

A chill scraped Haegan's spine. Deliverers. "Baen Celahar," Haegan muttered. "The first of my ancestors to take the throne." Given the name Zaelero II as king.

Tili nodded. "Aye." He angled his shoulder down and pointed. "In the center of the Crossing, ye'll see his statue."

Amid multi-storied buildings it was hard to see the statue. "Why here? That battle happened in Hetaera, leagues from here."

"Draorin, Baen's right hand, settled here. The city rose up around him and when he died, they built this." Tili motioned. "Look to the north. It's worse than the reports."

White walls were now blackened. Plaster crumbling. Sections of walls and buildings missing. "Why damage a city when they're looking for me?"

"That city represents everything ye are. Poired is looking to tear down every artifice that might give them hope." Tili shrugged. "I am surprised the statues still stand."

"Where are the Sirdarians?"

"Unknown. Perhaps hiding in the trees northeast of the city." Tili studied the land for several long seconds, giving Haegan time to work through his own thoughts.

What would he do if confronted by Poired's men? Haegan could just see himself wielding in a panic or rage and destroying the entirety of the city. Yes, that would make them want to crown him—officially—as their king.

Something in the air tugged at Haegan's awareness. He squinted, staring into the town as if he could see the people. Hear them.

"What is it?"

Haegan shook his head. "I know not. Something . . . something's not right."

Tili's gaze snapped to the city, his eyes darting over it.

"I think they're still there. Or someone is—maybe spies."

"How do you know?"

Wincing at the question made him look weak. "I can . . . feel them."

25

The Jujak and Haegan's friends gathered as he, Grinda, and Tili returned from the overlook. As they approached the group, Grinda tilted his head toward Haegan. "*Feel* them?" he asked in a lowered voice. "Your father had great wielding abilities, and I was with him all his years, but I never heard him say something like that, not at this great a distance."

Was he wrong then? Was it his imagination? Haegan shoved a hand into his hair—and immediately felt the restraint of the crown. "I cannot explain it. I just . . . know."

Reaching the gathered men a few strides ahead of them, Tili beckoned to Aburas. "Set a double guard. I want no surprises while Prince Haegan enters the city."

"What's wrong?" Tokar asked.

Though his friends joined him, Haegan noted that the Jujak hung back, uncertain of their place until General Grinda stepped forward. "We have reason to believe the enemy may still be in Baen's Crossing."

"What reason is that?" Tokar asked.

Grinda looked at Haegan, who hesitated. "I . . . I can feel them." Or something. He didn't know what it was, exactly.

The Jujak shifted, glancing at each other.

"Is this part of your being the Fierian?" Graem asked.

"I—"

"That's an impossible query to answer," came Drracien's voice, "since there has never before been a Fierian." The slick accelerant made his way through the armored Jujak, who moved aside readily to let him pass.

"Who is to know what abilities he might have? Pray he does not turn them on you."

"Why?" a Jujak asked.

"Ghor, leave it," Graem said.

"I've seen him wipe out twenty Ematahri with a few well-placed words," Tokar explained. "Fried them out of existence."

Haegan's heart thumped, his painful past laid bare, but he noticed the Jujak seemed less hesitant.

Because they are now afraid of me.

"What are we to do?" Graem asked.

"Ride into Baen's Crossing—openly," Grinda said. "We are there in response to the attacks. Ask questions. Commander Thurig has agreed to send some men into the city to blend in and ask around. Between us, we should find what we're looking for."

"What's that?" It was the one Graem called Ghor. Mistrust and animosity tumbled through his face.

"Da enemy." Laertes's voice piped up from between two Jujak.

Haegan's eyes found the boy, chin jutting, standing tall, though he was half the size of the men around him. "Yes," he said gently, "which means it will be no place for a boy."

Laertes's face fell, but Tili beckoned him over. "The lad will stay with me. I've yet to have the chance to train him, and now seems as good a time as ever."

Surprised at the deft attempt to protect Laertes's pride, Haegan nodded at Tili, then focused on Drracien. "Would you ride with me?"

Drracien's eyebrows shot into his shiny black hair, then he grinned. "Wouldn't miss it."

"Claerian," Captain Grinda called to one of the Jujak. "The standards."

Something in Haegan twisted and bent sideways as a lanky man went to his mount. There, he removed two sets of three rods, which he screwed together to form two long poles. Then he drew out two lengths of fabric—one the green field and gold crown with the tri-tipped flame, the sigil of House Celahar. Next came the gold flame on the red field, the emblem of Abiassa and the Nine Kingdoms. He handed one to another Jujak, then the pair stood ready beside their horses.

Graem met Haegan's gaze and nodded. "Mount up!"

With the Jujak creating an outer frame of protection as they descended the hill toward Baen's Crossing, Haegan rode flanked by the two Grindas and followed closely by Praegur, Tokar, and Drracien. They crossed the half-league with ease and speed, their shadows stretching long in the sinking sunlight. His gut roiled at the thought of riding in so aggressively. Yet, with the standards proclaiming their identity and loyalty, he could only hope the people of Baen's Crossing would see they were here to make a stand. And the enemy would see their attacks would not go unanswered.

Awe speared him as they approached the main gate. At a signal from the general, Graem heeled his mount and the beast surged ahead across the last hundred paces to the gate, hooves thundering. "Open in the name of Prince Haegan!"

Bile rose in Haegan's throat.

"Open in the name of the prince!" Graem shouted again.

Faces peered over the walls, then, "Open the gate! Open the gate!"

With groaning and creaking, wood surrendered. By the time Haegan reached the entrance, the gate yawned wide. They trotted in, taking in cobbled roads and narrow passages. Curious eyes peered from windows and doors. Marble pillars lined the sides of the main road as they slowed their horses to a walk, heading for the Sanctuary, sure the city seat would be nearby. The streets began filling with people, who trailed them the full ten minutes to the city center. Speculative eyes studied him. Some scowled and shook their heads.

"Are you truly Haegan?"

"He died ten years ago!"

"Nah, he was sickly."

"Well, he don't look sick to me!"

He wanted to stop and argue, prove himself, but there would be no defense, no frantic pleas of his identity. Only his actions could convince them that he was truly the prince, that though he had been sick—and might as well have been dead—he now rode into the city, well and healed and their future king. Because Poired had killed his father.

Beside him, Graem ceaselessly scanned the people, as, no doubt, did his fighters, who now rode ahead and behind.

A shout and the sound of a scuffle rose off Haegan's left flank. "Beg off," someone growled.

Haegan resisted the urge to look back, but when he heard the sound of a fist on flesh, he shifted his gaze—

"No," Graem whispered, edging closer with his mount. "Quiet and confident, an assured leader—that's what they need. Your men will take care of it."

After another bend, the entourage spilled out into the main city center, where the massive statue of Baen Celahar, later known as Zaelero II, stood in the middle of a reflecting pool. On either side towered the two head-quarters of the elected officials who held power: Sanctuary on the left, city seat on the right. On the steps of the former, a half-dozen Ignatieri waited behind the high marshal, who stared down his perfect, straight nose at Haegan. So much like Cilicien ka'Dur. The thought sent a shud-der through Haegan.

On the right, a man stood before the door to the city building, wear-ing a simple tunic that bore the emblem of Abiassa alongside another symbol, the Glass Dagger, used by Baen to slay Dirag the Desecrator. The mayor.

Claerian and the other standard bearer led the way to a central posi-tion before the great statue, while the remaining Jujak fanned out behind, creating a cushion between the crowds and Haegan's small party. Haegan had watched enough official processions from the tower to know the city's two representatives should present themselves to him in welcome.

But he was not officially set in. Would they acknowledge him?

Silence gutted the din as the crowds filled in every crevice and nook of the square. Here and there children laughed, oblivious to the painful void shrouding them.

Uncertainty fastened to Haegan, tempting him to shift. Look uncom-fortable. But he refused. Ever so slowly, General Grinda's hand twitched and drew up his thigh, a sign of his impatience at receiving no welcome.

Feet clapped against the cobbles, sharp in the silence. The mayor of the city strode forward from the city hall, straight toward the statue as if he might walk right into it. A sturdy fellow with no sign of gray hair or wrinkles, he pivoted and came directly in line with where Haegan waited.

The mayor bowed. "Your Highness," his voice rang out, echoing and hissing at the end. On a knee, the mayor waited.

Grinda waited.

Haegan wondered—waited. Was he to acknowledge the mayor now? No, *both* leaders were to present themselves. The hesitation of the Ignatieri thickened the already-palpable tension. Murmurs drifted through the crowds, the disrespect evident to all present.

Grinda cast a glance to his son. In response, Graem clicked his tongue, the command to his destrier. Reins clinked as the great horse hopped forward.

A patter of feet on the cobbles stilled Grinda and his son, but outrage roiled off the burly general.

Three Ignatieri fluttered into view on the left. The lesser two stopped at the fountain, but the third—a high marshal—continued, turning to stand before Haegan. He bowed but did not kneel. "My liege."

The generals seemed pacified, but still angry. As was Haegan.

Turning his gaze to the first man, Haegan spoke clearly, "Mayor, I thank you for your *ready* and warm welcome." His shifted his gaze with deliberate hesitation to the accelerant. "High Marshal, your reticence concerns me."

The accelerant did not flinch. "Forgive me, my liege, but there has been an attack—"

"And that is cause to disrespect the crown prince?" It was hard to project confidence when he felt anything but.

The high marshal stilled. "No. I beg your mercy." His oily voice sounded anything but apologetic. "It is only that you are not yet set in."

"How much more allegiance is needed before," Grinda grumbled. "Think you, the new Fire King, will ally himself with one who determines his actions on appearance alone?"

The dynamics of Ignatieri and the Fire King were intricate and myriad. Though Fire Kings were most often trained by the grand marshal, the king maintained superiority.

Haegan swung down off his mount.

Grinda grunted, clearly not pleased Haegan had dismounted, and got down as well.

Haegan stalked toward the mayor. "Please—stand that we may greet one another and talk."

The man came up, young eyes meeting Haegan's as the prince gripped his forearm and clasped his shoulder. "The days are dark and hard. I appreciate your reception. I would have your name."

The mayor's stiffness fell away and he smiled. "Jarain Fal'Raen. It is an honor, my prince." He bowed his head again.

"Thank you, Jarain." Haegan turned to the accelerant. Older. Annoyed. "High Marshal." Haegan extended his hand.

Hooded in apathy, the marshal's eyes showed nothing but disdain. "I am High Marshal Eftu, Haegan."

At his side, Grinda tensed at the informality and disrespect. But Haegan, remembering the lessons with Drracien, sent a spark from his hand to the high marshal.

The accelerant gasped, his ridiculous headdress faltering atop a narrow head. He steadied it, eyes bulging. "'Twas said you could not wield."

"I suppose it was also said I was crippled, sick, or dead." Haegan released the man. "Now, I would speak with you both."

The mayor nodded. "In the great hall, sire. It should be ready."

"Would you not prefer the elegance of Sanctuary?" the high marshal purred.

Haegan glared at him, reminded again of Cilicien ka'Dur. "I thank you, no." He nodded to Jarain. "Please." As they climbed the numerous steps, Haegan felt the strange unease again and let his gaze slide to the right, across the sea of faces in the city center, though they had become dim in the swiftly fading light. What was it? What lingered here?

Marble greeted them, opulence defined in the gold chandeliers of the grand foyer. The mayor held a hand to the left, where more of the same waited. A large tapestry depicting the pivotal battle of Zaelero against Dirag hung over the great fire pit. From there, two long tables spread out, draped in red satin and aglow from the twenty-four stick candelabras. Haegan raised an eyebrow at Jarain when he noticed the steam and wonderful aromas that rose from the platters of food nestled on the tables. "Sentries saw the banners, and we ordered preparations at once," Jarain said.

"Very kind," Haegan said, but his attention faltered as he caught sight of a door swinging closed at the far side of the room, a blur of fabric disappearing into the darkness.

Haegan was unsettled. It was with some effort that he focused on the mayor once more. "I beg your mercy, Jarain. I did not come for a feast, not when you and your people are so freshly grieved over the attack."

The man's face went white. "Thank you, sire. The grief is deep—my own father, the former mayor, was killed trying to stop the Sirdarian spies from escaping."

Haegan flinched. Closed the gap between them and took the man's forearm in solidarity. "We have much in common, Jarain Fal'Raen. As I'm sure you know, I recently lost my father at Poired's hand."

"Some reports differ," came the sniveling voice of the high marshal.

"The death of King Zireli is a great loss to the Nine," Jarain said, casting an uncertain glance at the high marshal.

"For your kind words, I thank you." Haegan motioned to the elaborate feast. "Come, I would hear of the attack, and we might as well enjoy the hard labors."

At the head table, Haegan sat with Jarain and High Marshal Eftu, as well as Graem and the general. Tokar, Drracien, and Praegur were brought in as Jarain explained how the Sirdarians had come up from the south with stealth and secrecy. "Once discovered, they fought their way out of the city, our guards giving chase. But . . . the Sirdarians escaped."

"They came with one purpose," the high marshal snapped.

"In pursuit of what?" Haegan asked. Did it seem a bit chilly? His gaze hit the fireplace, where flames danced and sap crackled. Its light a nice, ambient glow.

"The Fierian," Jarain said with a sniff. "I cannot believe anyone believes in that demon."

"He is no demon." The high marshal's eyes now narrowed and fixed on Haegan. "He is sent by Abiassa to be a cleansing fire."

They do not know . . . ? Amazement clutched Haegan that word had not already reached the people of the Nine that he had been named Fierian. Or perhaps it was only this far corner where his identity was not known. It was good. Better even. But would his credibility be questioned?

"Death and destruction," Jarain spat, flicking his wrist as if to banish the Fierian into lore once more.

"He does not tell the whole truth," the high marshal said.

"Honestly, Eftu," Jarain muttered. "Leave it."

But High Marshal Eftu was undeterred. "Whispers through the city were that the Sirdarian spies were asking after *you*, Prince Haegan."

The words thudded against his heart and conscience. "Were they?"

"They did not elaborate," Eftu droned, his words seeming too much an effort for the marshal to utter. "But speculation is rampant, and, since you are here, I can only imagine the rumors are true."

"And what rumors are those?" Perhaps the truth was not so unknown as he had hoped.

"Many, my prince," Eftu said. "Some say you murdered the Fire King, your own father."

Haegan considered the high marshal, trying to ascertain his position.

"Others say you betrayed your father and stole your sister's gifts. And there has been an even stronger rumor, mostly from the north—"

"I am here," Haegan said, "to rout the Sirdarian vermin from the city."

"Oh, they are already gone," Eftu said.

"No," Haegan countered, shouldering away another wave of coldness. "They are here."

Eftu frowned, leaving Jarain to sputter and nearly laugh. "I watched them leave, Prince—"

"Are you certain?" Haegan asked in a way that was not a question.

"Of course I am—they left the city."

"Then mayhap they left spies," Graem offered as he dragged a chunk of bread around the porcelain plate, slopping up gravy.

Jarain paled.

If the mayor had watched the Sirdarians leave, spies would explain why Haegan sensed something here. In fact—he'd tried to ignore the chill, but it was strong. Relentlessly strong. Right now. So cold and tainted now with such a foul odor that Haegan grew ill. He looked away, frowning. Swallowed, forcing back the bile rising in his throat.

"My lord, are you well?"

"Aye," Haegan managed as he stood. "If you will pardon me but a moment."

Graem was on his feet.

"Nay," Haegan said and held up a hand. "'Tis well. I shall return—"

"I have orders not to leave your side."

He looked to the captain, who stared back impassively. With a glance across the table, he met Drracien's gaze. Shoved a wake of heat at him, hoping he'd understand.

Out in the main foyer, Haegan pulled in a ragged breath. Leaned against a pillar for support and to gain his bearings.

"Are you well?" Graem asked.

"I—"

Drracien appeared, dark brows drawn together. A question in his eyes he did not ask. He closed the space between them.

Chin tucked, Haegan thought through the feeling. He angled in closer to Drracien. "Is it possible for me to . . . sense them?"

Hesitation guarded Drracien. He opened his mouth, then closed it. Frowned. "Why?"

"This feeling"—Haegan snapped his gaze away—"no, not a *feeling*." He gripped his head, again reminded of the circlet. He sighed. "Every now and then, I get a chill not related to the weather. But in there, in that hall, it was so strong I could *smell* something. It made me sick."

Dark eyes probed his, weighing. Considering. "I know of no accelerant being able to smell them," Drracien said. "But as I said earlier, nobody's been the Fierian." He shrugged. "It may well be."

"Reassuring." Rolling his eyes, Haegan turned away.

"We are in uncharted territory. Nothing is impossible and everything possible."

What if I'm wrong? What if there is no chill and no Sirdarians are here? Then he would look the fool, feeding the rumors of his madness, giving credence to the reports that he had killed his father. Pinching the bridge of his nose, he paced.

The chill returned. Icy. Painful. Wincing, Haegan drew up.

"My prince?" Graem reached toward him.

In the far corner a blur caught Haegan's eye. But almost as soon as he saw it, it was gone. As was the person.

Haegan shot in that direction.

"My prince! Wait!"

Darkness had fallen, but he sprinted into the night, rolling his fingers to illumine the way. A door clicked shut a dozen paces ahead. Haegan threw himself at it. Barreled out. Down a flight of steps, nearly falling.

He stopped and scanned the darkness, but he could see nothing.

He closed his eyes, shut out the distractions. Focused on the—

Cold. To the right.

He chased it, determined to capture this person. Conviction pushed him on. A Sirdarian. Around a corner.

A wisp of white fabric, like the servants in the hall had worn.

Spy. The word hissed through his mind. He sprinted down the hall, shouts coming from behind as the others struggled to stay with him.

"My prince, please stop. It's dangerous—"

But Haegan ran on, resolute. They would not get away with killing people. They would not hurt innocents while on a warpath against him, nor would he allow them to walk casually into the dark night and escape justice.

He pushed down the narrow street. Was it not enough to murder his own father and mother in front of him? And now, Poired sent his soldiers out to hunt him, kill his people?

A four-way juncture presented itself. Haegan would not be so easily thrown off. Not this time. He slid his eyes shut again. Focused on that stench. On the chill. But it seemed to have faded.

He turned a slow circle, trained on the temperature, the voices of his friends in the distance as they searched for him while he hunted this spy.

There. He nearly smiled and shouldered into the darkness. It was getting stronger now. He could feel it. The chill. The smell. He ran. Faster. Harder.

They broke out into a road and ahead, aiming for the side gate, a form rushed through the night.

"Stop," Haegan growled.

But it only seemed to fuel his quarry.

Palming the air, Haegan arced his hand down and up, then drew it and the heat back to himself.

When a distant scream rent the night, Haegan stopped, watching helplessly from twenty feet away as the person shoved out a spark. It hit someone, and they crumpled to the ground.

"No!" Anger shot through Haegan's veins. He clawed the embers he'd drawn up, gathering the fiery storm to himself.

Another ball of light appeared at the far end of the path. The spy was going to wield against someone else. Trying to throw him off. Stop him.

"My prince, no!"

Haegan punched his hand forward, palm open, ignoring the voice behind him.

"Nooo!"

Darkness shattered.

Light erupted.

Satisfaction spiraled through him as he waited for the images of night to return. The somber glow of the moon slowly unfurled its hem and spread it over the road. Over a body in the middle.

Haegan smiled. *Got him.*

From a building, someone rushed into the road. Knelt at the body.

"Is he dead?" Haegan demanded, striding forward. At least he had served the people. Protected them.

"Haegan, no. Please—come back," Graem pleaded.

"Princeling, you must come." Drracien said.

"Is the spy dead?" Haegan insisted, vindication heady.

"Spy?" a man spat, shoving upward. "This is no spy—this is my brother!"

Haegan frowned. "No, I—"

"The prince killed a servant!" someone shouted.

"And a child," said another.

"No." Haegan glanced back. The small frame—it'd been a child? "It wasn't . . . He—"

"The prince murdered a child and servant, just like he did the Fire King!"

26

"Sirdarians skirt the southern border of Ybienn and the Rekken continue to threaten from the north."

Leaning against his pelt throne, Aselan smoothed a hand over his beard. Sikir came to his side, looking for another ear rub. "Threatening but not attacking."

"Not yet," Byrin groused from the table. "And most likely, they dare not tempt Legier during winter's prowl."

"Aye," Teelh put in. "But the weather has been warmer than usual since the prince's departure. 'Tis but an invitation to them to move against the Northlands sooner."

"Scouts also saw Southlanders ride out under the escort of the Nivari."

"Southlanders? Ye mean the Jujak?"

"Aye." Byrin looked to Markoo, then both of them studied the table.

Their reticence to speak made Aselan hesitate. They would only act so if they felt their thoughts would be unfavorable to their cacique. What would be unfavorable at this hour? They'd already foretold attacks from both the north and south.

The Fierian.

His mind caught up with the news and put the pieces together. "The Fierian rode out with the Jujak."

Byrin gave a curt nod.

"South," Aselan muttered, imagining the reason, "to respond to the attacks."

"No doubt," Byrin agreed.

"And what about that gives ye cause for concern, Byrin?"

His man stood. "He rode out like a king."

Aselan leaned back against the throne. "King." Haegan had been gone from Legier's Heart less than a week.

"I would wager," Byrin began, folding his arms, "that he acts under the advice of General Grinda."

"Agreed," Aselan said. "The Fierian must show himself, must show that Seultrie is not undefended, that the Nine has a leader." His mind drifted to a pair of pale blue eyes, wondering how she would react to hearing her brother was taking the throne. "As long as he stays to his business, what concern is it of ours?"

"But Cacique," Bardin spoke clearly, "the Nivari rode with him."

Slinging his gaze to Bardin, Aselan considered the words. "Do ye worry about an alignment between Ybienn and the Nine?"

"Aye, and it should unnerve every man in the Heart," Bardin growled. "We have remained in the safety of the mountain with a tenuous agreement with Thurig. What if Haegan holds sway over him? What if he—"

"Mayhap that is why the cacique has held the princess," Capit offered quietly.

"Aye," Byrin said with a grunt. "Keep her here, and if war comes to Legier, she can speak on our behalf. Wise. Very wise, Cacique."

"Or be our hostage. A trade."

Grumbles and nods of grim agreement rippled through the room. Though Byrin's thought agreed with him, Aselan would not allow them to believe a lie. "The princess remains here because it is not yet safe for her leave the mountain. She would need a wheeled carriage, and that's not possible until the first thaw."

"That is what we tell them." Teelh nodded. "It is believable and will buy us time."

"Maybe she'll take a mountain man during Etaesian's Feast."

At that, Aselan laughed. "She would no more have one of ye than the scoundrel her father pledged her to."

"She was pledged? To who?" Teelh asked, his face a mask of worry.

"Jedric."

"He's a puppet of the Dark One!" Teelh shot up, pounding a fist on the table. "What if they learn she is here? That muarshtait Jedric could come looking for her."

"That is a fear we will concern ourselves with only when they enter the Northlands."

"Think ye they will come here?" Doubt and concern weighted Byrin's question.

"There has been no word of Jedric—or anyone—searching for her. She is believed lost in the battle for Zaethien." This turn in the conversation would not bode well. "They assume she is dead."

"Aye, but Haegan took the princess in front of Poired and his army, and now he goes to the Nine—they will soon know where their princess hides."

"Aye," Byrin mumbled, his gaze dark.

Aselan could not deny it. "'Tis a concern—but no more than the armies coming here. We train throughout winter as always. We have the Heart, and they are not trained in mountain fighting or living." It was why the Eilidan had remained in the mountains, concealed among the clouds, and rearing hardy children to not just survive here, but thrive. "Let us put our attention where it is best spent."

After a chorus of ayes, Aselan motioned to Teelh, who held the order of minutes. "What next, friend?"

"Ingwait and her Ladies of the Heart."

Grumbles spiraled through the cavern . . . until someone muttered a joke about Etaesian's Feast, then a shout of laughter went up. The doors were opened and in came the Ladies of the Heart. With women outnumbering men, the Ladies oversaw Etaesian's Feast and the Choosing. All in the hopes of bearing more sons to defend the mountain.

Aselan stood and welcomed Ingwait, their representative, but he'd rather work the kitchens than listen to the plans for the Bonding. It was yet two months out, but they required the permission of the cacique to proceed.

Forty mind-numbing minutes later, plans were approved—a celebration to officially start the week-long ceremony that included the Choosing banquet, the Honoring, and the final Joining Ring.

Formalities decided, Aselan dismissed the Legiera and headed to his cave.

"Cacique," Capit called from behind as he strode the stone passage. Aselan turned.

"For the Bonding, is the princess eligible?"

The cheek of him. Aselan stowed his annoyance. "Is she a citizen of Legier or the Cold One's Tooth?"

Capit shifted.

"There is yer answer."

With a smirk, Capit backed away. "Just wondering."

Aselan started again for his cave, shoving a hand through his hair. The counsel meeting had worn down his mood. And the thought of that impudent pup thinking he would have anything to induce a princess to select him for the Choosing . . . He snorted, doubting there was even a man in the Heart who would be enough to induce Kaelyria Celahar to betray her family or her oath to the throne and Nine.

Laughter spiraled from the left, drawing closer. He turned and found Hoeff pushing the princess's wheeled chair. Gray pelts tucked around her legs made her near-white hair brighter.

Hoeff said something to her, and she laughed again. Shaking her head, she covered her mouth. Was she always so happy? So lighthearted? It called to him, her laughter. He did not hear much of it. Not since Doskari died.

Those pale eyes found their way to him, and her brows rose. Her lips formed a perfect circle.

"Master," Hoeff said, his voice rumbling through the passage as they neared the juncture.

Safer ground lay in the murky eyes of the hulking giant. "Ye are acknowledged, Hoeff."

The Drigo bowed his head.

"We go to dine," Kaelyria said, her cheeks red. Were they so deeply shaded before now?

"I see."

"Excuse me, Cacique," came the stiff, annoyed voice of Ingwait from behind the giant. "Hoeff, yer help is needed."

Frozen in indecision, Hoeff looked to his patient, then to Ingwait. As a Drigo, he could not abandon his charge. Yet he was being called to help elsewhere. Hoeff was distressed, not sure which to serve. To Aselan, this smelled of a setup, especially after the words Ingwait had scalded his ears with before the prince left.

The bustling woman gave him a sniff. "Surely the cacique can push the princess to the dining room," Ingwait said, taking the arm of the giant. "Come, ye are needed."

A trap, definitely.

"If I am intruding or if this is a problem . . ." Kaelyria said, sensing his hesitation.

Aselan stepped behind the chair and took the handles. "'Tis well." He guided her wheeled chair to the next juncture and turned right. His mind tripped over the scent flowing back to him, saturating his nostrils in her essence of sowaoli petals and some herb he couldn't pin down.

The thrum of the chatter in the hall was a welcome change to the silence clogging the passages.

"Cacique?" a young man called from a table, where he sat with a half-dozen others.

"Aye, Matyon?"

"Have the Ladies meted out the details for the Choosing?"

Aselan sighed. "Aye."

"Oochak!" The shout echoed through the dining hall as he pushed the princess to the end of the head table. Carilla, a table wench, hurried over and removed a chair so the princess's chair could fit. Though he normally sat in the middle, he chose to remain with her so she was not alone. A moment later, Carilla returned with two trays of food and warmed cordi juice. Aselan sat straight as she set out the meals then hurried off to tend another citizen.

"Aselan," Kaelyria asked, hesitant. "I've been wondering. Do . . . do we pay for this?"

Surprised at the question, he paused. "Everyone pays—by carrying out their own duties to ensure we are all warm, fed, and healthy."

"But I carry no duty."

"Ye are a guest."

"Is that why you're not sitting in your normal seat?"

Again, he hesitated.

"She was waiting at your seat then hurried here, to adjust the setting."

He gave a light snort. "There is little ye miss."

"You do not have to nursemaid me, Aselan." Kaelyria's gaze did not rise to meet his as she set a napkin across her lap. "I recognize your duties are many and as their leader, you—"

"—still have to eat." He lifted a fork, flashed a smile, then dug into the pulled meat and vegetables. It was a good way to quiet her concerns and his own ramming thoughts. He should be above, poring over maps and discussing scout reports with Byrin. The ones not mentioned in the meeting hall. In the minutes as they ate, the silence grew. And grew painfully. Awkwardly. Obvious.

He should talk to her. Put her at ease, but words betrayed him just as Ingwait had. And of what use was he with small talk? He would wager she had neither time nor patience for it herself. She was, after all, a princess. No doubt King Zireli had been training her to take the throne, to—

"What is the Choosing?"

The meat caught at the back of his throat. Aselan coughed, thumping his fist against his chest. He dropped his fork and took a drink of juice. After wiping his mouth and taking another sip, he cleared his now-burning throat. "'Tis . . ." He coughed again. Searching the knots of the wood table for direction. How was he to speak of such a thing with a . . . a . . . an unbound woman? In fact, he questioned sitting here at the head table alone with her. But he could not abandon her.

Laughter drifted through the air between them. "I fear I have inadvertently stepped upon a precarious topic."

"Aye," he said, feeling the heat. Then he chuckled. "Aye, 'tis better put to one of the Ladies."

"Ladies—that's a formal title, aye?"

"Here among the Eilidan a cacique is chosen to guide the men, to wage war, and to protect the mountains. But the Ladies of the Heart are the true heart of the mountain, they oversee the women."

"And . . . they're all ladies?"

"Aye." Wait. Did she mean every woman was a lady? Or that all on the council were ladies? "No. That is—only women are among the Ladies of the Heart, if that is yer question."

She smiled, her eyes sparkling like ice on fresh-fallen snow. "Aye." But then something shone in them. "So, the women are the . . . the women are in charge?"

"Ingwait would like to think so," he said, then lifted his shoulders in acquiescence. "They oversee the daily activities of the Heart and the Tooth."

"The Tooth?"

"Legier's Heart"—he looked around the large room—"is here. And the Cold One's Tooth—the lesser mountain farther north, whose spine embraces Ybienn."

After sipping her juice, the metal cup dark and dingy against her fair complexion, she sighed. "Clearly, I have much to learn."

"Haven't we all?" He retrieved his fork to finish his midday meal. "Much is done differently here and for good reason."

"Such as?"

He pointed his fork around the hall. "Due to limited ventilation, cooking fires are restricted to this hall, so we eat communally. Everyone serves a function. The women lead and govern social affairs—bindings, births—"

"The Choosing." She smiled, and it seemed a knowing smile. Mischievous.

In truth, it surprised him. "Ye taunt me, Princess. Not many dare."

27

She had crossed the line. For a moment, she had been able to abandon the grief and longing for her family, most of whom no longer existed. Haegan was down in Ybienn, doing what she did not know, though she prayed to Abiassa that he was preparing some sort of retaliation against Poired for murdering their father.

"I beg your mercy, Cacique." Kae stared at her half-eaten meat and vegetables. "Your reprimand is just. I had no cause—"

His hand rested on hers. Large, callused. Strong. Warm. She missed warmth. It'd been in her bones, in her abiatasso from birth. Now . . . gone. Because of a tragic, misguided mistake. His touch sparked memories of her father. He'd done the same many times over when she'd grown frustrated or become impatient during a lesson.

"We are friends, Princess."

She dragged her gaze from his hand to his eyes. Dark, curly hair framed an olive complexion hedged in by a thick beard. His features were not hard but seasoned. Experienced. It made him seem sturdy, reliable. Aye, handsome. "Then use my name. Please."

Aselan swallowed and withdrew his hand. "'Twould not be right." His gaze skidded around the room. "Ye are still heir to the Fire Throne, and here, that is what ye represent. An enemy with a very long reach."

She caught his meaning, though she wasn't sure he intended it to reveal itself. "They fear me?" Why did that upset her so? Most of her life she had walked in authority with the Flames and her station. It was as much a part of her as breathing. "But I can neither sense the Flames nor wield. I am stripped."

"They fear what ye represent—and how are they to know with certainty that ye have not the ability to wield? 'Tis . . . uncommon that a powerful accelerant such as yerself would lose her abilities. That she would then come to the Heart—foreign territory—with no intent."

They doubted her. Kaelyria stared at him, her heart pounding. In truth, she was not used to being doubted. Or questioned. "And do you, too, think this?"

Aselan leaned forward, resting his arms on the table and burrowing closer. She thought the move was meant to inflict sincerity, but it came across as severity, for his shoulders were broad and thick. His arms well muscled. He lifted his eyebrows and looked over her shoulder. "They are my people, Princess. I am responsible for the thousands who live beneath the mountain. 'Twould be foolish to not at least consider the possibilities."

"What?" She heard the pitch in her voice and didn't care. "What possibilities?" This time, she leaned forward. "That I'm here to boil this mountain to slag? That I'm gathering information on how to best take your people down?"

His left cheek muscle twitched, his gaze resolute.

Her breast heaved with the pain of hurt and shock. "To what end, *Cacique*? To what end would I do that?"

"Lovers' quarrel?" came a taunting voice from behind. Aselan's second officer—*what was his name?*—dropped into a chair next to his cacique and immediately a tray of food found its way to him.

Aselan shoved to his feet. "Make sure she returns to her cave when she finishes, Byrin." His stony expression hardened as he turned to her. "Princess."

Kae watched him go, hating the way her eyes stung. Humiliated at his dismissal. Beneath the hurt, she discovered how . . . personal it all felt. His reproof. His rejection, which hurt most. She respected and admired him.

"Winning him with yer fiery charm, Princess?" Byrin peppered his food, then added some salt. Then more pepper. "What? Did ye spark him?"

She flashed the man a glare. "I can no more wield these days than you . . ." She stopped, unsure what to call him. "How am I to address you?"

"Address me?" With a chunk of meat halfway to his mouth, he hesitated then added yet more pepper.

"Yes, what title?"

"Handsome? Devilish? Rogue?" He stuffed the meat into his mouth.

Irritation rolled across her shoulders. "Have you no title as the cacique's right hand?"

"He has his own hands, Princess. He doesn't need mine."

Futile. It was futile. *Everything* was futile. Weariness clawed at her, and she suddenly found she had no humor for entertaining or enduring these people any longer. "I think . . . I grow weary. I would like to return to my"—she could not bear to call it a cave, which seemed so much like a prison—"room."

Byrin chewed his food, then glanced toward the kitchens and waved. A girl started from her post as he turned his attention back to Kae. "He's a cacique, a chief. Do not expect him to be yer best friend or lover. Thousands in the Heart depend on him." He sucked on his teeth, then stabbed a potato with his fork. "He gave his heart away once, and it got bludgeoned. Won't do it again. He'll stick to the icehounds for warmth at night."

Shocked again, she lowered her chin, cheeks flaming. "I neither expected nor asked for a lover, or friend, Master Byrin."

"Master?" He snorted and shook his head. "Throw away those high-born ways, Princess. They get ye nothin' here."

Carilla was there.

"Get her back to Hoeff," Byrin said without looking at either of them as he sawed a purple vegetable in half.

The girl wheeled her from the room. Shivering with indignity and a chill from the cool passage, Kaelyria hugged herself and silently screamed away her tears of humiliation.

"Don't be giving them no mind, miss—er, Princess."

Kaelyria worried the edge of the heavy blanket draped across her useless legs.

"They're the warriors. They're like that."

She understood. She'd fallen in love with a warrior, in her former life. Graem . . . Where was he now? Had he fallen in the battle at Fieri Keep? Why was she only now thinking of her Jujak?

Because, though she could not admit it then, she could be honest now. Graem had been a piece of her rebellion against her father's injustice toward her and toward Haegan.

A pack of younger men huddled in the narrow junction ahead. They were indiscreet about their stares at her. Their laughter barreled out as one got pushed to the front. He squared his shoulders and started toward them.

Kae's first instinct was to spark them. But then an icy fear cocooned her in the realization that she'd lost that ability. She swallowed. For the first time she didn't feel safe. She drew the blanket to her waist and knotted the heavy wool in her powerless fists.

"Go on with ye," Carilla growled, waving her hands at the men. "Or I'll be telling the cacique."

"Ye're a hag, Carilla."

"At least I got a brain, Vorku. Now, go on." Carilla caught a small boy by the shoulder and placed something in his hand, whispering in his ear. The lad shot up the stairs like an arrow. "There," she said, turning back to Kae. "Hoeff will be here soon."

"Are . . . are they all like that?" Kaelyria watched the half-dozen men hovering farther back, but not moving off as instructed.

"They're getting all wound up," Carilla said as she sat on the iron steps, her skirts gathered about her legs. "It's the Choosing. Does that to their weak brains." She laughed.

"What is it?"

Carilla's gray eyes widened. "Ye don't know? It's only the most important event each cycle."

"Why?"

"The Ladies hold a great celebration, and the whole Heart joins in. There's food, music, and games for a full week! On the night before the last, we all get to go into the great hall for dancing and feasting. The women who are given permission by the Ladies are allowed to choose a man for binding." She stabbed a finger in the air. "But only those men who lay their daggers on the table at the feast."

"It is very different in the Nine," Kaelyria said, her thoughts on the wily Jedric, who had given her chills. "I was pledged to a man I hadn't met, and then when we did meet, I wanted to run away."

"Blazes," Carilla muttered, shaking her head. "I wouldn't want to live there! Here, the women do the choosing. They pick their man. Then they go to their chosen that night. If he accepts, they . . ." Her eyes darted around.

"Oh." Realization crackled through Kaelyria. She'd thought they went to them on the dance floor, but this . . . "Isn't that . . ." She swallowed. "In the Nine, you could be arrested for entering a man's room alone."

"Only on this night 'tis allowed—and only if ye have his dagger. Ye must stand on the threshold until he accepts the dagger back." Carilla waved a hand. "The next night, there's the Joining Ring. That's when those bound are presented before all Eilidan."

"Have you done it?"

"No," she said with a grin. "But I go this year."

"Do you have a man in mind?"

"Oh, ye cannot tell a soul who ye're choosing. That way, if the man refuses, nobody knows but the two of ye. Yer name is clear and so is his."

"Does that happen often?"

Carilla laughed. "And what girl would admit to being rejected?"

28

"Don't stop! Don't stop!"

Haegan slowed and glanced back down the sloping hill to the city. Twin full moons shone brightly, and he easily saw the dispatch of horses flooding out of the wagon gate. If those riders caught up with them, or if he fled to the shelter of Nivar Hold, there would be war between the Nine and the Northlands.

The thought pulled him around. He couldn't let that happen. Not because of him. There was too much war and bloodshed to come. Kingdoms had to unite against Poired. Division helped only the Dark One in his quest to subjugate all of Primar for Sirdar of Tharqnis.

The world would be in ruin.

Because of me.

Tokar came about, shouting, "What are you doing?"

"I can't bring trouble to Ybienn." The future if he went north, took shelter with the Nivari, was perfectly clear to him. "I will not."

Graem joined them. "Baen's Crossing will seek a blood price for the child."

"It wasn't me. I didn't kill the boy." The face! He could not get the boy's face out of his mind—brown eyes like Thiel's, outsized teeth like Laertes. "I didn't kill him, but I will not be the one to bring war to Ybienn. Not when I can help it."

Heat faded to his left. Haegan detected it a split-second before he saw the tiny explosion. A spark, meant to incapacitate him, as had happened before.

Annoyed, he flicked his finger and sent his own spark, the two colliding in the air like a clap of hands. "Tempt not my patience nor temper this hour, Drracien."

"I had to try." He looked out over the lands with a heavy sigh. "If you go north—"

"They will blame Ybienn," Haegan said.

"Then we must stay in the Nine."

Haegan's heart slowed, the tendrils of heat spreading over his arms and losing the concentration in his hands. Balancing. "Agreed."

"Are you both mad?" Tokar asked. "There is nothing for leagues, and we are pursued. We *must* seek the safety of the Nivari."

And hand victory to Poired. "No."

"This is lunacy!" Tokar shouted, his anger strangling good sense. "We must go—the Nivari are waiting. We can debate what to do next when we're safe across the border!"

"I will not have their deaths on my head as well." But an idea sparked. "Haegan."

He gazed east, where moonslight caressed the jagged spine of the mountains that gave birth to the Great Falls. It seemed the place that had irrevocably altered his life, mocked him still. Glittered at him, taunting.

"The Falls."

Haegan snapped his gaze to the accelerant. So strange to have a solid ally in Drracien at this hour. "We know it—"

"*Know* it? We fled it. We nearly *died* in it," Tokar yelled.

"Indecision is about to kill us," Graem growled.

"Haegan."

He realized his name had been called before—Praegur. And there was warning in his tone. Haegan looked back to where Praegur sat atop his horse, facing north. Staring. Squinting. Haegan followed his gaze, but he saw nothing save the great Black Forest that separated Ybienn from the Nine. Two miles between them and that forest.

Wait. Something . . . the trees were swaying.

A vibration wormed through his body as he searched the branches from one side to the other. Again, the trees moved violently. "What's going on?"

"Haegan, the patrol!" Tokar shouted.

On the knoll, the men of Baen's Crossing were closing in.

"To the Falls," Drracien said.

"The Nivari are closer," Tokar countered.

"Haegan, this isn't good." It was Praegur's voice again.

"No," Haegan said. "We're not going to the Falls." Devastation waited for them if they fled. He felt in his bones. No . . . not his bones. It was deeper. What was deeper than bones?

Abiatasso.

Warmth spread through him, churning. *Stay. Stay, and I will defend you, Fierian.* But the others . . . Haegan turned to them. "Please. You go to the Nivari. I don't . . . I don't know what's going to happen."

Drracien snorted. "Don't try that, 'this is for your own good' muarshtait. We were set on your path for a reason. We stay."

Tokar let out a loud, frustrated growl. "Form a perimeter around him!"

Startled, Haegan watched as his friends encircled him. "No—"

"Quiet," Tokar shot over his shoulder. "And if we die . . ."

"I won't let that happen."

"Getting sentimental?" Tokar taunted. "I might have to write this down. But first—think you could summon those Deliverers to help out?"

"It doesn't work that way." Haegan wasn't sure how any of it worked, and he could not escape the distinct feeling that he didn't control any of it either. He was a puppet on this stage like everyone else.

Hooves thundered as horses rushed up the knoll. There were at least a hundred men, the heat of them buffeting Haegan's senses.

Interesting.

He had plenty to draw from should he have to defend the others.

"We are the Dagger," a man shouted, his horse stamping forward. "You will surrender yourself, Haegan Celahar—"

"*Prince* Haegan," Drracien corrected. "He does not take orders from a city patrol, he commands them!"

"Not until he's formally recognized as king and crowned in Hetaera," the man said. "Prince Haegan, come forward or we will draw you out."

Draw me out? They seemed unusually calm. Too calm to be arresting an accelerant blamed with murdering a man and child.

"That man was not who you believe him to have been," Haegan said, trying to negotiate his way out.

"And the boy?" came a deep voice that sounded like rocks in a barrel.

"I did not—" The words caught in his throat. "The boy was murdered by another accelerant—the man I was chasing killed him to distract me."

"Then you admit you are responsible for his death?" the gravelly voice said. "The penalty is death."

Haegan stared. "What?"

"Calb, easy," the leader muttered to the side.

"He killed my boy!"

The words thudded against Haegan's heart. "No!" He'd never be able to dislodge that memory seared into his mind. "I beg your mercy—"

"Mercy?" Calb spat. "I want your blood!"

"Careful," Drracien snapped, his hand a halo of light.

"Drracien, yield," Haegan said.

"That sounded a lot like wield," Drracien threatened, but the words were empty as the halo snapped closed.

Cold. A *very* cold chill at his back.

Haegan didn't want to appear to ignore the Dagger, but the odd sensation sliding down his spine drew his gaze to the side.

"Surrender yourself, my lord," the leader said. "You will face trial."

But Haegan held up a hand, his eyes on the south. Saw a wake dancing in the moonslight. Someone was wielding, but the glow was wrong. Not gold and red. Greenish-brown. Like dirt or moss.

From the dregs of earth and bodies therein
Come the sons of darkness and Zer'En.
Brown, green, and twisted hues,
Wield our Flames with icy cues.

"Incipients!" Drracien's shout stabbed the night.

Panicked, Haegan spotted a volley that roared into the sky. It looked like a river of fire, sailing up into the darkness. But it wasn't just one. There were at least five or six incipients sending their dirty brown flames skyward.

Haegan jerked the reins and faced the leader. "You knew." It seemed the volleys hung in the sky forever. "You knew the man I killed was an incipient. You knew!"

The man made no acknowledgement, yet his eyes told of his guilt.

"I see it in your eyes that you know this path is wrong."

"We have little choice," the man said, his voice and bearing weary. "Jujak are gone or spread thin. Many Ignatieri have fled—"

"Save Eftu."

The man's lips thinned.

"So, he's the leader of the incipients," Haegan pointed to the line of evil behind them, then looked up as the streams of fire grew brighter. "You fool! Can you not see they would kill you, too?"

"Incoming!" Drracien shouted.

But all Haegan seemed to notice was the change in the air. Cold. Very cold. The incipients were sucking all the heat from the people and the elements of nature. Freezing his ability to—

Something . . . changed. Something was different. Haegan glanced down. To the side. Frowned. *What?*

It wasn't warm, but in some strange, incomprehensible way he sensed *more* heat. More than ever before. It infused him. Roiled through him. Invigorated him. Strength not his own coursed through his veins.

This doesn't make sense.

The sky went as day. A long, thick blanket of fire speared the night, shattering darkness. It would reach them. They would die in a blaze of glory.

Well, in a blaze. The *glory* he wasn't sure about.

Tingling rushed up his fingertips. He glanced at his hands. Though he saw nothing, he felt . . . everything. A buzzing. An iciness hotter than anything he'd encountered before. As if something in him were drawing heat from . . . from the volley? From the incipient?

Separate from whatever it was that surged through him, the ground shook, vibrating like the drums in the Ematahri camp. But faster. More violent.

Shouts went up, drawing his attention to the guards. Horses reared. Shrieked. "What's happening?" Graem shouted, shielding his eyes, but keeping watch on the panicking Dagger.

The ground rattled.

A roar filled the sky.

Crack! Pop!

The noises came from the trees and mingled with shouts—as a unit, the Nivari poured from them, clearly visible in the moonslight. Though harried in chaos, they slowly formed up a hundred yards from the tree line, their backs to Haegan as they gazed at the forest. Apparently, they were as confused and concerned as everyone else.

Haegan looked to the woods. And his brain lied to him. Said there was a forest, but there wasn't. Trees flew this way and that, as if an enormous gardener pitched weeds.

What in blazes?

"Haegan!"

Drracien's shout pulled Haegan around. The accelerant had dismounted, wielding, dancing. Fast, frantic. A warbling wall of energy and heat sailed out as he tried to stall the blanket of fire. But Drracien was failing. Six to one. It wasn't a fair blaze.

Joining Drracien on the ground, Haegan focused on the heat he'd sensed thrumming through his fingers and shoved his hands toward the sky. Crossed them, then splayed across the canopy, forming a shield. It glittered and crackled as he worked to stop the volley from killing everyone on the field. He thought to speak the words useful against the Ematahri, but as he opened his mouth to utter the ancient words he had never learned, overgrown men hurled themselves in front of Haegan with bloodcurdling roars.

And in the space of a blink, as the giants' feet thudded to the ground and the din of combat faded beneath the hot-icy thrumming in his veins, Haegan heard different words escape his mouth. *"Ïmnæh wæithe he-ahwl abiałassø et Thræïho. Miembo Thræïho!"*

Drracien jerked toward him. Shot a look filled with panic. Shock.

As if dropping from the sky—their hurdles from the trees long and fluid—three more Drigo landed within a dozen paces of Haegan, pitching him off balance. Backs to him, they faced the enemy, clearly enraged by the sons of Ederac.

The middle giant—the largest and garbed in blue-green—fisted his right hand. Covered it with his left. And lifted both hands over his eight-foot height. He gave a primal shout that rattled the heavens. As if in response, the other Drigo did the same.

The Drigo stomped their feet four times. *Thud. Thud-thud. Thud.* Then jerked their hands to the side in unison. The concussion of their combined shouts knocked Haegan backward as if someone had punched him.

Haegan's heart crashed against his ribs. He scrambled back to his feet. "Drigo."

"Of all that's holy and . . ." Graem's words trailed off, wonder and terror vying for supremacy on his face.

"They've returned." Drracien's words pushed Haegan to interpret what he saw. What his mind refused to believe. The Drigo before him were no longer eight feet tall. They were at least twelve or thirteen. Their arms muscled like centuries-old trees. Their hair flowing like rivers of gold down their now-bare scaled spines. Beautiful and terrifying.

With brutal and swift actions that belied their monstrous size, the transformed Drigo crushed the incipients. Bones crunched as men were flattened into the earth. Breath stolen by the gruesome sight, Haegan could not move. Could not scream. Could not think. Shock held him fast as the giants delivered swift justice to the wicked.

Screams behind Haegan turned him in a daze to the rear, to where the men of Baen's Crossing had challenged them. But instead of a hundred men, there were four more Drigo. And only one man standing. The leader.

Haegan forced a swallow.

"Hae—" Drracien's word was clipped, losing the last syllable in a gasp.

Behind him, Haegan sensed it. That same thrumming in his veins. He turned slowly. And looked up . . . up . . . up.

His stomach fell as he saw the enormous shape moving toward him.

"Back! Back!" Tokar shouted at the morphed giant, rushing in with his sword.

A mere splinter to the Drigo.

Forehead melting toward his nose, the Drigo scowled at Tokar. Fury in his eyes. Death in his touch.

"No no no!" Haegan sent a harmless puff of heat against Tokar, throwing him backward a few feet. "Stand down."

"But did you just see—"

"Aye." He held out hand to the rest of his companions, pushing enough heat against them so they knew not to advance. "Nobody moves."

"More soldiers coming out of Baen's Crossing," Graem said directly behind him.

At this, the Drigo turned toward the city, and growled.

Haegan's stomach churned. It was not lost on him that this Drigo stood at his right hand, watching the soldiers flood out of the city. As the Drigo looked to the walls, then to the forest, his massive chest wall heaved breaths that sounded like loud snores. But he didn't seem out of breath. Just . . . loud.

His face had changed. At least, Haegan thought it had. Now there seemed to be sectioned plates. In fact, the Drigo's chest, legs, and arms even seemed segmented like a protective shell. *Armor.*

When he tipped back his head again to look the Drigo in the face, the creature was watching him. His upper lip seemed pushed against his nostrils. His eyebrow furrowed into his nose. Maybe that was why he was snore-breathing. But the eyes—they seemed to dig into the depths of Heagan's heart and pour light. Pure, unadulterated light.

The Drigo shifted back a single step, causing Haegan to wobble. The giant bent his right knee to the ground. *"Fhuriætyr."*

Fire roiled through Haegan's chest, as if answering the giant's call. He stepped between Drracien and Tokar, who struck out a hand toward Haegan. "Wait—how—"

But Haegan was locked onto eyes that were changing from red to orange. *Like a fire.* "'Tis well," he said to Tokar as he emerged from the protective circle of friends.

The giant held his hands out to the side, and instantly the other Drigo went to their knees. Haegan swallowed and skirted a sidelong glance to each giant but didn't allow himself to retreat.

The leader—*was he a leader?*—arranged his hands as he had moments before he and his brethren had morphed into the massive creatures that knelt before him now.

Tensing, Haegan expected to get hammered into the ground like the incipients. Instead, the Drigo touched fisted hands to their foreheads with a thud. They then struck their chests over the heart. Haegan winced at the sound. With a reverence that permeated the atmosphere, the Drigo stretched their right hands toward him, tucked the left behind themselves, and bowed before Haegan.

29

What am I to do with that? Haegan felt sick as he stared at the seven golden heads bowed before him.

"I think you are to release them," came Drracien's whisper.

"How?"

"The same way you summoned them."

"Summoned the—" Haegan jerked toward the accelerant. As he did, he recalled Drracien's shocked look when he'd uttered the ancient words. "I didn't—"

A roar jolted Haegan again. At this rate, his heart might surrender before the enemy did. What was the giant angry about? Because he hadn't released him?

Eyes that were now nearly golden and matched the flowing hair, stared back with expectant patience. "Thelikor serve."

Drracien's shoulder was against Haegan's now. "I think Thelikor is his name"

"You *think*?"

"You have a better idea?"

"I thought you were raised in the Citadel? Shouldn't you know?"

"And who keeps bragging about the books he reads?"

Haegan stared at the giant. "Thelikor . . ."

The giant seemed to smile at hearing his name. But with that sectioned plate rather than skin, it was hard to be sure.

"I beg your mercy, Thelikor," Haegan said.

"Thelikor serve."

He *had* served. And well—killing the enemy. Routing incipients from Baen's Crossing. "I thank you." It was earnest. And all he could think to say.

The Drigo seemed to purr, his eyes slipping closed in apparent pleasure as he inclined his head. Relief?

"Abiassa be praised!"

Like lightning, the air crackled.

Thelikor, though a dozen feet tall and massively strong, moved swift and true, like an arrow.

It was so fast, so sudden, Haegan didn't see the target until it was nearly too late. "Thelikor, wait!"

The giant froze, his clenched fist hovering over the ornately garbed figure of High Marshal Eftu. Arrayed behind him, a half-dozen awed Ignatieri cowered.

And Haegan knew without a doubt what he had suspected on instinct and intuition back in the Citadel. "Eftu, you've conspired against Abiassa."

The proud marshal shifted and looked to the side, as if gauging his subordinates' reaction. "No." His hands were raised as if to protect his head from Thelikor's fist, which had yet to drop.

Thelikor's growl fueled Haegan's determination. "He smells it on you." He walked toward the marshal, who seemed frozen. If the Drigo unleashed judgment, the marshal's arms would be twigs beneath a boulder. Another realization struck Haegan. Made him sick. Furious. "That is why the incipients were here, so close. You betrayed me."

"No, I'm here to help." Eftu swiped a hand over his mouth. "I—I just came beyond the wall to tell you that he's waiting for you to release him. He's in his heightened state, the vudd. It's painful." He peeked up at Thelikor. "See? I'm trying to help."

The giant growled, louder, angrier.

Which meant the accelerant was lying again.

"No more," came the tumbling-rocks growl of Thelikor as he reached toward Eftu, large fingers pinching at the high-collared overcloak that indicated his stature and supposed submission to Abiassa's will, and ripped it off the marshal, dragging him backward.

Haegan resisted the urge to tell Thelikor to stop. What he did, disrobing—*stripping*—the high marshal was only done at the guiding of Abiassa.

Behind Eftu the handful of accelerants watched, white-faced and frozen like statues. Haegan, anticipating more stripping, trained his attention on Thelikor. None of the other Drigo moved, but they had all closed in, tightening the perimeter. Thelikor scanned the accelerants, who quickly dropped into low bows. He spared them no more than a passing glance, then huffed. Turned back to Haegan and inclined his head in another bow.

"Thelikor," Haegan said.

"Thelikor serve *Fhuriætyr*."

Hot and powerful, the words of the giant brushed against Haegan's body—no, *inside* his body—like a warm, stiff breeze. The sensation was exhilarating and terrifying at the same time. The giant knelt again before him, this time, his arm resting on his knee so he could look at Haegan directly, as if ready for a fireside chat. Gentility rested in eyes that had been a storm of violence only seconds earlier. Focus and resolute dedication lined the smooth planes of his face.

Haegan struggled to believe what was happening. And more than anything at this moment, he wanted a little less . . . giant. "How do I release you? Is that what you need?"

He grunted. "Speak," he rumbled.

Haegan swallowed. The words to summon the Drigo had not been ones he'd known or learned. They'd arisen from his tongue as simply as air filled his lungs. He turned and glanced back at Drracien.

"Fierian," came a quiet, humble voice from the row of accelerants. A mandarin-collared tunic that cross-tied over the chest adorned one who could not be much older than Haegan or Drracien. The black and white trim on the overcoat gave a striking accent to the white pants and sash. "I might be able to help, Fierian."

"Conductor," Drracien spoke loudly, coming to Haegan's side protectively. "What do you know?"

The conductor hesitated, then bobbed his head. "You must release them in the ancient language."

That would make sense, since it was how he'd accidentally summoned them in the first place. Haegan angled his head toward Drracien. "I don't know the ancient language."

"I do." Unabashed, the conductor shifted forward. "I believe the words *exsaeilto Thræïho* will sever the abiatassan link."

Thelikor purred his agreement, his gold eyes shifting from the accelerant to Haegan.

"What does it mean?" Drracien asked.

"*Thræïho*—obviously—is the Drigo. *Exsaeilto* . . . well, there is really no transliteration, but it basically tells him to rest, which releases him from the vudd state."

Abiatassan link? The words spoken, Haegan waited for the change. For the vudd state, or whatever was going on, to lessen. But nothing happened. Thelikor remained as a kneeling giant-warrior before him. Haegan cast a questioning glance to the conductor. "Why didn't your words work?"

"Because I am not linked to the Drigo. Only Deliverers and the Fierian—and of course, Abiassa Herself—can command the giants. *You* must speak it, my prince."

Command the giants? "Thelikor, I thank you for your protection today." It seemed necessary to let the Drigo know of his appreciation. "I release you, Thelikor. *Exsaeilto Thræïho.*"

A rumbling noise, pleasant but loud, sifted the air. Again, Thelikor held his right fist with his left covering it, and touched his forehead, then his chest. "*Mwaheatiel embran, Fhuriætyr.*" He tilted his head back and splayed out his arms.

Haegan looked to the conductor.

"He said, 'You have but to summon, Fierian.'" The conductor shrugged. "Again, it's a loose translation. The ancient tongue doesn't have full equals in our language."

Thelikor pushed to his feet. He gave one last nod to Haegan, then started toward the others. Tokar, Praegur, and Graem grouped up tighter as Thelikor approached. Haegan held his breath, implicitly trusting that Thelikor would know his friends were allies of Abiassa. Was this what it was like to watch mountains move? As the seven giants stalked back to Ybienn's Black Forest, he squinted. They were growing smaller. Maybe it was just because they were farther away.

Perhaps both.

"Fierian."

Numb, rattled, and disoriented with the normalcy of standing on a grassy field, Haegan shifted back to the conductor. Stared at him blankly.

"We beg your mercy for our earlier disrespect." He bowed to the ground, forehead on the grass, fingers splayed out toward Haegan in total submission.

Weariness clung to Haegan. He rubbed his forehead and looked to the forest once more. Besides toppled trees, no trace of the giants could be found. It was a relief to see the Nivari standing in a loose collection near the forest's edge. They were on foot—not a single horse had remained nearby in the wake of the Drigo's entrance—but unharmed. "I know not what transpired within those walls before this morning, but from this day forward, you will be sure those within serve Abiassa."

"Of course," the conductor muttered into the grass.

"Get up." He was tired. Agitated. Feeling . . . empty. Again, he looked to the mountains, feeling a tug to go after the giants. "And speak to no one of my identity as the Fierian or of the giants. Already Poired seeks to kill me."

The conductor nodded. "Would you honor us with your presence at a feast on the morrow?"

Haegan blinked. "What?" *Feast?* "No." Annoyed at the thought when there were bodies on the plain and rot within the hearts of so many, Haegan turned away.

"You need rest," Praegur said softly.

He sighed. "Aye."

"We will happily provide you with a place to stay. And food."

Haegan squinted at the conductor. "What is your name?"

"Tiadith."

"You are high marshal now, Tiadith."

The accelerant's eyes widened. Hesitated.

"As Fierian, he says who serves Her and who does not," Drracien said.

"Thank you, Prince Haegan."

"Serve Her well . . ." The world tilted. Arms caught him. He let them, falling into the deep.

30

Bones crunched. Heads popped. Limbs splatted. Fire engulfed the room. The body of his father writhed. A hand reached out to Haegan and he lunged for it. In that moment, a Deliverer appeared.

"This is not yours—"

"Augh!" Fingers as daggers, Haegan plunged onward. Sailed through the phantom-like form. Where he'd expected resistance, he found none. It threw him off. He stumbled.

Something caught his leg and pitched him forward. Straight over the ledge of a cliff. Horror gripped him—the walls were not dirt. They were made of giants. Drigo. They stood, eyes blazing. Their bodies enlarged. Their anger rabid.

Haegan fell, feeling their searing disapproval. The fires of their rage. He threw out his hand, sending a blast of heat below to level himself and vault back over the cliff's edge. He landed, knees bent, shoulders stooped. Then drew straight.

As he turned toward his father, though he did not see it, he knew what was coming. The fist of Thelikor. Straight down on top of Haegan. He screamed.

Jolted upright, hauling in ragged breaths, Haegan shuddered through a cry. Sweat dripped into his eyes. He dragged himself free of the drenched sheets. Moonslight stroked the night and cast an eerie glow across the highly polished floor. Haegan shuffled to a water stand and gripped the edges. He gritted his teeth against the onslaught of images. His father's flesh melting away as Poired killed him.

Haegan swallowed. His grip tightened.

The crunch of incipient's bones. Flattened into the earth.

Stop—no.

His mother's agonized scream.

Heat thrummed.

"Augh!" Haegan pushed. The water stand exploded. He whirled and threw a fire ball at the bed.

A creak sounded to his left.

He flicked his hand in that direction in the same second his gaze hit hers. His heart stalled as the spark snapped Thiel's head back. Her hair blew away from her face. Shock widened her eyes. She fell back into the door, which cracked against the wall.

"Thiel!" he cried. "Thiel. What are you doing here?"

Shouts in the hall froze Haegan. Guilt nauseated him as he watched Thiel find her feet, hand to her cheek.

"You startled me," he said, crossing the room to her, his lame words ringing in his ears. "Are you well? How are you here?"

Wincing, she swallowed. "I disguised myself and hid among the Nivari." A shaky laugh. "Tili was not pleased."

He tilted her chin to see better. "I've scorched you." Anger churned. "I told you it was dangerous. They are hunting me."

Two shapes appeared in the corridor. Torches cast a dull glow upon Tili and Tokar.

Tendrils of smoke from the burning bed curled across his field of vision, entangling him in its choking stench and guilt. Haegan dropped his gaze, ashamed. Angry with himself, he turned away.

"Haegan."

Teeth grinding, he pivoted. Threw out a bracing blast. "Stay back." He shoved a warbling wall between them. "Please . . . don't." Had to get out of here. Escape. He backed up, feeling for the door to the outer courtyard.

Drracien slipped in and extended a hand toward the flames devouring the bed. With a roll of his fingers, he drew his hand back to himself and doused the fire. Smoke hung defiantly in the air.

"Haegan," Thiel called. "Haegan, please. Please don't go."

How? How did she know his thoughts before he did? "I have to." He turned away, expending the energy it took to maintain the wall.

"Ye've been through a lot, Princeling." Tili's words were firm and sure. But not angry. "We are yer friends. How can we serve ye?"

Haegan pivoted, his anger flaring. A halo of red rimmed the heat wake he'd erected. "I don't want anyone serving me! I only . . ." What? What did he want? He pushed his hand into his hair and fisted a tangle of curls. Thought to rip them out.

"Go," Thiel said quietly to the others. "Leave us." Surely someone would pose an objection to them being alone in his bedchamber, but no one did. A few seconds later came the click of the door.

Haegan moved onto the terrace, out of the smoke, away from her constant belief in him. On the path to a wading pool, he dropped onto a step. Stared at the rippling water.

Though her steps were quiet behind him, he heard them. Felt her calm, cooling presence. She was the antithesis to him. The cool to the fire. Peace to the rage. This hadn't always been his way. "I hate what I'm becoming."

She sat beside him.

"This is a burden I did not ask to carry. I merely want . . ." Wishing and lamenting were exercises in futility. He'd never been able to have what he wanted. In the tower, he had wanted to walk and run and train with the Jujak. Now, though he could do all those things, he wanted to be back in the tower.

"It's overwhelming."

He snorted. "An understatement."

"I believe in ye, Haegan."

"Do you?" He glanced to the side but couldn't bring himself to meet her beautiful brown eyes as he voiced the most painful part. "I hurt you."

"Ye didn't mean to."

"In a rage, I acted without restraint. Because of my folly, you were a victim." He shook his head. "I don't know why She chose me when—"

"It does not matter why."

This time, he did look at her. And winced at the mark on her right cheek. Half the length of his finger, the marred flesh was edged in black where he'd seared her. He yanked his gaze away. She should be far from him so he could not hurt her. "You should go to the Eilidan. They have a Drigo healer. His ministrations helped my sister recover from Poired's attack." He thought of Hoeff and his endearing ways. "Do all Drigo heal?"

She hesitated a beat too long before she said, "I have no idea. They've been gone for generations. But . . ."

Haegan looked up, and the pieces fell together in a gut-clench of realization. "You saw." The Drigovudd. The massacre.

Caught off guard, she flinched. Her eyes betrayed her.

"You know now what I've become. What I bring."

Thiel looked away, but when she spoke again her voice held neither judgment nor horror, but the ache of sympathy. "Haegan, we always knew what it would mean, yer being the Fierian." Taking his hand, she entwined their fingers. "I admit it became . . . real on that field. But regardless. I am not leaving ye, Haegan. Ye cannot send me away."

Frustration gripped him. Worry. "'Tis dangerous, Thiel. *I* am dangerous. Go to the Eilidan. For me. I don't want you with me."

"We are out of time, my prince."

Surprised at the intrusion, Haegan tore his gaze from the hurt on Thiel's face—far worse than the pain her wound had caused—and came to his feet. Looked across the courtyard to where the mayor stood with General Grinda and a half-dozen Jujak. Surrounded by the Nivari.

Jarain inclined his head. "Pardon the intrusion, but we have word Poired has taken Luxlirien and marches for Hetaera."

Haegan tensed, imagining the devastation in Luxlirien, picturing the terror that would come to Hetaera with Dyrth's attack. "We must go."

31

A strange taste carried on the wind. Haegan gulped back some water to banish the acrid flavor as they stood on the rise overlooking Hetaera City two days later. The caravan of riders, which included an official Ignatieri escort from Baen's Crossing—the new marshal had insisted—camped on the rise and now stirred beneath the cool breath of dawn. Haegan, however, sat on the overlook for the last several hours, staring at the city that could change his life forever.

A shout went up behind, and Haegan shifted toward the commotion. Four Ignatieri wrestled a fifth person between them. Tiadith rushed around the crowd toward Haegan. "My prince, we have a fugitive in our midst!"

Black hair flayed as a growl tore through the bodies. A wild mixture of panic and anger seized Drracien's face. Why had he not sparked them? Or seared them even? His temper was worse than Haegan's.

Outrage coursed through Haegan. "Release him at once," he ordered.

Tiadith gaped. "My prince—"

"Release him!" Only as the crowd around them stirred did Haegan realize the embers roiled through his fingers.

"But, my prince, he is wanted for murdering a high lord."

"And some say I am wanted for the murder of the Fire King. Will you arrest me as well?" As the attendants drew back with gaping expressions, Haegan hauled in a shaking breath.

Drracien yanked free from the brethren and strode toward Haegan with a fierce scowl. "They haloed my hands," he hissed, and he flung a withering gaze at the accelerants as he rubbed his wrists.

"Then you knew the charges against him," came a new voice. Another accelerant.

"What I knew is that this man saved not only my life, but the lives of my friends, the only ones who braved a perilous journey with me before safely delivering me to the Great Falls." Haegan pulled in a measuring breath. "I will extend you mercy for this slight . . . this one time." He weighed each of them, monitoring their reactions. Assessing who he might expect the most trouble from. In the shortest accelerant, the one with narrow, muddy eyes, Haegan saw trouble. "Have you an objection?" he challenged.

The accelerant wet his lips. "Our concern with him is outside your purview," he said, voice quiet.

"Outside my purview?" Would that he could singe this man's clothes to show what *purview* Abiassa had given him. Instead, Haegan slid closer. "Have you not heard that they intend to set me in as king?" He angled his head closer. "In the Nine, the Fire King supersedes Ignatieri law."

The man tremored with unrestrained emotion. "Does it mean nothing to you that he murdered High Lord Aloing?"

"What proof have you of his guilt?" Haegan cocked his head. "Produce it now, and I will deliver his punishment myself." Only as he laid out the demand did Haegan realize his folly. *Was* there proof of these charges against Drracien? The rogue had merely shown up in a cave and claimed ignorance. He had never fully related the truth of what made him flee the Citadel. "No proof, then?"

Silence snapped through the camp.

"Be at peace, Elgni," Tiadith spoke gently, then turned to Haegan. "If Marshal Drracien is not guilty, he should present himself to the Ignatieri to answer for his actions, to explain . . ." He inclined his head. "We beg your mercy, but Grand Marshal Dromadric himself reported chasing Drracien from the high lord's tower."

"Then you persist in accusing my friend," Haegan said.

"Justice will be done," Tiadith insisted.

"Not when the eyes of those trying him"—Haegan looked to Elgni—"yearn more for blood than truth."

Praegur came to his side as Tokar stepped before Drracien, forming a protective barrier. Incredible how the rogue had become an irrefutable member of their troupe. It was then, as even Laertes surged to the front next to Haegan, that he knew they were his family. They would lay down their lives for one another. "I have seen the kind of justice delivered by those with a single mindset, bent on punishing someone rather than meting out the truth. We will have truth!" Haegan shouted. "We will have *justice*."

"Prince Haegan."

At the commanding voice, Haegan shifted. Saw General Grinda plowing through the crowd that had formed around them. He'd always been grim-faced, but his dourness had deepened.

"I beg your mercy, my prince." Grinda inclined his head. "There is a contingent coming from the east."

"Sirdarians?" Is that what the odor was?

"Our own," Grinda said. "Jujak as well as Ignatieri."

Haegan's gaze swung eastward, though with the faces before him, he could not see. "Show me."

"Make a path!" Grinda roared, swinging his arms wide as the sea of bodies parted.

Haegan followed him to the easternmost ledge. Dawn yawned in the cool morning, brightening the lands and glittering against the white plaster Citadel and its Spire of Zaelero.

Marching across the great valley in precise columns came the Jujak. One hundred in each column. A total of eight hundred men. Awe speared Haegan as he watched them advance, rimmed by a thin black line on all sides—Ignatieri. At the rear came the banner of Dromadric and, of course, the Jujak carried the banner of the Nine.

"Am I friend or foe to them, Grinda?"

"She knows," Grinda responded gruffly. "We've sent word, but what poison has the grand marshal put in their ears as they handled the masses, the desperation?"

The general had long been known to be suspicious of the Ignatieri. But Haegan suddenly felt the same hesitation. Gazing on his father's army, Haegan wondered at the number. "So few . . ."

"The rest are coming. Tricky paths to evade Sirdarians. But they have their orders to regroup here. Also, some have orders to protect those fleeing the city, help keep order." Grinda pointed southwest, where it seemed another city had sprung up at the base of Abiassa's Throne. "The refugees."

Disbelief found a new ally as Haegan looked with new eyes at the small tent-city. He'd been here, months gone by, with Thiel—on that cleft. Where Zicri had skimmed his head and given him terrors.

"Blazes," Laertes said, choked on the same shock. "Dem what's got little 'ave taken ov'a da whole fields. I ain' ne'va seen nu'fin like it."

"Haven't, ever, anything," Haegan corrected absently, his mind struggling to take it in. The potential dangers that arose with people in desperate lives and situations.

In the past, wagon masters would set up camp there, but nothing like this, with structure to the layout. Nothing like this great a number. Not a patch of grass remained exposed between the city wall and foothill. How had so many come in such a short time?

Haegan glanced at the thick-chested general. "Are the Jujak here to protect them, or fight them?"

"Both," Grinda grunted. "Most are peace-loving. Just wanting a place to live and survive. But that creates pressure, stress, panic. They forget themselves."

Something in Haegan writhed. "We shouldn't be policing them. Jujak are for protection, not—"

"Aye." Grinda lowered his head. "But where am I to quarter the Jujak, my prince?" His voice was quiet but resolved as he made his point: Seultrie was taken. "And there are thousands more coming up the Throne Road and farther east, fleeing what remains of Luxlirien."

"Why? Why would they risk traveling here? When Poired has his eyes fixed on Hetaera City?"

"I sent word their prince was coming." Gray, weighted eyes measured. Probed with an intensity Haegan could only liken to what he felt beneath the Deliverer's gaze. Expectation. But more than that—necessity.

The Nine *needed* a leader.

"They should be told of Kaelyria."

"Begging your pardon, my prince, but in her condition, she is of no use to us. To them." Resolution carved long, experienced lines through

Grinda's ruddy face. "You're here. And the Lady chose you." He gripped Haegan's shoulder. "Be the man I always knew you to be, my prince. Make your father proud."

"Hitting below the scabbard, Grinda."

He grinned, his silver-threaded beard parting. "Sometimes, it takes your manhood getting jostled to find out who you are." His gaze sobered. "I know you fear this path. I see it in your eyes—the same look your father had before taking the throne."

He hadn't heard stories of his father like this. "Father was never afraid."

Grinda chuckled, his broad shoulders bouncing. "Aye, that's what he wanted everyone to think. But there were times even the most powerful accelerant wanted to walk away." His smile vanished, and he seemed to consider his words, the patch of beard below his lip rolling. "Don't run from this, Haegan. Don't you do it."

Thunder clapped through Haegan's chest. "I—I won't."

"I know you fear this path and would run from it if you could. We all would." Grinda squeezed his shoulder again. "But I won't let you. And I will have your back until my dying breath."

Hunger unlike anything Haegan had ever known coiled around his heart, tempting him to grab this thread of hope. Of courage.

Grinda must've seen the yearning because he gave a grim smile. "I had your father's back so he could do his job. It will be the same with you. But if you don't do your job, I can't do mine."

Haegan nodded.

"And I will kill you myself before I let you dishonor House Celahar or Abiassa—or yourself."

Shock pushed Haegan back a step so he could look into the eyes that had only seconds earlier pulsed with reassurance. Was he sincere?

Unlike Haegan, Grinda did not falter. "I am Jujak—Valor Guard. My oath is to Her first." He gave a cockeyed nod, the same one Haegan had often seen his father do. "Then to the Fire King."

"I will not shame you, my father, or Abiassa."

"You have good sense in that head—you're Zireli's son. I know you'll do the right thing. Ready yourself, Prince," Grinda said as he turned toward the guard huddled behind them.

"For what?"

"To ride out and meet your reception."

Haegan looked to the field of red, blacks, and greens. "What if they want to kill me? Arrest me as these"—he motioned to the Ignatieri—"attempted with Drracien?"

"Then they die." There was no anger in Grinda's expression or eyes. Only hard resolution before he pushed past two Jujak and the rest swallowed him.

Smoothing a hand over his face, Haegan could not help but feel that forces were converging at this point, on this field. Not just Jujak and Ignatieri. But light and dark. Good and evil.

Were there but a way to escape . . .

"Do we ride with you?" Tokar asked. "Down to meet the delegation, I mean?"

Haegan turned from the tide of bodies. Considered Tokar, Praegur, and Laertes. "I know not what dangers are coming," he said, glancing again to the valley floor, "whether they will crown me or kill me."

Tokar didn't blink. "I will help if they want to kill you."

Laertes stomped on his foot.

Tokar hopped away, grimacing. "What? I meant—help defend Haegan." He peered at Laertes, rubbing the top of his foot on the back of his opposite calf. "Pick on someone your own size. It was an earnest statement."

Laertes grinned, his blond hair tucked behind his ears to stay out of his eyes. "Den what's dat make us, iffin dem swords are Jujak? And da king's men be Valor Guard?" The boy scratched his head. "Dat makes us what, da Fire Guard?"

"Yeah, because he's going to set us on fire."

32

Had he wool for a tongue it could not have been drier. The green Celahar surcoat embroidered with the tri-tipped flame itched at the neck, but Haegan suppressed the urge to scratch. Instead, he sat perfectly still and stared over the green and gold plume adorning his warhorse's chamfron at the delegation of ten sent to welcome him. Grinda had explained he would have to formally stake his claim to the throne, but surely that could wait until they reached the city itself.

From his right came the Jujak.

"Negaer," Grinda muttered.

Haegan mentally nodded. He'd heard of Negaer. Hard man, even harder general. Commander of the Pathfinders. Though Grinda had called him ruthless, there had also been a hint of admiration. *Despite misgivings about methods, Grinda respects him.*

"Prince Haegan," Negaer boomed into the morning. "I am General Negaer, Commander of the northern contingent and Pathfinders. You are welcomed back to Hetaera. It is good to see you . . . alive."

Spine straight, shoulders squared, Negaer defined military command. His eyes were hard and focused. Unlike Grinda with his slight paunch, every muscle on Negaer seemed carved from steel. Years in the elements had leathered his face.

It had not escaped Haegan's notice that the fierce general had yet to submit himself to Haegan's leadership.

"You forget yourself," Grinda growled. "He is your king—"

"My king is dead," Negaer said evenly. "Murdered on the bridge of Fieri Keep."

Flames and screams raked Haegan's mind. He shrank back—but no. He must not appear weak. Could not flinch. "Then you saw that terrible battle." He sounded bigger than he felt. "You saw Poired cut down the king and queen with relentless cruelty."

"Aye." There was something . . . cold, hate-filled in the way Negaer answered. But this field was not the place to rout the truth.

Negaer let out a whistle. Immediately, the column of Jujak behind him split in two, facing the path they formed down the middle that was wide enough for two to pass unencumbered. Straight to the sea of red and black. *Like burnt blood.* The Ignatieri. It was an invitation to draw closer to Hetaera. Now, only the Ignatieri stood between him and the capital city.

Haegan started forward, Grinda at his side as his champion, and Negaer and Tiadith behind. As the Valor Guard brought up the rear, the sea of warriors became a single unit.

Two hundred paces separated them from the three hundred accelerants on the field. Did these accelerants know who he was? That he was the Fierian?

Two rows of five accelerants in plain black uniforms moved out in front of the high lords and grand marshal. Hands behind their backs, they went to a knee. Then to both. With an elaborate sway, they raised their arms over their heads, then splayed their palms on the grass, faces pressed downward.

The ten rolled onto their backs and shoved their hands, fingers held claw-like, to the sky. Fireballs shot up.

Grinda swung out a hand, stopping their column.

"It's not an attack. It's a welcome form," Tiadith said, his voice more pleased than Haegan had heard before. "For you."

The fireballs dropped and the accelerants spun the balls with their feet, as if riding them lying down. Then as one—they kicked and flipped themselves upright. They swung in an amazing, swirling pattern, arms like windmills. With each rotation, a new spark flew from their fingers. Blue. Red.

"How . . . ?" Haegan found himself envying the skill as much as the technique.

"They are the demonstration team," Tiadith said quietly. "They train relentlessly."

"Demonstration? To what end?"

"Recruitment."

Haegan nearly laughed. "Surely you cannot—accelerants are chosen by Abiassa."

"Aye, but we use the demonstration team to visit villages and ensure they know there is a safe place to train."

Haegan marveled as the accelerants swept into a straight line. The first one spewed a long stream of fire into the sky. Tipped backward. A second set of hands went up, adding to the flame. Then a third . . .

Haegan would've taken a step back, watching as the stream grew, both in enormity and length. The stream slowly coiled in on itself, roiling, crackling in the air, but he could not take his eyes from the display. Was it his imagination or had the fire stream morphed?

A chill rushed over Haegan, and he twitched beneath the cooling fingers.

And fourth . . . fifth . . . until they had all combined their wielding and created a massive creature. Wings spread out. Snapped. Like a canopy on the wind.

Sparks formed white eyes. Wings. A tail.

The accelerants were still moving—dancing—bringing the mighty animal to "life." Drawing back, the fire creature seemed to rear. Then lunged forward.

A wave of shouts and cries went up among the Jujak as the fiery creature glided overhead. "A raqine," someone said.

Haegan was not completely sure the Pathfinders were even breathing, for they had made no response to the display. They stood motionless, severe, like marble columns.

Haegan lifted a hand as the fire raqine roared over them, letting the heat trail across the tips of his fingers. The wake blanketed his senses. He craned his neck to peer into the sky as the raqine rose toward the sun, then exploded into fireworks.

But as he watched, something nagged at Haegan's mind. At his heart.

Was it right for these gifts, meant for the protection of Abiassa's children, to be treated as a sideshow? Were gifts being misused? He didn't know. It seemed harmless.

"Prince Haegan," Dromadric shouted from the other end of the field. "In the name of Our Lady, we welcome you to the Citadel of Zaelero."

With that, the accelerants pivoted and marched back toward the city, leading Haegan and the Jujak with great fanfare and fiery displays. As they crossed the main bridge, hooves clomping heavily against the wood, the citizens sent up a shout.

Haegan furrowed his brow.

Grinda grinned broadly beneath his trim beard. "Zireli's heir is come!"

33

Laughter lived here. That's what his mother used to say. Before he'd been poisoned. Before he'd been isolated from the world, Haegan had run the halls of Celahar Mansion, the great home used when his father-king was summoned to Hetaera to meet with the Council of Nine or the rulers of the other eight kingdoms.

"It is suggested, my lord," Grinda said, "that you make Celahar Mansion your home now that Seultrie is taken."

"Then we are to simply roll over like an obedient dog at the feet of its new master?" Acerbic words—not his intent but the result all the same. In his new role, it was imperative—whether he liked it or not—that he exercise lessons of diplomacy. "I beg your mercy. The travels have taken a toll on my manners."

He turned away from the others. The two Grindas stood by the fire with Negaer and one of his captains, while Dromadric and Adomath had planted themselves in two high-backed chairs, flanking Haegan like armies in attack formation. Tiadith moved between the two groups like a restless dog.

Haegan ignored them all, focusing instead on the bay of windows overlooking the city. Another tower of isolation. It wasn't really, but it had the feel of where he'd spent the last ten years—distant. Cold. Separate.

"Marshal Tiadith mentioned you were attacked at Baen's Crossing," Dromadric said, his voice deep yet oily.

Haegan clasped his hands behind his back, recalling the great shock when he'd realized incipients had come out against him. "Aye," he spoke to the window.

"An even greater tale has come from that story." A chuckle, hollow and disdainful, injected itself into Dromadric's statement. "That the giants have returned."

"They have." Haegan kept his tone civil, clean, still refusing to look at those gathered in his private quarters.

"But that's . . . absurd," Dromadric sniffed.

Haegan sighed.

"They were absurdly tall," Tiadith exclaimed with a nervous chuckle. "And powerful. Their voices like thunder in the heavens. I have never seen anything like it! And the way they knelt before Prince Haegan and waited for his command, then returned after they'd delivered Her justice to those wicked incipients . . ."

"This must make you very proud," Dromadric purred.

"Proud?" Grinding his teeth did nothing to alleviate the annoyance thrumming through his veins. He spun. "Proud?" How could any-one—"Think you I should be proud, watching even the wicked snapped in two like twigs? And grown men smashed to dust in a sickening burst of red?" He touched his ears. "Never will I forget those sounds—the sounds of death."

"No." Dromadric, in lesser regalia now but still ornate, surged out of his chair. "No, it was the sound of Her judgment on those who acted against the future king."

"King?" Haegan's voice pitched. But he caught himself. "Think you anyone in the Nine will want a king who is"—he pivoted to the accelerant at Dromadric's side, Adomath—"what was it you called me at the Great Falls? A scourge? An abomination?"

The high lord shifted. "I spoke out of ignorance," Adomath hissed.

"Yet the sentiment remains," Haegan said, his gaze returning to the crowds bustling through the city. "It lingers in your words like a fermented drink, stinking."

Stepping into the thick silence after Haegan's reproach, Grinda said, "Soon you will present yourself to the Council of Nine for the Contending. After that, a date will be set for your coronation."

Haegan closed his eyes. This should not be happening.

"That is," Dromadric said, "assuming the Council accepts you and your claim."

Haegan wanted to say he made no claim, but he did not want to sound petulant, or worse—repulsed, even though he was. As the only able-bodied heir, Haegan had a duty to step into the role of Fire King, especially now that he displayed Her gifts.

"They will, of course, want to see a demonstration of your gifts." Dromadric's long, narrow face seemed elongated by his uniform's pointy shoulders and arcing collar sweeping up behind his head. "Assuming you have a gifting."

He baits me. Haegan refused to turn, to acknowledge in any regard the grand marshal's words and insinuation. "You know well, after numerous visits to Fieri Keep," he said, watching a red-haired boy dart in and out of the crowd like a fish swimming upstream, "'twas my sister who was gifted."

"And of that—how is the Princess Kaelyria? We hope and pray for her safe return."

"As do I," Haegan said, not surprised the grand marshal knew of his sister's health.

He recalled sneaking through the city, all those weeks ago, trying to follow Drracien. Where was the accelerant now? He'd quietly slipped from their ranks and vanished. In truth, Haegan had been relieved to discover him missing. He'd insisted Tiadith and his Ignatieri let Drracien go but seriously doubted he'd hold the same sway over Dromadric.

"In the meeting with the Nine," Grinda said, "objections to your taking the throne will be raised."

"Good."

"How can you be so cavalier about taking the throne?" Reproach pinched the grand marshal's voice.

"My life has been engulfed in one battle after another, Dromadric," Haegan said, his voice bouncing off the window. "Cavalier is the last thing I feel."

"But the objections—"

"If an objection or complaint is presented that I cannot answer or give a reasoned response for, then I am no more fit to be king than the crippled prince who laid in a tower for most of his life." Only, he was that prince. And he wasn't. His reflection stared back at him. *Who am I?*

After a long pause, Haegan saw Dromadric's image in the window rise. "You are tired, Highness. We will leave you."

Finally. Haegan almost sighed in relief at the words, but he remained in place. Hands behind his back. Eyes on the city. Movement again reflected in the glass as Captain Grinda escorted Dromadric and Adomath out, then returned.

"They find you unresponsive," Negaer said tersely.

"You mean, unmanipulated." Haegan walked to the small round table where fruits, cheese, and cordi juice were set out. He took a chunk of the cheese and bit into it. "You forget—I spent my life listening to an accelerant. Where is my old tutor anyway? I thought he would be breathing down my neck the moment we arrived." Haegan would have words with the old man. *Did he truly poison me?*

"There are reports he is in the city, but we have no confirmation," Captain Grinda said. "I've asked the Ignatieri to keep us informed on the arrival of the Council."

The older Grinda sat down, reminding Haegan of a cross between his own father and King Thurig. It was an interesting idea, and a possibly lethal concoction. "What's on your heart, my prince?"

Haegan steepled his fingers, thinking. "Everything. Nothing." Then he shook his head. "Dromadric said the return of the giants is absurd—" He snorted. "But me? Me being king? I laid in the tower for ten years, thinking I would be nothing but a possible advisor to my sister. To stand here now, poised for the throne . . . that seems absurd."

"So, you have already changed your mind about the throne? So easily?"

"No." Shaking his head again, Haegan wrestled his own thoughts. "Yes." He growled. "I don't know. But admit it—this is insane."

The general's thick brows tangled together. "Why?"

"Because!" Haegan lifted his hands in frustration. "I have not the instruction nor preparation. My sister was trained. You should bring her from Legier's Heart."

"Aye, my prince," Grinda said sadly. "I know you love the princess. There has always been a strong bond between you two, but"—he shook his head—"she cannot take the throne. We all know it. And I mean not for my words to be cruel, but she is paralyzed. And as you have said, ill."

Haegan shoved to his feet and paced. "And who is to say she won't fully recover? The Drigo have gifts of healing. There was one there, tending her. She regained use of her arms."

"Arms." The general stared into his cup, his somber, ruddy face betraying his own sadness. "Are we to hope none will challenge her for the throne—and the Council will demand it with a perceived weakness. We all know that as well."

Negaer grunted. "Or how long are we expected to wait to see if she does recover?"

"As long as it takes."

Negaer's eyes went fierce. "Would you have us tell Poired to halt his attacks while we wait?"

Haegan growled and returned to the window.

"If you take the throne and your sister recovers," came Grinda's more gentle yet firm words, "you can step down or abdicate, should you then feel it still necessary."

Haegan wrestled with the logic, only to release the source behind his fear. "Can you not see I am ill qualified?" That odor, the one he'd tasted on the hill outside the city, hit his mouth again. Filled his nostrils. Stung.

Boards creaked as Grinda came to his side. "Do you see"—shoulder touching Haegan's, he nodded to the Citadel—"the spire?"

Gleaming, oblivious to Haegan's turmoil, the multi-orbed spire stuck defiantly into the sky. Red, blue, and green gems covered the three spheres sparkling beneath the sun's caress.

"You know the story, my prince, of Baen and his warriors, fighting their way into the city. His melding a glass dagger from the sand in his hands"—he held out a thick, callused palm—"and using it to end the life of Dirag the Desecrator."

Haegan didn't answer. Didn't dare move a muscle. Aye, he knew the story.

"Who was Baen?"

Confused by the question, Haegan flicked his gaze to the general.

"He was no one," Grinda said, his lips thinned in . . . disgust? "A commoner-general. Like me."

"Is this your way of saying you want the throne?" A thick slap to the back of his head startled Haegan. His eyes went wide. "You struck me!" He laughed.

"Aye, and you need much more than that, but I have respect for you."

Stunned at the words, Haegan stilled with his hand on his head, eyes locked on the general, commander of the Valor Guard. Grinda respected *him*?

"I know you haven't heard kind words most of your life. I know you lack belief in yourself, but remember that Baen was naught but a farmer who took up a sword to protect what he believed in." His chest heaved. "And he leveled the Desecrator and became king. It is not your birth that sets you apart but your heart."

The backs of his eyes burned.

"You leaped on the back of an animal you knew not how to control, to rush back to save your family."

Haegan swallowed.

"You fought—and hard. We saw it. We watched"—*were there tears in his eyes?*—"as that demon cut your father's breath from him. You." He tapped Haegan's chest with two fingers. "You stepped into Ederac's fiery maw to save the king."

"Why didn't you kill him?"

Haegan flinched at Negaer's intruding words. Looked to the side where the general stood.

No—no, he wanted to spend more time absorbing Grinda's words. His belief. The austerity in his voice.

"You were there." Intensity radiated through Negaer's expression. "You faced him on that bridge. *Why* did you not kill Poired, if you are so powerful?" There wasn't an accusation in his words. Only legitimate question.

But it dawned on Haegan as he met Grinda's eyes once more. "You said you were there."

"Aye."

"Did you see it—him?" Haegan looked between the generals. "Did either of you see the Deliverer who stood between me and the Dark One?"

The two exchanged a glance before shaking their heads.

"There were three, in fact," Haegan said with a shudder. "I very much wanted to kill Poired—and was going to. You are right that I had the power—at least, I think I did." He scratched his jaw. "I was livid, and I wanted him dead. Having watched him murder my mother, then attack my sister and kill my father—nothing was violent enough for him."

"Why didn't you?" Negaer again.

"A Deliverer stopped me. Told me it was not for me to kill Poired." Haegan remembered. Oh, he remembered. The fires. The screams. The smell of burning flesh. "But I was going to kill him anyway. Melt his flesh right off his bones. Sear the life from his lungs." Anger radiated through him, his words coming through teeth clenched in the agony of remembrance.

"Aye, we saw you advance," Negaer said softly. "But then you stopped. Next thing, you're climbing on the back of that beast and flying off."

Haegan drew up his sleeve and showed the marred mess on his forearm. "For my rebellion and my thirst for Poired's blood, the Deliverer gave me a reminder."

Captain Grinda grimaced. "Does it hurt?"

A wry smile tugged at the edges of his mouth. "Only when I think of it."

Grinda looked over his shoulder at the steely Negaer. "Are you satisfied?"

Negaer moved one step forward. Inclined his head. "I beg mercy for my reticence, Prince Haegan. I yield my sword and the Pathfinders to you."

Awe rushed through Haegan, thinking of the white-cloaked Pathfinders, the elite of the elite Jujak. And yet—

Negaer had doubted him.

And with good reason. Haegan was not worthy of this burden. He did not want swords. He did not want fealty. He wanted . . . out.

The taste. Again. What was that?

It didn't matter. He pivoted and stalked away from the soldiers. Away from the great responsibility bearing down on him. He reached the entrance to his private chambers, but the doors swung open before he could touch the knob. Haegan stopped short.

The valet tucked his chin, hiding his gaze.

Haegan's hands curled into fists. "Stop bowing." His heart pounded. "Stop yielding. Stop . . . just stop!"

34

"Well, well," came a sneering voice from a dark alley. "What pretties we have here."

Trale slowed to a stop, mentally tracking the four brigands who peeled from the shadows of the millinery. Astadia slid behind him, and he trained himself on her breathing. Normal. Calm. He had expected as much, but never failed to verify. It wasn't the first ambush they'd walked into. Wouldn't be the last.

Four men with foul breath had little chance of stopping them. But when he felt Astadia's shoulder blades bump his back, he stilled. Apparently, more had come from behind as well.

"Five," she muttered over her shoulder.

"Nine to two," Trale said to the mealymouthed man who'd spoken. "Not exactly a fair fight."

"Who says it have t' be fair?" a wiry man said around his sneer. "What you got in that sack?"

"Food, clothes, blankets—we're wanderers." Play dumb. Make them overconfident.

"Well, it seems you wandered right into our little city. Dues—you gots to pay dues." The wiry man had legs like wet reeds, wobbly as he exaggerated his taunting advance. "And we's the collectors. Right, boys?"

The others didn't talk. They stared. Menace in their eyes and weapons in hands. A club, a mace, a broken javrod, a dagger, a saber. Trale's gaze lingered on the last—curved and engraved with the double crescent moons. "Tahsca." Interesting. The man wielding the blade looked like any beggar on the street.

Wiry man grunted. "Wha'?"

"Your friend's blade—it's a Tahscan saber, from House Tahsca off the coast of Iteveria. They're the fiercest sea-faring warriors."

"We's don' care about no seadogs," wiry guy growled.

"So you haven't endured the Tahscan drums?"

"Why would we care about drums?"

If they had heard the Tahscan drums, they would care. A lot. Trale had once faced a Tahscan and spent months recovering. Which told him these men weren't Tahscans, though how they came by that blade, he could not fathom. A shame—if Trale could best a Tahscan, his blade would be at his service for life. That could come in handy. Of course, the blade itself could come in handy.

"We'll be taking 'dem arrows, missy," a man said behind him.

"Will you?" his sister asked, her voice annoyed.

Oh no.

Thwat! Thwat! The sound of two arrows hitting their mark, seconds apart, slapped the darkness.

"Bi'mwæi!" he hissed at her inability toward restraint, then took a step forward. Drove the heel of his hand into the face of the burliest thug. With a sickening crack, the man yelped and collapsed.

Steel glinted beneath the corner gas lamp and the waxing moons.

Anticipating their attacks kept him alive. Kept his enemies dead. He liked it that way. In a split second he assessed the threats: three attackers facing him. At least three engaging Astadia, but she could handle herself.

So, three.

Wiry Guy. Side of Beef. And Half Brain. The man's head had been dented. His brain most likely as well. Instinct told him Half Brain was the easier target, but he would not underestimate Half Brain as these imbeciles had underestimated lowly brother-sister wanderers passing through an abandoned city.

So. Side of Beef. Trale flicked his dagger at the big guy's chest. It bounced off with the clink of metal on metal and clattered to the cobbled path.

Frustrating.

Side of Beef leered. "Now, I use knife to kill you."

Wiry Guy was moving. So was Trale. Lightning fast, he slid closer. With his fingers tightly together for added strength, he stabbed a knife-hand strike into Wiry Guy's throat, then swept around and buried his spare dagger in Side of Beef. The big man fell with a meaty thud.

Cupping his throat, Wiry Guy wobbled . . . all the way to the ground.

The blur to Trale's left wasn't unexpected. He ducked as Half Brain's saber swept through the space where his head had been, and the man's searing stench made him cough. "In earnest, you must take your hygiene seriously."

Confusion clouded the man's face, quickly replaced by greedy blood-lust. He lunged. Caught Trale by the waist. Hauled him off his feet and slammed him against the millinery.

Air punched from his lungs, Trale strained to focus. *Focus!* He had endured worse. And if he did not, he would endure more. Only as he braced himself against the oaf did he detect the ultra-thin armor beneath the man's tunic. What in the celestials . . . ? More armor? Tahscan saber . . .

Worry muddled Trale's thoughts. He lingered too long on the questions. On the doubts. Almost didn't see the glint of steel slicing toward him again.

He bent sideways.

Tschink!

Heat sizzled along his ear. But the strike missed. With his hand as a knife again, he stabbed the man's neck.

Half Brain stumbled backward, gasping as he slumped to the ground. His eyes bulged and his sword came up again.

"In earnest," Trale said, "it's okay to die." He removed the dagger from his boot.

The oaf struggled to gain his feet.

Trale gritted his teeth. Dove forward. The Tahscan saber skimmed the back of his shoulder, but he felt nothing. He should. He knew he'd been cut but felt no pain, only the warmth of his own blood sliding down his back. Trale drove his blade into the man's jugular.

Spun to Astadia.

That's when it hit him. Fire roared through his shoulder. Nearly pushed him to the dirt as his gaze swept the alley. Six bodies were laid

out. But no Astadia. He searched the shadows, expecting to see her leaning against a building as she had many a time before, bored when his
battle took longer.

Wait.

Six? Trale spun. Pitched forward. "Astadia!" Grabbed the shoulder
of the first body—not her. The second and third. Panic vomited his
thoughts in a million directions. "Asta—"

She moaned. There, against the barrel.

He rushed to her and knelt, eyeing the dagger in her side. "Hold on."
He shoved his arms beneath her head and legs. "We'll find a pharmakeia."

"Nay!" a beggar of an old man appeared in the alley, his spine crooked.
"Nay, not like that." He wagged gnarled fingers. "Lift her like that and
you'll push the dagger in farther."

Trale's heart stuttered—at both the man's appearance and intrusion,
and the thought of causing his sister additional pain. "Who are you?"

"No one of consequence."

"And these men—are they also of no consequence?"

"Nay, they are Poired's mercenaries. Sent to route laggers. Subdue
or kill, but for this lot"—he nodded to the bodies—"kill was easier and
more profitable. Then they could steal what they would with no fear of
reprisal or having Poired take their bounty."

Strange. Being the victim of the very man who held their leash.

"Here." The old man shuffled aside and pointed to something. "Use
this to keep her straight."

Trale rushed there and found the remains of a wood crate. He could
make a stretcher, but how to move her once she was on it. "I can't carry
it alone."

"Who says you're alone?" The man snickered. "Here, help." He beckoned to someone out of sight in the alley.

A gangly youth stepped from the shadows and bent toward the pallet.
They hurried to Astadia and slid it beneath her unconscious form. Trale
helped the youth lift her from the ground.

"This way," the old man instructed, hurrying down a gas-lit passage
toward a darkened stoop. He pushed the heavy singewood door inward
then vanished into the darkness.

"What is this?" Trale asked, staring into the void.

"Shelter," the old man said around a laugh as light bloomed in a corner. A lamp flickered on a small table. He threw off his raggedy cloak and indicated to where a bed made of singewood—but no mattress—waited. "Place her there. Rauf, find water and clean cloths."

"Are you a pharmakeia?" Trale asked, as they eased Astadia to the bedframe.

"Near enough." He motioned to Trale. "Get the fire going. We'll need to boil the water."

But the appearance of the man, the empty house, the orders . . . "What do you mean 'near enough'?"

"I have the means and knowledge to tend your sister. Would you have me do that or stand here in debate with you?"

"This house—who owns it?"

"Whoever owned it, they are gone. Fled north from Poired's army."

It made sense. Too much sense. But it still rattled Trale. "Why are you helping us?"

"Would you have me leave you both for dead?"

"Dead? I bested them"—he nodded to Astadia—"as did she."

"Aye, but it seems that knife in her side and that wound in your shoulder would take your stubborn lives."

Shoulder wound?

"You look pale, champion. Would you sit?"

As if the man's words inflicted their own potion, Trale's knees buckled. He grabbed for the nearby chair and dropped into it, the legs groaning against the floor as he did. He reached to the fire in his shoulder. His fingers came away sticky, stained dark.

Rauf returned with a basket filled with items.

"Ah, just in time." The old man took clean lengths of cloth and a few other items in hand. "Now go on and start the fire. He'll be out soon, too."

No. Trale couldn't pass out. These men were strangers. They could prey upon them. Do horrible things to Astadia. He'd long ago promised that no man would ever abuse her again. Trale would never surrender their fate to strangers. And they had a mission . . .

His hand slid into his pocket, and he felt the touchstone.

"Keep it with you, Trale, and I will be with you. My thoughts your

thoughts," she had said. He should throw it away if he wanted to be free of the Infantessa. He'd been controlled all his life, bought from one master to serve another. He'd allowed himself to dream of freedom with Astadia. A fool's hope.

He hefted the stone in his hand. Gripped it tight. *Throw it away.*

Shuffling around, the old man set out tools and moved toward Astadia with a sharp instrument.

Alarmed, Trale tugged his hand free and surged to his feet. "Nay! What are you doing?"

"I believe I'm trying to save your sister's life."

Trale wavered, his ears hollowing. The edges of his vision blurred.

"Sit." Fire swam in the old man's eyes. "That blade was doused in poison. If you keep thrashing around, you'll speed it through your veins."

The old man must be right. There wasn't enough injury to warrant being so weak. So dizzy. Trale shook his head. Blinked. Swallowed.

"Stretch out on the floor. I'll tend you as soon as I remove this dagger and stitch her wound. Mayhap by the blessing of Abiassa you can be on your way by morning."

Trale grunted, easing himself to the floor before he dropped like a hot pot. He breathed awkwardly, a hot-damp fever rushing over him.

"Where are you headed?"

"North," he muttered, though he knew not why he'd answered.

"Ah, good. You might then catch the prince."

A sharp wave of clearheadedness snapped through Trale. "The prince."

"Aye. Zireli's boy—rumors are he's on his way to Hetaera. I've even heard tell he's the long-foretold Fierian."

The prince. The prince would be in Hetaera. Relief swam through Trale. They would find him. Capture him. The Infantessa would be pleased.

"I heard the Jujak are basing out of Hetaera," the youth put in. "The prince is making that the temporary capital. It's the main military center now."

Which meant that many more to evade.

Trale's limbs felt heavy.

"I believe they'll set him in as king there," the old man added.

King. Prince. Title did not matter.

Oh, blazes—his head hurt! He closed his eyes. Just for a minute. But he would somehow . . . get Haegan. The thought alone made his temples pound.

But in the morning.

I will not fail you, Infantessa. He laid his hand over the stone in his pocket. "So . . . beau . . . ful . . ."

35

"And are we accompanied by a judge again?"

Gwogh lifted his hood and slid it away as he met the kind smile of the only woman on the Council of Nine. "We never know, do we?"

"True enough," she said, hands clasped before her round figure. "It has been more than a month since we saw your protégé. How does he fare?"

"You are correct in saying it has been more than a month since *we* saw him." Gwogh too had stayed away, knowing the prince must find his way. Must find answers that he could own.

"Then you have not spoken to him of late?"

"Nay," Gwogh admitted as he nodded to Kelviel, Aoald, and Adek, who sat at the table. "My brothers."

"But you were to be his mentor, to guide him," Kedulcya said.

"The giants—is it true?" Adek asked, arms resting on the table. "The city is abuzz with reports of Drigo coming out of the Dark Forest to save the prince."

"I believe more than mere salvation happened there," Gwogh said with a smile as he eased into the chair near the head of the table. But not at the head. That was left empty. For Abiassa. Or Her representative. It was hard not to look at the empty space and wonder if a Deliverer occupied it. He shuddered at the thought, remembering how Medric had so swiftly and resolutely ended Baede and his rebellion, right in front of their eyes. By the Lady, he hoped they would not have another visitor. It could mean more judgment. More betrayal by one of their own.

"Have you informed the prince of the Contending?"

Gwogh gave a solemn nod. "He is a prince and knows it's part of the process."

The door creaked open, admitting Voath, Traytith, and Griese to the room and conversation. They wore weighted countenances, their countries crumbling beneath Poired's scourge. They were trailed by a person unfamiliar to Gwogh.

The room fell silent as the newcomer stopped by the door, his gaze flicking around the room uncertainly. "I am Falip Wrel. I have been chosen to represent Dradith since . . ."

"You mean, since Abiassa delivered your predecessor of his head," Kelviel said, his anger rife.

"Peace, Kelviel," Gwogh said, motioning Bæde's replacement to take a seat. "Falip, your work in Yoiand is well-known to us. We welcome you to the Council of Nine."

"We are gathered," Kedulcya announced, taking the lead, "to address the unique situation we find ourselves in—with the Fire Throne vacant and war breathing down our necks."

"It is not simply war and an empty throne," Gwogh countered. "It is the ultimate—final—conflict, foretold for centuries. And in Ybienn, this Council named the Fierian, who will lead the charge against the Dark One."

Grunts and nods filtered around the room.

"Prince Haegan is the son of Zireli, one of the fiercest, most skilled accelerants to hold the throne, likely as far back as his ancestor, Baen."

"I realize your intent," Kedulcya spoke, "but the prince's blood tie to Zireli merely guarantees him the right to the Zaethien throne, but delivers no guarantee of his holding the Fire Throne."

"The Fire Throne has been ruled from Seultrie for nearly two centuries."

"Because the Celahars have been victors in the Contending." Kedulcya nodded, her expression smooth. "As the previous Fire King's heir, Haegan is automatically entered in the Contending as Zaethien's candidate."

Gwogh's heart fell. He could not argue the Guidings, the laws which placed the Nine's ruler on the throne, but he had hoped . . . hoped to sway the Council against the Contending. "Time is short, my brothers and sister. Sirdar advances. We are facing things we have never encountered before. We cannot afford mistakes and pointless delays at this time."

"All the more reason to be sure we do not warrant another display"— Kedulcya nodded to the empty chair—"of Abiassa's judgment by disregarding the laws in place since Baen's Council."

"Aye," Voath said. "There are many questions regarding the prince's actions in the last few months, and a victory in the Contending will silence those objections."

Therein lay the caveat Gwogh feared—a victory.

"Indeed," Voath continued. "There has been talk of the prince's role in the death of his father."

"You mean, in trying to *save* his father," Traytith corrected.

"I mean—"

"Gwogh has a point," Falip put in. "Do we have the time to conduct a Contending? Choosing candidates—"

"They are all but chosen," Kedulcya countered. "It is common to maintain a list of Contenders in each kingdom."

"But Haegan's transgressions—"

"Transgressions?" A storm moved through Gwogh. "They are but accusations with no merit. Some conjured."

"But the accusations exist," Aaold said. "And they persist in the minds of the people. The Fire King is dead, as is the queen. The princess—"

"Princess Kaelyria," Gwogh interrupted, "is with the Eilidan, sick and paralyzed, but alive."

"With the Eilidan? In the Northlands?" Kedulcya seemed particularly put out at this news. "'Tis no fitting place for a princess."

"Fitting or not," Traytith said, "if she's there, we must confirm it. Voath, make a note to send a messenger. What of her gift? Was there mention?"

Gwogh sighed. "It is believed lost."

Silence stretched for a moment as each accelerant glimpsed the agony of such loss. Falip was the first to speak. "Lost. Then she . . ."

"Is no longer eligible to Contend, even if she were physically able," Gwogh finished. "The succession has fallen from her, and we cannot look back."

"Of course," Voath said, glancing around. "As for Haegan, there is another consideration—as Fierian, he is Abiassa's Chosen. Dare we presume to put him through a Contending?"

"But chosen ruler and chosen destroyer—"

"Not destroyer," Gwogh said quickly. "Chosen *Hand*."

Griese conceded with a nod. "Still, the two are mutually exclusive. Nowhere in the Parchments does it state one is the other. If that were the case, Zireli could have been the Fierian."

Kedulcya sat taller. "Except that Zireli did not fulfill the prophecies, and while the Parchments may not explicitly state the Fierian will be king, they also do not explicitly state he won't."

"Well said." Gwogh had long ago come to appreciate Kedulcya's logical mind.

"However," Kedulcya continued, "the allegations against Haegan are too numerous and too serious to be ignored. As Aoald has already pointed out, rumor has taken root."

"Forgive me," Falip said. "But I fear I am lately come and ill informed. Just what are these rumors?"

Voath cleared his throat almost apologetically and consulted a piece of paper in front of him. "Well, to begin with, there is Haegan's association with an accelerant accused of murdering High Lord Aloing. He's also known or supposed to be responsible for the deaths of twenty Ematahri warriors.

"It is also speculated that he conspired"—Voath's eyes skirted the room, avoiding Gwogh—"with his tutor to manipulate his sister into the transference, so he could steal the throne."

At this, Gwogh laughed. Hard. "My dear Council—to believe this one, we would have to promote Haegan to Foreteller. His mental prowess would surpass everyone in the world."

A few smiles went around the room, but Voath read on. "In the Citadel, the gossip is that his education was left to a stripped accelerant."

Gwogh sighed. "All at this table know I was not stripped. A decision was made, which we all accepted." He pointed to Voath. "That charge will be struck, as we cannot address the truth of the situation openly."

"Agreed," Kedulcya said firmly.

Nodding, Voath looked back at his paper, making Gwogh groan inwardly. Did all the world have a grievance against Haegan? "And among the soldiers, he is criticized for his association and relationship with the daughter of the Fire King's most renowned enemy, Thurig the Formidable."

"'Most renowned enemy,'" Gwogh repeated with a sniff. "They are cousins—distantly."

"Very distantly," Traytith said.

"And last I looked, the Northlands were not an enemy of the Nine."

"Neither are they friend," Kelviel added.

"You speak truth. What else, Voath?"

"The last is a serious charge of collusion with Poired—"

"Collusion!" Gwogh could not hold back his anger this time, but he swallowed his retort. "I beg your mercy. Go on."

"General Negaer himself reported that on the bridge to the Keep, the prince conversed with the Dark One, then mounted a raqine and left Seultrie to the enemy."

Gwogh tapped the table to stem his frustration. He could not help but think of the empty seat.

"It would seem to me," Kelviel said quietly, "that the Deliverers would have dealt with Haegan most severely had he colluded with darkness."

"Yes," Gwogh said, enlivened by Kelviel's words. "Yes, indeed."

"Perhaps they did."

Gwogh frowned at Griese. "Explain."

"He has an injury to his arm, given to him by a Deliverer."

Gwogh sat back, wondering how Griese knew this.

Kedulcya put both elbows on the table and her eyes settled on Gwogh with understanding and regret. "So you see, old friend, I fear the only way to proceed is to force Haegan to put the people's concerns to rest. There must be a Contending."

Kelviel nodded. "I agree. Prince Haegan must compete in the Contending. He cannot simply be handed the Fire Throne."

"Even as Abiassa's Chosen."

"Chosen *Fierian*. Not necessarily the Fire King."

"We must be prepared," Traytith said.

"And we must have faith," Gwogh countered, "in the will of Abiassa. She set the prophecies, and he met every one without even knowing!"

Kelviel sighed. "But as Kedulcya stated—the Fire King and the Fierian are not necessarily one and the same. We must be prepared to set someone on the throne in case they are not."

It was a lost battle. Gwogh stroked his long beard, heart heavy. Haegan would contend. And he would do his best. But the Contending was a series of trials that tested wit, leadership, wielding, and physical strength. The once-crippled prince, who had only just learned four months ago that he even had the abiatasso, didn't stand a chance against those who had practiced—*honed*—their gift for years.

The windows rattled, the floor vibrating beneath them. Gwogh frowned, then his gaze shifted to the glass, where he saw a wake of heat retreat.

"Can we search the Parchments?" Kelviel said.

"Are you concerned?" Kedulcya asked, eyebrows creased.

"Aye, because though the Council will have a voice—each of us will send our Contenders—there is another granted a voice in this."

"Dromadric."

Boom!

The windows shook again.

"Wha—?" Kedulcya was first on her feet, rushing to the panes of glass.

Gwogh went after, watching that wake of heat slide backward, to its owner no doubt. "There are few accelerants that powerful these days," he mumbled. Yet, in the air he could sense the young man's abiatasso. Haegan.

Another explosion sent the rippling wake streaking right for them.

Kedulcya screamed, spinning away and shielding her face.

Gwogh watched. Believed. Trusted. The wake rushed up. Smacked the glass. But did not break it.

"It's coming from the training yard," Griese announced.

"It's the prince," Kelviel said. "We should see this for ourselves."

36

Only his second day in the Citadel and Haegan stood in the training yard, dripping sweat beneath the glaring disapproval of High Lord Adomath. Why in the blazes had Adomath been chosen as his instructor? Months ago, the man had tried to get the Jujak to dispatch him to the eternal darkness. Called him a scourge.

If he was going to survive this, Haegan had to tuck aside that memory. Focus on the unorthodox training methods. Sending heat—and only heat—high into the heavens. Shake the glass, he was told, but don't break it.

"Again!" Adomath shouted from the raised dais at the corner of the training yard.

Gritting his teeth and drawing in a half breath—all he could drag into his lungs—Haegan snapped his head, spraying the sandy yard with droplets of sweat.

"What are you waiting for?"

Haegan glowered. He locked onto the high lord before stepping back with his right foot. Palmed his own chest as Adomath had instructed, then curved his hands out, sending the wake upward. His forearms and thighs trembled as he used his stance for additional strength. Wishing he could skim Adomath, sear some of that attitude off him. But even as the thought crossed his mind, he saw the marred mess on his arm. A reminder of the Deliverer who'd punished him for dipping into vengeance. Anger.

This time, the puny heat plume barely rose above the training walls.

"Weakling!"

The word stung. Painful echoes from his childhood. Haegan coiled his hands into fists as he stood beneath the reprimand.

"How are you to save this world if you cannot withstand training? Do you think our enemies will wait while you rest?"

He gritted his teeth.

"Again! Stronger this time, if you wish to sup."

He had missed the midday meal because he failed to impress the marshal. Already, he'd sent up a couple of dozen plumes. The exercise had grown tedious.

"Now, Prince Haegan!"

Huffing out a breath, Haegan cocked his head. Stepped back. Had no tolerance—

Shapes moved in the shadows of the observation deck, its canopy gently flapping in the afternoon breeze. Haegan could not make out who had joined them, but he resented having an audience witness his inability to more accurately control or sustain his gift. Yet, he knew it imperative to succeed. He would face Poired again one day.

Or would he? Why would the Deliverer say it was not his to kill Poired, then allow him to do it later? But if not Poired, someone stronger.

Sirdar of Tharqnis.

Fear crashed through him. His heat plume went sideways. Smacked Adomath. Flapped hard against the canopy, revealing those on the observation deck. All garbed in thick, dark robes. The Council.

"You must *focusss*," Adomath hissed, his own anger palpable.

"What good will heat plumes be against Poired or Sirdar?"

"Who said anything about either of them?"

"The prophecies," Haegan spat back, shoving his sweaty hair off his forehead.

A gentle word came from the observation deck but was not loud enough for Haegan to hear. Adomath pivoted, as if surprised by the presence of the audience, then gave a curt nod. He faced Haegan with a sneer. "They want a demonstration."

"I thought I was training, not performing. Am I a dog—"

"At this rate, I'm not sure you're doing either." Adomath snapped his fingers, and two conductors rushed onto the training field with targets.

They set them in a random pattern, then scurried out of sight. "Hit each target at the same time."

Simultaneously? Haegan looked at Adomath as if he'd instructed Haegan to split himself in four. How was he to do that? He considered the arrangement of the targets. Adjusted his position back and to the left. Then with a thrust of his arm, he sent a wide, thin wake barreling over the targets.

They toppled. All six. He turned to Adomath, whose face had gone red.

"All six with separated flames."

Frustration tightened the muscles in his shoulders. "You did not clarify."

"Straighten the targets," Adomath instructed the conductors, who complied immediately, then nodded to Haegan. "Repeat it. Correctly."

For a second Haegan considered defying him. Why was he being made to conduct like a child?

Because you don't know how to conduct.

Aye. And Adomath seemed intent on humiliating him with that fact. Condemning him. Criticizing. Eying the targets, he tried to think past his anger. To shove it aside. To remember what Thurig had taught him. There—*there* was a man, an accelerant, he could respect.

"Now—again. And strike each with a separate flame." Adomath's sigh carried loudly over the yard. "Remember—start here," he said, holding his hand to his chest.

It was an awkward technique that slowed Haegan. His mind tripped trying to wield with fancy forms. It scared him that he could not correctly wield. That he was a combustible tool. So he would comply. He was not the master here.

He palmed his chest, reaching out and sensing the elements. Drawing on the heat of those around. Of the city. Of fireplaces. He arced out. Flames spiraled from his fingers. But the angle was wrong. He saw it as soon as the fiery daggers shot out. He'd only struck four.

"You are a disgrace!" Adomath shouted.

Haegan spun. "Am I to be trained, or am I to be humiliated?"

"The humiliation is of your own making." Adomath nodded. "Again. Focusssss, Prince Haegan."

Anger roiled through him. He could feel it, the wake bubbling around his fingers. "Wrong wake," he whispered to himself. A piece of him tore off. He clenched his eyes. "I did not want this. I did not want to be this . . . scourge," he muttered. "I can't. I *can't* do this."

"Prince!"

Haegan flinched. Turned. Flung out some fiery daggers but knew instantly they would fail, too. He didn't have the right arc. Or trajectory. Or life.

"Failure!"

"We all know your view of me." Haegan jerked toward Adomath and hauled off his shirt. "You are not here to train me, but to mock me. To humiliate me. How long will you demean me from your pedestal?"

"I am—"

"Enough!" He threw his hands downward to emphasize the word.

In the space of a blink, a wall of glass shot upward from the ground. Dagger-sharp spikes glittered in the afternoon sun all around him. Pristine, beautiful. He stared at the pieces, disbelieving, then looked for whoever had thrown them at him.

A chorus of shocked gasps wove through the observation deck. Murmurs quickly followed, shaming him more that they'd felt the need to defend the high lord against him.

Haegan grabbed his shirt and started for the exit. Threading his arms through the sleeves, he hauled in greedy breaths. Fed-up breaths. Angry breaths. He tugged his tunic over his head and rounded the corner, falling into the damp, earthy darkness of the tunnels beneath the Citadel.

Ambient light flared, glowing brighter as a figure came toward him.

Haegan hesitated, feeling the embers churning still. All too ready to use them again. "Who are you? What do you want?"

"You are inordinately gifted," came a deep voice. Familiar. Yet . . . distant. Seconds later, the man came into focus.

"Grand Marshal Dromadric." Had he seen the eruption of Haegan's anger?

"Leaving so soon, my prince?"

Next to the Fire King, the grand marshal was above all, and as such, Haegan struggled to find balance in how to speak or act before him. But the elaborate overcloak seemed to sweep in the bitter scent he'd detected before. What was that?

Next to Dromadric, I am nothing. The thought filled his mind. "I beg your mercy, but . . . I seek solitude."

"I would imagine so after training all day with Adomath."

Was this a trap? Haegan would not trust any accelerant—except Drracien. And Thurig. "He is well-versed at prying the worst from me."

Dromadric chuckled. "He is good at that with most everyone, but he is also a very skilled accelerant."

"So I've been told."

"But he is not schooled in how to train the Fierian."

Was that a jibe? Mocking?

"Do you realize what you did in the end, when you let yourself loose?"

"I didn't—" The glass. He didn't want to think about it. "I . . . It's never happened before."

For several long seconds, Dromadric studied him. "Tell me, have you wielded before on sand?"

Sand? His mind tumbled through all the places he'd practiced and trained. The yard. The patio at Nivar. The forest. "No, most always on grass. Sometimes rock or gravel."

Dromadric gave an appreciative nod. "Do you know how you created the glass?"

Haegan hesitated. He knew lightning strikes on the beach sometimes created a pure glass. But . . . that was different.

"You superheated the sand—sparked with your anger, you made glass. Maybe anger isn't your problem."

"You mock me."

"Most certainly not. Especially not with the power you hold without putting a thought to it." Dromadric had a tall walking stick, which he switched to his other hand. "Would you humor me for a moment and return to the training yard?"

Annoyance rippled through Haegan. "I am tired."

"I promise this will be worth the remnants of your strength." Dromadric was already walking.

Haegan stood in the darkness, irritated. Why would they not simply leave him alone?

Mercies of Abiassa—he could do with Thiel's calming touch right about now. Hold her and pretend this training yard did not exist. That the glass had never happened. When he finally returned to the fading daylight, he found Dromadric standing in the middle of the yard, without his walking stick.

"When you threw your hands out, your anger roiling, did you think?"

Haegan blinked. "What?"

"Did you think? Or did you just do it?"

"I just . . . wanted Adomath to stop ridiculing me."

Dromadric nodded with a near smile. "Indulge me—tell me the story of the Ematahri you killed."

Affronted, Haegan took a step back.

Dromadric held out a staying hand. "I pass no judgment. Please—tell me what led to it, and what happened."

"They were attacking me and my friends. We had done nothing wrong, save mistakenly entering their territory. Five against dozens."

"They bore down on you?"

Haegan nodded.

"Then what?"

"I only . . ." He couldn't make sense of it. "I only meant to protect us."

"You wanted them to stop."

"Aye."

Dromadric made a grunt at the back of his throat, his eyes on Haegan. Studying him as if he were a horse for purchase. He was intrigued. Curious.

The scraping of metal against metal drew Haegan's attention. A dozen steel gates around the yard pulled up, leaving dark, gaping maws. Growling emerged before the heads of the—

"Icehounds." Haegan stepped back, the earlier taste again in his mouth. "What . . . ?"

Growling hounds stalked. But these were not the highly trained breed he'd seen in Legier's Heart. These . . . these had fire in their eyes. A thirst for blood.

"What happened?" Dromadric asked, whirling around with indignation. "Who opened the gates! Shut them!"

Immediately, they slid shut. Too late! And a mistake—now Haegan and the grand marshal were enclosed in the yard with the beasts. Haegan's heart shot into his throat as the dogs homed in on them. Circled. Foam dripped from their jowls. Razor-sharp teeth bared. He threw himself backward, bumping against the grand marshal with a yelp. "Help!"

There's no one there. The thought thumped his mind, and in a split-second check, he confirmed it. The observation deck sat empty.

We're going to die.

"Get back," Haegan shouted to the grand marshal. "Go for one of the tunnels."

"We haven't time," Dromadric said, his voice even.

"How can you be so calm?"

"They feed on our fear."

Haegan started at the words.

A hound lunged.

Haegan flashed out a hand. Felt the dog's hot breath and heard the jaws snap. In a blink, the dog was gone.

Another from the left. No—two. Haegan stabbed at the first. The dog yelped and vanished in a puff. The other, however, latched on this arm. "Augh!" He flicked his wrist, and the dog flew, engulfed in a ball of fire. Ash fluttered to the ground.

Before he could even register it, Haegan felt the attack from behind. Like a prickling along his nape. He roared as he stretched his back, throwing out his arms, hands fisted. Breathing hard, terrified, adrenaline coursing through his body, he pivoted. Turned a circle. The training yard lay empty. His heart thundered.

Dromadric stood with assessing eyes.

I just killed five dogs. "I . . . I think they're . . . gone." 'Twas cruel. "Why use dogs for training? 'Tis heartless."

"Yes," Dromadric finally spoke. "It would be. If they were real."

"What do you mean—they were! I felt their breath on my face." He lifted his right forearm. "One clamped onto—" Haegan stopped short. Stared at his arm. His unaffected, unbitten arm. No marks. Not a scratch. He blinked. Turned his arm over. "I heal . . . quickly . . ."

"That may be true, but there was no bite to be healed."

"I . . . I don't understand."

"The icehounds were in your mind, Haegan. I merely inflamed your thoughts, your fears."

Inflamed my fears? "That's not possible." Yet he knew it was. Had heard of accelerants with that much power. The thought terrified him.

"Not for an untrained accelerant, and the practice of inflaming is not allowed for any but the highest of our Order, but it was necessary."

"Necessary?" Haegan felt spittle at the corners of his mouth, tears burning his eyes. "Why? Am I dog that I must do tricks now?"

"No, what you are is the most powerful accelerant I have ever encountered." Dromadric stepped closer, tilting his head to the side. "Haegan, you don't need training because your abilities far outwield any in this Citadel, perhaps even mine."

"Even if that were true, I can't control it. Conquer it."

"Conquer it?" Dromadric sniffed. "My boy, anger is your fuel. As for control—well, you might not be able to spark others the way children do to each other, or split a flame into multiple parts—yet—but you *can* control it. The Flames did exactly what you, from your thoughts, told them to do with the icehounds. Each scenario where you've had this great explosion of power, the Flames obeyed. They protected. Yours is not an ambivalent gift meant to police the realm, as most here have."

Destroyer. Hated. Murderer.

A spicy, pungent smell struck Haegan's senses. Probably something used to kill the odor of the training yards. "If I cannot split a vein of fire into four parts . . . how am I to be the Fire King—"

"Fire King is a different matter." Something flickered through Dromadric's expression, but Haegan wasn't sure what. "But the Fierian is meant to *destroy*. It was written that in the days when darkness overtakes the land, Her anger would be the answer." The grand marshal patted Haegan. "That's you."

"But I can't . . ." Life was too precious.

"You already have. It has begun, whether you would have it or not. But do not lose heart in the Contending—"

"The Contending." He'd forgotten. Of course. There was always a Contending. His father and Thurig had battled it out. All his forebears had. But he'd . . . forgotten. Or secretly hoped he wouldn't have to participate.

How am I to be the Fire King if I cannot remember the laws?

"Yes—fear not. Losing the Fire Throne does not diminish your task as Fierian."

"Losing?" Haegan met the grand marshal's eyes. So, even the greatest accelerant had little faith in his abilities. *I do not belong here.*

Haegan had the strong desire to sneeze, thanks to the pungent odor again.

"You are chosen as Fierian, Prince. Be grateful. I am sure your father would not fault you—after all, you've had no formal training. We cannot expect a boy to become a man overnight, even if he is the Fierian. You were probably Her choice because of your inexperience."

• • •

Gwogh pulled himself into the shadows as the tall form of the grand marshal cast a shadow at his feet. Dromadric soon swept past the dark alcove that concealed Gwogh and strode down the corridor. Earthy, pungent odors trickled into the air. And it wasn't the straw-strewn floor he smelled.

Grief tore at Gwogh, who waited until the passage was empty once more, then peeked into the training yard. The prince sat on the edge of the dais, holding his sweaty tunic. Head down, shoulders slumped, he looked defeated.

I have failed you, my prince.

Gwogh had known for a decade the boy would be the Fierian. He'd trained and tutored to equip him with the best knowledge. Challenged him in duels of wit to prepare him to face any political adversary. But he had not prepared him for the one thing he must face first—himself.

Warmth spiraled around Gwogh, sending a strange chill up his spine. The scent was sweet, aromatic, specific—it pulled him around. Though he knew what—whom—to expect, his heart still wobbled, as did his confidence. Abiassa knew every thought. She knew he had failed. Was it time for judgment?

Wrapped in shadow but also in light, the august Deliverer met him with a steady, piercing gaze that he felt to his toes.

Gwogh inclined his head. "I am here but to serve."

"Fear not for the boy," Medric said. "She has ordered his steps."

"Then you heard—" The Deliverer did not need to hear. His kind walked the Void and talked with Abiassa. "I fear Dromadric attempts to turn the boy against the path. I believe he hopes Haegan will fail the Contending."

"The Contending is a tool of man."

Heartsick still, Gwogh nodded. "But you know—you know Dromadric . . ." To speak it, to give voice to the evil he had just witnessed, the twisting of words and Legacies, Prophecies . . .

Medric said nothing.

So he did know. Of course he did. "Then why have you not delivered us from his faithlessness, prevented him from infecting Haegan—the Fierian—with doubts?"

"Trials are wrought by fire, not by deliverance."

"But you intervened regarding Bæde."

"You question Her?"

Gwogh sighed, struggling to tame his response that was spoken in truth and frustration. "Nay."

"It is hard to understand Her ways when your eyes are darkened by your own pursuits and blurred by the cares of this world," Medric spoke, his voice seeming to be everywhere at once. "Give care not to the empty pursuits that will bring Dromadric down, but to the purpose She has given you, Gwogh."

Desperation clung to hem of Gwogh's robes like the dust and dirt of the passage. He wore them heavily, weighting his heart, mind, and abiatasso. "I beg your mercy," he muttered, not to the Deliverer, but to Abiassa.

"Your heart is right, Gwogh. This is why She chose you." Medric gave a nod, something severe snapping through his vibrant eyes. "However, the throne must be protected so that darkness does not seep in through cracks while the world looks to the east."

"How?" Gwogh moved forward a step, hope sparking in his chest. "How can it be protected?"

"You will find the answer in Baen's Blood Oath."

37

A rich green canopy dangled overhead, embracing Trale and protecting them both from the elements. He held the stone, wondering if perhaps the Infantessa had protected them. It might make sense. From the growth of stubble on his own chin, he judged they'd been unconscious for several days.

They had wound the eastern path to Hetaera on the mules they'd found tethered outside the small hut. The old man and youth were gone. In their place—food, fresh clothes, and a few coins. When he and Astadia had finally sorted out how long they'd been out of it, they'd raced through the city, scurrying to make up the time lost.

"I don't like it," Astadia said as they paused at the lip of the woods and stared over the open valley. A short rise predicated the great city. The tops of buildings peeking over looked deceptively small. "Things are wrong."

He'd felt it, too, but she looked for reassurance, and they could not afford hesitation now. "You're only saying that because it was easy."

"Yes," she bit out. "Who leaves money and mules and clothes for strangers? Two badly injured strangers? And how are our injuries nearly whole?"

"Your complaining is injuring my ears." It didn't make sense—she was right. And he didn't have answers. At least not ones someone in possession of their faculties would believe. What good would it to do throw out meaningless theories?

Trale dismounted and led the mule off trail. "We should walk from here."

"The spire," Astadia said. "Look!"

He glanced through the trees and squinted, the sun unrelenting this morning. But he saw the Spire of Zaelero, and on it—the Celahar standard. "Infantessa be praised."

Astadia whipped toward him. "'Infantessa be praised?' You jest!"

Trale swallowed. "His standard—it means the prince is there."

"Aye, but that has nothing to do with the Infantessa."

He didn't know why he'd intoned her name. It embarrassed him, but he didn't need his sister's jabbing. "He isn't king yet—there will be an entire process, approval by the Council of Nine, the induction, then his formal coronation." He slung his pack over his shoulder. "We need to get him before any of that happens."

"Are you crazy?" Astadia lifted her leg over and slid off the mule. "We won't get anywhere close to him now that they intend to set him in."

"We'll find a way."

"How? It'll be impossible."

He spun to her. "Since when have you been such a complainer? When did you decide the life of an assassin was too difficult? It's adventure, remember? That's what you said."

"It was a way out—of the boredom and abuse," Astadia growled. "We agreed to do this and save our lots until we could escape. A way out of that man's clutches and prison. I would've done anything to be rid of that place and him."

"And you have, so don't grow a conscience now. The Infantessa wants Haegan, and we'll bring him to her."

"But why? What does she want him for?"

"I think she wants to save him." Trale wasn't sure where the words came from, but once spoken, they seemed truer.

Astadia scoffed. "You cannot believe that."

"I do. She was . . . earnest." Beautiful. Sensuous. He wanted to get this done and return to her as quickly as possible. "I didn't detect malice from her."

"But you detected her curves, no doubt. Took a clout to the knees because of your wandering eyes." She touched her temples, shaking her head. "Did we meet the same Infantessa?"

"Are you jealous, Astadia?"

"What?" Her green eyes bulged. "You're my brother—why would I be *jealous*?"

"If I do this for her, she might favor me. Invite me to stay at her court."

Stilled, she frowned. "Have you lost your faculties? You are nothing but a hired killer to her. She says go, you go. She says kill, you kill."

"And if she keeps me—"

"*Keeps* you?" She slapped the back of his head.

"Hey!"

"What is wrong with you? Whatever that old man gave you to eat must've been drug laced. We are saving to escape, Trale. Do you recall?"

He scowled. "Of course I do . . . but . . . we don't have enough resources." Trale shrugged, wondering if she was right. Had the old man drugged his drink or food? It would explain why he'd slept so hard. And long. Days, they'd slept. But he'd woken refreshed. Not hung over or battered, despite the injuries. "Regardless, we have a mission. Whether Poired sends us on it or the Infantessa—we obey. As they command."

He slapped the flank of the mule, who nickered but didn't move. "We have a prince to catch."

• • •

LEGIER'S HEART, NORTHLANDS

From this snowy vantage, he could stare across the realms. It seemed a thousand leagues spread out, intersected by the forests of Ybienn and the mountains of the Great Falls. Spring was fanning its warm breath over the more southern plains. But here, on the mountain, a blanket of snow still held spring at bay.

Aselan lifted a foot and set it against a boulder, then leaned an arm on his leg as he contemplated the political changes of the Nine Kingdoms. Of the prince who'd gone out from Ybienn a week earlier. Made of sturdier mettle than he realized, Haegan still had much to learn. And he was facing one colossal nightmare. Scouts had brought word that Poired was marching toward Hetaera. If he took that . . .

The subtle crunch of a boot alerted him to company. When no further noise was made, Aselan knew who'd joined him. Few knew of his thinking spot. "Have ye come to reprimand me again?"

A snort. "I could no more reprimand ye than we can tame the raqine." Byrin came closer, his boots crunching in the foot-deep snow that washed the area in a pristine blanket of crystal-white. "Ye look to the south."

Aselan nodded.

"Because of the princess?"

Pushing up, Aselan scowled at his first. "I look to the south because a powerful enemy wages war there. I weigh our future, our options." He planted his feet firmly and stuffed his cold hands in the pockets of his heavy cloak.

"Think he'll take Hetaera?"

Aselan's gaze traced the distant terrain—just beyond that lay the thriving country and its extravagant capital. "He is powerful and shrewd. Hetaera must be taken to solidify his hold on the Nine. If he succeeds . . ."

"The Nine are lost," Byrin finished his thought.

"He is a gifted accelerant, cowed into service by Sirdar, a Void Walker, if ever there was one. The Nine are headless and thrashing for direction." That very morning he'd received word of the Contending. He almost pitied Haegan. Aselan had enough to contend with in the Heart. He did not envy the thin-blood the troubles of nine realms.

"Void Walkers are supposed to be the hand of Abiassa."

"Think ye that only the good walk there? It's a chasm between worlds." Aselan scratched his beard, then smoothed a hand over it. "If Sirdar is to stake his claim as supreme ruler, Poired must break the backs of the Ignatieri as much as the governors. And that can only be completed in Hetaera."

"What of the princess?"

Aselan sighed. "Ye are relentless in mentioning her."

"But it must be asked—she is the heir to Seultrie."

"A right she has surrendered, as a cripple and stripped of her gift."

"So ye do not think her a threat?"

With a scoff, Aselan folded his arms over his chest, still watching the horizon. "A threat to what?"

Byrin gave him a shrewd look. "Then ye no longer believe 'It would be foolish to not at least consider the possibilities'?"

Aselan turned a scowl on him.

Byrin raised his hands in mock surrender. "Yer words, Cacique."

"And I meant them. But she has been here over a month now and caused no stir."

"Except among the men."

With an acknowledging nod, Aselan ignored the tightening in his stomach. The thought of anyone bothering her . . . "I am not surprised. She is beautiful." And alluring and intelligent.

"I came upon her in the cantina," Byrin said. "She asked of our plans to defend against attack."

Did she? "What did ye tell her?"

"That she need not worry."

"And that went well, I'm sure."

"She said she was not worried. She had ideas."

Aselan arched his eyebrows.

"They ain't half bad, either," Byrin conceded.

"What's this?" Aselan laughed. "Are ye going soft on her?"

Byrin huffed. "'Tis her own fault—batting those snowy-blues around."

A smile tugged at Aselan. It made sense—why Byrin saw her as a threat. Aselan could relate. She was infectious. He had given her more thought than he should, considering the situation and wars springing up around the planet. But 'twas of no use to speak of her. To entertain thoughts of her. "Things are changing. I never thought I'd see the day when the Rekken would come out and brazenly attack Langeria."

"Ye think they'll come here?"

"There is no reason for them to come," Aselan said, but then added, "except for a show of might. And that has always been their vice." Thick clouds clung to the mountain peak, shielding the men from the sun and blue sky. "We should be on alert. Train harder."

"But we're here, in the Heart. No one has ever dared attack."

"And that is why we must expect it. We are not impenetrable or impervious."

"But we have the safeguards."

"And far too few men." It had always been a struggle to keep a decent band of fighters ready when the few men within the Heart were also farmers, tanners, blacksmiths, and herbalists. And women had outnumbered men for generations. Even he had no heir. Neither did Byrin or his brother.

"This mean ye'll be placing yer dagger at Etaesian's Feast?"

Turning, he slapped Byrin on the shoulder. "Ye first."

"Oh, I intend to."

Aselan stopped short and considered the burly man. "In earnest?"

"Aye," Byrin said, his expression serious. "I'm no young man, and as ye said—we need more men."

Startled at the thought of Byrin binding himself to a woman, Aselan searched for a response. "Have ye someone in mind?"

Byrin, close to Aselan's thirty-four years but grayer and burlier, dropped his gaze. Guilt. Embarrassment. What was this? Who . . . ?

Ah. "The princess." Why did that annoy Aselan?

"Ye know well the women choose," Byrin groused. "And the likes of her probably won't have nothing to do with a mountain goat like me, but . . ."

"I would not be so sure." And that annoyed Aselan more. Kaelyria had dismantled every preconceived notion he held of her. She was sturdier than he'd expected, more resilient, more intelligent. More beautiful. "Her will is strong."

"There's that," Byrin said with a frown. "But 'tis her royal blood and titles. She wouldn't have someone as lowborn as meself. And I'm not sure I could tolerate her highborn ways and demands."

"'Tis not a fault, simply a fact, but here"—Aselan nodded to the cleft rising above them—"she seems settled and content *not* to be highborn."

Byrin stared at him, then grinned. "So I have a chance?"

"Why would ye ask me? I have no idea what chance ye or any other dozen men have."

"Then why ye be fisting yer hand?"

Surprised, Aselan slid his hand back in his pocket. "I have work to do—as do ye. How's the nest?"

"Quiet. I think 'tis nearly time."

Aselan nodded, making his way through the snow-laden thicket back to the hidden entrance to the Heart. But he glanced to the south one more time, his worry complete about being tangled up in the war.

"Tell me we'll avoid engaging," Byrin muttered as he climbed the rope ladder.

"As long as we can." They descended into the Heart. The two parted ways at the main juncture, and though Aselan felt a powerful tug to check in on the princess, he forced himself to his cave. There, he went over notes, scout reports, inventories. But his mind kept swinging south. War.

He bent forward, rubbing his knuckles. What he wouldn't give to seek his father for sage counsel. Talk to him, weigh options.

Here, the men were ready to defend to the death their home, the Heart. But was there a way to avoid war? An honorable way? He had been set in power here because of his marriage, but it did not mean he was ably equipped. He hadn't really thought of himself as inadequate—he'd long known he'd do anything for the Eilidan—but this . . . a single bad speck of judgment could eradicate every mountain dweller. That guilt would not only be carried through Eilidan history, but would be a black mark against his father and the Nivari, merely by blood-association. He'd shamed his father and Nivar enough already.

"You look distressed."

Aselan raised his eyes only, peering beneath the rim of black curls shielding his face. How had she rolled that chair to his door without his hearing? He leaned back with a long-suffering sigh. "Much to consider in light of what's happening in the Nine."

She held out her hand, asking if she could enter.

Aselan started from his chair.

Kaelyria flashed her palm and smiled. "I'm able." White-blond hair swinging over her shoulder, she rolled up to his desk. "It's nice to regain a little of my independence."

"Rightly so," he said, his gut tight as her scent swirled around his head, tangling his thoughts. "I'm sure ye were quite independent in Seultrie."

She gave a groan-laugh. "You have no idea." Hands in her lap, she sat as the epitome of elegance. "I'm sure Nanny said at least a few unkind words about me to the other servants." Nose wrinkled, she scrunched her face. "I was quite spoiled. Things were perfect—I had all I wanted. My father was king." Her voice broke. Eyes glossed. She looked away. "I beg your mercy. It was an unexpected thought."

Instinct told him to extend a hand of comfort. Instead, he sat rigid. "'Tis a fresh wound."

"Too fresh." She brushed a tear from the corner of her eye. "I was even the perfect sister." Shaking her head, she lifted the tail of her gold chain belt and feigned fascination. "In truth, I was pompous and selfish. Visiting my crippled brother made me feel like a good person, made me look good."

Aselan felt the frown slide across his face.

"See?" She nodded. "There you have it—even you believe it selfish."

"Ye mistake my frown for disdain. Yer actions may have reflected well upon yer person and name, but I doubt ye did it solely for yer reputation. There is no doubt of yer love for Haegan. I believe ye to be resolute and true."

Did that sound like pandering? Flattery?

Her blue eyes glittered at him. "It is no wonder you are cacique."

It surprised him how her words slid over his weary soul like a warm balm. "Why is that?"

"You have a way with words—a dignified way—and with people."

He laughed, pleased she thought him dignified.

"No, it's true. I see how they respect you. Though you aren't Eilidan by birth, you are their cacique and their loyalty is absolute." She smiled. "I've had conversations in the cantina with Carilla, whom I believe has more than a few fond thoughts of you."

Heat climbed into Aselan's face, dismissing the image of the young girl. "She's but a child."

"She is of child-bearing age. Isn't that what is important to a ruler?"

"Not just."

"Well, she is not the only one who has bestowed generous praise on you or your appearance. I've heard some say you are handsome."

He could not help but stare into her pale eyes, searching after the answer to a question he dared not ask—had *she* thought that of him? She found him dignified, but that was far from handsome. He swallowed and shook his head to dislodge the thought. "*Handsome* does not protect the Heart or her people."

"So you embrace it?"

He started. Did she think him vain? "No, I—"

"Peace, Aselan," she said around a smile. "I tease you."

He breathed a laugh. "Aye, and well."

This time, she laughed. "My brother often said the same." Uncertainty flickered through her gaze. "You mentioned the Nine—have you word of Haegan? Tell me what's happening out there."

Should he tell her? About the giants, the Rekken, the incipients?

"Think not to hide truth from me, no matter how painful. I read people better than most read the Parchments." A smile wobbled on her pink lips. "Already I see in your eyes concern. Come. I would have the truth, Cacique."

Aselan leaned forward, his fingers grazing the sheer material covering her arm. "He is well—at least, that is the last report my scouts have."

Wary blue eyes held his. "You wouldn't speak just to quiet my fears, would you?"

He smiled. "I probably would, but in this, I speak truth. There was an altercation at Baen's Crossing, but he is well. I'm sure, mentally, he's challenged, though."

She frowned.

"'Tis said yer brother summoned the giants back from the land of the ancients."

Kaelyria gaped. "You mean the Unauri—like Hoeff and Toeff?"

He nodded. "Many witnesses give testament that the Drigo transformed into their advanced state."

"Vudd—but they lost that ability centuries ago."

"So 'tis said."

"You jest," she said with a laugh. "This strains credulity."

"There is more, better." Again, he nodded. "The Drigo wiped out a band of incipients, who ambushed yer brother and his friends. Then the leader of the giants silenced a faltering accelerant. Stripped him of his powers and robe right there."

She laughed. "How I would have loved to see that!" Her words were wistful and awed. "And the Nine?"

"Poired advances toward Hetaera."

The princess sighed, worry weighting her ice-blues. She did not belong here, as much as he might will it. 'Twas more fitting that she be with her brother, her only family. Not among mountain dwellers and cold weather. She'd chosen to remain here to heal. And she had done that.

"We should look into seeing ye down the mountain soon."

She cocked her head and raised an eyebrow. "Are you sure 'tis safe for me to see the passages? That I'm not a spy?"

The words stung. He looked down. "That was a conversation I handled badly. I regret using the truth so."

"But it was still truth." Her fingers brushed his arm, and he met her open gaze. "You were looking out for your people, and any good ruler would. I should not have let my emotions blind me." With a sigh, she leaned back and looked away. "If you wish me to go, I will go. But"—she lifted a shoulder in a shrug—"I have nothing to go back to." Her hand fluttered to the chair she sat in. "My . . . condition. They would look down on me. I would be no more than a pitiable creature there."

What was she saying? "'Tis yer home."

"I have no home now. It is besieged. Where would I live?"

"Yer family keeps a house in Hetaera, does it not?"

She looked down again. Swallowed. "I do not want to be pitied . . ." She placed her other hand on his, stirring something strange and deep in his gut. "I heard them. The unthinking, cruel comments hurled through-out the realm about Haegan, 'the poor crippled prince.' They only knew he could not use his body, not that his mind was sharp and alive." Her gaze rose to his, saturated in wretched fear. "I do not want to live like that. I know it's horrible to admit, but"—she wet her lips—"here, I am accepted. At least, as much as can be. I don't feel . . . The people here are different, kind. They care."

He didn't speak. Couldn't. Not with her holding his hand. Hope clawed through him like spring on the mountain.

She smoothed a hand over his and straightened her shoulders, the princess in her emerging once more. "I seek asylum and refuge with the Eilidan, Cacique. Will you grant me this request?"

His heart thumped against his ribs with each breath.

"Of course, it is not my will to retain"—she swallowed—"my titles here. I know that wouldn't help my situation. I'd take on duties like everyone else. I mean, obviously I can't do anything that requires stand-ing, but I could write. Or translate reports. Or . . ."

His mind tripped. Fell against the chasm his hope trod across. "Ye would embrace the way of the Eilidan?" A drum banged in his chest.

Blue eyes snapped to his. "Yes." Then she blinked. Seemed to gather the remnants of her dignity, modestly doused in embarrassment. "I mean—for a time. Perhaps just until Haegan settles somewhere, after the wars."

After the wars. His thoughts rampaged, plummeting down that chasm. He could hardly envision that future with the wars just starting. "Ye will have to request permission from the Ladies. My authority rests in protection and defense of the Heart. Theirs in everything else. If they approve, then I will present it before the Legiera, though I daresay that won't be a problem."

"No? Why?"

"Half have inquired if ye are eligible for Etaesian's Feast."

Her cheeks reddened and she drew back, releasing his hand.

"Have no fear. I assured them ye have no interest in taking an Eilidan as yer bound."

"I only just arrived . . ."

He nodded. Of course. Focus on the asylum. "If ye will put it to paper, the request can be made—for asylum."

The smile that returned besieged his heart. The Lady help him—he'd probably do anything for this princess.

38

Icy blue eyes glared down at him, stunning Haegan with a silent reprimand. One he'd often perceived in those eyes. Chastisement. Disappointment. He had never lived up to the great warrior and statesman Zireli Celahar had become in his lifetime. And now in death, his father seemed greater than before, though his visage had been relegated to oil and canvas in the Honoring Hall of the Citadel.

Larger than life. Fiercer than the Lakes of Fire. The Crown of Flames tangled amid citrines, the purest of stones on Primar, the representation of the abiatasso, sat atop his trim golden hair. Somehow, the fiery crown had seemed to enliven his father's eyes—as if they needed enlivening—which were strikingly blue. Zireli had been the name and king who struck fear and respect into the heart of the Nine like no other since Baen. Even now, Haegan's heart faltered, knowing he had failed him.

Would that you were here to instruct me . . .

But then it wouldn't be Haegan facing the Contending. It wouldn't be Haegan chosen as the Fierian.

Abiassa had known. Known the enemy would kill his father. Steal everything Haegan had in life.

"He was resplendent."

The kind voice turned Haegan toward the woman who stood a head shorter and considerably rounder. She had been in Thurig's home. Been one of those who had upended his life with the confirmation of the Fierian prophecies. A Council member. Haegan glanced back to the painting. "Aye."

"Not practicing?"

Haegan hesitated, pushing aside his annoyance as he slowly shook his head. "Between sessions." He sighed, a weariness having dug itself bone-deep in him. "I beg your mercy—I recall meeting you in Ybienn, but . . ."

"I am Kedulcya." She motioned to the carpeted hall and started walking.

He had neither the temperament to endure a lecture nor the energy to fight one. So he fell into step with her.

"At the end of the week, the Contending will begin."

"Dromadric mentioned it."

Indignation flashed across her features. "Did he?"

"Along with the truth that he did not believe me capable of winning."

Hands clasped beneath her ample bosom, Kedulcya could not hide her disappointment.

It pained him that no one believed in him. Truth be told, he did not believe in himself. "I must win," he said, more to himself than the Councilwoman. "I do not want to be the first Celahar in two hundred years to fail."

"One hundred eighty-three." As if it made a difference or lessened his shame. "What you must remember, young prince, is that all your fore-bears were trained nearly from infancy to win that throne."

"Your words are meant as comfort, but I must beg your mercy as it does nothing to dull the blow."

"No," she said with a long sigh. "I supposed it would not. The Contenders will start arriving soon. I urge you to learn all that you can of each one. Were you to . . ." Her gaze darted around nervously.

"Lose?" Anger and hurt writhed through Haegan's chest.

"It will be imperative that you form an alliance with the winner. I've already spoken to the other Council members to ensure ready and defin-itive support for you as Fierian."

Haegan could not believe his ears. "How well you have planned for my defeat, Kedulcya."

"I—"

"If you have no further need to detain me, I would be alone with my thoughts and inabilities."

"Prince—"

"Good day, ma'am." He clapped his heels together and bowed, then pivoted and stormed out of the Honoring Hall, barely resisting the urge to send a furious spark against the canvas of his father's image.

• • •

NIVAR HOLD, YBIENN

Beneath each hand lay a cauldron of emptiness. Thiel stood at her wardrobe, one hand fingering the leather forearm plating with the braided bands, a sign—she had thought then—of Cadeif's protection. The other hand held Haegan's tunic from when he'd gone into the Great Falls. She'd delivered him to Ybienn for tending and healing, and the tunic had been discarded by the pharmakeia. Stained, torn, it resembled the prince more than ever.

Uselessness created as big a hole in her as Haegan's absence had.

"Ye did well."

Thiel closed the drawer and shut the doors of the wardrobe, then turned to her mother. "When?" It felt strange, almost another symbolic gesture—putting the past, Haegan and Cadeif, behind her. But the former she didn't want behind her. She wanted him in front of her. Right here.

"Had ye not roused yer brother, he might have been too late to secure Yedriseth that night." Her mother nodded to the hall. "Come, walk with me."

Thiel resisted the urge to sigh, knowing another discussion was coming about how to be a lady. But she went to her mother, who took her arm and threaded it through her own.

"I know the ordeal with Yedriseth is weeks past, but we have not had the chance to discuss it. Tell me—how did ye know?"

Thiel shrugged as they glided slowly down the residence hall. "Different things I saw and heard. It just hit me, and I knew . . . Then when I heard the shouts, it was confirmed."

"What things?"

Lifting her skirts as they strolled, she frowned. "Why does it matter, Mama? Haegan was saved—and now he's gone."

Serenely, her mother led her down the stairs to the first level. Her mother had always been the master of cruel silence. The one that whispered fears and torturous punishments, ones often more sinister in Thiel's mind than what was later meted out.

"When I was sixteen and being groomed for the court, my younger sister was but twelve." Mama went quiet again, a distant memory seeming to flicker through her eyes. Aunt Cicaelia had married an Outlander and vanished into the wilds. At least, that's what Atelaria and the more embellished stories said. "She was adventurous and a tomboy and disregarded most every rule I was forced to obey without question. I was so angry with her."

"Because she was not a lady," Thiel supplied.

Her mother glanced at her, a lingering sadness in her expression. "No, for being free, for *living*."

What . . . ? She didn't understand.

Mama toyed with the ribbons and pearls that dangled from her waist. "I was so afraid of letting propriety go, of having someone look down on me for running with my skirts in hand, or laughing too loud and drawing attention." Her mother paused beside a large window overlooking the gardens. She released Thiel's arm and turned so they were facing each other. "It is true—a queen must be elegant and graceful. A strong emblem of her king, of the people she represents."

Of course. As she thought. Thiel forced herself to nod, swallowing her groans.

"But Thiel, a queen does not need a sword or spear to wield power."

She'd heard this one before. "Her word."

"No." Ferocity tightened her mother's lips. "Her silence."

Thiel squinted, trying to comprehend the meaning. "I don't—"

"Tell me about our trip to Councilman Raechter's home."

Thiel blinked. "But I already wrote this down and showed ye."

Her mother employed that cruel silence.

Thiel refrained from rolling her eyes and looked out the window instead, thinking back to the event. "The food was delicious. There were a lot of people—"

Her mother stopped her with a finger. "What did ye see that was not acknowledged or spoken?"

Mind pinging, she saw the councilman and the girl. She flushed.

Her mother nodded. "Yes."

Had she earnestly known about that?

"And at the monastery—what happened there? Ye were changed when we were reunited on the lawn. What transpired?"

"I'm not sure. Just that it . . . wasn't right. There was an argument between Yedriseth and the man, but there was more. He wasn't just angry with a stranger. There was a relationship, a connection between them."

"See?" She tucked her chin, peering at Thiel. "We women are wired for relationships. To love. Yes?"

Thiel's thoughts wandered to the shaggy-haired prince with icy blue eyes.

"We are the subtle swords of our husband's kingdom. I can enter a home and learn things there that yer father will never know, because men talk politics, strategy, and war. If it is not spoken, he will not learn it. Ye saw things others missed when the focus was on the one with greater power. More importantly, ye paid attention to those things, and in the end, it saved Haegan's life." She smiled and drew her away from the window, walking again, through the hall, through a room. "Knowledge is power, my sweet daughter."

Why was her mother telling her this?

"You must be ready to be strong—not in physical might, but as a shrewd, cunning queen. Haegan will need you to be so."

Heat flushed her face. "If I ever see him again . . ."

"There is only one way to find out," her mother said.

Surprised when her mother stopped, Thiel realized they stood in the library opposite her father's receiving room. Why were they in here?

Voices broke through the narrow sliver in the door, which she only then realized stood ajar. Thiel pretended not to notice—it wasn't polite to eavesdrop—but Mama nodded to it.

Thiel inched closer, peeking through. Her father and Tili stood with their backs to the door, facing someone, but also blocking that person from her view.

"We leave at once," came the person's voice.

Gwogh.

"Sometimes," Mama whispered in her ear, "silence is not better." With that, she gave Thiel a nudge, urging her into the room. "We must fight for what we know is right."

Thiel slipped into the room, and her brother and father parted like curtains.

"Ah," Gwogh said with amusement. "I hoped ye would show, Thiel."

She entered, clasping her hands before her to hide their trembling. Feeling as if she'd stepped into a well-plotted trap, her mother in collusion. "Why would that be?"

39

The Inner Court of the Citadel boasted a serene landscape that included gardens, water fountains, cobbled paths, and well-designed seating arrangements that blended with the natural elements. The Eternal Flame, a cascading wall of fire that represented Abiassa, illuminated the center. Shaped like an octagon, The Citadel boasted mirroring courtyards on all eight sides—plus one: the main entrance jutting from the grand façade. The tri-tipped flame encircled with a crown had been carved over the ninth arch—Celahar/Seultrie. His family had stood as guardians over the Nine for generations. Victors in the Contending. It was now his turn to continue that legacy.

Or shame them.

Haegan tugged on the stiff embroidered hem of his green doublet. It snapped tight against his shoulders, the gold threads catching the rising sunlight. The gold citrine, a symbol of his position as the heir to the throne, poked into his left breast. Over his heart.

He stood alone, as he would battle in the Contending to persuade the Council and the kingdoms that he was ready to assume the role of Fire King.

Taking the Seultrian throne was one thing—he was heir by blood. Taking the Fire King throne . . . that was a challenge he wasn't sure he was up to. But he must contend. He could not shame his father's memory by not even trying.

"Haegan!"

At the excited voice, he shifted, his highly polished shoes glaring in the morning sunlight. The world tilted, the axis returning to its right position as, swathed in tiers of pale coral, Thiel rushed from the double doors he'd only moments before exited.

"Thiel!" He caught her into his arms, crushing her against his chest. Savoring the warmth of her, the softness of her in a world of hard realities and cold betrayals. Heartache vanished. Trouble faded. Life roared. Her presence had always quieted the storm in him. It was good . . . so good to have her in his arms again.

He pressed a kiss into the crook of her neck, then cupped her face. "What are you doing here? When did you arrive? How are you here?"

She laughed. "One question at a time, tunnel rat." She smiled, her hair in a complicated braid that crowned her and coiled around her head. But then her gaze shifted. "Are ye well?"

Haegan shrugged. He didn't want to talk of that. He wanted her to talk. Simply to hear her voice. "It matters not."

"Aye, it matters all," she said, her eyes dark against her olive complexion. "Ye're . . ." She shook her head, frowning.

He didn't like that. Needed her to smile. "Why are you here?" Distraction was better than the dark truth at this hour.

"Gwogh visited my father. They asked me to return, said ye might need me."

He smiled. "They were right."

"Prince Haegan?" the Ignatieri sentinel called from the side. "It's time, sire."

Frustrated with the distraction, the reminder of what lay before him, Haegan held up a hand. "A moment. Please."

Destroyer. Scourge. He would kill countless people as Fierian. *What right does a murderer have to be Fire King?*

Yet to reject the throne was to reject all his father and forebears had fought for. He looked at the Zaethien sigil, synonymous with House Celahar. The Tri-tipped flame in the crown. The Lady. The King. The Flames.

Could Haegan have two out of three?

"Haegan?" Worry creased Thiel's brow. "What—"

"Will you be here . . . after?" He cast a sidelong glance to the doors, then back to her. "Please say you will be here."

"Of course." But she clung to him, frowning.

He pressed another kiss, this time to her lips, lingering.

"I beg your mercy, Prince Haegan," the sentinel spoke. "We are ordered to send you in."

The doors swung open.

Haegan lifted his chin, squeezed Thiel's hand, and stared into the Sanctuary. A massive hall with eleven columns standing in a circle around the tri-tipped flame inlaid in the marble. He strode forward, eyes on the dais that held the Council of Nine. The dense, dank air was thick with the heat of the packed room. Ignatieri. Jujak. Nobles. They stood in cordoned off sections, forming pie-shaped assemblages that left yawning gaps from each of the nine doors to the dais.

Alone, Haegan strode into the Sanctuary and straight to the inlaid Flame. He knelt and stretched his right hand forth, touching the middle tip, showing his allegiance not to the Council but to Abiassa.

He stood and straightened his doublet. "I am Prince Haegan," he said, repeating the expected words. "Heir of Zireli and Zaelero, kings of Zaethien and the Nine. Hand of Abiassa."

"Thank you, Prince Haegan," Kedulcya of Kerral said from her lavish seat. "If you would remain where you stand as the other Contenders are presented, please."

"Vid!" High Marshal Adomath shouted from the right side of the Council table.

From his left, Haegan heard the firm thud of approaching steps. A man at least ten years his senior marched forward and bowed over the Flame in ceremony as Haegan had. Broad shouldered, stern faced, the man stood. "Agremar Ro'Stu, son of Kenbrin Ro'Stu, Electreri of the Viddan Council and master sentinel."

A sentinel. Haegan shifted nervously, his gaze bouncing to the dais.

"Thank you, Sentinel Ro'Stu. You are welcomed."

"Dradith!" Adomath announced.

Though Haegan heard no steps, he saw an olive-skinned girl gliding forward. Were her feet even touching the ground? She made it to the center without effort or acknowledging him or the sentinel. On his left, the girl bowed before the Flame and the Council.

"Ociliama Herra, princessa and daughter of Oci and Liama Herra, co-rulers of Dradith." Her words were heavily drenched in the accent of her people which thickened her *S*s and lightened her *R*s.

She was no sooner welcomed than Adomath called, "Caori!"

Clipped steps clacked through the Sanctuary. A girl in a swirl of dark blue came forward, her face swathed in satin and her brown eyes fringed with dark bangs. She swept up to the Flame, bowed elegantly, then straightened. Chin high, she smiled. "Henem Comed, daughter of Brid and Hecno Comed. Electreri."

Electreri? And a master sentinel? Was he truly so horribly outmatched? Haegan searched out Gwogh at the Council table, but his old tutor looked to the newcomer with a placid smile.

"Kerral!"

In sauntered Degra Breab, daughter of Ang and Ahn Breab, also an Electreri. With her large, dark eyes and thick, black hair, braided and pearled, Degra Breab was stunning. She'd make a great queen.

Not for him. But for . . . in general.

"Praenia!"

The pronouncement brought Cypal Webst, daughter of Marq and Rovi Webst. Electreri as well.

Wicalir produced an intimidating contender in Dewyn of Adrili, who wore a doublet and the emblem of the Light Throne on his cloak. A prince, too. And an Electreri.

He is more suited than I. They all are.

Lera sent Kenro Chfra, son of Keach Chfra, Commander General of the Leran army. Electreri.

Of course.

And with each name announced, Haegan's confidence fell away. Relief rushed in at the selfish thought that he would not win and take on the responsibility of the Fire Throne, though he knew he should not embrace the thoughts. A Celahar had been on the throne since Zaelero II. Nearly two centuries.

"Hetaera," Adomath announced.

In sauntered a spritely girl barely in her twenties. Dark hair, bright eyes. She presented herself with a snap and an easy smile. "I am Arak Kcep, daughter of Duke and Duchess Wrenkyle."

"Thank you, Miss Kcep. With the others, please." Kedulcya glanced to the side before pulling her shoulders back. "As is required by the Guidings that govern the Nine," she said, her voice loud and formal, "a voice is given to the Citadel, a state in its own right among the Nine."

A figure moved from behind the curtain—Dromadric. Something in Haegan curled into a ball, like a frightened child in the dark of his bedroom, anticipating whomever the Grand Marshal would add to the Contending.

Walking without a military bearing but with hefty confidence came the final contender, wearing the overcloak of . . .

"A marshal," the girl on his left—*Henem?*—whispered.

Yes, a marshal. Highest rank of the accelerants entered into the Contending.

There is no hope for me.

That earthy scent hit Haegan again, but he ignored it as the marshal announced himself.

"I am Tortook Puthago, blood of Ahnri Puthago, chamberlain of Hetaera."

"Welcome, Marshal Puthago. Take your place with the others."

Whirling in an arrogant gesture, he slid Haegan a bored look, then stood beside Prince Dewyn. He looked five or six years older than Haegan, his blond hair shorn close. His jaw tense as he bowed with a flourish.

Insane. He could summon giants and speak a language he'd never learned, but he must contend in areas where he'd had little training. At a time when war was upon them.

Kedulcya took in a slow breath and let it out. "Now, Contenders—"

"I beg your mercy." Gwogh raised his hands to the crowds as he lumbered to his feet.

The hundreds gathered fell quiet, including Haegan. Did Gwogh have a way to stop this, to deliver him from having to contend? He would gladly and quickly take the Zaethien throne, but this . . . this game?

"I beg your mercy, Mistress," Gwogh called loudly, "Not all contenders are present."

As the mistress glanced down the line in which Haegan stood and counted, Haegan and the others did the same, wondering what Gwogh meant.

"There are nine contenders, plus the Citadel's," Kedulcya reassured them all in a partially pitched voice, motioning toward the line of accelerants. "Ten contenders."

"Aye, perhaps." Gwogh offered a strange smile. "But I have not presented my contender."

Frowning, Kedulcya motioned to Haegan. "There he stands."

With a sardonic smile, Gwogh breathed, "No." His hands went behind his back. "Prince Haegan is not the contender I refer to."

What? He wasn't Gwogh's chosen champion? How could that be? Then who represented him? Haegan frowned. As did most of the Council. Haegan fought the instinct to step back. He held his ground, refusing to reveal his own uncertainty in front of this crowd. Even his own mentor did not believe in him? The one who had poisoned him? Anger flashed over him.

"I don't understand."

"None of us do," Dromadric said, an edge in his voice.

Gwogh moved to the podium, his arthritic hands gnarled as he gripped the edges. "As the heir of Zaethien, last ruler of the Nine, Haegan of Seultrie has the inherent right to compete in the Contending. In essence, Haegan is the one the others will contend against."

"But he needs a representative," Kedulcya said. "If you are representing Haegan—"

"Mistress, who would you say represents the Fierian?"

Haegan pulled in a sharp breath and looked down. He did not want that name. Did not want anyone else knowing . . . He felt the tremors, the looks, the disapproval radiating through the room.

"Abiassa."

"Aye." Gwogh gave Haegan a sardonic smile. "As all can see, Haegan is not my contender. He is far better represented by Abiassa, no?"

A nervous laugh sifted the tension in the room.

"It took some research," Gwogh went on, "but I was able to locate a writ penned under the authority of Zaethien, heir of Baen, who was—as we all know—later known as—"

"We do not need a history lesson," Dromadric snapped.

Gwogh smiled, his eyes nearly disappearing beneath the wrinkles and bushy eyebrows. A grunting laugh echoed from him. "I'm afraid you do—I did. We all do." He held out a hand and Laertes rushed to the dais with a large, bound book, delivered it to Gwogh, then whirled around and returned to his spot.

With what seemed to be a deliberately slow turn of pages, Gwogh leafed through the book. "Ah, yes . . . in the unlikely—no, no." His finger trailed down the page, then to the next. "Yes, here." Gwogh held up a finger. "I quote—'regardless of upbringing or residence, regardless of training or loyalty, if there is found to be any of Baen's blood to exist outside the realm or within, that person will have the explicit right to contend for the Fire Throne."

Dromadric chuckled. "I think you've lost your wit along with your hair, Gwogh." He nodded to the ten. "That is why we are here, the Contending."

"Mm," Gwogh said with a smile, clearly not affected by the grand marshal's insult. "It is also why we have an eleventh contender—Baen's Blood Oath." He lifted his gnarled hand to the door. "General, please."

General Negaer stood stiffly at the door Haegan had come through, then pulled it open. Against the bright morning sun, a lone figure stood silhouetted. Head up. Shoulders back. The man strode into the Sanctuary with authority and confidence. Once the doors closed, the uniform—dark blue and bearing a sash of royalty—could be seen. He seemed unfazed by the stares of the hundreds as he came to a stop at the Flames.

Haegan gaped. "Tili."

40

The Nivaran gave no indication he'd heard his name. Haegan couldn't move. Couldn't think. Tili? A contender? Since when?

"You should bow," Degra whispered to Tili and indicated the inlay. "On the Flames."

Instead, Tili locked his gaze on the Council, unmoving.

"Announce yourself," Agremar muttered.

Tili hefted a sigh. "I am Thurig As'Tili, rightful heir of Nivar and Ybienn." He inclined his head slightly. "Northlands. Son of Thurig the Formidable and commander of the Nivari Guard."

Stricken into a stunned silence, the Sanctuary was captive to the moment.

"But he's not even a citizen of the Nine!" Cypal Webst objected.

"His loyalty isn't to the Nine. It's to Ybienn," Prince Dewyn said.

"Everyone knows Northlanders can't wield," Ociliama Herra countered. "His claim is void."

"He's gorgeous," Degra Breab purred to the other girls, making Henem and Cypal giggle.

Even as the objections poured from the contenders, Haegan felt a trembling in his own being. One that shifted from shock to disbelief.

Tili.

Tili had come to take the throne. Had Haegan's time in Ybienn shown him to be so weak that Tili felt he stood a chance to steal the Fire Throne?

Breathing became a chore. Embers warbled around his fingers and mind, fanning into outrage.

Gwogh stood at the edge of the dais. "Thank you, Prince Tili, for coming." He turned his wizened eyes to the crowd. "I present my representative for the Contending. True, he may have been born in Nivar Hold and raised in the Northlands, but he bears the same blood as our own Prince Haegan."

Gasps and murmurs shot around the room.

"They share a great-great"—he rolled his hand in a circular motion—"grandfather. Baen Celahar had three children—"

"Blasphemy," Tortook shouted.

Haegan flinched.

But his tutor slid a hand toward Tortook, snapping his mouth closed beneath a wake of heat that even Haegan felt. "Baen, who became Zaelero when he took the throne, had three children with Queen Nydessa, one of whom was Ybienn, the second-eldest son and great-however-many-grandfathers to Thurig, who fathered our fine young prince here."

"But Northlanders can't wield," came Ociliama's objection again.

Yes. Wielding. That—that's how they'd disqualify him. Yet . . . Gwogh would not have gone through the trouble of bringing the Ybiennese crown prince here if he could be disqualified.

Gwogh smiled. "Prince as'Tili?"

Nostrils flaring, Tili glowered up at the aged accelerant.

Tili hated the Nine. So why would he be here among "thin-bloods" but to rule them?

He is a dangerous enemy. The thought came unbidden. Haegan wrestled it away, remembering the prince who'd teased him. Mocked him. Had it all been a ruse? What of Thiel? Had she known what Gwogh and Tili plotted? Is that why Gwogh had her come—to soften him?

Haegan couldn't breathe. Couldn't think. Heat rushed over him. Anger choked. Calm. Calm down. The sight of Tili drawing his hand from his cloak, still glaring at the Council, and rolling his hand over and producing a pure blue-red flame stunned Haegan.

"But he's Ybiennese," someone on the Council gaped.

Gwogh returned to the table and hefted the large book. "Here is the *Tenants of Wielding and the Guiding of Wielding*. In it there is no record stating the Fire King must have been born within the Nine to take the throne. It merely states he must have noble blood and be able to wield.

The Fire King must represent the Ignatieri, as well as the citizens of the Nine." He nodded to Tili. "As Thurig's heir and able to wield, Prince as'Tili is qualified."

"This is wrong," Haegan heard himself say. Though his heart rammed in rapid succession, he tried to calm himself. "So the Northlanders wish to steal the throne, to add to the wars already besieging us."

Tili scowled at him but gave no reply.

A chorus of *ayes* went up, some shouting for Tili to go back to the frozen wasteland. Others saying he should have a chance to prove his incompetence—everyone knew Northlanders wouldn't survive the south.

"Contenders," Kedulcya spoke loudly, drawing down the tension. "Sir Gwogh is correct and Prince as'Tili's contention for the throne is accepted." When more objections started, she lifted her hand and spoke louder, this time to the eleven. "Contenders, in a moment, please exit to the rear. You will immediately gather your belongings, report to your assigned quarters, and remain there for the duration of the Contending. You can request use of the training yard at any time. Meals are served at first light, high rise, and dusk. You may interact with each other, but no one else."

Haegan cared not about interacting with anyone. Except Thiel. He wanted to know. Wanted to ask her about Tili.

Since he was first in, Haegan brought up the rear, roiling in annoyance as Tili fell into step beside him. "Think not that I will give mercy for this."

"Think not that I intend to ask, thin-blood," Tili bit back.

"'Tis *my* father's throne." Haegan kept his gaze straight ahead as they stepped into the sunlight of the courtyard.

Tili turned to him, cuffed his arm. "I no more wish to rule the Nine than ye would the Northlands. But I will not disgrace my father as ye have yers."

Haegan gaped. "You dare—"

"Earn it, thin-blood. Earn it well." He spun and collided with a flutter of fabric. "I beg yer mercy, mistress."

Degra Breab curtseyed low. "And I beg yours, Prince as'Tili."

Tili gave Haegan one more warning look, then stalked across the courtyard. When he did, Haegan saw Thiel. The two talked quietly, gave a brief hug, then Tili vanished down the passage.

You were never good enough for her. Even she knows you won't win.

Haegan stormed toward her. "You knew? You knew why he was here, yet you said nothing to me. He is as deceptive as Dirag the Desecrator, coming here to steal my father's throne."

Her hand flew fast and true. Stung his cheek. "How dare ye!"

Anger unabated, Haegan stepped in. "Is it the power? Is it that you think I will not win, so at least your brother can take the throne and secure you a life of luxury?"

Hurt and anger flashed through her eyes. "Ye know me better than that, Haegan—or at least, I thought ye did." A crease formed between her eyes. "What has happened to ye?" She shook her head, stepping away. "Ye are not the man I knew." Another few steps backward. She started to turn, hesitated, but then left.

Haegan sniffed. *Let her go. You're from different worlds.*

That smell . . . it was here again. He wiped the tip of his nose, trying to rid himself of the spicy scent. What was it? It was giving him a headache.

A flicker of black and red Ignatieri robes whisked onto the garden path leading from the Sanctuary to the Citadel.

Watching Thiel walk away had been akin to having the earth rip open between them and gape like a deep, black chasm. Emptiness. Darkness. Coldness. He stood alone in the courtyard, emptied of accelerants and contenders. Alone.

41

Thiel threw open the door to the residence chambers Gwogh provided for her and Tili—before her brother's plan to betray Haegan was announced before Abiassa and everyone. She swung around and slammed the door. It rattled, the locks catching. She kicked it with a growl.

"I guess you heard the news, too?"

Thiel spun, startled to find her friends in the seating area. "What are ye doing here?"

"We come t' talk wif yous about da trial—it's not fair, whats being done t' Haegan," Laertes said. "I fought your bro'va what's da prince was his friend."

"What is going on?" Tokar asked, arms folded. "You show up with them and suddenly, your brother is making a move for the throne."

Praegur stood near the window, arms folded loosely but his expression tight. His silent disappointment was nearly as scalding as Haegan's words.

And enough to push Thiel past the point of reason. "And naturally—like Haegan—ye think I knew and am party to this . . . this . . ."

"Betrayal?" Tokar arched an eyebrow.

Thiel wished she could wield. Wished she could spark that smug look right off Tokar's face. But he was right. It *was* a betrayal. An enormous one. "I did not know about this."

"But yous came wif dem t' da city," Laertes said.

"Aye, because Gwogh said . . . Oh, blazes of flames and fury." She shoved her hand through her hair and dug her fingers into her scalp.

"I am a fool! Gwogh told me Haegan needed me, that what he would face . . ." And she'd played right into it. Thiel growled.

"Tili," Tokar said. "He knew, though?"

Though that's what he asked, Thiel knew that wasn't Tokar's question. "I . . ."

Laertes looked up at her from beneath the golden fringe of hair. "Was dat *aye* or *I*?"

Thiel moved to the overstuffed chair in the corner and sat, pulling her knees to her chest. She straightened the skirts. "Would that I could say he knew not the plan, that he—like me—came to Hetaera as support for Haegan, but . . ."

Thiel couldn't help but look at Praegur, wishing for sage words. Warm comfort of his wisdom. Part of her hated that his words were now only for Haegan. But she saw—felt—his sadness. His grief. She shared in that.

"He knew." Finality coated Tokar's words as he lowered himself to the sofa. Perched on the edge, elbows on his knees, he stared at the fire. "I didn't think your brother capable of that. I trained under him, respected him . . ."

Grief churned through Thiel. "I want to believe there is some explanation. He liked Haegan."

"Don't have to *dis*like the former king's heir to seize a chance at power."

Thiel closed her eyes. This could not be right. Tili didn't want the Nine. What was happening? "Haegan blames me, too. He thinks I conspired against him, withheld what Tili intended to do."

"Bet that ticked him off."

"He all but called him Dirag the Desecrator."

Tokar's eyebrows rose. "Amazed he didn't singe you."

"I think he might have, if I hadn't slapped him." She pinched the bridge of her nose, then punched to her feet. "How could they do this to him? It's bad enough that there are ten other contenders . . ."

"And who are dey t' steal Haegan's frone from 'im?" The lad shook his head. "It ain't right."

"*Isn't* right," Thiel corrected, then groaned. "Blazes, now I'm doing it." She cast a look across the room to Tokar, who seemed especially put out. "Is there anything we can do?"

Tokar folded his arms as he sat back. "It's in the Guidings—the Law."
He shrugged.

"I know," Laertes said, eyes wide. "He's your bro'ver and will listen
t' yous. So, go and tell him he should back out. Not t' do dis evil 'fing."

It was a simplistic approach. A naïve one. "I fear my brother would
no sooner listen to me than any of you. His mind is set—and to remove
himself now would be to shame our father." She sighed, but then drew
up the dregs of her determination. "But I will tell you this—my brother
will hear from me."

"But they're sequestered," Tokar said.

Thiel grinned. "Since when has a rule like that kept us from entering
a place?"

"Never—but this is the Citadel. Guarded by sentinels, and security is
high with so many of their best in one place." Tokar shook his head. "And
to be honest, now that I'm training with the Jujak, I don't want a mark on
my record that stops me from becoming a full recruit."

"Well, I'm going." Thiel punched to her feet. "My brother owes me an
explanation—as does Gwogh."

Praegur grunted. Tapped the window, nodding to something.

Thiel hurried to his side. Saw her brother, sack slung over his back,
crossing the large cobbled area. She sucked in a breath and whirled for
the door. She sprinted out of the residence and down the staircase, using
the balustrade to spin her in the direction of the side exit. Thiel burst into
the afternoon with a mission and scanned for her brother.

There. Nearly at the Citadel barracks. "Tili!" She plunged across the
lawn. The distance wasn't great but it seemed to take forever to reach
him. "Tili, wait!"

On the steps, he turned, looking in her direction.

She raced the last thirty paces and slid up next to him. "What are ye
doing?" she said around a jagged breath.

The planes of his face were smooth, hard. "Entering the barracks."

Narrowing her eyes she leaned into him, panting. "Thurig as'Tili, ye
know full well what I mean. Why are ye doing this?"

"Thiel, go back to the residence. Wait for him. He—"

"He'll what? *Need* me? That's what ye and yer conspirator said, is it not? But he won't." Her heart thumped hard. "He believes me to be a part of yer plan to steal his father's throne."

"The throne is Abiassa's," he said.

With both hands, Thiel shoved him back. "Ye dare."

He dropped his sack, probably instinct, and held up his palms. But she'd been in the training yard with him enough to know it was a tactical move, a stance he could readily respond from. "Thiel . . ." Warning hung in his tone.

"Does Papa know?" Her nostrils flared. "And Gwogh—how? Why? Haegan struggles enough as it is—"

"*Aye.*" Terse, intentional meaning streaked through his answer and eyes.

Her breath caught. "Ye mean to do it. To take the throne—" She gulped fear and adrenaline. "Tili, ye promised to have his back. Did ye mean so ye could drive a dagger in it?"

Hurt knotted his brow. Tili retrieved his sack. "Go back to the residence, Thiel."

She punched him. She hadn't intended to, but the anger erupted. Forced her to act.

His muscles contracted. His jaw muscle popped. Fists clenched. But instead of sending her to the ground, Tili turned and entered the barracks.

"He was right—ye are as Dirag reborn!"

• • •

Haegan stood in the training yard, bouncing flames back and forth in a ridiculously absurd test of skill. His partner on this, the fifth round, was Henem Comed. She bounced a volley back to him, and he returned it, though it went wide since—in earnest—who cared about this exercise?

She laughed and lunged to catch it, her dark hair spilling out and the headdress slipping around her shoulders. Henem ignored the covering, grinning as she reignited a volley and tossed it to him.

Dromadric's words rang in his head: that he wasn't meant to patrol, that he would not win the Contending. What then was the point of participating?

"We came to Fieri Keep once." Henem's words drifted through his bad mood.

What did he care, too, if she had been to his home? He had spent his days up in the tower, so he had not seen her.

"You and I went out to the dunes by the Lakes of Fire."

Haegan snapped out the volley. Scowled. "You are mistaken. I was crippled—"

Her smile wavered. "You were only five when I came."

"Oh."

She sniffed. "Of course, the queen was furious with you for soiling your clothes. And me for turning my hair black with soot—it was blonde then, like yours."

He wished he remembered. Or cared. Which was atrocious of him, but it had not escaped his notice that the contending females had been paired with males. As if to test alignments. Did Henem hope for a husband, if she failed the trials?

"I'm sure you've forgotten," she said, her words hushed in embarrassment.

"I beg your mercy. My"—he wouldn't admit he couldn't remember—"thoughts are elsewhere."

"I imagine, with all of us vying for the Fire Throne." Henem lifted a shoulder in a shrug. "I want you to know, I'm here because I was told to come. But I won't win."

Neither will I. They both glanced over the training yard. Puthago and Degra were engaged in a battle of wits, it seemed, with dagger-like volleys of words pitched back and forth along with the flame.

"Puthago is vicious," Henem said, "but he's also lazy. It gives an advantage. He takes the shortest route in the hope it'll work. But he doesn't do well with strategy, which is one of Degra's skills."

Haegan watched Puthago throwing short, quick bursts. And Degra countered, using more intricate wielding, her returns swinging wide. Puthago narrowly avoided a graze to his temple. His eyes widened and his lips thinned as he shoved a burst at his partner.

Which Degra slid back—in a high arc.

"Ha," Puthago gloated.

The arc stabbed straight down. Seared a line down Puthago's cheek.

He cried out, holding his hand to the burn. Eyes flamed. Anger flared and he overreacted.

Haegan saw it before it happened. The blast that could kill. Without thinking, he thrust a hand out. A glowing white trail seared the air and knocked Puthago off balance. His blast went wide.

Only as Puthago came to his feet did Haegan realize what he'd done.

"Flames!" Henem said with a smile. "How—it was so fast. How did you do that? I had just seen his searing when you were already countering."

Haegan had no answer. But remembered Dromadric saying his wielding obeyed his thoughts without his trying.

A bell gonged, ordering them to switch partners. Adomath stood on the observation deck and handed out the new assignments, pairing Haegan this time with Degra. They moved to the outer edge and went through the mind-numbing rituals that accelerants called forms.

"Don't think because you stunted his volley, that I owe you anything."

Haegan frowned. Had he said anything like that?

"You're a weak scourge, Fierian."

The insult cut. But Henem's words tugged at him—Degra used strategy. Got in her opponent's head, defeated her foe. Was that her plan? To make him doubt himself? Too bad he didn't have the ability or training to inflame her thoughts.

"They should take your throne away."

"Angering me only makes my gift more powerful, Degra."

"Does it?" She arched an eyebrow. "Show me."

Her greedy gleam made him realize he'd given away a tactic. Yes, he was more powerful, but he was also less focused. Less able to control what happened. It just sort of . . . happened. As if someone else controlled the wielding.

He should distract her. Over her shoulder, Tili wielded with Cypal Webst. "They seem a good pair." Only because of the comment Degra made in the Sanctuary did he take that route. Her pandering to the prince, whom he'd once called friend.

She looked back, holding the wake between her fingers. Then without looking at him, she flicked the ball.

Haegan quenched it and tossed it at her.

Hand up, she bounced it back.

Was he dead yet? Because that would be better than this. Bored. So bored. So annoyed. He hated it. Hated sparring. Poired was out there raping the land and killing citizens of the Nine and Haegan was here . . . *vying for a throne.*

The gong rang again, and he headed toward the deck.

"Now we begin the inflaming trials," Adomath said. "Kenro, report to the grand marshal's chamber. The rest of you—lunch. You'll eat and study until you are called."

Tili moved with purpose out of the yard, narrowly avoiding bumping Haegan's shoulder. Haegan gritted his teeth. But . . . up in the viewing stand, he noticed something. He wasn't sure what, but his mind had snagged on it. He scanned the faces. Saw no one he knew. Of course. Only family members were allowed—Thiel could have come, but she hadn't. And Haegan had no family here.

His thoughts jumped to Kaelyria. How was she?

The face.

Haegan hyperfocused. Darted his gaze over each person. His mind registered shock—Drracien? He stood behind someone.

Just then, like a wisp of smoke, Drracien disappeared.

"Thin-blood," came Tili's taunting call.

Haegan looked back.

"Food. Ye're a little pale."

Anger plucked at Haegan, but before he moved, he again checked the stand. Drracien wouldn't be foolish enough to come here. Would he?

Haegan stowed his specially-treated gear to protect against burns, and headed out. He walked the narrow boardwalk between the training yard and the Citadel. The boardwalk had plastered walls on both sides that were kept in pristine condition. Even the locked doors were highly polished Caorian oak, a very expensive wood he'd only seen in Fieri Keep and Nivar Hold. Haegan came upon one, scanning the carved images. A battle scene. Zaelero.

Would he ever rise to be as great? Or would he shame the name of his ancestor?

As the thoughts and questions tumbled in his mind, he noticed the lock. Not latched. Alarmed, he nudged it open. Peered carefully past the step that led down into a meadow, the warmer weather just coaxing new life from the grass. A half league away, a copse of trees provided twiggy shade.

A figure moved there. Female.

Wait. He craned his head. "Thiel?" His heart skipped a beat, though he reminded himself he was angry with her. But had she been waiting? To apologize? He checked both sides of the boardwalk, then plunged into the field, shutting the door behind him. If someone locked it, he'd be caught.

But he didn't care.

He jogged across the open field. "Thiel?"

To the right, she moved deeper into the trees.

Haegan slowed as he came upon her spot. "Why are you seeking me out? I thought—" He stopped short. The face wasn't familiar. No—it was. But not Thiel's. "Who—"

From the side. He felt it. A shift in the air. In the tension of the way the breeze moved. Haegan lifted a hand. Pain scored his cheek. Flung him backward. His head thudded against a tree. He slid sideways.

The attacker was on him. Pinned him to the ground and threw another punch. Haegan remembered Aselan's training. He thrust two fingers at the attacker's throat and the man fell away.

Haegan pulled himself up.

Saw a glint of steel. They were going to kill him! "Augh!" He threw up his hand. The next few seconds blurred. The attacker swung back and upward, somehow suspended in the air above him, hand extended with the dagger.

Haegan scrabbled away, finally looking at his attacker's face—and stilled. "I—I know you."

A girl. Eyes were frantic, but she didn't move.

That's when he realized he'd somehow haloed her as Thurig had done to him many, many times. Haegan snatched the blade, his touch breaking the halo. She dropped hard, her forehead bouncing off the ground. She rolled to the side and moaned.

The man was on his feet.

Haegan set his right foot back and held the dagger toward him. "Stand down, or I will kill you."

"With dagger or fire?"

Haegan flexed his jaw. "Whatever it takes." And it hit him, the sprigs of new foliage behind the man. The girl. "You . . . you two were at the Great Falls."

The girl came off the ground, heel of her hand to her chin, stretching her jaw.

"What are you doing here?" he demanded.

"Easy." The man motioned placating hands at Haegan. "We're not here to kill you."

The girl shot him a look of surprise.

Sister. That's right. "Your sister disagrees." What was her name again? He'd only heard it once, but it was something like Asteria.

"Astadia wants to kill you for beating her."

Yeah. Astadia. She was a lot like Thiel. Not as pretty, but just as feisty. Haegan flipped her dagger. Holding the blade, he extended it to her.

Her eyes widened as she tentatively took it.

"You aren't here to kill me?"

Astadia looked to her brother. Shook her head.

The brother sighed. "Our intention is not to harm you—"

"Good, since you gave your word at the Falls not to harm me or my friends." He shrugged. "So, you lured me out here for what purpose?"

"We are to take you back to Iteveria."

Haegan blinked. "I will go nowhere with you."

Shouts went up from the training yard. His name carried on the wind.

"They've noticed I'm missing," Haegan said. "If I were you, I would leave the city before I have time to alert the Sentinels or Jujak."

The man took a step forward, hands still out wide in a gesture of peace. "If I could have just a word first . . ."

42

As soon as the thin-blood entered, Tili locked onto him. It'd taken Haegan too long to walk from the yard to the chow hall. Tili lowered his fork when he spotted the knot on his cheekbone. And a scrape. What happened?

Haegan accepted a plate of food from the server and made his way to an empty table, where he sat at an angle, shouldering Tili out of his view. His head low, he scooted the food around his plate, not really eating. What weighed on the prince's mind? Who had he encountered that left reminders, yet did not provoke the prince to report the incident?

Tili lifted his plate. Stood and moved to the table with Haegan. He slid it down. "To whom do I owe the thanks?"

Though Haegan's gaze slipped a peek, he did not raise his head. Or respond. Lips went tight. Jaw muscle twitched beneath fuzz.

Settling on the bench, Tili hooked his arms around his plate, focused on the prince. "The knot—looks like ye got punched. Who can I thank?"

Haegan jerked his head down. "Nobody. I walked into a door."

Now he lies. "The Contenders will enjoy hearing that," Tili said, finishing off his bland meal, missing Ybiennese food, with its spices and meats and vegetables. "Ye're making it too easy for them."

"Them?" Haegan stabbed a small piece of meat and lifted it to his mouth. "Or you? And what do you care as long as you win?"

"So 'tis fair to be petulant and shame yer father?"

"Don't," Haegan growled.

Tili held his gaze. Let the prince think what he would about Tili's motives. But he would not abide abuse toward the prince or any of those he considered family or friend. That he'd been attacked and hadn't reported it . . . "Who punched ye?"

"I told you—"

"Ye *lied*." Chin tucked, he drove his gaze into Haegan. "I saw more strength in ye in Ybienn than here. I know not what's chipping away at ye, but get yer head on straight or ye guarantee losing that Fire Throne, Princeling."

Haegan's gaze flickered. "That would make it easier for you, so why do you care?"

"I do not need anything made easy for me. But the Contending—'tis not only about wielding, thin-blood. 'Tis the head—and ye have a good one, if ye dare use it."

"Why are you doing this? Why come for the throne? You don't even like the Southlands."

Tili nearly looked away. But he must focus the prince. "Where were ye? What took ye so long to come from the training yard?" Maybe another tactic would work. "If ye were with my sister, blazes help me, I will put ye down."

Haegan scoffed. "You think she did this to me?"

"She didn't?"

"It wasn't Thiel, but by the Lady, I wish it was. I'm so sick of this. Poired is out there, and we're in here—sparring."

"And ye are ready to face him?"

"Aye," Haegan hissed.

Tili set a challenge in his eyes and barked, "Because ye finally have control of that gift?"

Shoving up, Haegan snorted. "I don't need lectures. I would try, rather than hide in here with you, oath breaker. "

"Ye should *try* something other than simpering and scurrying away like the tunnel rat Kiethiel calls ye."

Haegan leaned over the table, breathing heavily.

Tili came up, meeting him. "If ye worked to deserve that gift ye have, if ye were focused on being the Fierian, ye would have a chance." He straightened, stepped back, then tapped the metal plate. "This Contending will prove one thing."

"What's that?"

"That any one of us on that throne is better than ye!"

• • •

Heat warbled around his hands, surging from the pit of his stomach as he watched Tili stride away. Haegan flexed his fingers, the Northlander's reprimand ringing in his ears. It been the final knife to his courage. As if Astadia's dagger *had* cut through him. He wished it had. Then he would be dead. Freed of this curse.

"It's not true," came a soft voice from his left.

Haegan shifted his gaze enough to see the sleeve of Henem's tunic beside him. He felt the wood bench creak as she joined him.

"I wouldn't be better," she said. "I might have abilities with the Flames, but I'm not a ruler. Much to my father's dismay."

If she was looking to someone for binding, she was aiming at the wrong target.

Henem leaned closer, her hair brushing against his arm. "Did you know—"

Why wouldn't she just leave him alone? He huffed and turned to her. "I am pledged." Not technically but close enough.

She drew up. "I beg your mercy?"

"I'm pledged to someone else. I love her." Though he was furiously angry with her. But he held his ground with Henem.

"As am I. We marry at the next full moons." Her brows rippled in confusion. "Wait—you thought—" She laughed.

Haegan punched to his feet and stalked away. Only as he moved did he see Kenro sitting at the table with his head in his heads, his expression blank. Beside him, Ociliama rubbed his back.

Haegan hesitated.

Ociliama shook her head.

Inflaming. Why would the marshals let those already interviewed return to the mess hall?

To scare us.

Haegan stalked out of the dining hall. The inflaming was all about manipulating thoughts. Dromadric had done that to him already. It'd been terrifying, but . . . not terrible.

"They use your worst fears."

He stopped and looked over his shoulder to Degra, who sat on the half wall, her legs hugged to her chest the way Thiel often did, all trace of her former animosity gone. "Who does?"

"The high lord and grand marshal—they draw out your greatest fear."

He turned toward her, noting the way she drew away from him. "You've already been?"

A nod.

"What is the point of exposing a fear?"

"To see how you react to your worst dreams. To simply know what that fear is, so we face it."

But it was handy information for the grand marshal to know every-one's fear, wasn't it? "Dromadric did that to me in the training yard a couple of days ago—used a fear against me to exploit my gift."

"Are you really the Fierian?"

Haegan shook his head and lifted his shoulder in a halfhearted shrug. "So they say."

"In Kerral, they teach that the Fierian is the savior. He'll free us from the plagues."

Haegan snorted. "How?"

She shrugged. "I don't know. But there's always an illness of some kind. The air is rife with it, and the waters are contaminated. It's why most are leaving."

"But my father spoke highly of Kerral. He loved it there—the rugged terrain. How long has it been like that?"

"Last two years. It's bad. I was so relieved with Mistress Kedulcya plucked me from the training yard."

"Prince Haegan!" Adomath called across the courtyard.

Haegan spotted Adomath standing at the entrance to the high tower, where the offices and classrooms were.

"Your turn," Degra said.

Haegan started toward the high lord, but Degra caught his arm.

"Just remember," she whispered, "You're only as strong as you think you are."

Which meant he wasn't strong at all.

43

Blindfolded, Haegan was led through a maze of passages. But then the hand of his guide fell away and Haegan waited. A cool breeze swirled around him, tinged with a spicy—*that* spicy—scent. He'd really grown to hate the chill in the air away from the Lakes of Fire. "What is that smell?" he muttered to himself.

But wait . . .

The last time he felt that chill someone had been wielding. The incipients in Baen's Crossing. As he remained in place, the temperature dropped. So . . . the strange chill and smell. Were they associated with incipient wielding?

No, that wasn't possible. He stood in the great Citadel.

An ache spread up his neck. Freezing yet burning. His head—his head throbbed, like his brain was swelling and pushing against his skull. Haegan gritted his teeth against the sensation, turning his head to try to ward it off. He rubbed the base of his neck, trying to loosen the knot that sent shooting pain up into his head.

A taste, bitter and minty, coated his tongue.

Nausea swirled.

Haegan fisted his hand, braced against it. He would not be sick. No weakness. He must fight. Must retain the right to the Fire throne.

Why? You don't want it.

It was true. He didn't want it. He'd shown himself to be more than incapable. He disgraced his father's name, shamed him. His father, the mighty Fire King. One of the most powerful since Baen. And he had Haegan for a son.

Failure. Embarrassment.

"You can remove the blindfold," a voice spoke calmly.

Haegan tugged it off. Blinked rapidly as he took in the setting. The training yard. He groaned. Must he show his ineptitude again? The gates squeaked and his heart hitched. *No, not again.*

Six massive icehounds, their fur dingy gray and eyes glowing, stalked him as they emerged from the shadows.

Wait. *They're not real.* He remembered. Dromadric had done this before. Haegan relaxed, though his mind wrestled with what it saw, what it smelled.

Smelled? He didn't recall a smell last time.

The closest one snapped.

Haegan watched it, not moving. He'd be strong. Show them. Besides, this was conjured from his fears. Did they think he wouldn't remember this scenario?

Another lunged into the air.

For fun, Haegan flicked a spark.

The icehound came unheeding.

It's not real. It's not real. Instinct drew up his arm.

The hound clamped on. He stared in confused horror as the icehound's teeth sank into his flesh. White-hot pain streaked through him. "Augh!"

He dropped to his knees, the agony unbearable. The teeth were like blades; all sliced his skin at once.

Alarm shot through him. The hounds were real. He had to protect himself. They'd tricked him. He flung up his arm. Light exploded and with a yelp his arm was free. Haegan searched the yard. The hounds that remained lay unmoving.

A man bent over one of the bodies.

Blond hair. Green tunic. Tri-tipped flame and crown.

The man rose, slowly turned.

"Father!" A tickling sensation in his forearm reminded him of the bite. He wrapped it with the tail of his shirt as he started forward.

Flames roared, separating them.

He lifted a hand to protect his face, arching away from the inferno. No, this wasn't possible. His father was dead. Killed by Poired. Was the fire real? Each step he took made the heat hotter. The flames louder.

That's when he noticed his father yelling something. Waving him back. "No, don't come for me." He then turned and knelt at the hound again.

Only it wasn't a hound. "Thiel!" She lay curled on her side, her dark hair spilling over the ground. And blood. So much blood.

Haegan cared not what flames stood between them. He threw himself forward. Fire tore at his clothes. Singed them. But he was through.

His father was gone. "Father?" Haegan looked around.

No, he's dead.

But Thiel . . .

She lay at his feet now, blood haloing her head. They wanted him to think he'd struck her with his blast. But he hadn't. He'd struck the hound.

Was she real? Or wasn't she? He hated this game. Why keep throwing scenarios then erase them? It only strengthened his resolve not to be afraid.

The hound was real. His father wasn't.

He had to know if Thiel was real. Haegan knelt . . . and stretched out a hand for her. But he drew it back, feeling foolish. She couldn't be here. This was the inflaming.

His stomach roiled. That smell filled his nostrils again.

Haegan reached toward her. Touched her. Real. Soft, warm. "No!" He rolled her over. Her arm flopped to the side, limp. "No! Thiel, please!"

But she wasn't moving. Wasn't breathing.

"Please!" It couldn't be true. "You can't die!" He pulled her into his arms. Her lifeless form slumped against him.

Anger roiled through him. He howled.

Crack!

Haegan blinked way the tears. Light flooded the training yard. He glanced about, confused at the change. But Thiel . . .

He looked to her.

And shoved back with a shout.

She was gone. In her place a stuffed target.

Haegan climbed to his feet. Swiped at the tears. Fought the anger. "This is useless," he shouted. "Are you done yet?"

Adomath emerged from a side chamber. "The test is over, Prince."

Breathing hard, shaking off the belief of Thiel's death, he ground his teeth. "This is a waste of time."

"Everyone must be tested." Adomath pointed to the boardwalk. "You can go now."

Exhausted, furious, Haegan huffed. Stomped out into the passageway.

A howl rent the afternoon. Darkness spread over the sky. The claxon at the city gate sounded, its wail piercing. Shouts and orders rang out on the other side of the wall. Haegan scaled it and saw Jujak and Sentinels sprinting toward the main gates with shouts of "Poired!" and "The Dark One attacks!"

Boom!

A concussion pitched Haegan backward. He caught himself, then jumped from the wall. He sprinted through the streets, aiming for the main gate. People screamed and shoved. Dogs nipped at his heels.

He pushed through, determined to make it to the front. He would not let Poired kill another person. Not one more.

But you're weak.

Haegan slowed—then reprimanded himself. He could not be weak. Could not fail.

Where were the Grindas and Negaer? Jujak clogged the streets, warning the people back into their homes.

"No," Haegan shouted, but his voice was lost in the chaos. "Not in their homes. To the fields!" If they stayed in the structures, they'd burn with them. "To the fields. Get to the fields!"

But nobody listened. They ran. They screamed. They fell. They raged.

Haegan must get to the gate. It was the only way to save Hetaera. To stop Poired and save the Nine as well. But it was like trying to wade through a churning sea, so thick were the citizens and panicked animals. They pushed against him. Forced him back.

He shoved his hand forward, wielding. A path cleared, the people nudged out of his way. *See? I can do it.* Control. He had control.

Within seconds, he was at the foot gate.

General Grinda sat atop his horse.

Wasn't he too exposed? "General"—even as Haegan spoke the name, the general looked at him, then to the side—"you should move back."

Then Haegan followed the general's gaze. Off to the right, Kaelyria sat in a wheeled chair. "No!"

Arrows thudded into Grinda's chest. A fireball knocked him off his mount. He dropped on a sea of people, who carried him away in their panic.

"No! Nooo!" Haegan gripped his head. Not Grinda! He was like a father to him. He had to get to Kaelyria before—

"Fierian," a voice roared into the static din. "Face me!"

Haegan swallowed, watching as the bridge cleared of people, toppling aside until Poired Dyrth was revealed in the act of beheading his sister.

"Nooo!" Haegan's gut churned. He felt sick.

You'll only fail.

Poired grabbed Kaelyria's bloodied head by the hair and lifted it from the ground, then cast it aside. "You're the last Celahar, Prince. Let's end this!"

I can't do it. Anger pushed him around the thought. He crossed his arms. Drew them to his sides. Then shoved out. The shot was perfect. Spirited straight toward Poired. Powerful. Thrumming.

The Dark One froze. Looked shocked.

But the flames rippled. Sputtered. Died.

Poired roared, his laughter haunting and menacing.

"No," Haegan breathed. It was a perfect shot. How had he missed?

Because you can't control it. You're weak.

He tried again. This time, the volley died even sooner.

Poired laughed harder. "You are so weak. A disgrace."

"No."

"It is good Zireli is dead so he cannot see the failure you are!"

Haegan shoved outward but nothing happened.

Poired leered. "Dried up, Fierian?" With but a puff of air, an entire mountain of fire barreled at Haegan.

He dropped and shielded himself, feeling the searing heat wash over his spine. He lifted his head, peeking through the flames . . .

And saw another man. Lying in a dark, dank corner. A gnarly beard wreathed his face. Eyes nearly swollen shut. His lips were cracked, bleeding. His limbs hung out of the clothes like sticks. Vacant eyes stared at Haegan.

Then the skeletal man lifted his head with a vestige of former dignity. And he knew. *Knew.* "Father."

A bony hand reached toward Haegan, his father giving a guttural cry. Haegan surged forward. "Father!"

Hiss. Clank. Pop!

The world snapped away.

44

"Grand Marshal! Grand Marshal!"

Gwogh hurried in the opposite direction of Adomath, who rushed toward their brother, who had collapsed in his chair. Gwogh raced to Haegan's prone form and knelt. Blood seeped from his nose.

"Kedulcya, we need your gifts," Gwogh called, but when he looked up, she was tending the grand marshal. "Leave him. This boy is our hope, our future."

She hesitated for a moment, then came to him. She moved her hands over Haegan's body. "His signatures are"—she shook her head—"phenomenal. So high, I can't get a reading." Forlorn eyes came to Gwogh. "I can't do anything."

"You must."

"I don't know where to start!"

"Start where it's hottest—he overexerted."

With a huff, she focused her healing efforts, eyes closed. Hands trailing an inch over Haegan's body. Down then up. Up then down. She finally came to rest over his head. She frowned. Screwed her brow tight. Her fingers moved as if she were massaging his muscles. But she massaged air.

"He's . . . I think he's fine. Just . . . resting." With a reassuring nod, she climbed to her feet and returned to the grand marshal.

Gwogh motioned to Kelviel and Griese. "Remove the prince to the sofa." As the men did so, he watched Kedulcya. "How is the grand marshal?"

"He needs a pharmakeia." She wrung her hands. "He has significant injury to his head and heart."

"What is wrong?" Adomath demanded. "This has never happened! He's done the inflaming on every accelerant in this Citadel."

"Yes," Gwogh said, his voice grave, "but never on the Fierian."

"What does that mean?" Adomath growled. "He is the grand marshal!"

"None of us has the answer." Gwogh could only offer that, as it was the truth. And any speculation at this point would be foolish.

"We are in uncharted territory," Kelviel agreed.

There was something in his voice that drew Gwogh's attention. But the pharmakeia from the first floor rushed in to tend the grand marshal. A few moments later, four sentinels came in with a cot to transfer Dromadric from his office to his bedroom under the pharmakeia's supervision.

"Are you well?" Gwogh asked Kelviel.

The Hetaeran representative nodded. Then shook his head. "I saw him again."

Gwogh's chest tightened. Dare he ask? "Who?"

"The Deliverer."

Eyes wide, Gwogh tried to take it in. Looked around, half expecting to see Medric again. "The same one?"

An almost imperceptible nod. "Only at the end. Right before they both collapsed.

"What did he do?"

Kelviel gave a sharp shake of his head. "Stood between them. It was like he thought that should be enough." He rubbed his forehead. "Then his sword vanished and he snapped out his arms to them."

Gwogh glanced at the prince again.

"And light—light exploded. When it cleared, Haegan was down. And the grand marshal. He severed the connection." Kelviel stared as if still seeing the Deliverer. "To protect him."

"Haegan, yes . . ."

"No, Dromadric."

"Tell no one of this."

"I have no desire to." He frowned. "But why not?"

"If Medric has appeared—if he had to intervene . . ." Gwogh did not want to voice his thoughts. He let his gaze drift to the door they'd carried the grand marshal through. "Let's remove the prince to the mansion."

"Not the barracks?" Kelviel asked.

"No, there will be no more trials for him. At least, not from the Contending."

• • •

The scent of jasmine and cordi dug through his brain. Haegan shifted, felt something solid at his side. He pried his eyes open.

A round face peered up at him. Beautiful brown eyes. Rosy lips. A smile to make all aches go away.

When he leaned forward, he froze. Inflaming? Was he in the trials still? He sucked in a painful breath.

Thiel pushed up. "What's wrong?"

Haegan tensed. Swallowed. "My neck . . ." But he blinked. "How . . . how are you here? We're not allowed visitors—"

"I snuck in," she said, smiling softly. "Should I get the pharmakeia?"

"No." Haegan lifted an arm. Groaned. He pried open his eyes again. Though he lay on his bed, it was the one in Celahar Mansion, not the barracks. And Thiel had been lying beside him. A good thing her brother had not known her whereabouts.

The trial—seeing Kaelyria murdered, though through Inflaming— haunted him. "My sister . . ." He dropped back against the pillow. "Why does my head hurt so much?"

"Sir Gwogh said it was the inflaming," Thiel explained. "Though he gave no further explanation. Just that ye must rest. But I saw the worry in his eyes, so I came."

He rubbed his temple. "I had no idea what was real and what wasn't." With a sigh, he closed his eyes again. They'd made him think Thiel was dead. He looked at her. Touched her arm. "Real."

She smiled. "Aye."

"I feel like a Drigo pummeled me into the ground," Haegan said, trying to swallow against a dry mouth. He coughed.

"Water," Thiel muttered as she lifted a pitcher from the stand and poured a glass for him. "I hear ye fared much better than the grand marshal."

Haegan frowned. "Is he"—*what if he'd killed him?*—"well?"

Thiel handed him a glass. "I heard he is recovering but very ill."

"The trials." Haegan felt a stab of panic, which made everything hurt all over again. "I need—"

"Ye're not in them any longer," Thiel said.

"But the throne—"

"I'm pretty sure ye more than proved yerself, whatever they were after," Thiel said, annoyance on her pretty face.

"I injured the grand marshal—they will not easily grant mercy for that," Haegan snapped.

"Please, don't worry about it. Rest. 'Tis important. Ye were badly injured."

She placates me. "You would have your brother win the trials?"

"Do not start that again." She scowled. "I would have ye well enough to do what Abiassa wants of ye."

Evading the question. "I thought you believed in me. But you showed up with your brother, who is trying to take the throne."

"Haegan, please—"

"Why don't you leave, so I can rest."

Hurt roiled through her face. "I only want—"

"I know what you want," he growled. "Go on. Go. I need to rest and do not need you milk-maiding me."

"Milk-ma—"

"If you will excuse us," came Gwogh's gravelly voice. "I would have a word with the prince."

Thiel whirled, startled.

"And I am sure it is only our prince's exhaustion concealing his manners at this hour," Gwogh said. "And I will grant mercy for your presence here, Princess."

Guilt-ridden at his treatment of her, Haegan stared at the cup he held, relieved when she hurried out the door. "What happened to me?" he asked, anxious to have the massive memory gap filled.

"What do you remember?"

"Besides that"—he shook his head, the world tilting—"nightmare?" He waited for his vision to clear. "Nothing."

"The inflaming. Can you tell me what you saw?"

A whirl of thoughts and images swarmed him. Around a moan, he said, "It's all muddled."

"Take your time."

Haegan considered his tutor. "You only say that when you're digging for information."

"With a very large shovel." Gwogh smiled. "When you're ready."

With another groan, Haegan launched into a detailed account of what he'd experienced. The hounds. The attack, Grinda, Kaelyria. Poired.

"You are afraid you can't protect her," Gwogh said when Haegan mentioned Thiel.

"Aye," Haegan said, hating himself for ordering her out of the room just now.

"And when you faced Poired? What happened then?"

Haegan swallowed. "I tried to wield, but nothing could touch him. Everything fell short. Then shorter and shorter, until I could no longer wield at all. Then he blasted me. I ducked, threw up a shield to protect myself, and as it rushed over me, I saw him."

"Poired?"

"No." He could see him still. "A bearded man. In a pitch-black area. His skin seemed to glow. I think it might have been a cell. But he was ghost-thin with a thick, dirty beard. Then he lifted his head." Haegan swallowed. Hard. His heart thrummed, remembering. Aching. "It was my father. Next I knew, I woke up here."

"Mmm," Gwogh said, nodding. Thinking. He sighed. "Your greatest fear is not the icehounds, or Thiel dying, or Grinda or anyone else you know."

"It's failing my father."

Gwogh tilted his head. "I fear not—I think perhaps, you fear that maybe he survived, that he lives to see you fail the legacy he would have left."

Haegan knew the truth of it, though he'd never let the thought into his mind before. But hearing it from Gwogh . . . "When I was with the Eilidan, I met a reader."

Gwogh gave a nod. "I've heard of her."

"She was bizarre. Has some weird ideas. She gave me something."

"Did she?"

"Top drawer." Haegan pointed to the bed stand. "Would you hand it to me?"

With a curious look, Gwogh moved to the drawer. Tugged it open. Taking a step back, he inhaled quickly, snapping his hands tightly to his sides. He slammed the drawer closed. Took a shuddering breath. "You test me, my lord prince."

Haegan narrowed his eyes. "You withhold things from me."

"Only in the interest of protecting you."

"Is that what you were doing when you poisoned me?"

Pale, Gwogh looked to the stand again, as if he could see through it. "Wegna told you this?"

"Aye. And she showed me I'm the only one who can open that book."

"The *Kinidd*," Gwogh said with a sigh. "The holy writs."

"That book, penned supposedly by Abiassa, and I'm the only one who can open it."

Gwogh shifted, and it seemed the old tutor began to understand what Haegan was thinking.

"Wegna said I struggle to control my gift because of the poison and the Falls."

Gwogh gave a slight nod.

"What does she mean?"

"That had I not poisoned you, you would have grown up learning to control what was in you."

"In me? You mean . . ."

"The abiatasso has been with you since birth."

Indignation thrummed. "And you—you *poisoned* me? To what? Stop it?"

"Stop it? No, that could not be done. I did it to hide you."

Grief crashed in on him, suffocating the breath he tried to take. The one person who had filled his days, made him laugh, believed in him . . . "Someone should have hidden me from *you*!"

"I understand your anger—"

"Do you? What if this gift could have protected Seultrie? Saved my father?" Haegan's anger vaulted over his exhaustion. "Because of you—they're gone. And you even want to take the throne from me and give it to Thiel's brother!"

"No. That's not—"

"Leave!" Haegan shouted, feeling the warbling in his hands and not caring. "Leave me at once!"

45

Thiel stepped through the door to the darkened library within the Citadel. Books on shelves lined the walls, and stacks sat at the base of the shelving and some even on tufted benches. Somber glowing stone lights gave the library a warm feel. Or perhaps that was the result of the massive fireplace behind a heavily carved table and embroidered chair, also carved. Just as the gray-bearded man sitting in it was carved with lines of age.

Torchlight spilled over his long, scraggly hair. "Come in, child," he said.

It surprised Thiel that with her skills of stealth he'd heard her though he'd worked intently, his gnarled hand clutching a pen as he wrote in a large tome. She should not be surprised at his keen awareness. Accelerants could detect the slightest hint of warmth in the air, indicating someone's presence. "Laertes said you would speak with me."

Head still down, he extended his free hand over his desk. "Have a seat."

The space between his desk and the shelves gaped in the absence of anywhere to sit. "Where?"

Sir Gwogh looked up, and his bushy eyebrows bounced. "Oh. There was a chair there . . . once." He grunted and glanced around. "Ah, there. Move the books and bring it closer."

Beneath the window sat a chair piled with books. Thiel complied, removing the books before dragging it to his desk and sitting. A puff of dust plumed around her. She sneezed and rubbed her nose.

Sir Gwogh kept writing, the silver glasses perched on his nose catching the firelight.

After a few moments, she cleared her throat. But drew no response. It felt worse than being a little girl trying to interrupt her father at Nivar. But after nearly a quarter hour sitting silently, she cleared her throat again.

Nothing.

"Sir Gwogh—"

"Be patient, child. The others are not here yet."

"Others?"

But of course, he gave no reply, his pen scratching over the paper. Soon, however, a voice came skittering down the lonely halls, delivering Praegur and Laertes into the musty library.

"I done wha' you said, Master Gwogh, sir." Laertes strode to the desk with a bounce.

Sir Gwogh nudged aside a paper, lifted a candy, and handed it to the boy.

Laertes took it, unwrapped it, and popped it into his mouth. Then around the lump, he said, "Now, dat's awful nice of you, sir, but dat's not wha' you went and promised me."

Gwogh's lips twitched. He smirked at the boy. "Bold and efficient," he said, tugging at a lap drawer. Something clanked softly in his hand—coins? He passed it over to Laertes.

"See, sir? I knew you was good for it."

Thiel sniffed a laugh, then stood. "Why are we here?"

Threading his fingers, Sir Gwogh focused on her. "Are you bored, Kiethiel?"

"I beg your mercy?"

"Are you bored?" He sat forward, arms resting on the book he'd been writing in. "You are an adventurer—you've survived years out there with only two teens and a boy. But you sit here, idle, doing nothing in a land that is not your own."

She might as well be standing naked before him. "I'm here for Haegan. Remember, you asked me to come be his support."

"Mm, yes." Again, he sat back and nodded. "But I'm afraid that's turned out poorly."

"Aye." This wasn't about his concern for her state of boredom. But what he wanted, she couldn't discern. "But I will be here—"

"I want you to be here for him in another way," Gwogh said as he pushed to his feet.

"Sir?" Surprise made her look at her friends. Praegur only frowned. Laertes was intent on finishing the chewy candy he'd been given and prying into a book from a nearby stack.

"I am sending you out of the city—"

"I'm not leaving." She jerked straight at his audacity.

"You are," Gwogh said. "And once you hear what I have in mind, you will go willingly."

It sounded like a challenge, something she had never walked away from. And she could not deny how much it tugged at her heart to help Haegan. With one more cautious glance at her friends, Thiel lifted her chin. "Very well. Tell me."

"What is coming—we, none of us, are prepared. But we can work toward being such, so that when the great war is through our door, we will not only survive, but perhaps even win."

"We will win, 'cause Haegan's da Fierian what will scorch Poired an' his dark dogs."

A kindly smile flickered through Gwogh's thick beard before he let out a long sigh. "Yes, Haegan is the Fierian. His task is singular: to face the Dark One in defense of—"

"Da city," Laertes said, prying a sticky piece of candy from his teeth.

"No, my friend. Abiassa cares not for the city, but for the people. She has set this time—Haegan's life—so that his purpose and Her will intersect to be the salvation of Her people at the appointed time."

Hiding her frustration with the storytelling grew more difficult.

"But Abiassa does not intend the fight to be Haegan alone—he is an integral part—but I believe . . ." His gaze fell on an envelope with a green wax seal. "I believe we must send emissaries to the Nine's neighbors to garner support."

"Garner support?" Thiel repeated, her voice pitching. "I am no politician."

"No, nor would I have you be one," he said.

"I'm confused."

Beside her, Praegur shifted. His scowl was deep as he angled closer to the accelerant.

Laertes's eyes widened. He held up a finger in solution. "Dem Ematahri."

Thiel sucked in a breath. Coughed. "*What?* No." She held out her hands. "No, that is not happening. I've left him—*them*. Twice. There will be no mercy and plenty of judgment. Have you *seen* their judgment?" She had. And she would never forget Cadeif's dark eyes when she had shown up with Haegan.

"You must go to the Ematahri, Thiel, and convince them to come when they are needed."

"I can't—they won't listen to me."

"You must."

"I can't! They—"

"Do you love Haegan?"

She snapped her mouth shut, nostrils flaring.

"He will need support, and you can bring it to him."

• • •

Haegan leaned across the bed and drew open the drawer. Lifted out the *Kinidd*. He traced its edges, awed by the steel interlocking triangles secured onto the leather. *My symbol.* It felt prideful to think that, but it was truth. What did the three interlocked triangles represent?

It smelled old. Musty. The pages were crisp and scritchy, not like the notable stationery missives from his father and Fieri Keep. Within its binding were tellings of Baen, Zaethien, Ybienn, along with sketches of the great battles. Haegan turned the page and stilled. A sketch stared back of not just someone from the Histories, but—"Father." He dove into the story, which recounted the Contending that put his father on the throne. There hadn't really been a champion from any of the Nine. Even Thurig, who topped the list, was no match for Zireli Celahar.

Haegan flipped back to the History of his grandfather, Zaelero V. He was good and powerful. The kingdom was mostly at peace in his rule, so there were no great feats save being dubbed the Gentle King. An ironic moniker, considering his role as Fire King relegated to his hand swift justice, which meant death at times.

Kaiade. Great-grandfather. Defeated a rogue band that came from the Violet Sea, the Rekken. He dealt them a brutal blow, banishing them to the frozen tundra north of the Ice Mountains. He'd been dubbed Mad Kaiade, not because he lost his faculties the way Queen Ybaenia had, but because he'd pursued the Rekken with so much relentlessness that he nearly lost his hands to frostbite.

Haegan flipped back several more generations. Wondering why this book had nothing but Histories. He could cull information from the droll texts Gwogh had used for a decade of thumping Haegan over the head. Regardless—there was Zaethien, first son of Baen, who'd named Zaethien after one of the six warriors who warred and defeated Dirag the Desecrator. Abiassa had made the six Deliverers, and subsequent victors who held the Fire Throne often used the names for their sons.

Haegan slapped the book closed. His forebears were mighty men. Powerful. Strong. Leaders. Beloved.

Who am I? A once-crippled prince who can't seem to find his way.

He threw himself back against the pillows and closed his eyes. Pinched the bridge of his nose.

"Is it working?"

Haegan jerked up, startled by the intruding voice. No, more by the owner of that voice. "Drracien."

The rogue sat against the ledge of a now-open window, legs crossed and arms folded over his chest. "So, is it working?"

"What?"

"Your pity party."

Haegan huffed. "Leave off. I have no patience for—"

"Nay," Drracien said, pushing from the ledge. "You have no patience, period. Not for yourself, nor for the trials you tread."

"Aye," Haegan growled, prying himself off the bed. "In that we agree." He went to the dressing area. He stuffed his legs into his pants and tugged them up. A cold weight pressed against his thigh. He drew a stone from the pocket. A sweet, earthy scent drenched him. Haegan stilled, his senses and confusion warring. Where had the stone come from?

"Where is your beauty?"

Snapped out of the fog, Haegan glanced at Drracien as he finished dressing. The rogue lifted a cordi from the tray that also held a pitcher of water, crackers, and cheese.

"My beauty?"

After chomping into the fruit, he motioned toward the door. "Thiel."

"Oh." Guilt hung like an anvil around his neck as he joined his friend, sliding the stone back into his pocket. "I was never good enough for her anyway."

Drracien frowned, frozen. Then grinned. "She finally saw I was the better man?"

Glad the rogue made light and didn't demand to know what was wrong, Haegan poured a glass of water and went to the seating area by the dwindling fire. What hour was it? He glanced at the clock on the mantle. Nearly ten.

"I won't ask," Drracien finally said, "but I think you're a fool to let it happen."

"Let what happen?"

"Thiel get away." Drracien took up the chair with another cordi in the same hand that held a cup by its handle. Seated, he set the warmed juice and fruit down, then dug in his pocket. Crackers. Cheese.

Haegan chuckled. "Have you not eaten today?"

Lifting a shoulder, Drracien stuffed a couple of crackers into his mouth. He pointed to the tray. "Just had a cordi."

There was no fight left in Haegan. He shook his head and dropped lazily onto the settee, staring into the fire.

"Very well," Drracien said. "I'll bite. What ails you?"

Haegan frowned. "Of what do you speak?"

"I just climbed through a window after vanishing on the high plains, and all you ask is if I've eaten?" He stuffed another cracker into his mouth. "And why didn't you report those two who attacked you?"

Haegan started. "How—"

"Nay," Drracien said, holding the cordi up. "You will not distract me. Why—they attacked you. Gave you a knot."

"How would it look in the midst of the Contending trials if I were to admit that I went willingly to a place I shouldn't have been, and in doing so, I got attacked?"

Drracien nodded, chewing a chunk of cordi. "Good point." He slurped another bite. "But that's not why you didn't report it."

"I beg your mercy," he said, incredulous.

"No need to beg." Drracien finished the fruit, then tossed the core right out the open window he'd climbed through. "But will you be honest with yourself? And with me?"

"What is honesty but a tool your enemy can use against you?"

Drracien pulled straight. "Is that what I am to you?"

Haegan blinked. "Nay." He worked to dislodge the thought. "I am not sure why I said that." After clearing his throat and mind, he nodded. "Why are you hiding? Why are you scaling walls in the dark?"

"Because it's challenging?"

"I've never seen you cower—even when the assassins hit us near the Great Falls."

"Speaking of—"

"Not yet." Haegan pointed at him. "Drracien . . . what's going on?" It wasn't hard to put the pieces together. They'd first encountered him south of Hetaera. And they'd gotten the impression he was running from something, but as he'd said at the time—weren't they all? Questions had been tucked aside as Drracien became an asset and friend. "I've kept no secrets from you. I've trusted you implicitly." He snorted. "I still do, though they named you a murderer."

Drracien slowed in his chewing and slid a wary glance at Haegan.

"Come. We are friends, are we not? We've protected one another. Though I daresay you've protected me more than I have returned that favor." Haegan nodded. "Tell me why they pursue you."

Swallowing, Drracien looked at the remaining crackers and cheese in his hand. "It's a long story."

"The best ones usually are."

"I think . . ." Drracien's lip bulged as he swiped his tongue around his teeth. "I killed High Marshal Aloing."

Shock ripped through Haegan. "You *think*?" He fought to not lunge up. But this rogue may very well be the last friend he had left. "Of the people I've met, you possess the most candid and honest character—albeit a bit petulant—so, I struggle to accept you could take another's life. He was your mentor, was he not? What happened?"

"He was." Drracien nearly smiled. "I know not what happened. I was summoned from the training yard, where the sparkers had at least another hour of instruction. When I got to his office, he chastised me for sparking Tortook."

"Puthago?" Haegan asked, his voice rising. "He's a Contender."

Drracien grunted. "Be wary of him."

"I am. Go on."

"Aloing antagonized me. More than ever before. He'd always been hard on me, but not . . ." Distance grew in his gaze, drawing him into the past. " . . . not cruel. But that day he was. As if he *wanted* to anger me. Next thing I know, we're throwing bolts. Me deflecting, begging him to stop. But I'm getting angrier. And he's not letting up, pushing . . . pushing . . . It finally overtakes me. I throw a blast at him." Drracien hauled in a shaky breath. "Struck him in the temple."

Haegan watched his friend, saw the pain on his face. "Seems anger has impeded the both of us." His laugh was hollow, and they both knew it.

"Next thing I know, they're at the door—the grand marshal and other high lords—demanding the door be opened."

"What did you do?"

"I sailed out of the window onto the roof of the governor's mansion—across one rooftop after another. Dromadric's deadly bolts pursuing me."

"Did he want to kill you?"

"Dromadric? I'm sur—"

"Aloing. Why else would a powerful accelerant challenge his mentee?"

Drracien sniffed. "Even if he wanted to kill me, I do not think he could."

Arrogance? He'd known Drracien to be sure of himself, but downright arrogant? "A high lord—"

"Has decades on me in training." Drracien nodded. "But I had outwielded him more than once. It's why he set me as a marshal. Why he put me to instruction."

"Then why antagonize you?"

"I have asked the question a thousand times. As he died, he begged my mercy. Said . . . it was for my own good."

"What was?"

He snorted. "If I knew, would I be wandering the frozen plains of nothingness with you?"

Haegan smirked. "Aye, you would. I don't think you could survive without controversy in your path."

Drracien laughed, but it was a bitter sound. "You know me well." His dark eyes bounced to Haegan. "How could forcing my hand to kill him be for my own good?"

"How can destroying the land bring healing, and yet—that is the task before me."

Drracien hung his head. His gaze drifted to the city lights in the distance, and his smile faded. "I must beg your mercy, Haegan. I cannot walk this path with you as long as you are quartered within Hetaera."

"Is there not a way to . . . defend yourself? Tell them what happened."

"And what? Expect them to believe one of the most revered accelerants of our time committed suicide by mentee?" Drracien moved to the window and palmed the ledge. "All evidence points to my guilt." His words were void of emotion, but his expression roiled with turmoil. "I just don't understand it."

"What?"

"Any of it." He flopped around, crossing his arms. "He sought me out. Brought me to the Citadel. Trained me. Mentored me." Drracien shook his head. "Why force me to kill him? Why tell me to run?" His brow knotted and his expression waxed in grief. "He took everything away from me. Why?"

Haegan sagged. He had no answers. None. Not even for himself. They were both in a quandary. "We are both saddled with burdens we did not ask to bear."

"Aye, but you got the girl."

Though Haegan snorted, he could not voice the thought that robbed him of any pleasure he found in having Thiel as *his*. He did not want to talk about their confrontation, about her betrayal.

"Listen, I came to warn you about Dromadric."

Haegan frowned.

"Do not trust him."

"Is this your anger over him chasing you from the Citadel speaking?"

"No, this is me, who saw him work your fears against you in an attempt to trip you up in the trials, warning you."

"You saw? Where were you?"

"I've learned to be invisible when necessary. But I will never be far. I know you don't believe in what's happening to you, but I do." The petulant accelerant seemed to find a conviction. "She chose you. Don't let them take that from you. You fight." He tapped Haegan's chest. "Fight with every spark in and around you."

Haegan looked away. He didn't want to fight.

Voices scampered through the hall, bouncing against the door. A thud on the wood made Haegan jump. "Go," he hissed, spinning around.

But Drracien was already a black blur in the window frame, vanishing into the night.

Quickly, Haegan dove beneath the thick comforter and tugged the *Kinidd* back onto his lap. "Enter."

Two Jujak entered. "We beg your mercy, Prince Haegan, but the Council requests your presence at nine bells."

Haegan sighed. "Thank you."

The soldiers exited, and Haegan waited until the door was secured before throwing off the covers and hurrying to the window. "Drracien?" He leaned out the ledge but saw nothing.

A swirl of cold night rushed in. Coiled around his head. He drew back, then paused to take in the city. Lights had dimmed and only a spark here and there gave a dull outline to the perimeter. The Citadel's wall of Flames glowed brightly, casting its light over the inner city.

The moons ducked behind fast-moving clouds, and Haegan let his gaze travel to the hills. To the moment when he'd believed himself welcomed and cheered as the next king. Then he set foot in the city and everything changed.

Eleven Contenders.

And who was he among them but an unskilled accelerant? Though he completed his academic studies, he had little experience. He had never led anyone anywhere, except maybe Gwogh to madness.

Gwogh.

Was it guilt that then compelled him to leave the Order and act as tutor? *He poisoned me.* And now? Now he would have me be the Fierian. But not the Fire King.

I am not good enough for anyone.

Disgust wove through Haegan. He glanced to the Mier Woods as a ray of moonslight struck it.

A flash caught his eye. A shape. Moving in the woods. It blended into the darkness. Haegan hurried to his armoire and drew out his telescope. At the window again, he lifted the long glass to his eye. Scanned the tree line. Trees. Brush. But no fire. No person.

He lowered the telescope. What had he seen?

It happened again, as he watched the movement with the naked eye. Haegan snapped up the glass. Spotted Trale Kath at the edge of the woods. And he didn't look happy. His sister was there, arms wagging in apparent frustration.

An argument.

The silent scene played out, the sister pointing at Haegan—no, at the city—and shouting at her brother. Who shook his head. Stabbed a finger to the ground.

We stay.

Haegan lowered the glass more slowly this time. How he knew that's what Trale said, he wasn't sure. But he did. Why were they staying?

To assassinate me.

They could've done that the other day.

Haegan used the telescope again. The amplified image of Astadia Kath's face filled his glass. But—no, there was something. "Blazes," Haegan hissed, nearly dropping the telescope. She was aiming a crossbow directly at him. He stumbled backward, the glass wobbling in his hand. He steadied it, reminding himself they were at least a half league away.

Still, she fired.

His mind wrestled—they were too far from him, were they not? Then why shoot? Even as he asked the question, the arrow arced high. Then came down.

And bounced backward.

Bounced? Off what?

He remembered the protective heat shield he'd thrown up in the inflaming test. Had someone raised a protecting shield? Against what? Did someone in the city know the assassins were there?

Drracien?

Haegan pulled the window closed and paused. Why would they stay? Could they reach him?

Trale had said in the courtyard that they weren't here to kill him. But to take him back to Iteveria.

Why would they think he'd do that?

Because it would solve a lot of problems.

The thought pounded against his conscience. Against his agony to be free of this great responsibility of being the Fierian. A scourge.

Something he could no sooner fulfill as a weak and incompetent prince than he could as the Fierian. He'd been tested and measured . . . and found very lacking.

He returned to the bed and drew the covers to his chest, though it would do no good. He could not hide here. Not from the assassins. Not from Abiassa. His elbow thudded against the *Kinidd.*

Haegan turned on his side and opened the book again. He rather enjoyed the sketches of his forebears and skirmishes. And there were some of great keeps. When he turned the page, he hesitated.

Smoothed a hand over the spine so it would lay flatter on the bed, his fingers seeming to ignite the words his mind saw. It was the prophecy. Written, of course, in the ancient tongue. And yet, somehow, just as he could speak the words, he read the words. Words he did not know. Yet, he found comprehension.

"*Who can stand against Abiassa's Fhuriætyr? The armies will be at his back. The enemy before him. All will meet his fiery judgment and succumb.*

Answer his call, Thræiho. Let your mighty hand wield his scythe. Slice down every adversary.

Defend him, Deh'læfhïer. Let not his blood be spilled or you will surrender your life.

The chïphlïæng will be his emissaries, delivering death to those who oppose the Fhuriætyr.

In the day of Riætyr, none will remain beside him. None will prevail against her champion. Arise, Fhuriætyr!"

Delivering death. Fiery judgment. Slice down every adversary. None will prevail.

How? How was that to be true when Haegan could not pass simple tests? When his wielding could not rival even that of a sparker or conductor?

Chïphliæng.

Haegan stilled, recalling Gwogh explaining the word meant siblings. He slowly pushed his gaze to the window. Let his mind travel past it to the woods. To the sibling assassins.

46

"Just bed down!" Trale snapped, his patience thin. "You're tired."

"I'm angry," Astadia spat back. "There's a difference. We should *not* be here. We *should* be in that city, finding a way into the palace to drag the prince back to the Infantessa."

"Yes," he growled, rolling out his pallet, wishing he hadn't slipped the touch stone into the prince's pocket. He felt empty, lost, without it. "And you proved there's a protective barrier."

She'd been furious at that. Neither had known the barrier existed until she'd tried to show him they were too far from the city for her to target the prince. Which wasn't their mission anyway. But Astadia seemed bent on death.

"But he has the rock?"

Trale nodded, thinking of the nondescript stone. Gray and smoothed by a river, it seemed innocuous. But it'd hummed, filled an emptiness he hadn't noticed before. "Though I wish I hadn't."

Astadia huffed. "I swear if she gave you a dirty handkerchief, you'd carry it around like a treasure. Why a rock anyway?"

"She asked me to take it to him."

"We need to leave. None of this makes sense." She shifted to him. "Please, Trale. Trust me on this. 'Tis not right."

He rolled his eyes. "She didn't ask us to kill him, which is what Poired wanted." He shot her a fierce look. "Is that your will, too? I seem to remember at the Great Falls you developed a weakness for the prince." The words were meant to cut.

And they did. Astadia ducked. Fisted her hands. "I must *do* something. We aren't diplomats. We're *assassins*."

Trale felt something on the wind. It smelled . . . strange. "Shh," he hissed, rising. "Someone's coming."

Astadia hopped to her feet soundlessly, dagger in hand.

Trale drew the Tahscan saber and waited, listening. She pointed to his right, and he angled there as a shadowy figure strode straight for them.

Jujak? Sentinel?

Not dressed right. And they'd be louder. Arrogant in their defense of the city or the prince. Accelerant? Even more arrogant.

A small light-halo blossomed at the man's waist level, shielded by his form. It cast an eerie glow over his features.

Shock tore at Trale. "Prince Haegan."

Resolution gouged hard lines in his face, tightening his lips. Eyes hooded in determination, he hunched as if he moved against his own will.

"Far enough," Trale said, lifting the Tahscan blade to his throat.

The prince's hands flexed, heat warbling . . . then dissipating. "I will go with you." His words sounded forced. "But we must leave now. We have only until dawn before they discover I am missing."

47

Sir Gwogh stared at the Sentinel. "You are sure?"

"Aye, sir. We found this on his bed."

The hastily scrawled note to Thiel simply read, *"I beg your mercy. 'Tis not what I want to become."*

"Thank you." As the messenger of bad news left, Gwogh called to him, "Sentinel."

The man turned. "Sir?"

"Speak of this to no one. The Nine is in enough chaos."

A curt nod. "Understood, sir."

"Summon the Council members to my chambers at once."

"Aye, sir." And with that the Sentinel left.

Heart heavy, Gwogh moved to his writing desk and sat. Haegan had nearly a full day's head start. The final trial was still three days away, but he doubted they'd be able to track the prince down before then.

He stared at the simple words that carried so much hurt and fear. "I have failed you in so many ways, my prince." He pushed his gaze to the window. "Where have you gone?"

•••

HETAERA CITY, HETAERA, KINGDOM OF THE NINE

"Behind you is Mount Medric, which has stood watch over the Citadel and Hetaera City for all time," Adomath announced from a watchtower that had not been on this plain yester-morn. Standing at the center, he was flanked by the Council of Nine. "Please, Contenders, position your-selves in the circle marked with your sigil."

Tili made his way to the attacking raqine and stood with his arms folded, quickly noting Haegan's sigil remained empty. It had been sev-eral days since their confrontation in the chow hall. He had not seen the prince since. The other Contenders were whispering about the prince's glaring absence, some suggesting he'd been disqualified. Others rumored he had taken deathly ill after the inflaming.

Which could not be true. Surely someone—Thiel or Gwogh—would've come to him with the news.

"The mountain," rang Adomath's nasally voice, "has been divided into eleven sections, one per contender. Each mirrors the others as closely as possible in trial, if not precisely in terrain."

Tili glanced toward the stretch of land they called a mountain and wanted to laugh. A mountain was the Cold One's Tooth. Or even greater—Legier. This was a nub of a hill overlooking a pompous city.

Fences raced up Mount Medric to the crest. As he turned, Tili caught sight of more than forty people from the Citadel spilling onto the plain with the early morning light. Dew glittered like diamonds across the tawny field. A soft breeze petted the blades of grass, stroking them gently with a fragranced hand as the forty drew closer. A lone figure stood out. Nearly a hand taller than the rest, Tokar wandered onto the field.

"Each Contender will be assigned a contingent of four," Adomath explained, motioning to the crowd of newcomers. "You will have no choice in your unit. The mission is exactly the same for each Contender: Find and safely deliver the jewel to the peak, where the Nine will be waiting."

Tili stood with his arms folded and feet shoulder-width apart, watch-ing as Tokar stalked to him. So this is how they would test him.

"I did not want to come," Tokar said evenly.

"In that, we are alike, tenderfoot."

Tokar scowled at the moniker forced upon those vying for the Jujak. "You may have found me lacking for the Nivari, but I will prove you wrong."

Tokar's annoyance pleased Tili, especially considering that dark look the youth shot him. He focused on the next person coming his way, a Kergulian, and extended a hand. "Tili."

"D'wyn," the man said, nodding.

After him arrived a twig of a boy, who reminded him of Haegan when they'd first met. "Tili," he said, again offering his hand.

"Twig."

Tili flinched. "Mercies?" Was this a jest?

"*Chwik,*" he said, this time clearly pronouncing his name.

Mayhap he was less than even the missing prince. It would take an effort not to call him Twig. Tili heard another approach to his right and turned. A honey-haired girl stepped to the sigil, and the twig withdrew. Chwik gawked at the girl who had beauty to rival the warm, dew-covered fields.

Tili inclined his head in a slight bow, refraining from taking her hand. Nivaran etiquette frowned upon that between an eligible man—especially a prince—and a woman. "I'm—"

"Prince Tili." She curtseyed. "I know." Her smile was doused in flattery and flirtation. "Everyone knows you. All the ladies talk of the handsome Ybiennese prince contending for the Fire Throne."

Her flirtation cloyed at him. "And yer name?"

She giggled, and he tried not to cringe as she introduced herself. "I beg your mercy. Darielle Jurden at your service."

With a slight acknowledgement, Tili turned to face the tower again.

"Blazes," Tokar muttered. "Do they all fawn at your feet?"

Though he wanted to ask if Tokar was jealous, Tili saw the deep blush coloring Darielle's cheeks and the shame that came with it. "Give care with yer words, tenderfoot. No matter yer feelings on a subject, one never has right to cause injury to another."

Tokar shifted, casting a quick look at the girl.

With a huff, Tili wished for Aburas, Zendric, Etan, and Pesh. Or any one of the Nivari. Instead, he was saddled with a rogue, a twig, and a flirt. And D'wyn. The Council seemed set against him.

Brilliant.

"You have till full tilt to reach the peak," Adomath said as first-years rushed along the field, delivering supplies to the Contenders. "Each unit will have the same equipment: a torch, a rope, a stone light, a pouch, dried meat, paper, and a book."

The items lay before them. While the others bent to study the objects, Tili focused on Adomath.

"Should you or all your team die, a whistler will be fired to alert the other teams. First to reach the peak and present the jewel to the Council will win this round. Tomorrow at the Grand Feast, they will also have the seat of honor."

Tili frowned. "How many games are we to best? What score is expected before a decision is made?" *When will this futility end?*

Sir Gwogh came to his feet and approached the high lord, whispering to him, then he spoke to the teams. "Within this course are four trials, but overall"—Gwogh's gaze rose to the mountain—"this is the final test, Prince Tili. The Council will weigh each test and what came out of it to determine who will take the Fire Throne. Points alone do not guarantee victory."

Relief rushed through Tili. Thoughts of home tugged at him. Then he thought of Haegan and a lump of foreboding settled in his stomach. If Haegan remained absent . . . He looked to Gwogh, but the aged accelerant turned his gaze to the Contenders.

"It has been a long week of training and examinations," Gwogh said, "and I know you are all tired. Draw on your strength and do your best. Wield when it matters. Use every resource at your disposal. And seek Abiassa's wisdom. Beyond all else, recover the jewel!"

Adomath raised his arm. "Contenders, to your section."

Tili motioned his unit to the area marked with the standard of Nivar. The sight of it was a lone comfort in this humid setting, so far from his father and mother. The raqine. The chill of Legier.

"It's warmer here than in Ybienn, yes?" Darielle asked as she strode beside him.

Tili nodded, refusing to be annoyed so early in the day.

"What's it like there? I've never ventured that far north."

He doubted she'd ever ventured anywhere. The smell of Hetaera clung to her clothes and loose-bound hair. "Cold," he answered. "The breath of Legier always blows along the neck."

"The neck?"

"The villages at the base of the mountain."

"Oh."

At the standard, Tili found they would be armed as well. Bows and training arrows. He threaded his arm through a bow and shifted it to his back, lifting a handful of arrows and stuffing them into the back of his shirt, since they were not afforded a way to carry them. "Arm up." He nodded to the gear lying in a heap.

As his unit bumbled their way through the armor and weapons, he stuffed on gauntlets. "I would know yer strengths, each of ye."

"Tracking." D'wyn lifted a pair of greaves and handed them to Tili. "I grew up on a mountain like this. Learned to track animals." He, too, took a bow and arrows.

"In Nivar, we track as well in mountains and snow." He clapped the man on the shoulder. "It will be good to have another set of eyes. And Chwik?"

The twig started, eyes widening as he slid his hands into gloves that looked two sizes too big. "S—sir?"

"What strengths have ye?"

Geared and ready, Tokar snorted.

"Arrogance is the quickest way to the Fires and defeat." Tili focused on the twig again. "Strengths?"

"I—I . . ." Blue-green eyes darted at the others. He shrugged. "I have none."

Sparring dagger in his boot, Tili patted the twig's arm. "All are gifted with strength in one way or another, my father says." He gave an affirming smile. "When ye are on yer own, what do ye do to pass the time? What do ye enjoy?"

At this, Chwik lowered his head even farther.

"As in, have fun?" Tokar taunted. "You do know how to do that, right?"

Tili scowled his remonstration at Tokar. Then he jutted his chin toward the twig, encouraging him to answer.

"Sketch, read." Chwik shrugged again, stringing the pouch, the parchment, and book over his shoulder. He looked at the bow and arrows, but didn't take any. "My father is the Keeper of the Parchments in the capital."

Tsss. Tokar shook his head and turned away.

Darielle struggled to strap on forearm plating.

Tili stepped over, holding her hand between his elbow and side. "What of yer strengths, my lady? Besides yer beauty?"

She took in a breath, then let it out in a giggle. "I've been trained in the Citadel—"

"Ye're an accelerant?" Tili stilled, peering into her eyes.

"Oh no," she said, nearly laughing again. "No, I came to the Citadel because I have a way with languages. The best scholars instruct the accelerants, and if you're keen enough, they allow you to learn alongside Abiassa's Chosen."

He scanned her face, surprised. "So, intelligence." One would not think this squirrel of a girl had much lurking beyond her beauty and flirtations.

"Contenders, enter the corral."

Tili guided his four into the staked-off area and closed the gate. "Remember," he said, working his way to the front, "shoot nothing, do nothing without my command."

"But," Darielle whispered, her voice piqued, "I thought you would wield. That we'd . . ."

"We're a unit," he said. "We work together. Think not that they put ye here for me to show off my ability to wield. This must be done together."

48

Dawn had cracked the void of night leagues past. In a queue sandwiched between Trale at the front and Astadia behind, Haegan made himself keep moving. His feet ached, but he would not mention it. He did not believe the assassins would care one spark about his discomfort, when this is what they did for a living. Traipsing across countries, in and out of cities.

Besides, guilt forbade him from complaining about this path he'd set himself on. What was he doing? Walking straight into the enemy's hands?

I would not have won regardless. The throne was lost to me.

Haegan's sinuses ached, the warm scent stronger, so much that he could smell almost nothing else.

After miles of walking in silence, Haegan wondered about his captors. "What sort of person chooses to spend his days spilling blood and ending lives?"

A sharp thud between his shoulders made him stumble—Astadia had shoved him. He felt the heat of hatred roiling off the sister.

"Just shut up and walk," she ordered.

Haegan looked to the brother. Older, stronger. His shoulders squared as they trudged up a knoll peppered with heavily sapped trees. Sap . . .

"Don't even think about sparking here," she growled. "I'll thump you over the head and you'll wake—"

Trale snapped up a hand and dropped to his knees.

Confused but following the lead, Haegan did the same, heart

pounding. What had the assassin seen? Astadia sidled next to her brother, watching.

Tucked out of sight, Haegan waited, looking back in the direction they'd come. He could see for leagues from this vantage. Hetaera stood tall and proud in the distance, the Spire of Zaelero stabbing the sky. Had they noticed his absence? What would Gwogh do when he realized his prized puppet was missing? Would Thiel be okay? His heart ached at the thought of her discovering what he'd done. Though she would likely hate him, she would also be disappointed—hurt.

I am no warrior.

Thiel is more a fighter than me.

I do not deserve her.

I would bring shame to her and her family.

It would not have worked.

A hand gripped the edge of his cloak and pulled.

Haegan scrambled around.

"Move," Astadia growled.

"What—"

"Quiet," she hissed.

Haegan frowned at her, but she pointed to a pond. What was so significant or threatening about—

A shadow shifted.

Panic thrummed against his chest.

Not shadows. Sirdarians. Watering their horses. Four officers stepped toward the pond, their uniforms making it appear as if blood spilled from the trees. Blood-red uniforms to denote the dedication of their lives to the will of Sirdar. Red cloaks attached to epaulets. Silver braids corded the chest. Buttons glinted in the morning light.

As he watched, more blood—a lot more—spilled out around the small body of water.

So many? Haegan's thoughts pinged. They weren't coming from the south, as had been expected. They were closing in from the east. Which meant they were flanking the city.

Not good. Did Duke Maer'ksh and Dromadric know that an incipient horde lay beyond the plains?

"Are you going to turn me over to the horde?" Haegan whispered as they backtracked.

"Keep moving," Trale bit out.

"I have to notify the Jujak—"

Like a whip, Trale spun. Cuffed Haegan by the throat. Lifted him off his feet and pinned him to the ground. Dark hair hung over darker eyes. "If you would die on this hillside, open your mouth again," he said, his voice a deadly whisper.

Startled, Haegan clenched his jaw.

Trale hopped up and started moving again, not waiting for Haegan. Not concerning himself with the prince at all. The sister was no better, trotting behind her brother without so much as a backward glance. Were they not afraid he would go back?

Back to what? I have nothing left there.

They were afraid. The thought struck him with such clarity, Haegan scrambled to his feet and hurried after them, remembering how Tokar constantly reprimanded him for being so noisy. Not wanting to give Trale more reason to knock him to the ground, Haegan watched his step. Walked as quietly as he could. And most importantly, kept his thoughts to himself.

Which is not to say they were quiet in his head. His thoughts bounced here and there, landing back on his guides' fear. Yes, they were afraid of something, but not of him. Did they not know Haegan was the Fierian?

They hiked northwest, if Haegan's sense of direction and skills with topography were accurate. Skirting north of Vid. Would this not take them away from Iteveria?

Why did the Infantessa want him anyway?

I would like to see her.

Trale stopped and turned. Glanced back. Scanned the tree-dotted plain. "I think we're clear." He nodded to Haegan. "I beg your mercy, but it's said the Sirdarians have unusually keen hearing. One wrong sound and they'd have been upon us."

They didn't want the Sirdarians to know. "You take me to the Infantessa, but not to Poired."

Trale's expression seemed to soften. "She asked us to deliver you, alive."

"So she can kill me herself?" Why had he thought this was a good idea?

"I know you doubt us," Trale said, glancing at his sister, who glowered still, "but I am not convinced her intent is to kill. She is good."

Astadia snorted and looked away.

Haegan frowned. "If she does not want me dead, then what?"

Perhaps an alliance?

Where the thought came from, he didn't know.

His nose dripped, and he wiped it again. Maybe if they put more distance between him and Hetaera, the smell would dissipate.

Farther from home, from his friends? And this was a good path?

Again, he didn't understand his own actions. Walking out of Hetaera with assassins bent on delivering him to the Iteverian Infantessa, who was said to be the spawn of Sirdar . . .

The amusement, the light that had flickered momentarily in Trale's eyes vanished. He frowned, his gaze darting over the earth. "I . . . I am not her voice. Only her instrument. She asked for you. We do as she commands."

"Yes," Astadia snapped. "Now, can we actually *do* it?" Her eyes held fire. "Or would you two like to spend the afternoon chatting like lovesick dogs while the Sirdarians close in?"

• • •

HETAERA CITY, HETAERA, KINGDOM OF THE NINE

Like a sign of the times, the screech of evil in a world protected by Abiassa, a whistler streaked into the sky. Gwogh watched the fiery-orange ball arc over the mountain and felt a tinge of sadness that someone had failed.

"That's a record," Adomath chuckled from his chair on the tower platform. "What, forty minutes?"

"Forty-two," confirmed Voath as he pointed to the western half of Medric.

"Who?" Gwogh asked. The Contender must have failed only moments into the second challenge. Sentinels had just confirmed all ten had survived the first obstacle—navigating a maze cut into the overgrown grasses.

Marshals had come out in the night and scorched the area, hardening the waxy field so the grasses were not easily bypassed, thereby allowing swaths to be cut out and traps set in.

"It's Ociliama of Dradith," Voath said, slumping in his chair.

"No surprise there," Adomath murmured. "It's a practically failed state anyway. Should be absorbed into Vid."

Mm, it would make things easier for Sirdar, now wouldn't it? Gwogh thought.

"Nay," Falip objected from his chair. "We are stronger than we have ever been."

Gwogh glanced at the new Council member, impressed with his courage in contradicting the grand marshal's faithful ally.

"As seen by your Contender," Adomath taunted.

"She was not my choice," Falip confessed. "Her family has money Dradith badly needs."

"There is no shame in failure," Gwogh injected into the contest. "Each test was made to be challenging. "

Kedulcya nodded. "The huts particularly so."

"What of the shriekers?" Aoald asked. "The beasts already got one."

"Beasts," Adomath said with a guffaw. "They are but two hands in length."

"Aye, and they're vicious with those hooked beaks and dagger-sharp talons. They hate the sight of people and attack relentlessly."

"They have arrows," Adomath said with a smirk. "Let's hope they use them wisely."

• • •

The copse of trees seemed welcoming, but there was a strange quiet emanating from it that raised the hairs on the back of Tili's neck. "Is there a way around?"

D'wyn shook his head, then nodded both right and left. "The fence cuts directly through the trees."

Tokar eyed the fence. "Let's follow it up. At least we'll have protection on one side."

"And nowhere to go if we're set upon," Tili said, noting Tokar's annoyed expression. The guy didn't like being countered. Too bad. That was the way of things—suggestions, improvements. Someone suggested something. Someone improved upon it. Kept everyone alive.

Tili pointed up the middle. "Straight through. If we're separated, move north. Always north—that's our endpoint. Going back means failure. Find the separation barrier and wait there. Understood?"

They nodded.

"Single file. Bows ready. Stay close." As they lined up, he tugged Tokar to the front. "Take point."

"Why? So I die first?"

Tili bit back the retort on his tongue. "Go. We're waiting."

With a huff, Tokar slid into position and advanced. Tili trailed the team, sweeping up and around. Behind. Up, around, behind. Eyes out at all times. He moved quietly, listening to the others. Noting them as he took in the landscape.

"Weird quiet," Chwik whispered.

Aye . . . Using his abiatasso, Tili reached out for warmth but found little. There was something out there, but not big enough to be human. Nor did he detect the eerie chill that would indicate accelerants in their path. That was similar to what he'd detected as he watched Haegan and the Drigo face the incipients. But this . . . this was different. Slightly. Annoyingly. What was there?

The strangeness bathed them as they ventured farther into the trees. It wasn't a forest, not like Ybienn's southernmost Black Forest, so named because no light penetrated the canopy. But the vegetation was dense enough to drape the day in shadows.

"I . . . don't like this," Darielle murmured, her hand going to Tokar's shoulder as she trudged onward. "It feels like it did when my sister and I were hiking. Shriekers—"

"Quiet," Tili hissed, slowing, gaze skimming the upper branches.

Something changed. The air. He wasn't sure. A strange, trilling sound broke the silence.

"Shriekers," Darielle gasped. "I told you!"

"Go! North! Don't stop!" Tili lined up his arrow on the first inbound bird. Its keening vibrated against his ear drums. A sound meant to distract its victim. Tili released the arrow, slinking backward over the forest litter.

Sighted the next. Fired.

He heard the pluck of another bow and release of arrow to his left. Tili worked the right. Sent another shaft through a bird.

Poof!

Hesitating, Tili sorted what he saw. The birds—they weren't birds.

"They aren't real," Tokar announced. "They're only flames."

"But if they touch ye—sear yer clothes—ye're still dead in the trial."

"D'wyn, Chwik, get Darielle to safety." Tili nocked another arrow. Felled the next flaming bird. And another. Tokar was his counterpart, dropping just as many.

"Last arrow," Tokar called.

"Go!" Tili tested how many he had left—five—then drove another.

A whistler shot into the air.

Darielle cried out.

Tili swung around, staring down the shaft of an arrow as two shriekers descended upon her. She hunkered down, arms over her head, screaming. Her position gave Tili the opportunity. He released the arrow. It flew true. Sailed into the first.

Pooof!

And right into the second. Another puff of smoke.

Someone yelped.

Tili kept walking backward, protecting the rear. He aimed at a shrieker. And stumbled. The arrow went wide. *Blazes!*

The shrieker spiraled in on him. *Death kill.*

He grabbed for an arrow but knew he'd be too late. His heart hammered. Would he lose so quickly?

An arrow sailed overhead. *Poof!*

Tili scrabbled around. Hauled Chwik to his feet. "Go. Run, Twig." Thrust him north. Nodded at Tokar, who'd just saved his life. They were moving. Running. He saw the lip of the woods. Sunlight. "Go go go!"

Hearing the stampede of feet, he pivoted, trotting backward as he fired another arrow at a shrieker. And another.

"Your right!"

He heard the warning and reached for another arrow—gone! Tili's heart jammed. He threw himself toward the lip of the forest, straining for security. Heat blazed over his neck and shoulder. He ducked. Dove into the sunlight.

Poof!

Hands pawed at him, pulling him upright. He stumbled a step then caught traction. Sprinted for the fence.

"They're gone!" Darielle said, glancing back. Slowing.

Tili's heart was still firing hard, but he braved a look toward the trees once more. She was right. The shriekers were gone.

"The woods," D'wyn said. "That was their perimeter. Couldn't go past it."

Tili ran his hands over his face and then through his hair. Gripped his knees. Then his temple. Rubbed. Thinking.

"That was close," Tokar said. "Good thing I saved you."

Though arrogance filled those words, Tili could not deny it. "I owe ye."

Tokar squinted in a hidden smile. "No." He cocked his head. "We're a unit, remember? You go down, we all go down."

Surprise lanced through Tili. That was a mark of maturity he hadn't expected from the thin-blood.

"Did you hear the whistler?" Darielle asked, her voice stricken. Haunted. She shivered. "That was the second one in this challenge alone. Another Contender failed."

"A head of pride sinks in the river of life," Tili said, quoting the proverb his mother taught him.

"We know that what comes at us is conjured," D'wyn said. "Those birds were inflamers—worked out of flames by accelerants. We don't have to worry."

Tili pointed at the dark-skinned man. "Think like that, and ye lose the trial on this spot."

Beside the Kergulian, Chwik was making notes on the parchment. He'd scrounged a scorched stick to use for writing. Tili craned his neck to see what he recorded. A list of some sort.

Tili glanced at the next fence and nodded. "We must be prepared. The Council is not doing this for bloodshed but to test the mettle of the Contenders."

"Lucky us," Tokar muttered. "Chosen to get the flames scared out of us so you can prove you're worthy."

"Think not that this is about only me," Tili said. "Whoever takes the Fire Throne—all of ye on this field will know their mettle. Doubts will be erased, and from these forty-four, that word will spread. Confidence in the new leader will spread."

"So you like this?" Tokar scowled.

"Like? Nay."

"Can't you just lose?" D'wyn said. "I mean, then we could all go home." The Kergulian may well have strength, but he had more doubt.

"And where is the honor in that?" Tokar growled.

"Easy," Tili warned then focused on D'wyn. "Tokar is right—I do this to honor my father's name. If I cast about without purpose, I lose. Nivar is blemished, shamed."

"Besides," Tokar said. "I don't like losing."

"Sir."

Tili looked to Chwik, more than a little annoyed with D'wyn's taste for passivity. Chwik drew a stack of arrows from behind him. Handed them over.

Tili frowned. "Where—?"

"When you shot them, they fell to the ground." He shrugged beneath his mop of dirty-brown hair. "I picked them up. Thought we might need them."

With a laugh, Tili took a handful and gave the others to Tokar then patted Chwik's shoulder. "Well done, Twig."

"I . . . it's Chwik sir."

Again, Tili indicated the next fence. "Line up and stay close." He positioned them with Tokar again the lead—*am I always the bait?*—then D'wyn, Darielle, and Chwik.

Taking up the rear, Tili readied himself. "Go."

Tokar slid around the corner and the unit snaked around behind him, clinging to the fence until they got their bearings in the new setting.

Only . . . there wasn't anything to figure out. A thin swath of field narrowed in the northeast quadrant, effectively pulling their gaze to a lone glass dome. Something was under it. He couldn't quite tell what with twenty-five meters between them and the glass.

"Too easy," muttered Tokar, holding his position, which forced the others to do the same.

Tili trotted up to where his point man crouched. "Agreed." There had to be a catch. A trick. Something.

With a gasp, Darielle drifted closer. "The jewel!" she exclaimed and started forward.

Tili caught her arm and pulled her back, giving her a stern look. "Nobody moves until we all move."

"Grass is wet around the dome," Tokar muttered

Realization dawned on Tili. "That's because it's not glass. It's ice."

The girl shrugged. Pointed. "Then use your wielding." She shrugged again. "Melt the ice, retrieve the jewel. Then take it to the peak. Pretty straightforward."

"Which means it's not," Tokar said.

As the tenderfoot echoed the words in Tili's head, he scanned the fence. The grass. Looked back at the woods. If something came out of there, they'd never see it because they'd be facing the wrong way.

"So what do we do?"

"It's obvious," Darielle said. "Skirt the fence and come up along the outer fence line to the dome."

That might work. But Tili wasn't convinced. Still too easy. But maybe the challenge was that the jewel was frozen inside the ice dome.

Screaming, a whistler sounded over the mountain.

Darielle jerked her gaze skyward. "I suppose—"

Another whistler went active.

"Two?" She whirled to him, eyes wild. "Two more contenders lost? That makes four gone." Ashen, she placed a hand on her stomach, looking to the dome.

"Okay," Tokar said, swinging his bow in front of him and nocking an arrow, ready for whatever was going to come at them on this challenge. His determined gaze met Tili's. "Thoughts?"

Tili scanned, and scanned again. What were they missing? "D'wyn, what do ye see?"

"The grass," D'wyn said with a bob of his head toward the field.

Adjusting his position, Tili eyed the field. Squatted, tilting his head to take in a better vantage. His gut clenched. "Minefield." He stretched an arm out, pointing to variation in the patterns, broken bits of dried grass used to conceal the mines. The Council wouldn't wound anyone with real explosives, but they'd used something to mark those who would die.

"I think Darielle's suggestion is valid," D'wyn said. "Skirt the fence around to the dome."

"They'll have thought of that," Tokar added.

"Aye," Tili said, crouching lower and assessing the perimeter, "but the Council anticipated more contenders would just rush across the field, believing the dome was the challenge." He straightened and turned to D'wyn. "Ye lead. Slow and easy. Watch for the mines." To the others, "Fall in behind. Step only where he steps. If ye die, ye die alone."

Darielle widened her eyes and slipped behind Chwik, who'd kept his head down and mouth closed.

Maybe he sounded too harsh. "So, don't die," he added. "D'wyn, go."

They trekked slowly along the fence, most watching the ground. Tili bounced his gaze from D'wyn, down the line of the unit, and out to the field, then back to his unit.

A hand snapped up.

But Chwik and Darielle didn't see it, their gazes on their feet.

"Stop," Tili growled to them.

She glanced back at him, but she was still moving forward. Didn't see Tokar and Chwik step to the side. Her foot—

Tili lunged, hooked an arm around her waist and pulled her up and back against his chest. Arms swinging out, she yelped. Flailed. "Keep still," he hissed in her ear.

A whistler streaked into the air.

Darielle froze, as did Tili, but then he lowered her, the back of her head against his shoulder. "Wa—was that for us?"

"No." He pointed to the ground. "Mines. Eyes forward at all times. Let's move."

She twitched a nod, her frame rigid.

He'd broken nearly every rule of propriety manhandling her, but she hadn't been eliminated. And that was the point. They advanced on the field without further incident, sidestepping two more well-laid mines before coming upon the dome.

D'wyn scanned around the dome. "It's clear."

"So, five Contenders are gone," Chwik said as Tokar squatted before the dome, studying it. "That leaves six."

"Five," Darielle corrected, wide-eyed. "Prince Haegan didn't show."

The thought struck Tili hard. Haegan hadn't shown. Still . . . "We need to focus. There are two more trials, and we've spent nearly half our time."

Darielle motioned to Tili. "Use the Flames. Melt it. You can see the jewel there, and we can't go forward without it."

Why did it still seem too easy? And dangerous?

"Aye, wield," Chwik said, a greedy gleam in his eye.

"Wait," D'wyn said. "Look at the ice."

Tili leaned in closer.

"There are . . . specks in it."

So not just ice. Then, perhaps . . . "Explosives?"

D'wyn nodded. "My speculation is it will react to whatever we use—whether wielding or daggers—the blade could ignite it."

"Can it be turned over?" Tokar asked.

"The weight of it, though," Darielle commented.

"Let's try," Tili said, going to a knee. He scraped around the bottom. "'Tis set in firm," he mumbled. Dug down. And down. "Blazes," he growled. "'Tis inches deep."

"Maybe wield and shield," Darielle said.

"Too risky," Tili countered. "One wrong manipulation and we're all—"

Another whistler screamed into the sky.

"The Lady and the Flame," Darielle whispered the oath. "Those things scare me every time. I'll have nightmares for weeks after this."

"Everyone dig," Tili said.

They all went to work, using daggers or hands to scoop out the marsh-like ground. Mounds of soggy earth bled through their trousers, but they managed to free it. Then they all pushed, Tokar and Tili guiding the dome onto its side, the ground giving a slurping suction.

"Careful!" Tili shouted, afraid any impact could ignite one of the pustules. Back in the muck, he wiped the base clean. "Just as I thought."

"What?" Tokar leaned from the other side.

"The pustules are only about an inch deep." He placed his hand on the ice and focused a light heat only in the bottom center. The melting was slow at first, then quickened. "D'wyn, while I'm doing this, sight a path to the next fence."

"Aye," D'wyn said.

Tili's hand slid up inside the dome.

"Easy," Tokar said softly, his breath shallow.

"Almost there!" Darielle nearly squealed.

Tili trained his mind on the process. On melting as little as possible. His fingers neared the jewel. He stared at the red orb, distorted through the wall of ice. His fingers inched closer . . . closer . . . His arm nearly in up to the elbow, he felt the tension release. Grab the jewel, get to the next objective. It'd—

Plish!

In stricken, awful horror, he struggled to register what had happened. One second the orb was there. The next, a red river rushed down his arm.

"No!" Darielle gasped, covering her mouth. "No, no!"

Tili extracted his hand and studied the crimson residue on his forearm.

"You ruined it." Darielle fisted her hands. "They told you to be careful. That was our only hope to win."

Disbelief held Tili tight.

"You stupid fool—that's what happens when a Nivari is put on Mount Medric. You really think you'd be a good king? Look—"

Tili was on his feet. Warned himself to calm. To be respectful. "It wasn't the jewel."

She stumbled backward, but—blast her, if she didn't nearly step on a mine again—Tili tugged her forward. "What? But we saw it!" Her cheeks were stained the same color as his forearm.

"It was gelatin." Tili shook out his arm, then planted his hand on his belt. "It was a distraction and cost us time." He roughed a palm over his jaw, then pointed to the fence. "D'wyn?"

The Kergulian nodded. "It's clear."

"Let's move. Get to the fence and regroup."

49

SOMEWHERE IN UNELITHIA

"It would be easier to hate them if they were mindless," Trale said, his stomach pressed to the rooftop as they peered down a street that had emptied at the rhythm of marching Sirdarians. They would soon round the corner and come into view.

This morning, Haegan and his guides had crossed into Unelithia. Not via the traditional route with papers presented at the border. That would have been too easy, even though they had no papers and risked arrest. They could've even taken the difficult route, walking the Nydessan Highway and risking their pockets to thieves and lives to mercenaries.

But no, Trale led them through the wasteland, across the vast Citrine Lake, and then had them scale the great wall of stone lights, which left their hands scalded after the hour-long climb.

Haegan watched in a nervous anticipation. "It's said in Seultrie that Sirdar controls them." If he was captured, they would kill him or turn him over to Poired. Who would kill him. Either way he was dead. As he waited with the assassins, Haegan could only hope the two who flanked him had honor.

Honor among murderers. Did that even exist?

Trale inched lower as the column of soldiers stepped into the torch-light and headed toward them. Haegan followed, anxiety clawing at him, shredding his courage. They should not be here, out in the open. Were the moons bright? It could betray their presence.

As the shinking-thuds of Sirdarian boots grew louder, Trale patted his shoulder. Pointed behind them to the rear of the building. Where was he going? Haegan, staying as low as possible, circled around and scrambled after him, stunned when Trale sailed into the air, over the edge of the building.

Disbelieving, Haegan stopped cold.

Astadia ran past him.

Jarred by her movement, Haegan started forward. As he drew closer, he saw the other rooftop, lower but there. Relief coursed through him, but still he hesitated a fraction before pitching himself off the edge. He tripped on landing and shoved out his hands to break his fall. Dirt and tar scored his palms. He came up, wincing but refusing the whimper that crawled up his throat.

Trale leapt to another rooftop with his sister right behind him. Limbs aching, Haegan worked to keep up. After a half-dozen ups and downs and sprinting between buildings, he ached for a breath that didn't hurt.

He had lost his mind, chasing assassins across rooftops. "Whe—" Breath trapped between as gasp and gust, Haegan tried to swallow. His throat was dry. His lungs burned. He swallowed and pushed not to lose his guides. If he did, he'd be alone in a city filled with Sirdarians. Ruled by Sirdar under the Infantessa.

Haegan rounded the corner after the siblings. And stopped short. Darkness and shadows gaped before him. Where had they gone? He took a few tentative steps, searching for them. "Trale," he hissed into the emptiness.

Something plunked him in the head.

He cringed and rubbed the spot. Turned a circle. Where were they? Panic began a slow march through his chest, thudding harder, faster, with each breath he took in isolation.

Was this their plan? Lure him here to be apprehended? Surrounded by enemies, by those who would see him crushed, he was ripe for the capture.

"Trale," he growled through clenched teeth.

Another rock struck his head. He looked up, spotted an iron ladder. But nobody there. A shape moved beneath the moonlight along the edge of the other rooftop. Astadia was scurrying out of sight again.

Haegan hurried to the dangling ladder. Leapt and caught it. Oh, Lady of Mercies! His arms ached. Muscles burned. Trembling, he hauled himself up. Hooked his arm over the first rung, but his weight nearly forced him to surrender. Teeth gritted, he reached for the next rung. Drew up his leg. His knee struck the iron. It rang with what seemed like an ear-splitting clang. He slipped, dangling.

Below, a flash of light danced beyond where he hung. Blood spilled out of the building, a pub by the raucous noise coming from within. Sirdarians gathered outside the door, talking amongst themselves. A couple of them donned silver helms with red plumes.

Dread rushed through his veins. If he could see them, they could see him. He dared not move. Dared not fall. Iron dug into his armpit, sharp and cruel. A burn radiated through his joint. Raced down his bicep. He gripped his elbow to support himself, hopefully take some of the pressure off his shoulder. Off the iron cutting into his flesh.

Drop. He should just drop and crouch. Pray they didn't see him. It'd be faster. And he wouldn't be in pain any longer.

But he would need to untangle himself from the ladder—without noise. He gripped the bar with his left hand and tried to haul himself up.

"No," came the frantic, urgent whisper from Astadia.

At the same time, iron rattled.

The ladder clanked. Dropped another rung. A loud clang and vibrations jarred the rung from his hands. Haegan fell. Landed hard. Pain shot through his head, which hit the ledge.

"The roof!" came a deep, angry shout.

Blazes!

A soft thump near his shoulder startled him.

"Up now, or you'll get us all killed." Astadia grabbed his arm and yanked him to his feet. Half dragging him back the direction they'd come.

"No," Haegan barked. "The Sirdarians are coming."

"Shut up and move!" After releasing him, she raced to the edge. "C'mon."

Haegan was at her side quickly, looking for an escape. The drop was easily three meters into a pitch-black alley. But he'd shatter his leg if he jumped. The wall of the stairs from the building pressed against his left shoulder. "How are—"

"There," Astadia instructed. "On the ledge."

Which was half the width of his hand. "Have you lost all reason?"

"Never had it in the first place," she muttered, climbing over and walking along the ledge as if it were a sidewalk.

Blazes. If he didn't, he'd be shown up by this girl. And caught by the enemy. Swallowing his fear and pride, Haegan ventured out, using the stairwell for support as he balanced on what felt like a wavering reed. He flattened his stomach against the wall, palms pressed to the still-warm plaster. Now his limbs trembled for another reason. But if Astadia could do it . . .

"Up," came the lone, hissed command.

Haegan carefully tilted his head back to look up at the top of the stairwell. A foot above him. But gravity tugged at him.

"Whoa," he grunted, flattening himself again.

"Up," Astadia insisted.

How was he supposed to get up there. "How?"

"Jump and grab the ledge."

"You *have* lost all reason."

"Now or they will find you."

Haegan huffed. Peered up at her, unwilling to peel himself away from the wall. He crawled his fingers up the wall. Insane. He could ride a raqine across leagues, but climb a wall? Fingers gripped the ledge. Fear gripped him.

A vise-like grip clapped onto his forearm. Another onto his other. Trale must've come back, thank the Lady. His shoulders rose above the wall and he bent forward, using the assistance to make the last few inches. He rolled to offer his thanks to Trale.

But only a pair of angry green eyes met his.

"We have seconds"—her lips flattened and nostrils flared—"to make this jump. Do not cower behind the crown, Prince."

"What—"

Astadia pivoted and came up, already running. She sprinted the five feet diagonally across the stairwell roof and threw herself into the yawning darkness. It felt like she hung there for eternity before dropping onto another ledge, rolling out of the momentum. She came up and spun around, waving him on.

There had to be at least five, maybe seven feet between the stairwell and that roof. Might as well be a hundred.

"Now or die," she said.

Haegan pushed himself up. If she could do it . . . With all he had in him, he lurched from the roof. Shot forward. Launched into the air. Proud of himself for making the leap.

Astadia's eyes rounded and her mouth opened. Alarm rippled through her face. She spun and dove farther into the darkness.

Where was she going? Panic stabbed him.

Pain snapped around his ankle.

Yanked him back down onto the roof. Bounced. Air punched from his lungs. He arched his back, groaning. Squeezing his eyes. When he blinked, Haegan stilled. Blood smeared the sky above him. Towering over him, silver helms grabbing the moonslight, were six Sirdarians.

Alarm shot through him. He thrust a hand toward them without thinking, refusing to be taken easily.

A strange, burning metal clamped his wrist. Nausea roiled. Pain scorched his temples.

50

Ambush. Tili eyed the knoll at the base of Medric with speculation and dread. It was the perfect spot for an ambush. But what would they encounter? More shriekers? Landmines? Taking a knee, he steadied his nerves. Took a moment to rest as he considered options, how to get around the smaller ambushes.

"What are we supposed to do?" Chwik asked quietly.

"The knoll," Tokar said. "There's something on the other side. "

"There is also something on this side," D'wyn said quietly.

"I haven't heard a whistler in a while," Darielle said. "How do you think the others are doing?"

"D'wyn." Tili turned to the man. "How many traps do ye see?"

"Only three, but the pattern . . ." The Kergulian gave a baleful shake of his head. "They worked hard to conceal the others, but there are more. I'm sure of it."

"Agreed," Tili said. "Whatever we're supposed to do is on the other side of that rise."

"My legs and arms hurt," Darielle said. "My back, too—everything hurts."

Tili focused on the land and ignored the girl's complaints. She was sent to test him as much as this trial, he was certain.

Chwik moved around Tokar and came toward Tili.

Then he dropped. Screamed.

Tokar was there, holding Chwik's arm as he hung over the lip of the in-ground trap that had given way beneath, saving him from dagger-like spikes sticking up from the belly of the pit. Of course, they weren't real, but the danger most likely felt raw and virulent to the one dangling over them.

D'wyn whirled around and helped pull him to safety. Chwik dropped to his knees and vomited.

Darielle drew in a breath. "How many traps did you say?"

"I'm sure there are dozens," D'wyn said, his voice ominous.

"This is ridiculous!" Anger colored Darielle's cheeks, and she fisted her hands. "Choosing a king is one thing. Sending him on a course like this—"

"Is preparation for what's to come." Tokar's words were even but laden with foreboding.

"Poired," Chwik said.

Or perhaps even the Void Walker, Sirdar.

"Concern yerselves not with what we cannot address now," Tili said. "We have an obstacle course before us. We need ideas." He looked at each of them, willing them to drag their minds from the drowning dread. "Tokar."

His gaze went to the field, then the knoll, but he slowly shook his head. "I'm fresh out."

"D'wyn?"

"The traps—we have to avoid them."

Lightning-sharp unit. Stowing his frustration, Tili turned. "Chwik?"

The twig also shook his head. "I . . ."

"Have mercy on me, my Lady," Tili muttered.

"The rope and stone," Darielle said. "Tie the rope to the stone, cast it ahead as we walk to test the ground."

Tili considered her. Then the field. "That might work." He nodded, moving. "Good thinking. Twig, give me the stone and rope."

The boy blinked. "You mean Chwik," he said, digging out the stone and rope from the pouch.

Tili tied the stone and tested the length of rope. "Behind me," he barked. He tossed the rock, holding the rope, and let it thump against the ground, then dragged it back toward himself, allowing it to bump across every inch of ground in the line he intended to walk. Toss, thump, drag, advance. Toss, thump—*Crack!*

The ground fell away.

Tili stilled, his heart amped.

A whistler screamed through the afternoon.

Tili glanced over his shoulder. Three. That left just three Contenders. Maybe he *should* fail. He was not interested, no matter how pleasant he found the weather or fair the ladies, in spending the rest of his years here. Binding himself to a Southlands woman. Raising a family. Leagues—an entire country—from his own family. He might indeed have a bit of the rogue blood his father always accused him of, but he was a Thurig through and through.

But Haegan had not shown.

He veered right. Toss, thump, drag, advance. Toss, thump, drag, advance. Annoyance gripped him at the number of traps—half the field—but also at the layout. It forced them to come straight at the knoll. No protective cover. No strategic flanking.

They knelt at the lip of the knoll and stared up. Rubbing his jaw did little to help him think. No great inspiration came. His father had said he stroked his beard because it made his brain work better. An old habit become fodder for mocking by his second-eldest son. Now that son found himself doing the same.

He lowered his hand to the side, and aimed his fingers toward the rise. He reached out, sensing the heat. Yes, there were several on the other side.

"Up and over," D'wyn said. "I see no traps on the knoll."

"That's because the danger is on the other side."

"I will lead," Tokar said.

"No, it's—"

"I know you would have all the glory," Tokar said with a sardonic smile, "but if you die, it's over. If I die—you still have a unit. The trial continues, and maybe my death will mean something when you get to the top with the jewel."

"Can you sense them on the other side?" D'wyn asked.

"Aye," Tili said, gaze still on the grass.

"Accelerants? How many?" Darielle leaned forward.

"Nay, just people. Too many." A true enough answer that would allow him to conceal the fact that his wielding abilities were not advanced. That his father had forbidden wielding, so he'd hidden it for most of his life.

"Let's flank."

Tili frowned. "'Tis not—"

"Not so far, yes—but far enough. Two columns versus one. I still crest it first, draw their attention, and then you attack."

"Aye, I like it." Even as he went to his knees, Tili slid the bow to the small of his back, securing it beneath his belt. Arrows tucked in his shirt.

Tili motioned them against the ground, then led Chwik and Darielle up from the right side. Even before he could start low-crawling, elbow over elbow up the small hill, Tokar and D'wyn were halfway up.

Hurrying, he came within inches of the crest. Laid his head flat, looking at Tokar. Tili drew his bow. Nocked an arrow. Met Tokar's gaze once more and nodded.

Tokar went up with a cry to draw attention.

Tili came up a breath later.

"No!" Tokar shouted.

A strangled cry from behind.

Something cuffed his ankles.

He went down, his chest thumping against the earth. Tili heard the whir of an arrow. Right past his ear. Stunned that he was on the ground, stunned that he'd nearly taken an arrow, he looked back at his feet, at the weight pressed on them.

And found Darielle hugging his legs. She scrabbled backward, cheeks aflame. "The Lady and the Flame. I saw the—it just came loose."

"What came loose?"

"The fence." She looked to the barrier. "It was a false wall."

With a sigh of disgust at himself for missing it, Tili stayed low. "Good job." He glanced to Tokar again. Then the knoll. It sat empty, save three small pyres. Heat signatures. He lowered his head. He'd sensed the heat from the pyres but hadn't guessed that they were a ruse, and by entering the trap, he'd unleashed flaming arrows.

"Stay low," Tili said as they all continued low-crawling to the next barrier. He dropped back against it. "I could've died."

"But you didn't," Darielle said with a smile. "Because we're a unit."

"No whistler," noted Chwik with a shake of his head. "Three of you remain."

"One field to go, but we still have no jewel." Tokar dropped against the wall.

Tili closed his eyes, resting. Whatever was coming would not be easy. Without moving, he eyed the others. They were all tired. "Ready to hit this?"

"More than," Tokar said.

"No matter what happens on this rise," Tili said, "ye are all the finest in my book."

"Book," Chwik mumbled, then scrambled for the pouch and lifted the book. "What do you think it means? It's blank." He fanned the pages.

"Let me see." Tili hefted the tome.

Darielle gasped.

So did Chwik.

Tili glanced down at the stained parchment that once had been blank, but now, black lettering scripted itself by an invisible hand, filling the page.

"How in blazes?" Tokar muttered.

"Your hand!" Darielle's eyes were bright. "You're an accelerant—your hands are naturally warm."

"There is an ink made of the same materials as the stone lights," Chwik said. "It reacts to heat. Just like a stone light illuminates, so does the ink."

Darielle took the book. Her fingers, dirtied and scratched from the Contending, trailed across the lettering. "It's about the jewel!"

Tili clenched his jaw. "Read it."

"I . . . I can't—it's fading." She held it out to him. "You must use it, if you intend to succeed."

Surrender was not in his nature. "Use the stone light," he instructed. "It has heat."

"What are you afraid of?" Tokar asked with an incredulous laugh.

Tili ignored the taunt. Nodded to Chwik. "Ye thought of the book. Use the stone light with it."

With a slow nod, Chwik retrieved the book and stone light. Touched it to the page. Chwik shot him a look, then back to the book. "It's not working."

Darielle lifted her chin. "As I said, you must use your gift if you intend to win."

Tokar frowned at him. "That's just it—you *don't* intend to win. Do you?"

Feeling exposed, Tili snatched back the book, his breaths coming in heavy gulps. Jaw tight, he set his fingertips to the edge. The words spilled across the page as heat from his hands radiated over it. *". . . and in the dawn of the fourth day in the heart of the dark maw amid dirt and grime, the jewel glows bright. Years beyond its age and shrewdly cunning, the jewel summons the one sent. Sharp and fiery, the jewel draws in the weakhearted and humiliates them in their arrogance. Sought after but hidden, the jewel will be as lightning to the Deliverer. The one who climbs the higher path and stands before nine stones with the jewel in hand shall be revealed as the great champion and made wealthy and ruler over all."*

"So," Tokar said, tucking his chin as he apparently thought through the words. "If you climb to the peak with the jewel in your hand, then you win."

"It sounds like that," Darielle said.

"Yer words hesitate."

"My whole body hesitates—out of exhaustion." She brushed a loose strand of hair from her face. "Nothing has been what we've expected, so I wonder at the words and worry at the course."

"Aye," Tili said. "Ye and I both." He climbed to his feet. "Let's get this done."

They hiked for an hour. Faced no challenges. But sweated and ached horrendously. Had they missed something? He peered over his shoulder at the steep climb they'd already made. Then back to the crest. Halfway. He grunted.

"Did we pass it?"

"What?"

Tokar shrugged. "Whatever we're looking for."

"If we knew what we were looking for, he might be able to answer that," Darielle said.

"Tili!" D'wyn's voice echoed out.

He shifted, stabilizing himself as he turned to the Kergulian, who stood on a small outcropping. "Ye find something?"

"Aye." D'wyn waved them over then bent forward and seemed to be absorbed into the rocks themselves.

"A cave," Chwik announced.

51

"Drink." Hoeff's overly large hands and fingers were deliberately gentle as he nudged the cup at her. "You drink. Heal."

Steam spiraled up from the bitter brew in the clay cup. She had spent months drinking this concoction, and though at first she'd recovered nicely thanks to his ministrations, it had been more than a month since there'd been additional improvement. She had given up on regaining the use of her legs. In truth, she was merely grateful for the use of her arms and torso. How her brother had endured such a cruel fate for so long, she could not fathom.

"Drink," Hoeff growled.

With a sigh, Kaelyria lifted the cup to her mouth, held her breath, and guzzled as quickly as she could. Handing off the cup, she squeezed her eyes shut as the last bitter liquid slipped down her throat. She dreaded that first breath afterward, when the lingering taste invariably hit her.

An explosion of tart and sour choked her. There. She shuddered and shook her head. "Could you not add some warmed cordi or honey to it?"

Hoeff frowned. "Medicine not to taste good."

"Then you are doing your job well, dear sir." Kaelyria reached for the cup of water beside her chair and drank it greedily. The awful aftertaste remained.

In the doorway appeared an older woman, sprigs of gray hair escaping a dark red cap. Bosomy, she hugged something to her chest.

Surprised at her presence, Kaelyria pulled her shoulders a little straighter. "Matron Ingwait."

"May we enter, Princess?"

We? "Please." Kaelyria motioned to the bed, the only remaining place for them to be seated. "And please call me Kaelyria."

Matron Ingwait smiled as she entered with two other Ladies. One was tall—very tall—and the other reminded Kae of her own mother but with brown hair. And far more wrinkles. "It is generous of ye to allow us such informality."

Kae wheeled her chair to face them. "Nonsense. Titles were necessary in the Nine. Here, they are an encumbrance."

"Ye are kind. This is Matron Tnimre"—the tall woman—"and Matron Entwila." Ingwait gave another wide smile. "The Ladies of the Heart have met and considered yer request for asylum."

For some reason, Kae's insides twisted and made her nauseous. She wanted to cover her stomach to calm those nerves, but she would not betray herself. Instead, she folded her hands in her lap. "I am grateful you have considered my request, and I am happy to answer whatever concerns or questions you have. I know there was one about my . . . position."

"There was," Matron Entwila said, her voice light and airy. "But no longer."

A bubble of excitement rose through her system. "No?"

"We've spoken with the cacique, who has considerable knowledge of ye and yer family, and who has spent a notable amount of time with ye since yer arrival," Matron Tnimre said. "He has given a glowing endorsement and advocates that ye be allowed to do as ye wish."

Why did that set a cage of butterflies free in her stomach? And heat—on the mercies of Abiassa—in her face. "He has been instrumental in my ability to integrate among the Eilidan. The Cacique is very patient with my many questions."

"Mm, quite," Ingwait said. "Which is why we are assigning ye to help him in his duties."

Kaelyria started. "I beg your mercy?" He didn't need her help, and she knew strong men like him—her father included—did not take kindly to having a woman "help" them in their duties.

"Aselan is a very capable cacique, and we in the Heart are blessed to have him as our leader, but," Matron Entwila said with a light but condescending tone, "well, he just is not good with the paperwork."

"Good?" Matron Tnimre scoffed. "He's terrible. Months behind!"

Kaelyria smiled, nodding. "My father was the same. He could rule nine kingdoms but could not manage to even get letters written. I often helped him—he said it taught me how to rule." She dropped her gaze, startled by the memory. Worried by it as well. "Oh, I didn't mean to imply that I want to rule. Only that—"

"Ye understand what it takes for a kingdom to function."

"Aye," Kae said with a whoosh of relief. "Exactly."

"Which is why ye are especially well suited to assist our cacique. Ye have language and writing skills. And while we do teach the children to write and read, none in the Heart have had the formal instruction ye've had, nor the experience."

"I see." Why were her hands sweating? "And he agrees?"

"Oh, he has no choice, my dear." Matron Ingwait had a mischievous look. "Ye see, the Ladies of the Heart oversee all matters pertaining to the Heart, but the men and our protection are managed by the cacique. If civil matters are not resolved by the Ladies, then the conflict is presented before him."

"It's a fascinating system," Kaelyria said. Of a sort, it was as if women of other kingdoms, who carried out their roles without complaint and with skill in their advancing years, had a formal title here. Ladies of the Heart. "So . . . do I need to sign something?"

"No, my dear. Ye are Eilidan now. No need to buy or swear allegiance."

That seemed rather simple.

"With all rights that all Eilidan woman have, including Etaesian's Feast and Choosing rights."

"Oh." Kae's heart stuttered at the thought of the ceremony where women and older girls chose the man they wanted to be bound to. "Oh, I won't—"

Matron Ingwait held up a hand. "Hold yer peace. We have a month. Things may change."

"In a month?" Kaelyria laughed, then thought better of it. "I do not mean to mock you, but"—she motioned to the chair—"what man would choose someone in my condition?"

"But ye forget, Kaelyria," Ingwait said, "the woman chooses."

"Does not the man have a say?"

"Aye, they do—but no man has ever rejected a Choosing."

"No man?"

Ingwait smiled as she stood. "Ye should report to the cacique's office at yer earliest convenience."

"You mean tomorrow?"

"Are ye busy now?"

"Now?" Kaelyria squeaked, reaching for her hair.

Ingwait's smile spoke of understanding. Of knowing. "Duties must be done, my dear," she said as she strutted out of the cavelike apartment.

Kaelyria wished for cleaner clothes. For some of her dresses from Fieri Keep. For her lady's maid, who'd worked gorgeous knots and braids into her hair. She fingered the braid that hung over her shoulder. *I am so plain* . . .

She sniffed a laugh. Choosing rights.

Even if she were ready for that, he wasn't. He'd made it clear he would not take another bound. Not after losing his first one. And what did she have to offer? No dowry. No title.

But at least she was here. She was an Eilidan. She felt safe. Tucked away from Poired and his menacing voice that tore at her mind. Pinching the bridge of her nose, she tried to shut out the terror of that time.

An ache made her stretch out her leg.

Kaelyria sighed, rubbing her thigh. Then froze. Looked at her leg. Stretched out. Her breath caught in her throat. She couldn't move. But she did. And though it took several long, painful seconds, she was able to return it to the rest on the chair. Stunned, she giggle-cried. Cupped a hand over her mouth. Did it again.

52

Tili ducked into the cave. "D'wyn?" When no answer came, he paused and turned to Chwik behind him. "The stone light." Elan would be amused at the thought of Tili crawling through caves in a mountain, considering he'd ridiculed Elan for being willing to do so. He could wield and provide illumination, but until he knew what, if any, gases lurked in the cave, he would not risk it.

Chwik went to a knee, digging into the pouch.

Inching forward, Tili crouched in the darkness and eyed the passage, which vanished into the darkened void. "D'wyn." His voice carried but then bounced back.

There must be a sharp corner or switchback ahead.

"Here," Chwik said, extending his hand.

Tili took the stone light and let it rest in his palm. Slowly, a glow arose from the stone. He held it out, toward the darkness. Light bloomed, chasing the black farther into the cave. A knock against his knuckles warned him the cave was growing smaller. "Had to be a cave," he muttered as he went to all fours, the stone light carefully tucked in his right hand.

A few feet in, the opening banked right. Tili turned the corner and lifted the stone light again. "D'wyn?"

Silence and darkness stared back.

With a huff, he continued in. Even if this was the wrong way, he had to get his man back.

"Tili!"

He looked up and found eyes staring back. "D'wyn!"

"This way. Hurry."

That gave him the motivation to move faster. "What did ye find?"

No answer came. He glanced to where the others were following, then continued. An opening gaped at the end, and he unfolded himself from the tunnel. Holding out the stone light, he swept the large area.

A small boy sat on the lip of a large boulder. Blankets gathered around him. His hand shifted in the blanket, but his eyes were on Tili.

"He won't let me come closer," D'wyn said.

Tili crossed the space in four strides. "Who are ye?"

"They call me Nagbe," he said, his voice quiet. Almost hoarse.

Tili folded his arms. "Why are ye in this cave, Nagbe?"

"'Tis where I belong." Serene brown eyes held Tili's. He pushed stringy black hair from his face. Yet still held that left hand beneath the blanket. The boy's eyes shifted to the hole, where Tili heard the others coming through. The boy must be a part of the trials. Must know why they were here.

"A lad?" Darielle said, coming to Tili's side, staring at Nagbe. "Poor child."

"Think he knows where the jewel is?" Chwik asked.

"Hello there," Darielle said to the boy, approaching him. "Do you know of the jewel we must find?"

Now-somber eyes held hers. But he didn't speak.

Tili turned to Chwik. "The book."

The twig dug it out and passed it to Tili, who opened it and scanned the wording again. Nothing stood out, though he was sure it contained a clue of some sort.

Darielle pressed in close—too close, batting those eyes at him. "What does it say?"

He extended it in front of her, gaining some distance. "Read it."

With a pout, she squinted at the page. " . . . in the heart of the dark maw amid dirt and grime—"

"Sure fits this," Tokar said, looking around.

Nagbe watched them, curiosity in his brown eyes. But his upper arm muscle flexed as he fidgeted with something in his hand. A shiver ran through his thin body. The blanket moved only slightly.

Tili went to Tokar. "Ye have the jerky?" He ignored the frown Tokar shot him before handing over the jerky from the saddle bag. "Hungry, Nagbe?"

The boy straightened—but only slightly. Another tremor raced through his spine.

"Cold, too," Tili said, eyeing him. "I'm glad we have warm clothes and have been moving. We are not as cold as ye must be."

"What are you doing?" Tokar asked.

Ignoring the question, Tili held up the stone light. "Here." He tossed the stone light to Nagbe. "This has warmth. It'll help some."

"But we need that!" Darielle objected as the light sailed through the air.

Nagbe threw up his arms to catch the stone light. And in the process, flipped the blanket away. There, in his lap, glowed a red orb.

Darielle's gasp shot through the cave.

Brows knotted, Nagbe scowled at Tili. "'Twasn't right, throwing the rock so I'd reveal it."

"And how much more cruel yer hiding what ye knew we were after."

"Those who seek must use wisdom," Nagbe said, his voice even, but perhaps tinged with a remnant of anger.

"Please," Darielle pleaded. "We need the jewel. Would you please give it to us?"

Brown, bored eyes stared back at her again.

"Please," Darielle said, nearly in tears. "We can't finish without it."

"What would it take to open your heart?" D'wyn asked. "Abiassa says we should all open our hearts to the plight of others."

Heart. Book in hands, Tili watched as he thought of Aselan. He closed the book, infused with an idea. Strode between the others. Stood before the boy. "Nagbe," he said, holding out his hand. "Would ye journey with us to the crest?"

"Why would I?"

"Because I see the cold ripping through yer body, and I can ensure ye receive shelter and food."

"You only want the jewel," Nagbe said, holding it up in an open palm.

"Journey with us," Tili said. "At the top, once ye see my word is true, ye can decide about that."

"But I am unable to walk," Nagbe said.

"Then how did you end up here?" Darielle asked.

"I was left here," the boy said.

"I will carry ye," Tili said. "Come with us."

Nagbe held Tili's gaze for several long seconds. "Thank you, sir. I would be glad for some sunshine."

Tili bent toward the boy and lifted him from the boulder. Nagbe clutched the jewel to his chest as Tili strode toward the opening. It was rough, getting the boy up the narrower sections of the tunnel, but once they were in the open, Tili hoisted him onto his back. "Tokar, tie him to me so that my hands are free for the climb."

They used the rope and crisscrossed it over their backs, with the boy's arms wrapped around Tili's neck. Nagbe had a solid fifty pounds on him, adding to the strenuous climb, but Tili kept moving.

"There've been no whistlers," Chwik said. "Unless one happened while we were in the cave."

"This challenge wasn't particularly *challenging*," Darielle commented.

Tokar stayed close, making sure at all times that Tili had what he needed and offering assistance where required. They soon found their way onto a footpath that arced up to the crest of the hill. Soon the top of the nine stone columns came into view. With each step the unit took the columns seemed to grow bigger. Taller.

"Blazes," Nagbe whispered as the Council of Nine became apparent on their stone chairs.

Tili froze. *Something is wrong here . . .*

Tokar uttered an oath. "A Contender's already there."

At that moment, Agremar Ro'Stu came into view, standing on a small platform before the Council. Three of his four stood off to the side, chatting idly.

"And look," Darielle said, their unit slowing when they reached the top. She pointed to where Tortook Puthago approached the nine with three of his four.

"He lost one, too" Chwik mentioned.

"Aye," Tili muttered, a strange chill tracing his spine. He hesitated, loosening the knot of the rope at the center of his chest. Darielle assisted, removing the rope and coiling it, as Tili sorted what he saw. What he felt. The thrum in the air. "Something's wrong."

Tokar came to his side, hefting his bow. "I feel it, too."

"Feel what?" Darielle pointed toward the platform. "They're waiting for us."

As if confirming her words, shapes bled from the trees behind the raised surface.

A wall of fire shot up around the Council members. Chaos ensued, the Council leaping from the platform.

"Run! Run!" one of the younger members shouted. "Incipients!"

53

Chaos. Fiery, terrifying chaos.

With the boy in his arms still, Tili shrank down the mountain. "Back," he spat to his unit. "Back down—"

Like an effigy, a shape went screaming away from the platform, engulfed in flames. So, this . . . this is what he'd been sensing. The chill. The strangeness.

Shrieking momentarily masked all sound as someone near the columns sent up a whistler ten times the intensity of the ones used in the trials. Trying to warn the city, most likely. The sound cut off abruptly when the Councilman died.

Darielle cried out, turning away, tucking her head. Tokar held the girl, fury in his expression as he looked to Tili.

"Here." Tili passed the boy to Tokar. "Go—take them back down. Flee to the Citadel. Don't look back."

D'wyn glowered. "Run? We should fight!"

"And what? Die? They are Poired's army—would yer blade win against dark fire?"

D'wyn swallowed. "He said—this wasn't supposed to happen."

Shock stunned. Then rage tore through Tili. He grabbed the Kergulian by the tunic and hauled him off his feet. "*Who* said? Who did this?"

"Dromadric."

"Tili!"

He turned, ready to drive his fist through D'wyn's face, and found one of the Council members running toward them. "Hurry—west side.

There's a hidden tunnel. It'll take—" The Councilman's arms spread wide. His mouth opened, eyes bulging with shock as fire engulfed him.

Tili drew back.

Darielle screamed as the Councilman died in a heap.

Tili homed in on the row of four incipients advancing, using tactics that were fluid and focused. "Get them to the tunnel," he said to Tokar, eyes locked on the enemy.

"But—"

"*Go!*" Though he had not been trained in the Citadel, Tili had spent countless hours in the Black Forest, teaching himself. He stretched his arms forward and with his right hand, he pulled back as if drawing a bow. He listened to the thrumming in his gut. Held it, the vibration growing . . . growing . . .

Release.

Tili plucked the air, flicking three fingers, which sent a volley of heat and fire across the outcropping. At the last second, it split into three.

The incipients crumpled.

"Good," someone said beside him. "They aren't used to the way you wield, so you have an advantage."

But Tili's gaze was on the sea of red sweeping across the peak of the mountain. Where were Haegan and his Drigo-summoning abilities when they were needed? There were too many enemies. Too few good guys.

"There." A hand stretched in front of him toward a handful of Sirdarians, focusing on Puthago's unit, all huddled in a circle, holding each other. "Together. Move east toward the tunnel as we go."

Tili spared a glance at the accelerant, surprised to find a younger councilman—Kelviel, if he remembered correctly. Shoulder to shoulder, they advanced, wielding, drawing the enemy's fire. Kelviel motioned with his hand, making a mouth that opened and closed.

A body, burning, turned to a smoking corpse.

Tili swallowed. Regretted it, tasting the foul stench of burning flesh. A shower of fire vaulted toward them.

Tili dove to the ground, rolled, and came up with bolts flying. Shooting one after another at the attacking horde. Though his unique method helped him gain ground, there were too many. For every two he took down, a half-dozen more seemed to bleed from the mountain in their red uniforms. Fifty? There had to be at least fifty advancing. They'd flow down the mountain and straight into the heart of the Citadel. Right into the city. There would be no stopping them.

A dark figure emerged in the flames. He looked as Dirag the Desecrator must have looked when Baen faced him in that impossible alley.

"Onerid," Kelviel panted. "Poired's right hand."

"Let's chop it off," Tili muttered, sending a spray across the platform.

Kelviel placed his hand over Tili's. The heat intensified. Flared to twice the breadth and temperature, startling Tili.

Shouts came from behind. It sounded like Tokar and Darielle.

"Stay focused," Kelviel warned. "If we lose—"

The air before him warbled like a clear pond rippling beneath the wind's breath. Tili was lifted off his feet. Flipped backward. He hit the ground hard, groaning. He clawed onto his knees, staring through a sweaty fringe of hair at the advancing incipients.

Movement, white and innocent against the fury of the attack, caught his attention. Darielle rushed straight at Onerid.

"No," Tili breathed, looking between the girl and the general. And only then seeing the small boy in the middle.

Nagbe was on his knees, holding his palms out at the infamous general. *Knees!* He wasn't paralyzed! He was an accelerant, a ruse in the trial. But he was a boy. And he'd get hurt.

"No!" Tili pushed, staggering to one foot. Then the other. He pitched himself across the distance.

"No, it's too late," Kelviel warned.

But Tili launched himself. Each step painful. Torturously slow. He locked onto Nagbe. "No! Back!"

Darielle skidded to a stop, uncertainty and terror etched into her ache-streaked face. She scrambled away, heading in the same direction as the others.

Pawing the air. Each step a dig of his feet into the earth. Anything to propel him faster. His heart slowed to an infinitesimal pace, which felt much like what his feet had taken. *"Nooo!"*

From Onerid came a sea of fire. Racing Tili. Daring him to reach the boy before the flames.

Tili threw out a halo, praying with all the embers he had that it would protect the boy.

A breath.

The fire surged.

Another step.

It warred for supremacy.

Nagbe's gaze dragged to Tili, his mouth open. His young face smudged and surprised. He looked for help. A flicker of hope in his eyes, clinging to the promise Tili had uttered in the cave. To see him to the top. To get him to safety.

Tili vaulted into the air.

The flame struck Nagbe. Focused now. Powerful. The boy flipped, twice. A strangled shout-cry clawed up Tili's throat. The boy hit the ground with a sickening thud.

The agonizing, surreal pace snapped closed.

Tili slid across the rocks and dirt. Sucked out the air, forbidding the flames to eat the boy's body. He scrambled the last few feet to the limp frame. "Nagbe." Snatching the boy up, he was on his feet.

Onerid roared.

Though Tili hesitated, meeting that fury-engulfed gaze for a split-second more, Kelviel and another Councilman swept in front of him and faced off against the general. "Behind the rise," Kelviel shouted.

Tili hesitated for but a second. Stumbled backward. Nearly tripped over Puthago's charred body and those of his team. He squeezed out the reality and pushed himself over the knoll, clutching Nagbe tightly against his chest. "Hold on," he grunted to the boy.

Tokar was there, watching. Waiting. "Hurry!" He waved, holding what looked like a door of grass. Beneath the cover, inches-thick iron.

Hefting the boy into a better hold, he heard the fight raging as he hurried through the smoke. He had no sooner cleared the opening than Kelviel and the other dropped in behind him. "Nagbe," he said, glancing at the boy's face, half blackened from Onerid's strike. But his eyes were closed. Was he breathing?

They secured the door, welding shut behind them. "No time to stop. Go," Kelviel breathed. "All the way down."

"Take them. I'll adjust the dials," the other said.

"Abiassa guard you, Aoald," Kelviel said as he turned to Tokar and Tili. "We must hurry." Light bubbled around them, evidence of the man's wielding and guiding them. Rumblings and tremors shook the shoulder-wide tunnel as they hurried down . . . down . . . down . . . the mountain.

They slipped through a couple of passages, Tili's heart in his throat. Just had to hurry, get Nagbe to a pharmakeia. He'd be well. Had to be. *I will not lose him.* Not the jewel of a trial, but the jewel of a precious life.

What felt like a solid twenty minutes later, the ground leveled, and they approached the next door. The boy wasn't breathing. Hadn't twitched a single muscle. *Just keep going . . .*

"No, this way," Kelviel turned toward an empty wall. He pressed his hands in two corners and the wall surrendered. Hissed back. "Go."

They entered a small, hidden passage that led to the right, then banked hard left. After one more corner, they stood on rickety stairs overlooking a cavernous space.

Structured. One section lined with rows of long boxes. Another with shelves of jars. "The catacombs," Kelviel whispered. "We'll be safe here. At least for a bit."

Tili slowed, navigating the treacherous steps, realizing they were as steep as his thoughts. As the ledge hope had leapt from. Grief had thrown him from. *Nagbe . . .*

On the lower level, he stopped short of where a small gathering waited, close enough to be heard, but far enough not to be seen. Tili slumped against the wall and closed his eyes. Pulled Nagbe to his chest. Crushed him hard. Choked back tears, swallowing against the rawness in his throat. He slid to the dirt floor and buried his face against the boy's neck.

Grief yanked a sob from his chest. He gasped. Surrendered. A sob. Another. Hand trembling, Tili cupped the boy's face. Remembered his eyes—bright once they'd reached the peak. His foolish, naïve courage at facing Onerid.

Nagbe's face blurred beyond his tears.

I failed you.

54

Hiel-touck! Was he supposed to work with her in the same small space? He would not begrudge the need for the wheeled chair, but it was so cumbersome in a cave, whether a sleeping cave or working. He could not argue—she needed a duty. And he would as soon have her here with him as he would anywhere she might be . . . bothered.

Ingwait. This was her doing, and not to ensure he caught up on his records. But to implant Kaelyria in his path. Conveniently, right before Etaesian's Feast.

Aselan sat back in his chair, paper in hand. He tapped a pen against his lip, scanning the document.

Kaelyria bent over a table to his right, transferring numbers from receipts to a ledger. She'd been working quietly for an hour now.

He, on the other hand, had stared at the same document for most of that time. And still had no idea what it said. With a huff, he flicked it onto the table. It fluttered to the corner. And slid off.

He lunged to catch it.

But it flipped direction and slid right beneath her chair.

Of course. Of course it had to do that.

That paper wasn't too important. He could pick it up later. Irritated, he snatched the next one on the pile. *Focus!* Reading the first line, he realized it was a report from the Outlands scout. The sentence was a fragment, but spoke of uncertainty about the direction the cacique would want to take. About what? Where was—

Aselan let out a long sigh. Closed his eyes. Then looked to the paper on the floor. Beneath Kaelyria. He needed it.

"Keep sighing so heavily and you will take all the air from the room," she said softly, amusement in her tone. Then she glanced at him over her shoulder, elbows on the table where she worked. "My father was notorious for sighing when he was annoyed."

He pushed his chair back and stood. "No annoyance." Unless one considered his annoyance with himself. "If ye'll grant me yer mercy," he said as he went to a knee.

Kaelyria's eyes widened and she straightened, watching.

"A paper," he mumbled, ducking his head and leaning beneath her chair. "It slipped beneath yer chair."

"Oh! I'm—let me move." She swung the chair back.

"No!"

Her chair rolled over his hand.

He groaned.

"Oh mercies!" Her eyes bugged and she reached for him. "Aselan, I beg your mercy. What—how horrible."

"It is well," he said, flexing his fingers and finding no damage. She was too close to him. Too distracting. Why did she have to be here?

"I'm in your way," she said softly, forlornly.

"Nay." 'Twas but a small lie. "The office is small."

"Of course it is, especially with this chair." She nodded, wheeling backward. "I'll ask Matron Ingwait to reassign me to somewhere more . . . with more room."

He caught the support of her chair. "No."

"I do not want to be a bother to you, Aselan."

"'Tis well," he said again, retrieving the paper. "Please—continue yer duties. They are duly appointed and ye are . . . efficient." He needed to leave. "I must find Byrin and speak with him about this report."

Aselan strode quickly down the passage, away from his thoughts, his guilt—both over leaving her just now and his inability to harness what he felt. As he rounded the corner, a loud clatter stopped him.

It'd come from behind, the passage. The office! Had she fallen? He spun back, jogging toward the office. "Kaely—" He stopped short.

She stood before him, hands braced against the table she'd been

working on. The wheelchair against the far wall. Her own legs supporting her, though she leaned heavily on the table. She tucked her chin and
a silent cry jerked her body.

"Kae . . ." He moved closer, stunned that she was standing on her
own—weakly, but she was doing it. "Ye can walk?"

She shook her head, a strangled sob shoving tears down her face.

He touched her back. Noticed her limbs trembling. Aselan supported
her by wrapping an arm around her shoulder. She collapsed against his
chest, crying. Instinct drew her closer. Held her tight as she sobbed.

"Please," she said. "Please don't send me back."

He guided her to the wheeled chair. "Kae, sit."

"No," she growled. "I will *not* sit in that chair one minute more. I want
to walk again. I want to be strong." Her glossy blue eyes begged him. "Let
me stay. Let me prove to you that I can do this."

He leaned back, staring hard into her snow-blue eyes. "Ye are strong,
Kaelyria. Stronger than any woman I've met."

Disbelief spiraled through her gaze as she held his. And he could feel
her rapid heartbeat against his side as he supported her. Felt her curves
pressing into him out of necessity, though he told himself not to notice.
Red rimmed her eyes, product of the shed tears and weeks of strain. A
strange ache wove through his chest. He brushed the loose strands of hair
from her cheek, trailing along her soft skin, too. She shuddered beneath
his touch. Her lips were full and red. Her breaths growing uneven as
attraction spiraled between them.

Her warm, warm fingers traced his face, his beard, making it hard for
him to breathe. To think. He pulled her closer. Leaned down, aiming for
her mouth.

Laughter shot through the passage, smacking Aselan's thoughts back
into line. He swallowed, cursing his weakness as he grabbed the top rail
of his chair. Jerked it closer. "Here."

She dropped heavily onto the wooden chair, hands propping her as she
studied the floor. Aselan squatted in front of her. "Ye are strong, Kaelyria.
That ye can stand—Hoeff said it was impossible."

"I believed him," she said, "but he also said we should not stop trying.
Whatever he has done, it is working."

Aselan smiled. "I am glad to hear it."

She searched his eyes. "Are you?"

His gut clenched. "More than I care to admit." No one had ever been so bold with him before, but Kaelyria was a princess, used to demanding answers and summoning submission from those around her.

"I have nothing left, Aselan. No home. No dowry. Even my brother is gone from me."

"But for a time."

"Still, I am alone," she said. "I have no purpose. I am . . . lost."

"Ye are not alone, nor are ye lost." He nodded around them. "The Ladies have welcomed ye, and the Legiera will protect ye."

She looked down, as if he'd said something wrong. "My—my father sent Haegan to the towers when he fell to the poison. He severed their close tie."

"And ye thought I would do the same?"

"I made you angry with the chair and being in the way. Then you stormed out." Tears slipped free, her chin dimpling. "I can stand. You saw—please let me stay."

He cupped her face, looking up into those icy blue eyes. "Kae . . ." A kiss. That's all it would take to quiet her fears. And ignite his.

"Cacique!"

Deflated, Aselan rose to his feet, noticing Kaelyria turn her back to the door to hide her face.

Byrin came into view. He slowed, looking between Aselan and the princess. Then thumbed over his shoulder. "They've brought a thief to the hall," he muttered, still gazing, measuring.

"I'll be there." Aselan waited for Byrin to nod and back away before turning to Kaelyria. "Work for as long as ye will here." He allowed himself to touch her shoulder. "Ye are always welcome."

He might has well have told her to clean his laundry, too. He had never been good at flattery or flirting. What was he to say to her? He could make no open commitment. As cacique they depended on him. But would not two minds, trained for leadership, work better than one?

Yet . . . he had lost one love. Could he risk another?

55

"What is your name?"

Haegan would give neither his name nor any other information. He knelt in the middle of the cell, watching a large rat scurry over the chain that secured him to a rusted iron hook embedded in the ground. Odd bands cuffed his wrists, a strange thrumming emanating through them and the cell. The energy brought a bitter chill that raced across his shoulders and dug into his bones. His head ached, his nose dripping like a leaky tap.

The rat boldly sped past the guards, right into a small corner hole.

It was then that Haegan realized the tiny pieces of rock beneath him weren't rock. They were rat droppings. How many were holed up in that corner? Disgust made his stomach clench. His skin itched. He wanted to push up. But 'twas a fitting end to his rebellion against Abiassa, was it not? He had not been forced from Hetaera. He had not been coerced. He'd walked out of luxury and stature . . . straight into imprisonment.

But I did not want to be the Fierian. Anything is better than that.

Trale and Astadia had sure vanished quick enough. For the first few hours, Haegan waited for rescue at the barred window. But none came.

"Your name." Boots shined glossy black, the Sirdarian stood over him in his crisp blood-red uniform.

If they didn't know his name, maybe the sibling assassins had not betrayed him. They had promised the Infantessa wanted him. But what was the word of an assassin? He would not provide any information. Would not answer their queries.

Pain exploded across his temple, his teeth clacking from the blow. He found himself lying on his side, a metallic sweetness in his mouth.

"One more time," the Sirdarian said, his words menacing as two guards hoisted Haegan upright again. "Name!"

Lip and head throbbing, Haegan spit blood from his mouth. Giving his name would only get him killed.

Another blow—this time to the other side of his head. He toppled again, pain scorching his temple. A kick to his face snapped his head back. His eye began to swell.

Anger rose. He curled his fingers to wield, but he felt a searing fire rush back along his hand and arm. What . . . ?

"Shielding," Sirdarian grinned. "They turn the current of heat back on you."

"Captain." A guard rushed into the cell and whispered to the officer.

The heavy shield around Haegan's wrists made his shoulders ache, so he rested his hands on his legs as he knelt.

Shouts preceded an eerie silence that seemed to stretch in and snake around Haegan's mind, making it . . . itch. The earthy, spicy sent filled his nostrils as the strange, insistent feeling needled him. He groaned, desperate to be rid of it all. What was it?

The guards snapped to attention.

Haegan stilled, wondering at the change.

From around the corner came a billowing sea of amethyst. Four—five—six guards in purple and silver marched in, then broke off to the sides, revealing a petite woman with russet hair and a green gown. She wore a crown of stars and a sheer veil that framed her round face and poured over her shoulders and thick, curly hair. Gems in the crown glittered beneath the prison torchlight. Her pale brown eyes settled on Haegan. Then widened. "Captain," she said, her voice as satiny as her gown. Yet sharp as the points on the stars. "*What* is this?"

A man in a black suit with amethyst stitch-work along the cuffs and shoulders stood between them and the woman. "The Infantessa," he intoned, "asks, 'What is this, Captain?'"

The captain shifted nervously. "Please tell her highness, it is an interrogation. She shouldn't—"

"And have you *my* permission to interrogate this man?" An odd mix of empathy and that bitter, discordant stench of fury swam at Haegan.

"The Infantessa asks, 'Do you have my permission to interrogate this man?'"

The captain lowered his gaze. "No, your majesty."

"The captain says, 'No, your majesty.'"

Majesty. Your Highness. Infantessa. This—this was the woman who asked for him? She seemed but a child. Too young to have the experience and knowledge of even his father.

"Remove the shielders at once," she commanded, and her lackey repeated the order.

"Yes, your majesty," he said, lumbering in and disengaging the clamps. The annoying thrum fell away, and Haegan slumped beneath the relief.

The Infantessa waved the suit aside. Glared at the captain. "And of course, you know the punishment for such crimes, yes?"

Eyes wild, the captain nodded. "I do, your majesty."

She extended a hand to Haegan. "Come."

"The Infantessa says to come," the suited man said.

Even as Haegan struggled to his feet, in his periphery he saw the captain draw his dagger. Haegan hauled in a sharp breath—would the captain murder him right here, before their monarch?

Instead, the captain turned the dagger on himself.

"No!" Haegan lurched.

But the captain drove the blade into his own heart.

Horrified, Haegan staggered with a yelp that died in his throat.

He deserved it.

The thought shook Haegan. How did a man deserve that? What justice—

The Infantessa reached toward Haegan's face. Despite the captain committing suicide beside her, she wagged her fingers. "Come," she said again, as calm as before, as unaffected as before.

"The Infantessa says, 'Come,'" the black-suit said.

"No," she said to the man. "I would speak to him."

Confused at the strange formality and sickened by the captain's suicide, Haegan accepted her hand. She tucked her arm through his, pulling him from the room. With one last backward glance, he noted the other guards were stunned and hadn't moved. What . . . ?

Royal guards swarmed in around them, protecting and marching them out of the dank prison, down long, stone halls without ornamentation. Straight out of the building. Right to a waiting carriage of brilliant purple and gold.

Two guards waited and opened the carriage door. Held out their hands in assistance. She glided right into the gilt box and sat facing forward.

Something writhed in him, down deep—distant—as he neared the carriage. What was it? He slowed, but felt a bump against his spine. Hesitation held him fast. A roiling in his gut. There was that smell again . . . bitter, yet sweet. A stench but not.

A guard's chest brushed his shoulder. A subtle thrust of his chin told Haegan to enter. Where else was he to go? Back to the cell?

Haegan climbed the two steps. Faced backward. He stole a peek at her, but it felt wrong to gaze upon the Infantessa. Especially knowing he must look a fright with the swollen-shut eye and busted lip.

"I do apologize," she said, removing her long gloves. "The Sirdarians have a ridiculously high code that"—she sighed—"they sometimes take too seriously. I mean, killing himself over such a small infraction." She clucked her tongue. "I would have overlooked such a display, but not the harm he visited upon you."

He would not have survived there anyway. "I thank you for removing me, but . . . why?"

"You are my guest, Haegan."

Surprise swam through him, heady. "You know who I am?"

She laughed, hands gracefully placed in her lap. "Of course! I sent dear Trale after you. But the poor boy just hadn't anticipated that you might need a little extra looking after."

"He was very good to me." Haegan felt the need to defend the man. Would Trale find himself driving a dagger into his own chest when the Infantessa spoke to him next? "More patient than I'd expected of his kind."

"His kind?" Her voice squeaked, and she bobbed her head from side to side. "I suppose he isn't up to your moral standard, but Trale Kath is loyal to the core."

"I have no doubt." Haegan's stomach roiled, so he looked out the window, guessing his nausea had to do with the rocking of the carriage. "Where are we going?"

"To Karithia." When Haegan glanced at her, she smiled. "My home."

'Twas then he realized he had expected the Iteverian sovereign to be as old as his parents. Her reputation, legacy, even her voice and maturity declared it so. But in her face, youthfulness. Beauty. Eyes as brown as the hills. Hair reddish-brown, thick, and curly. No woman was her equal.

Thiel would—

A sharp pain stabbed through his skull. "Augh!" Haegan grimaced and hunched, pressing the heel of his hand to his head.

"Are you well, Haegan?"

"Aye," he gritted, ashamed she would see him like this. "A little pain— probably from . . . prison."

"I am disappointed about your cruel welcome to Unelithia," she said. "Be assured it will not happen again."

Relaxing as the pressure eased, Haegan nodded his thanks. They raced through the city, unyielding of the people, who screamed and leapt out of the way. As they tore past them, he saw more than one face etched in fear.

No, in abject awe.

They really love their queen.

"So, you are the Infantessa Shavaussia."

She smiled, her complexion so pure, a beautiful paleness rivaling opals. "That is my title and diplomatic name. You may call me Nydelia."

"Like Nydessa."

She gave a nod. "Exactly. My mother was Nydessan when my father took her."

"Took her."

She breathed a laugh. "I'm afraid their story is not as romantic as your parents', Haegan. My mother was a concubine."

And yet, Nydelia was chosen as the heir to Iteveria. "I remember my father was very sad to hear of your father's passing."

With a sniff, she looked out the window. "As were we all."

He knew diplomacy. Knew political speech. And that had a ring of antipathy to it. A shout went up outside, and the carriage slowed but little before careening through a bejeweled gate. "Home at last," she said sweetly.

It took another five minutes of winding roads and climbing hills before the carriage pulled to a stop. The door opened, and the Infantessa stepped into the morning light.

Haegan exited and was immediately struck by the glittering of the tiered city set into the hills below, as if the dwellings knelt at the foot of the castle. White structures. All white. Everywhere. Stacked tightly, they crowded the mountain, some peeking from green foliage and trees.

"Sir," a stiff voice said.

Haegan turned to the voice—a guard.

"This way," he commanded.

Only as the towering man moved did Haegan see the golden castle. He'd heard of it—though Gwogh had rejected it as vanity. *"What lies within must match the splendor without to earn the title 'beauty,'"* his old tutor had warned.

Clearly, Sir Gwogh had not met the Infantessa, or he would have instantly declared Iteveria not simply beautiful, but resplendent. Minarets and towers gleamed in the bright sun. Balconies reaching out over the portico sparkled and shimmered.

"Sir," the guard prompted.

Haegan started for the portico and entered through a massive set of glass doors. Glass? Was the Infantessa not concerned with safety?

Who would want to harm her?

A butler greeted him with a low bow. "Prince Haegan, welcome to Karithia, the seat of Iteveria and the blessed halls of our beatific Infantessa Shavaussia." He held out a white-gloved hand toward the monstrous balcony. "I am Paung, butler of Karithia. If you would follow me, I will show you to your room."

"Room?"

He inclined his head as he walked. "It is one of the smaller rooms, but since our generous Infantessa will host a gala in a week's time, she must reserve those suites for dignitaries."

"Of course." Haegan blinked, surprised at the jealousy spiraling through his chest. Why would she not give him, a foreign prince, a nice room?

Paung led the way up the grand staircase, then turned left. He strode down a shorter hall before climbing another flight. A catwalk spanned the open staircase below and gave birth to a hall of rooms. At the far end, Paung pushed through a pair of doors, strode to a bank of windows, and nudged apart two sets of glass panels.

A salty breeze swept in from the balcony that stretched the entire length of the room. Haegan's breath backed into his throat as he stepped outside and gazed at the glittering body of water reaching to the horizon. "The Nydessan Sea," he muttered, any further words lost in awe.

Water crashed against rocks far below. The palace sat atop a mountain and was built into the cliff overlooking the Nydessan Sea. Blue-green waters stirred a foamy wake then drifted back out to sea. He had never seen anything so beautiful. Though he'd heard of it in the Histories, he'd forgotten. And never expected to see its splendor.

"I hope this is acceptable."

"It is more than acceptable." *See? I was right to leave.* Here . . . He could stay here. *Live by the sea. In peace. A place fit for a prince.*

Paung smiled and bowed. "Of course, the Infantessa has seen to your other needs as well." He went to shuttered doors and drew them apart. A room—no, a closet the size of a full room—had been stocked with tunics, coats, trousers, shoes.

Surprised yet again, Haegan crossed the bedroom and stared at the array of clothing. "How did she know my size?"

"There is little our Infantessa does not know," Paung said. "The bed will be turned down each night by the staff and made again in the morning. They will come and go without bother to you. Should you need anything, your attendant can take care of it."

"Attendant?"

Paung motioned to the corner, where a man stood as still as a statue in a dark green suit. "Thomannon will attend you during your stay."

The servant clapped his hands against his thighs, then bowed curtly. "Sir."

After acknowledging the man, Haegan took in the room. The bed—exquisite and large. The posts two-hands in breadth. Rich, brocade tapestries draped its sides. A sitting area with a fireplace looked out onto the balcony. In an adjoining room stood a table set for one and a buffet server supporting a bowl of flawless-looking fruit as well as a tray bearing crystal glasses and a decanter of cordi wine.

"Your meals will be served there, except for the eve meal, when you are expected in the main dining hall."

"Where is that?"

"An escort will deliver you when it is time," Paung said.

Haegan followed the butler to another room with a marble tub and a glass enclosure.

"Ah, your shower."

"Shower?"

Paung pointed to the lever. "Pull, and it will open, feeding water from the falls into the enclosure. The drain carries the rest back to the sea."

"Incredible!"

"King Adin was quite the innovator," Paung said as he returned to the entry, gripping a knob in each hand. "Enjoy the view. If you have need of anything, ask Thomannon."

Haegan again glanced at the statue-like man, then back to the butler. But the doors were closed. *Click.* Locks? Had he locked Haegan in? For what purpose? He went to the doors and tested them. "They're locked."

"All doors are secured at all times," came the rumbling voice of Thomannon. "To keep the Infantessa and her guests safe."

Was her safety so jeopardized that they must lock guests in? *But the safety of a sovereign is important.* Disquieted, Haegan returned to the balcony. He palmed the warm stone and stared out. Breathed in deeply, enjoying the moisture on his face. This was something he'd not experienced before. Lakes of Fire? Searing heat? Aye. But cool air bathed in the salty breath of the sea?

Yet something niggled at Haegan. Pulled at him. What, he couldn't be sure.

"What is the hour, Thomannon?"

"A quarter past first chime."

Haegan nodded. "And the next meal?" His stomach rumbled at the thought.

"Six chimes." Thomannon inclined his head. "I could send for food if you are hungry."

"That would be appreciated," Haegan said, pointing to the bath chamber. "May I shower now?"

"As you will." Thomannon moved across the room and vanished into the bathroom, where a squeak preceded a whoosh of water. He started the shower. "I will lay out fresh clothes, my lord."

Strange. This was the life he'd had in Fieri Keep, with an aged tutor and a manservant to serve him. But having legs, being able bodied, it felt odd to have a stranger waiting on him with such expediency.

But he did not deserve this.

Why? You are a prince!

Perhaps. But he should guard against growing lax and at ease in an enemy capital. What would Father do?

Why? The Infantessa said I'm her guest. Courtesies. They were courtesies expected of any noble house, extending kindness to a visiting dignitary. And that's what Haegan was, essentially, wasn't he?

The thought that nagged at him as he undressed plucked once more—louder. What if the Infantessa found out he was the Fierian? Could she use him? Why would she?

56

Palms pressed to the cool stone, Tili stared down at Nagbe, peacefully sleeping in Her embrace. *I failed you.* With a heavy sigh, he pressed his hand on the dirty brown hair. The boy would not be washed or ceremonially cleansed in preparation for burial. Nor would he be afforded a spot in the earth, but a box in a cave because of the war roiling aboveground.

"We must hurry," a woman whispered to Gwogh, who stood to the side.

This boy . . . he represented everything in Tili's life. Alive, he'd represented a new beginning, a youthfulness. Dead, he represented failure, an end to all things hoped for.

"Prince Tili," the woman insisted.

Annoyed and agitated, he ground his teeth. "This boy's death is on yer head," he growled, pushing a glower to the woman. "Ye used a *child* as a pawn in this trial. Now he lies dead, and ye wish me to—"

"No one could have known Onerid was coming."

"Clearly, someone knew," Tili countered. "D'wyn said the grand marshal paid him to sabotage my unit. Dromadric is in league with the Sirdarians."

"Your anger is justified, Tili." Gwogh's face was contrite, remorseful. "But there are things we must discuss, and we must soon leave the catacombs."

Again, Tili glanced at Nagbe, memorizing his little face, then he nodded, took a step back, and tucked his hands beneath his armpits. Grief folded into the length of fabric two sentinels placed over the boy's frame.

"Come." Gwogh's voice was a homing beacon, luring Tili back to the present, as he guided him to where the Council—what remained of it—had gathered.

But one step jolted Tili. He pivoted. "Thiel." His heart crashed. "She was in the city."

"I sent her away this morning."

Tili breathed a little easier as they joined the others around a table littered with cracked stones and bronze plates. Agremar stood with his hands behind his back and gave Tili a weighted nod.

Towering at the head of the table, Gwogh remained respectful as he proceeded. "The day is dreadful and has robbed this world of greatness and beauty," he said. "But six of the Council remain, and—"

"We should be up there fighting," Agremar growled. "I lost three of my unit—many others were killed. They are defenseless—"

"The city guards and Ignatieri are well trained, Agremar. Generals Grinda and Negaer will recover quickly. If Onerid is to be stopped, your presence or absence is unlikely to be the deciding factor." Kedulcya gave the Viddan sentinel a long look—stern, but not unkind. When he nodded, tight jawed, she continued, speaking firmly into the thick tension. "The purpose of this Council is, first and foremost, to ensure the Guidings and laws remain in place to guide the Nine. As such, we have before us a great quandary."

Tili shifted on his feet, thumbing his lower lip. Thinking of the people aboveground. Of his father in Ybienn.

Gwogh took over. "Because the Contending was not completed, and because only two of the Contenders even reached the final stage—"

"Three," Tili said. Beside him, Tokar shifted in his boots.

Gwogh nodded. "Three, but only two made it to safety." His smile faltered. "And only one of you brought the jewel to the peak."

Gaze drifting, Tili found himself looking at the draped body of Nagbe.

"The jewel," Gwogh said softly, "was not the gem, but the boy."

"So it is," Kedulcya said, her voice raspy, "this Council has voted to put into effect the Pelaeris Protocol."

Tili frowned.

"By a two-thirds vote, which is all that remains, sadly," Gwogh said, "we have elected a temporary leader, a steward, to hold the throne and be the representative of the Nine until . . ." He sighed. "Until we are whole once more and can make better sense."

Kelviel came to Tili, handing him a sealed parchment. "This decree is your official title as Steward of the Nine."

Heaviness tugged at Tili's shoulders as he slowly, reluctantly accepted the decree.

"Tili," Gwogh said. "It is urgent that you go with your guard"—a half-dozen Jujak emerged from the hall—"and ride with all haste to Vid. They have readied your mount."

"Vid?"

Kedulcya nodded. "The Viddans have regained control of their kingdom, and we will convene there in one month."

Hefting the parchment in his hand, Tili nodded. He started toward the guard, then paused and turned back. "I would have Tokar ride with me."

Gwogh inclined his head. "As the steward wills."

How had this day come? Jaw clenched, Tili followed the guard deeper, lower into the catacombs. They rounded a twist in the passage. A damp, pungent odor smacked him. Sewers. He snorted. Fitting, considering their situation.

"I'm surprised you asked for me to come."

"Ye proved me wrong," Tili said, willing to accept the truth.

A man waited in the tunnel ahead. At their approach, he pivoted and inclined his head. "Draorin, Steward as'Tili."

Tili grasped the man's forearm, startled by his strength. "Well met, Draorin." Did every person in the Nine name their children after Baen's Deliverers?

"We ride east," Draorin said.

"Aye, and fast."

"Tili." Gwogh came up the tunnel after them with a heavily bedecked guard, whose gold cord stretched from shoulder to waist and was secured to his belt. Valor Guard. Haegan's man.

Gwogh motioned to him. "This is Colonel Marz Chauld. He has volunteered for your guard."

Colonel Chauld stepped forward. Clapping a fist to his chest, he gave a curt bow.

Tili appreciated the ready respect but it didn't answer his question: "Yer offer is well made, Colonel, but don't ye have someone else to protect?"

"Share your report, Colonel Chauld," Gwogh said.

Chauld again gave a curt nod. "Sir, our spies report Prince Haegan was seen crossing the plains of western Vid two days past in the company of two Iteverian assassins."

Assassins? Tili scowled. "He is captive then? Are we—"

"No, sir." Chauld's voice was severe. "Not captive. The prince travels *with* them, sir."

"With *assassins*?" Tili scowled at Gwogh. "He is smarter than that. Everyone is smarter than that."

"Aye," Gwogh said, and his face—Tili's gut clenched. His expression betrayed the same pain Tili had seen on his father's face when Thiel had been taken, all those years ago.

"I do not understand."

"Most don't."

"If he travels with them," Tili said slowly, "he either trusts them or is using them for some means." But even Haegan wasn't foolish enough to try to manipulate two Iteverians assassins. "Or . . ." He squinted at Gwogh. "Ye have an idea."

"I must warn you, Tili, the Unelithian lands are rife with mercenaries, and a very powerful incipient."

"Unelithia? I thought I was going to Vid."

"That is the official word, but I now fear our prince has gotten himself into a situation far more deadly than he could imagine," Gwogh said gravely.

"Sirdar himself?"

Gwogh shook his head. "An inflamer, the most powerful I have ever encountered, one who can inflame thoughts and turn them against the person so subtly, so skillfully, the person loses themself in their own desires. This inflamer is a master. I, myself, narrowly escaped her clutches decades past."

"Her?"

"The Infantessa."

57

"Look. I might not 'ave da smarts t' talk right, but I knows fings," Laertes said as he stared across the clearing. They'd borrowed mounts to leave the city, then made their way here.

"What things?" Thiel swung the pack free from her horse and proceeded to untack the animal. The horses would have to find their own way back. She glanced to the Citadel in the distance, swallowing hard at the blackened haze covering it. Then she searched the blue sky above.

Laertes followed her gaze, squinting. "You shore it's coming?"

"I'm sure."

He seemed to accept this, and jumped back to their previous conversation. "I knows dat what fills the sky ain't from celebration fires."

Thiel felt a knot in her stomach. "No, ye are right. It's not celebration fires." At least not Hetaeran celebration fires.

"Dems da dark ones, ain't it?"

"I think so," Thiel said with a sigh. Had Haegan escaped? Tili? She looked to Praegur, afraid for the ones she'd left behind. Afraid for herself and her companions.

Praegur shifted, watching the city. He too, apparently, was conflicted about leaving Haegan. But then his face smoothed of the concern that had rippled through it a second past. He met her gaze, confident and calm, and shook his head.

"He's not there?"

Praegur shook his head again.

Relief rushed through her. "We should go." But they couldn't. Where was their ride?

A shadow grew larger and larger, swooping down on them.

With two massive thwaps of her furry wings, Chima alighted in the field. The horses bolted, and she chortled, as if amused by their fear. Her fiery eyes blinked at Thiel. Being with the raqine did something to her courage, to her belief that hope still existed when the capital was burning and Haegan was . . . somewhere.

Laertes whooped. "I knows dat dem dark ones will fink twice—or tens—'bout messing wif' a beau'ful girl what comes from da sky on a raqine!"

"Aye, but let us hope that the Ematahri won't panic. And that Chima will help them listen to us." Really, what worried her more was being accepted. Because that would involve expectation. Though her feelings for Cadeif were deep, they had never been the same as what she felt for Haegan. But, after their argument . . . she'd never felt so mixed up.

A warm, wet nose nudged her hand.

Thiel glanced at Chima, her dark red coat nearly black in the stretching shadows. Chima gave a low, mournful chortle. Could she sense was happening in the capital?

Even now, Chima stalked into the open, slinking down. She lifted her snout into the air and sniffed—through her mouth, taking in deeper scents. She rolled her shoulders, shaking back and forth. A high-pitched shriek—almost undetectable to the human ear—streaked through the night.

"What's she doin' dat for?"

"She's calling to him," Thiel whispered. *Just as I am.* But he would not be coming. He had told her to leave. He'd been so angry. Which was unlike him. And strange.

She turned to Chima and touched her ear. "Laertes."

"Wha'?

"Time to leave. Ye first—we must ride with the smallest at the front."

"I ain't neva' rode one of 'em." Eyes wide, Laertes swallowed as he came closer. "Me mo'vah wouldn't even let me drive da wagon what we had 'cuz she said I would crash it." He motioned to Chima. "What if I crash her?"

"She will never surrender that much control." Thiel smiled. "And I will be guiding her. Ye do not have to worry." She nodded to Praegur, who aided the boy onto Chima's back.

The raqine's spine rippled.

"Whoa-hoa," Laertes said, then laughed as he planted his hands on the side of Chima's neck.

"Be careful there. She's sensitive around her neck," Thiel warned as she hoisted herself up. No sooner had she felt the pressure of Praegur's chest against her shoulders than Chima stood. Gave another high-pitched signal to Haegan, who was probably impervious to her calls, then trotted into the clearing.

Her wings thwapped out.

Laertes stiffened, glancing to either side at the strong span.

"Relax," Thiel said. "When we tense, we also tense our legs—it can impede her."

"Oh." He swallowed. "Right."

Carrying three people required more effort, but Chima handled it with ease, tearing across the plain with near-frightening swiftness. Laertes struggled against the wind, but Thiel nudged his head down as she leaned into him. The wind force would only worsen once they were airborne.

And Chima leapt higher.

Laertes yelped.

Thiel smiled, closing her eyes as gravity surrendered to the creature of myth. Who was more real than most things people believed in.

As the wind leveled off, consistent and a roar in their ears, Laertes straightened. Pumped a hand in the air and gave a long, victorious cry. It was hard not to smile. And Thiel had to admit—she'd missed this. Feeling the wind in her hair. The fresh, crisp air. Watching land blur past below their feet and Chima's agile body. Missed Chima. Zicri. Racing Tili through the skies, though they would never admit such mischief to their father.

For three hours, they soared to the south. A tap on her shoulder made her look back to Praegur. He pointed to the ground. Hundreds of feet below them, she noticed a blackened area, but didn't recognize it. As Chima continued her course, Thiel saw in the far distance the Lakes of

Fire. But that meant . . . she twisted to look back toward the blackened patch. The Throne Road! The forest on the eastern side had been burned!

She snapped around to the front, scanning. A gorge ran the length between the Siannes and Ematahri land, which rested on the border of the Outlands. From this vantage, she detected movement. What was it? "Chima, descend low! North."

The commands were simple but effective. Her father and brothers knew them in both the plain tongue and the tongue of the ancients. It didn't matter—she just needed to scout the gorge.

"What's wrong?" Laertes asked, glancing back at her.

But Thiel focused on the gorge. "Low and fast, Chima," she shouted, Chima's ear close to her as the great beast turned and dipped down.

"Whoa!" Laertes shouted.

They dove and had to hold on tight, but Chima soon leveled off and soared over the gorge.

Thiel's heart rammed into her throat as she sorted what had drawn their attention. Three columns of Sirdarians. Marching through the winding gorge. Straight for Ematahri land. "Up, up, Chima!"

They went vertical, straight up into the clouds. "Fast and true," Thiel shouted.

With powerful flaps of her wings and an arch of her back Chima rumbled with a formidable growl as she lurched forward.

Like an arrow, she shot through the sky. The wind tore at them, unusually warm in this season and so close to the Siannes. They sailed to the edge of Ematahri territory, and Thiel guided Chima down. "Hurry," Thiel said. "They saw us."

"Da blood cloaks?"

"No, the Ematahri."

"But I 'fought dis wasn't deir land yet?" Laertes said, following her and Chima into the thick woods. Praegur brought up the rear.

"'Tis not. But they have scouts. Trust me," she said, shouldering into her pack. "They've seen"—movement ahead—"us." She just hoped it wouldn't be—

"Etelide."

Heat rushed up Thiel's spine and across her shoulders as Chima stopped beside her. Slowly, she came around to her left and looked. Her heart tripped. "Cadeif."

Taller than her by a head and a half, stronger by leagues, he stood with a spear in one hand, a sword in the other. Thick black coils dangled down shoulders and nearly reached the center point of the crisscrossed bands that had been dyed in the blood of his enemies. Formidable like her father, gorgeous like none other. Around his neck now hung a stone. A green stone.

Thiel drew in a slow breath.

"You are forbidden from entering our lands," another warrior—Zoijan, Cadeif's longtime friend and first fighter—barked. "When you were here last, because of your twig, we were visited by the Lucent Riders."

Thiel kept her gaze low. "I beg yer mercy, Cadeif. There is so much—so very much happening." She braved a look at his terse face.

Dark brown skin. Corded neck and muscles that had crushed enemies. He left no doubt what he could and would do. She reached toward Chima, the raqine giving a purr in response. But it was a different sound—not friendly but a nervous warning. "I know ye . . . I know we are not on good terms, but I would ask that ye hear me out."

Cadeif stared. Only stared. Anger coiled around his singewood-dark eyes.

"Tell us why we should not kill you all right now," Zoijan demanded.

Chima bent down and rumbled a low growl.

"We flew over the gorge," Thiel said with a shaky breath. "Sirdarians are coming."

Zoijan pried his angry glare from her and looked to his archon.

Still staring at her, Cadeif flicked a nod. Zoijan snapped out commands, and four Ematahri peeled from the shadows and sprinted across their path and into the other side of the woods. They would try to get a high vantage to verify her story.

"Ye should prepare to"—telling them to leave was like telling a dog to stop panting—"fight. They will be here by nightfall."

"We know," Cadeif said, his expression unaltered. "We invited them."

58

Darkness fell over Iteveria and bathed Karithia in an iridescent shimmer from the water tumbling past the balconies. Of course, Astadia Kath could not see that from this room—a servant's quarters buried far below the main levels and stuffed with ten bunks, a small fire, and hay for sitting. Their custodian, as they called him, stalked down the stone cellar, verifying all his hostages were in bed. Though *he* didn't call them hostages—such terms were forbidden—that's what they were. Movements closely monitored. Clothes provided. Meals served once a day. Still, this was a vast improvement over what they'd had camping with Poired.

But Trale, the obedient hound of the Infantessa, lay upstairs in a real room with real bedding and real food.

As the custodian came back by, returning to his office, Astadia lay motionless.

The witch of Karithia had a power over Trale that went beyond natural. She didn't know what her brother saw in the hag, why he fawned and followed her around like a leashed dog. But enough was enough. They'd delivered the Zaethien prince as commanded. Yet she hadn't released them. And Trale showed no interest in leaving.

Astadia would change his mind.

Snoring rattled through the cramped quarters.

She threw away her thin blanket and slid from the bunk, toes silently finding the floor. Trale had taught her how to slip in and out of a room—just like the one she fled now—without being noticed. She rushed through the darkened passage and up a level. He'd also taught her how to pick a lock—the one at the single high window tonight—and quick as a mouse, she was scurrying along the ledge of the palace, an empty chasm gaping into pitch black far below. She didn't care. She'd climbed bigger. Higher. With carefully placed hands, she scaled the bricked walls. Sidled past the main dining hall and up to the third level. Astadia went quickly but skillfully along the balconies to Trale's.

His guard stood with his back to the terrace, an ever-watchful guardian. She had to get the man outside to catch him by surprise. She tossed a pebble at the glass.

Plink.

The guard glanced over his shoulder but simply shifted his stance. Stayed.

With a huff, Astadia picked up another. Threw it harder.

Thunk!

The guard turned. Scanned the terrace.

Come on, she willed him outside.

His hand went to the lock.

Yes.

He flicked it and slid open the door. As he walked the balcony, his gaze went to his right. She came from the left. Slipped up behind the tall man. Hooked an arm around his throat and pulled back, pressing his head forward to cut off his air supply. He struggled, but she held tight.

When he finally went limp, she caught his hefty bulk and dragged him back into the room, so he wouldn't be seen by another guest who might not be able to sleep. She laid him in front of the door, then leapt onto the bed.

Trale came up, dagger in hand, his age-old instincts still intact.

Blade to her throat, Astadia grinned. "Hello, brother."

"Astadia," he said with a growl, slumping back. "What are you doing here?"

"I want a warm bed," she said sarcastically. Then slapped his temple—only then noticing the knot on his forehead. "What happened?"

"Nothing." He pushed her away and finally saw the guard. He shook his head. "You can't do things like that in her home. She will be angry."

"Why do you care about her? We did our job, Trale. It's time to leave." Feet tucked under her, she hugged herself. "I don't like it here. It's wrong."

"It's not wrong. The Infantessa is very good to us."

"You mean, like only giving you knots on your thick skull instead of chopping it off?"

"She's not like that!"

Astadia scowled. "You are the one who told me she was dangerous."

"I was misguided."

"Mis-*what*?" Astadia's heart thundered. "What is wrong with you? We need to leave. *Now*. While she isn't awake. We can be out of Iteveria before sunrise."

"No," Trale said. "I need to stay here. She needs me." He shook his head, eyes taking on more clarity. "The—the prince needs me."

"Needs you? She's using you!" Why could he not see that? "And that prince deserves whatever he gets, coming here of his own will. She—"

The guard groaned.

"Out," Trale ordered. "Quickly!"

"I want to leave this place," she hissed, hurrying to the door. "Make a plan, Trale, or I leave on my own. I won't wait forever." Out the window, she slid the door closed. Hopped to the ledge of the balcony and cast a glance back. Her brother helped the guard up, telling him he must have been tired because he'd fallen and hit his head on the glass. *He protects her but not me.* Betrayal sluiced through their relationship.

She eased over the rail and shuffled toward the next balcony. About to lower herself, she caught sight of a dull glow through the glass. It was Prince Haegan's room, wasn't it? A shout went out, and she nearly leapt backward, forgetting for a heartbeat that she stood over nothing but open air. She held fast, trying to sort what was going on in there.

The prince shouted again. She angled sideways and saw him. He thrashed in the bed. Dreaming.

The light—the light was coming from him. *That's right.* The prince was an accelerant. She'd heard rumors while traveling the Nine to capture him. Some even said he was the Fierian. Wouldn't that be a riot—for the Infantessa to have the enemy of Sirdar in her very home? Served the witch right. Astadia didn't care if she had the prince of the Nine or the Fierian or anyone else hostage. The Infantessa could not have Trale. Astadia would fight to the death for him.

A shadow moved. She flicked her gaze to it. Saw nothing. But then—

Astadia sucked in a breath. And froze. The Infantessa stood just inside the prince's room, hand extended toward him. What was she doing to him?

Haegan screamed. Arched his back, lost in some hellish nightmare. One created or agitated by the Infantessa.

It was cruel. Wrong. She was wrong.

Light blossomed. Grew. Spread over Astadia. She looked down, realizing she was fully illuminated. When she glanced up, the Infantessa stared back, glowering. Then shoved her hand at Astadia.

A burst of fire barreled out.

Astadia twisted around. Jumped off the ledge. Heard shattering glass. And dropped. Straight. Down.

59

Exhaustion weighted Haegan as he slipped into the chair at the dining table with Trale. Here it was, the evening meal and he felt like he'd just awoken. Sleep had been elusive, staved off by nightmares of unreal proportions, where he could not discern reality from fiction.

But his father—*his father!* Burning alive. Writhing in brutal agony in a dark, dank cell.

"Are you well, Prince Haegan?" Trale asked.

Haegan looked up, feeling the dull ache of exhaustion along the ridge of his brow. Torchlight felt like daggers behind his eyes. His sinuses were packed. "I am well. The Infantessa has been so kind—it is an honor to be here." A strange nausea swirled. Most likely from the headache. And lack of sleep.

"You look as if you could use a rest," Trale said.

"Aye," Haegan admitted, but he noted the dark circles beneath the assassin's eyes. "Am I mistaken, or are you tired as well?"

"I have trouble sleeping—comes with my line of work." He paused, looking troubled. "Have you seen my sister? I can't seem to find her."

"That's because she left Karithia," came the authoritative but soft voice of the Infantessa as she entered with four men.

Haegan and Trale struggled to their feet in her presence.

Lowering his head until she took her place, Haegan knew the assassin was anxious to speak of her notable pronouncement. The butler drew out her chair, and she slid in front of it, sitting as the chair came under her.

Trale and Haegan sat, as did the newcomers, who seemed to perch

RONIE KENDIG

strangely tall in the presence of the Infantessa. Haegan could not help but note the strange chill that ate at his bones had grown worse. His joints ached from it.

"Please," Trale said, "Infantessa, could you tell me of my sister's departure? It's most unusual. We never leave one another, if possible."

She shrugged. "I think she was jealous of me, with all the lovely attention you bestow upon me, Trale. Her custodian said she left Karithia in haste."

"When?"

Nydelia lifted a hand. "This morning, I suppose, but honestly"—she batted her eyes at them—"I couldn't be sure. Planning a ball in Prince Haegan's honor has taken all my time, I'm afraid."

"A ball?" The thought wearied Haegan, and he did not think it possible to further exhaust him. "To what end? I am only a guest."

"Oh, surely you know how important you are, Prince Haegan," she said with a laugh. "The prince of the Nine, *here*?" She scoffed. "The dignitaries are *dying* to meet you!"

"I did not think my presence would be welcome," Haegan said, irritated that she would so widely announce his location.

"You are sadly mistaken, my prince," she said. "Besides, if we are to marry, you must meet our allies."

Haegan froze. His mind would not process her words. "Marry?"

She sipped her soup and slurped it delicately—everything she did was delicate and pretty—before setting down her spoon. "Of course. That's why you came, isn't it? To secure an alliance?"

"I—I came because Trale said you sent for me." *An alliance would be good.* The thought startled him, but he was too tired to fight trivial things.

At this, the man on her left slid her a glowering look.

"Sent for you? Oh, I think our dear Trale must have misunderstood," she said.

"Yes, I misunderstood," Trale muttered. "I beg your mercy, Infantessa."

She touched his hand, then petted it. "You are such a dear, Trale."

Something . . . something wasn't right. It burned at the back of Haegan's mind. Wrestled to be free. The thought fought the restraints of exhaustion. What . . . what was he going . . . to think?

He would be King of the Nine. *I will need an heir. Nydelia is pretty and strong.*

"My *uncle* is here to approve of you, Prince Haegan," she said, pointing with her fork that held a chunk of meat. "Isn't that right, *Uncle?*" Sliding the meat into her mouth, she seemed especially happy.

But her uncle did not. Dark eyes, burning with hatred, seared into her, then turned to Haegan.

He blinked. Familiar. Very familiar. Panic jammed his heart. Fire roiled through the man's irises. The Desecrator!

'Tis your imagination. Surely he would not be here.

And then there was a smile on her uncle's face. "Of course, but I'm surprised you have found anyone good enough for you, Nydelia."

She laughed, a sound melodic and light.

Yet heavy. Dark.

Haegan gripped his head. His thoughts were a tangled mess.

"Are you well, my dear?" Nydelia asked, lifting her glass of wine. "You seem a bit peaked."

"Tired," he muttered. "I . . . I haven't slept well."

"Perhaps you should go rest. The ball is in two days, and you will need to be in your best shape."

"Of course." Obediently, Haegan set aside his napkin, stomach rife with nausea. "If you will excuse me." He pushed back and stumbled out of the dining hall. Though there existed a strange thrumming, it was dull. Easily ignored.

But the Infantessa—she wanted to bind with him! *What an honor!*

60

"You nearly ruined everything!"

Poired stood motionless before Infantessa Shavaussia, working to barricade his own anger against her. Careful to protect his thoughts. It wasn't that she could read minds, but she was the most powerful incipient he'd encountered—outside his own abilities. She could take every little sliver of doubt a person possessed and work it against them. "You treat them as playthings. He is the prince—"

"And I have relegated him to a fawning puppy." She drew off her gloves as they entered her sitting room. "Wine," she demanded of Paung and continued to her wide veranda overlooking the sea. "Have you found the girl's body yet?"

"Nay," the servant said.

Poired's fist clenched.

"With the tide," the servant continued, "it will take a few days for it to be washed up."

This time the witch had overstepped. "Killing the girl—she was mine! You asked for their help, I allowed you—"

"Yours?" she snarled. "She is a captive of Sirdar, and as such—"

"You go too far!" He could not stop the sneer. But he did manage to hold back the fire. "What if he had recognized me? You play with them like pets, and it will bring your destruction!"

"My abilities protected you, shielded you." Her eyebrow arched as her gaze traipsed his trim physique. "What it this, Poired? Why so much anger over a dead girl? She's an assassin. No one."

Fury tremored through him. But in a breath, he regained himself. "Give him to me. Give me the prince. I will end this and guarantee your continued . . . amusements."

"No," Nydelia said, then sighed. "And don't you dare touch him, or I will dig in that half-bald head of yours."

Poired slammed a volley at her. Pinned her against the wall. But even as he did, he felt her claw his mind. Refusing to allow her entrance, he released her. "Do not toy with me, Nydelia. Haegan is the Fierian."

A trickle of laughter rumbled through her. "Aye, and it is so much fun, watching his mind twit here and there, trying to sort everything." She giggled. "Trying and failing. He really is a weak-minded *twit*." She cackled.

"He may be young and inexperienced, but he is strong. Even I can see it's taking longer than normal for Haegan to succumb to your plyings."

"But he *will* succumb," she bit out, eyes dark. Desperate. When Paung returned with a tray of wine and glasses, she poured a very full one. "It is easy to convince him, to take every little insecurity and doubt and inflame it. Brilliant, really." She gulped her drink, then pointed at him. "And you're wrong, he's not strong."

Poired took a step forward. "He is. I sense that one day, your inflaming will no longer work."

"Of course it will! Everyone has doubts. All the time," she said around a swallow. "But there are some more difficult to inflame—the sister, for example. I had very little success with that thickheaded brat." She shrugged and dumped back her drink. "But that's one problem solved."

Poired drew up straight. Clenched his fists. Turned his thoughts back to the prince. "If word gets out that you have him here—"

"*Have* him here?" She snorted. "He came willingly. As a guest."

"You used my assassins, thwarted me—"

"*Your* assassins? They are tethered to Sirdar. As for Haegan . . ." Then she gave a giddy laugh. "I daresay, if anyone attempts to make him leave, he will protest. Loudly. Maybe even kill himself."

"He is the Fierian. It is foolish to think you can—"

"Don't call me a fool," she said with a glower. Then lifted her shoulders casually. "According to prophecy, the Fierian has a will for justice, to see Her way done." She gave him a rueful look. "There is no one beneath my roof who wills to be that instrument."

"When Haegan is angered, his Fierian abilities are . . . unmanageable," Poired said, remembering the encounter at Fieri Keep. "Something stopped him, but I daresay, had he stayed and fought, it would have been a bloody and long battle." All the more reason the prince had to die.

"You are so alluring when you talk strategy, but I have no reason to fear his anger because our dear prince is here of his own will."

"But how long will that last?"

"However long I want." She lifted her legs off the settee and turned to him, eyes narrowed. "You seem to think he *has* a will. Haegan has given himself to his doubts, which makes him mine. With each doubt that deepens, he surrenders any other opportunity. It will not take long to fully immerse him."

"He is the only one who can interrupt Sirdar's will. It's too dangerous to keep him alive. What if he overcomes your inflaming?"

"Overcomes," she guffawed. "That has never happened."

At that moment, his hatred of her greater than ever before, Poired wanted to kill the prince just to anger her. To pay her back for the girl.

But maybe it was his fear of failing and losing the one precious thing he had left on this planet.

Poired stilled. Fear of failing? He snapped Nydelia a glowering look, detecting that she'd gotten in his head. With a stomp, he sent a superwake into her. Slammed her back against the couch, nearly toppling her over it. "Stay out of my head!"

She readjusted on the sofa, wiping a trail of blood from her nose. Glowered. But then her smooth confidence slid back into place. "Really, that wasn't necessary. Go back to your war, Poired. The prince will not bother you, nor our lord, any longer."

"Kill him before it's too late!"

"I will . . . eventually." Another bounce of her shoulders. "But first, I will have a little fun destroying the hero of the Nine."

• • •

HEART OF LEGIER, NORTHLANDS

Aselan sat at the head of the elder table, sipping warmed cordi and watching the dancing and games. It had been hours of laughter and merriment. He recalled a decade ago, being brought to Etaesian's Feast. The celebration had seemed wild and unencumbered to him then, a young man of twenty and four, plagued with rebellion and anger toward a father who wanted nothing but to raise him in the legacy of Nivar. To one day sit on the throne and rule.

But a pair of brown eyes had swayed his heart. And within ten months, she abandoned him in the Heart. He dragged a finger over his lip, remembering all too well the raw agony of watching life slip out of her. Ingwait had hurried their dead child away. But he followed. Took his son before she placed him in the bier. And held him. Named him, as Doskari had wished.

"Will ye set yer dagger?" Petru asked in a rather loud shout, the fermented cordi loosening his tongue.

Aselan ignored him. Watched the pretty server girl smile at him. Recalled what Kaelyria had said of her, how she found him handsome. It could be his fear, that by setting his dagger on the table, he might end up with a girl like her, one not well-suited to him. Yet all women who participated had approval from the Ladies before going to the man's cave that night.

Still, it was why he would not set his dagger. Another choosing for him? He would not. Entirely too much risk.

A glimmer of light caught the pale blue of a satin gown, ushering a woman into the hall. Heat surged through his chest as he watched Kaelyria walk, unaided, into the festivities. Confidence had not returned to her, but strength had never left. He'd seen that since she first woke beneath those pelts after Chima had delivered her and her brother to the mountain.

Aselan stroked his beard and set aside his stein. Several men went to her, asking for a dance. Was it unkind that he found pleasure in her refusals?

Would she refuse me?

Somehow, he found himself crossing the room, the clot of men around her frustrating. But the crowd parted. He held out a hand to her. "We have a seat for ye, Princess."

A smile trembled across her lips as she placed her soft, warm hand in his.

"No fair," someone whined.

Aselan found pleasure in that, too. In her touch. In the way she glided to him. "Ye grow stronger."

"Not really," she whispered as he escorted her to a seat beside Ingwait, as propriety dictated. She smiled as he drew out the chair and helped her onto it. "Thank you for the rescue, Cacique."

He gave a curt bow and returned to his place, lifting the stein again and gulping from it. As the dancing ended, the men returned to the table and the food was served. Loud chatter and laughter filled the hall.

"Ye know," Byrin said as he plucked a thick leg of turkey from the plate. "'Twas a low blow."

"What was?" Aselan stared at the meat and potatoes, but he had no stomach for food.

"Walking her to the table—ye took her right out of their arms."

Good. "She was in no man's arms."

"Aye, but what ye did ensured she would *never* be in anyone's—except yers."

"Ye exaggerate." Aselan took a bite, so he didn't have to talk. But Byrin was right. And Aselan could not feign ignorance, though he'd like to. He didn't want anyone else trying to claim her or win her favor.

Which made no sense because he would not set his dagger. 'Twas not fair to her. Or the men.

He threaded his fingers and rested his elbows on the table as the men fell into idle chatter, nerves buzzing as they anticipated the Hour of the Daggers. Aselan pressed his mouth against his hands, thinking. Weighted with a tug to do it. To abandon fear and what-ifs.

But she is a princess.

And there were a thousand what-ifs tied up in that title.

But ye were born a prince.

She'd been so warm, so willing in his arms a couple of weeks past when she'd cried. When he held her, felt the silk of her hair against his hands. The heat of her breath as she cried into his tunic. And the clear longing when he'd considered kissing her.

Laughter erupted from the Ladies' table. Kaelyria had her head thrown back, holding her stomach as she laughed. She really was so beautiful. Her laughter infectious. They liked her. Accepted her.

A small girl—*was that Vork's little one?*—rushed up behind Kaelyria and set a wreath of flowers on her head.

A shout went through the hall, then a ringing applause. The wreath had named Kaelyria the fairest of the ladies. It would garner her a new dress by the seamstresses. Kaelyria thanked the little one and hugged her. And those icy blues came to Aselan. Did she know how very beautiful she was? What she did to his mind and will?

Matron Ingwait stood, clanking a fork against a cup. The hall quieted, the men slapping each other on the back. "Behind the pelt throne, the table waits for the men to place their daggers. As ye all know, we will continue dancing throughout the night. The men will leave their daggers and return to their caves. The feast will end when the last eligible woman who has applied for the Choosing selects a dagger."

Whoops and hollers went up. Aselan glanced toward the thrones, imagined beyond them, the table waiting to change the lives of the Legiera.

"In two days' time, we will gather here again to recognize the newly bound couples."

More shouts went up and bled into another hour of dancing and singing. Shouting and revelry. Annoyance gripped him when Byrin defied Aselan's unintentional claim and pulled Kaelyria to the dance floor, with her offering objections the entire way.

Aselan gritted his teeth. Fist balled, he watched the whole dance. Swore he would punish Byrin. Give him extra duties on the peak with the ice and snow. Perhaps cleaning the raqine nest. Without armor.

A gong clanged.

The men roared, pumping their fists. And without any further instruction, they all but shoved each other aside to round the fabric divider that separated the pelt throne and the table. 'Twas time for the men, whether or not they had decided to enter the Choosing, to pass by in ceremony, then leave the hall.

As cacique, he was to remain until all men left the hall. Once he saw Byrin nudging the last male through the door, Aselan came to his feet. Avoiding blue eyes, he gave a stiff bow to Matron Ingwait, surrendering his place as leader. He made the long walk behind the pelt throne.

Slowing at the table, he smiled at the offering—there must be close to fifty daggers. When had he ever seen so many?

'Twas not desperation but hope. He touched the daggers with his left hand and drew out his own with his right. He held it over the others in both hands.

Would she refuse me?

He could only know one way.

Heart in his throat, Aselan set down the dagger. Was he being foolish? She was young, beautiful. What would she want with a burly mountain man like him? He buried it beneath the others, somehow feeling less . . . foolish. And strode out the side door as the others had. The halls were empty, the thrum of anticipation great.

Ye are *a fool.*

Regret spun him back to the door, but the thick wood swung shut. A solid click told him it was locked. *Hiel-touck!* He huffed a breath. *'Tis done.* He forced himself to his cave, set his chair against the far wall and sat. Bent forward, he rested his elbows on his knees and again pressed his mouth to his knuckles.

Ye are a blazing fool. Thinking she would choose him.

He glanced at Duamauri, who watched him patiently beside his mate, Sikir. "Ye would have been smarter, aye?"

Sikir squinted.

"Aye." Aselan sighed. He must resolve himself to accept what may come. Humiliation. An ill-suited match.

Duamauri's ears twitched toward the entrance, and Aselan's heart vaulted into his throat. He watched the tapestry over his cave entrance, willing it to stir. But he remained there, each quarter hour sinking his hopes. Ones he had known better than to have. Why would one who'd seen the Nine, who'd lived with riches and luxury, choose this life? Choose him? Concealed in a mountain. With naught but a stone home and wooden chairs. A pelt. And icehounds.

Fool. He pressed the heels of his palms to his forehead. Pushed his hands through his hair. Might as well bed down. Face the humiliation of retrieving his dagger from Ingwait tomorrow. She would love this. His insipid pride on display when his dagger was the only one left unclaimed.

Aselan drew off his tunic and reached for his bed shirt.

Heads swiveling up, his hounds let out a soft growl. Air stirred behind him. He pivoted. And his heart stopped. The tapestry shifted. Kaelyria entered, hesitating at the threshold, hands cradling his dagger.

61

Pain wrenched his shoulders as two Sirdarians hauled him down the passage. His legs were weights. His vision blurry. But he had enough sense to know they were dragging him through the Citadel.

Drracien jerked. Shoved his feet under him. Pitched himself backward. Jerked again. Thrust a hand—He stilled, staring at the Tahscan steel rimming his wrists. "No." Shielders. They'd shielded him, stifled his ability to wield.

One of the guards laughed, yanking him forward again.

The halls shifted. They must have drugged him, too. This . . . this did not feel right. Did not feel normal.

Seconds—*hours?*—later, he was tossed to the ground. Four more guards knelt around him, bolting large iron shackles around his arms and legs, securing him against the obsidian marble. He slumped, his cheek against the cold surface. "What are you doing?"

The guards retreated to the wall even as the air changed. The squeak of boots heralded someone's approach. Their person marched around his outstretched arms, and the slick-booted toes stopped inches from his face. "Hello, Drracien."

Straining, he stared up into darkness defined—Poired. His stomach heaved. "No no," he growled, thrashing against the restraints. Whatever his intent, it would not be good. And Drracien wanted no part in it.

"Diavel, now." Even as Poired's voice coiled around his mind, there came the lurking shadow of a creature. It stalked forward, head down, purr-growling. It circled Drracien, its breath rancid. A raqine. Wisping in and out of sight.

Drracien shook his head, yet couldn't look away. What was going on? The creature was there, then not there. Half raqine. Half Void Walker.

Histories, Legacies, Parchments, lessons swirled into one massive vat of panic, spilling over Drracien. *By the Flames—a black raqine.*

The creature lunged at him. Rows of razor-sharp teeth sank into his shoulder.

Excruciating pain—like being burned alive from the inside—exploded through his shoulder. Then his chest. His entire body. Until Drracien felt sure he would explode. He howled in agony.

• • •

Poired watched in morbid fascination as Diavel stalked back from the boy, circling, snarling, snapping. Drracien's screams rattled the windows. The guards shifted, but Poired steadied them with a single hand. He waited. Watched.

He winced as the boy thrashed, head bouncing off the black floor like a ball. Poired had gone through the shift as well. Traversing the Void before his time. Blood appeared at Drracien's nose and the corners of his mouth. Then he lay still. Embraced in death.

A guard started toward the boy.

Without looking, Poired flicked a fiery dagger through his heart. The guard fell dead. Poired crouched, forearms on his knees as he studied the boy. How long would it take him to return?

Ragged and reeking, a breath trickled from Drracien. Dark eyes blinked. Took in his surroundings, confused. No doubt catching up on the last ten years of his life.

Poired stood. Moved to the dais. With a snap of his fingers, he freed the restraints.

Dragging himself to his feet, Drracien looked at the guards. He stumbled and staggered as if drunk. His gaze slowly drifted to Poired. Awareness, understanding, filtered into the eyes so like his own.

"Do you remember who you are?" Poired asked.

Drracien held his gaze. Defiance wavered in his eyes.

Poired extended a hand and pulled on the dark embers coiled in Drracien's abiatasso, eliciting a grunt from him. Only a grunt? "Do you remember?"

Those eyes stared back. "Aye."

"Aye, what?"

"Aye, Father."

• • •

CASTLE KARITHIA, ITEVERIA, UNELITHIA

Shouts went out through Karithia.

Nydelia shot from her bed and her servant was there, robing her as they rushed toward the door. "What is the matter?" But she felt it. Felt the sickeningly sweet aroma. "No," she rasped.

Her guards stood in the hall, hands on their hilts.

Maybe she had been wrong. They weren't rushing about, but staring . . . "What is it?" she asked, tying the belt.

"The prince," one said. "He's gone down to the lower levels."

Anger rushed through Nydelia. She seized it and threw a bolt at the guard. It struck his throat, and he collapsed as she stalked past him, fury building. Down the grand staircase, she saw torchlight scampering across the marble floor. Into the open doorway to the lower levels. Four guards stood, staring into the darkness.

Imbeciles. Clawing the air with her right hand, she pinched her lips. Drew heat from the palace and aimed it at the four. They fell in a heap on top of each other. They had failed her, allowing the prince to venture even to the main level. Her foot hit the floor quietly, and she became aware of the cold air. The very, very cold air.

She turned a slow circle. Such a drop in the temperature could only mean one thing—a very powerful accelerant was wielding. "Where are you?" she whispered. Poired had been right. Haegan had proven more difficult to inflame, but she'd never cowered from a challenge.

"It will be your destruction."

"We'll see about that," she muttered angrily.

The air tingled. Strange. Burning. Yet icy. It made no sense.

Voices came up the stairwell. Livid that the prince had gotten so far from his quarters, she turned to singe the first person who came out of that well.

Stone light glinted on long, blond curly hair as Haegan came into view, his gaze vacant. Holding his arm, the custodian was behind him, darkness in his eyes. Two guards followed.

"What's—"

The custodian held a hand to his lip. "Sleepwalking."

With a roll of her hand, she influenced Haegan's dreams to a lulled state that would return him back to his suite. With a nod to the guards, she ordered them to ensure the prince's arrival back in his room. "Did he see . . . ?" she hissed.

"No," the custodian said. "I was down there, talking with our guest, when the guards gave warning. He never made it far enough. Those dreams torture him, make—"

"Tortured with memories," she seethed. "*He's* calling to him."

"Impossible," the custodian said. "That's the stuff of raqines, not accelerants. And he was never that strong, and I cap his ability."

"You think too highly of yourself."

"I was trained by the best," he said, his eyes hooded with arrogance and loathing.

"Had Sirdar not sent you, I would have killed you long ago." Agony exploded across her temple, knocking her sideways. Gripping her head, Nydelia cried out against the excruciating pain.

And like a flash, it was gone.

The custodian frowned. "My lady?"

Startled, uncertain of what had just happened, she slowly straightened, carefully removing her hands. She gathered her skirts and hurried back to the third level. The guards were waking a groggy Thomannon, and Haegan now lay asleep in his bed.

Another blast of pain nearly sent Nydelia to her knees. The aroma smothered her. She stumbled. *No no no.*

"My lady?" her servant was there, catching her arm.

"What was that?"

"My lady?"

"I know."

They both turned to find Haegan sitting up. His eyes were focused but his voice . . . empty of emotion, conviction. "I know what this is," he said. He climbed from bed, went to the balcony, and slid back the door, then moved to the balustrade.

Giving an uncertain glance to the guards, Nydelia followed the prince onto the terrace. "What are—"

Electricity shot through her as she saw him. Standing like a pillar taller than any building in the city, he stood in full golden armor on the Iteverian shore. Head helmed, arms shielded and hands protected as they held a monstrous blade, he stared straight ahead—at her. Thrilling. Terrifying. Unmoving.

"Do you see them?" Haegan's voice was empty still. Droning.

Them?

"Fires of Sirdar, how many are there?"

Nydelia sprinted out of the room and up to the rooftop terrace. Panting hard, she ran from one side to another. "Five, there are five!" she shouted as the guard and Haegan joined her. But there weren't six. So maybe . . . Her mind struggled around the missing one. "They have encircled Karithia."

"My lady?" the guard asked. "What is wrong? Is there an attack?"

"What do you call those, if not an attack, you imbecile?"

"What, my lady? I see nothing."

"Do you not?" she screamed angrily, her pulse throbbing in her temples. "They stand over the city."

"Who?"

"Baen's Deliverers," Haegan muttered, staring at one in particular. "Why are they here? They told me not to kill him."

"Kill who?"

"Poired," Haegan droned, his mind a wasted space, drowning in his doubts and fears. "They told me it was not mine to do."

"*Nydelia!*" a voice resonated through the air with such ferocity, the building shook. "*Release the Fierian or face judgment.*"

• • •

Relegated to myth and legend, Baen's Six converged in the Void, their bodies column-like statues in the world as they surrounded Iteveria where the Fierian was held hostage. "Draorin, report."

"I am with the paladin," he said.

"Is he safe? And the Council?"

"Three are lost, but the paladin and the guardian are well. Fleeing the Citadel."

"Good," Medric said. "Drive the paladin east. He must converge here."

"What of the Fierian?" Draorin inquired.

"Fallen," Medric managed around a heavy heart. "We will ensure she releases him. He will not die here."

"She is defiant," Kaiade added. "And furious—he is resisting, though he has allowed his doubts to rule him."

Draorin nodded. "The Infantessa will not easily surrender the Fierian. She will fight to her last breath to stop it from happening."

"Aye. But it is written that she will die at his hand," Draorin said with a smile.

"So be it," Medric growled. "Let us introduce her to that end."

ALPHABETICAL
CHARACTER INDEX

Aaesh—Aaeshwaeith Adoaniel'afirema; servant girl in the Heart

Aburas—high-ranking officer in Thurig's guard/army

Arak Kcep—daughter of Duke and Duchess Wrenkyle; Contender for Hetaera

Adek—member of the Council of Nine

Adin—former king of Iteveria

Adomath—an Ignatieri, who condemned Haegan before the Great Falls

Adrroania Celahar—queen of the Nine Kingdoms

Agremar Ro'Stu—son of Kenbrin Ro'Stu; Electreri of the Viddan Council; master sentinel; Contender

Ah'maral—wagon master

Aloing—deceased high marshal; trained Drracien

Aoald—member of the Council of Nine; nasally voice; member for Caori

Aselan—Cacique of Legier's Heart

Astadia Kath—Iteverian assassin; sister to Trale

Astante—Jujak major

Atai—female servant in Nivar hold

Atelaria—Thiel's cousin; Neron and Laralith's daughter; from Langiera

A'tia—woman on farm

Bardin—member of the Legiera

Bæde—member of the Council of Nine; killed by a Deliverer for taking a bribe and betraying the Council

Baen Celahar—first Celahar to take the Fire Throne; assumed name Zaelero as king; fought the Mad Queen

Byrin—right hand of the cacique; member of the Legiera

Cadeif—Ematahri warrior; archon; claimed and protected Thiel years past

Calb—citizen of Baen's Crossing

Caprit—Member of the Legiera

Cerar—Ematahri clan Haegan wiped out

Chima—female raqine; bonded to no human; larger than Zicri

Chiphliæng—enemies of the Fierian; siblings

Chwik—skinny young man who's part of Tili's unit in the trials

Cicaelia—Thurig Eriathiel's younger sister

Cilicien ka'Dur—disgraced accelerant

Claerian—a Jujak under Graem's command

Cypal Webst—daughter of Marq and Rovi Webst; Electreri; contender from Praenia

Darielle Jurden—honey-haired girl, part of Tili's contingent in the trials

Degra Breab—daughter of Ang and Ahn Breab; an Electreri; contender from Kerral

Deh'læfhïer—mentioned in the Parchments as the defender of the Fierian; Deliverers

Dewyn of Adrili—prince from Wicalir; Electreri

Diavel—Poired's raqine

Dirag the Desecrator—slain by Baen Celahar before he became Zaelero II

Doskari—Aselan's late wife

Draorin—Baen's (Zaelero's) right hand

Draorin—Deliverer

Dromadric—grand marshal of the Ignatieri

Drracien Khar'val—fugitive marshal; friend of Haegan, Thiel, Tokar, and Laertes

D'wyn—Kergulian man who's part of Tili's unit in the trials

Ebose—Zicri's brother; raqine

Ederac—Epitome of evil

Eftu—high marshal of Baen's Crossing

Eldin Gwogh—tutor to Prince Haegan; master accelerant; member of the Council of Nine

Elgni—Ignatieri from Baen's Crossing

Eliatzer—servant at the Hetaeran Sanctuary

Entwila—one of the Ladies of the Heart

Eriathiel—wife of Thurig the Formidable; Thiel's mother

Etan—Nivari warrior

Falip Wrel—new member of the Council of Nine; replaced Baede

Faus Sharton—Ybienn ambassador to the Nine

Fhurïætyr—mentioned in the Parchments; seemingly the Fierian; also means Reckoner.

Filcher—man who kidnapped and abused Thiel when she was 12

Galaun—attendant of High Marshal Aloing

Gaord—male servant in Nivar Hold

Gelas—Marshal in charge of Luxlirien

Ghor—Jujak under Graem's command

Griese—one of the Council of Nine

Grinda, Graem—secret love of Kaelyria in book 1; son of Kiliv Grinda

Grinda, Kiliv—Jujak general; one of Zireli's top three

Haegan Celahar—prince of Seultrie; heir of the Fire King; Son of Zireli

Henem Comed—daughter of Brid and Hecno Comed; Electreri; contender from Caori

Holdermann—Ybiennese councilman

Hoeff—Drigo; Toeff's twin

Inele Larrow—Ybienn ambassador to the Nine

Ingwait—elder of the Ladies of the Heart; oversees relational and social affairs

Jarain Fal'Raen—new mayor of Baen's Crossing

Jedric—nobleman from Vid; Kaelyria's betrothed

Kaelyria Celahar—daughter of Zireli and Adrroania; princess of Seultrie

Kaiade—Haegan's great-grandfather

Kedulcya—member of the Council of Nine; from Kerral

Kelviel—member of the Council of Nine; Hetaeran; black hair

Kenro Chfra—son of Keach Chfra, Commander General of the Leran army; Electreri

Kiesa—handmaid to Princess Kaelyria; Grijani

Kiliv Grinda—Zireli's general

Klome—raqine keeper in Nivar Hold

Korben—accelerant

Laejan—general; Jujaky

Laertes—young boy from Caori; one of four companions Haegan joined

Lanct—Jujak lieutenant

Laralith, Duchess—wife to Neron; Thiel's aunt

Lumira—Countess of Langeria; mother of Peani

Maer'ksh—duke in Hetaera

Makule—second in command of Nivari army

Mallius—Jujak; lieutenant

Markoo—one of the Legiera

Marsel—possibly the cook in the Heart; possibly in Nivar Hold

Marz Chauld—colonel in the Valor Guard

Matyon—young man in the Heart

Medric—Deliverer

Nagbe—boy in the cave during the trial

Naudus—Nivari fighter; Lieutenant

Negaer—general in Zireli's army; commander of the Pathfinders, an elite force of trackers and fighters

Neron, Grand Duke—Thiel's uncle

Nydelia—Infantessa

Ociliama Herra—princessa and daughter of Oci and Liama Herra, co-rulers of Dradith

Onerid—general under the command of Poired Dyrth

Pao'chk—great healer

Paung—butler at Karithia

Peani Clarentia Ibirel—Yaorid's daughter

Pesh—another captain in Thurig's army

Poired Dyrth—commanding officer of Sirdar's armies; enemy of all who follow Abiassa

Praegur—a Kergulian male; one of four companions Haegan joined on the journey to the Great Falls

Raechter—Ybiennese Councelman

Raleng—Ematahri; twin of Ruldan; serves Cadeif

Rauf—young man; lanky; helps old man help Astadia and Trale in the village

Rekkens—foreigners from the north, across the Violet Sea

Ruldan—Ematahri; twin of Raleng; serves Cadeif

Seraecene—daughter of a Ybiennese council member

Shavaussia—see Nydelia

Sirdar Demas of Tharqnis—Fallen One; Lord of Darkness; of Tharqnis; enemy of the Fire King and Abiassa

Tarien—servant

Teelh—Byrin's brother

Thelikor—Drigo warrior leader

Thiel—daughter of Thurig and Eriathiel of Nivar; one of four companions with Haegan on the journey to the Great Falls; also called Etelide and Kiethiel

Thomannon—Haegan's manservant in Karithia

Thræïho—mentioned in the Parchments; will fight for the Fierian; also called Drigovudd, or Drigo

Thurig Asykth—king of the Northlands

Thurig Eriathiel—duchess of the Northlands; wife to Thurig

Thurig as'Osmon (Osmon)—youngest son of Thurig

Thurig as'Relig (Relig)—third eldest son of Thurig; second-eldest acknowledged son

Thurig as'Tili (Tili)—eldest acknowledged son of Thurig

Thurig Kiethiel (Thiel)—daughter of Thurig; love interest of Haegan; claimed by an Ematahri (see Cadeif)

Tiadith—conductor in Baen's Crossing

Toeff—Drigo; Hoeff's twin

Tokar—one of four companions Haegan joins on the journey to the Great Falls

Tortook Puthago—blood of Ahnri Puthago, chamberlain of Hetaera; contender from the Citadel

Tnimre—one of the Ladies in the Heart

Trale Kath—Iteverian assassin; brother to Astadia

Traytith—member of the Council of Nine

Unduhar—traitor connected to the story of Manido and Ruadh

Verilla—Zoijan's sister and consort to Cadeif

Viloren—grand marshal; one of the most influential thinkers and accelerants of the last century

Voath—member of the Council of Nine

Wegna—old woman who lives in Aselan's library

Yaorid, Earl of Langeria—Northlands earl

Yedriseth of Haroessa—a guard for Yaorid; of the House of Haroessa from Langiera

Zaelero II—first Celahar to take the Fire Throne; born Baen Celahar; fought the Mad Queen and restored the Nine to the ways of Abiassa

Zendric—officer in Thurig's army

Zicri—male raqine; bonded to Tili; somewhat smaller than Chima

Zireli Celahar—king of the Nine Kingdoms; the Fire King

Zoijan—Ematahri warrior

Glossary Of Terms

Abiassa's Fire—the gift of wielding the Flames, possessed by only certain individuals

Abiassa's throne—a cliff formation resembling a throne; overlooks most of Hetaera; Great Falls visible from atop the throne "seat"

abiatasso—the gift in the essence of a person who has the ability to wield

accelerant—one who can wield the Flames

Alaemantu—also, Law of Alaemantu; custom of giving one night's hospitality to travelers

Archon—leader of the Ematahri

Auspex/Foreteller—held by Poired for the delivery of messages and orders from Sirdar

Baen's Crossing—village on border between Ybienn and the Nine

Bandra oak—a sturdy wood

boarbeast—big boar creatures with tusks; killers

calming—the exercise of relaxing one's emotions

cacique—title used among the Kerguli for their leader, their chieftain

Caori—one of the Nine Kingdoms; capital city of Luxlirien has Sanctuary

Castle Karithia, Iteveria—seat of Infantessa

Catatori Ocean—beyond the Iteverian sea

chïphlïæng—people or creatures that will be the emissaries of the Fierian

Choosing, the (aka Etaesian's Feast)—Eilidan custom for marriage rituals

Citadel—the central Sanctuary in the Holy City in Hetaera

cold-palm—a cutting nickname to anyone who cannot wield the Flames

Cold-One's Tooth—mountain peak nearest Nivar Hold

cordi—fruit

dallion—silver coin

Deliverer—an ageless minister of justice and discipline; powerful; answers only to the will of Abiassa; also called Lucent Riders, Void Walker, Light Bringer

Destroyers—demons

Drigo—ancient race of giants whose only goal is to serve

Drigovudd—the Drigo in their enhanced state

Duamauri—Aselan's icehound

Eilidan—people of Legier; Aselan's people

Emahtari—fierce forest dwellers; a threat to any traveling the Way of the Throne/Throne Road

Etaesian's Feast—see "Choosing, the"

exsaeilto Thræiho—words to release the Drigo from their vudd state

Fieri Keep—home of the Celahars, who rule from here on the Fire Throne

Fierian, the—a prophesied accelerant said to bring about the destruction of the Nine and the eradication of the Lakes of Fire

Fiery Mount—the range of mountains beyond Fieri keep that feeds into the Lakes of Fire

Fire King—king who rules the Nine and is the most powerful accelerant

Flames—reference to the gift bestowed on certain individuals; sometimes an epithet

goli birds—glittery sea birds

Grija/Grijani—warriors of the High Plains; Zireli's mother said to have been a Grijani

Great Falls—a waterfall blessed with miraculous healing every 100 years during the Year of Feasts as a gift from Abiassa

Harket's—mercantile shop in Luxlirien

he-ahwl abiałassø—the untranslatable word for the power the Fierian will wield, roughly means "all consuming"

Hetaera—largest city in the Nine; contains the Holy City; close to the Great Falls

hiel-touck—oath used in Legier; Asykthian

Holy City—the seat of the Ignatieri; the largest Sanctuary; contains the Citadel, where accelerants are trained and commissioned

icehound—very large wolves who only exist in cold-weather climates

Ice Mountain—nickname of Maon Targo

Ignatieri—holy order of accelerants; refer to each other as The Brethren

incipient—one who can wield but has turned against Abiassa

Infantessa—the queen of Iteveria

Iteveria—twin city to Nydessa, within Unelithia

jav-rod—spearlike weapon

Jujak—the elite, royal guard of King Zireli

Karithia—palace in Iteveria

Kedardokith—a rite of Ematahri warriors to claim the lives of outsiders as their own; intended for protection; once claimed, always claimed

Kerguli—a race of people from the desert Outlands of the far west

Kindling—a time of healing concurrent with the Year of Feasts

kyssups—enormous trees with roots thicker than most trees and grow partially above ground

Lakes of Fire—the lava lakes near Fieri Keep; a blessing of Abiassa and connected to the Flames

Legier—largest mountain overlooking Ybienn; home to the Eilidan, a race of mountain dwellers

Lucent Riders—the name given to the Deliverers by the Ematahri

Luxlirien—largest city closest Seultrie; also known as the Light City; capital city of Caori

Maereni—Poired's elite thirty guards; ruthless; assassins

mahjik—magic, especially dark magic

moonslight—light of twin moons

Mount Feuria—the mountain overlooking the Lakes of Fire

Mount Legier—formal name for the largest mountain; also known as Legier

muarshtait—animal droppings

needling—some form of punishment for initiates

Nivar Hold—seat of power in Ybienn; residence of King Thurig

Nivari—Thurig's army; commanded by his son, as'Tili

Nivar River—river near Nivar Hold

Nydessa—twin city to Iteveria; birthplace of Sirdar and Poired

paladiums—gold coins, high-value

pharmakeia—a physician who uses herbs and the Flames to bring healing/restoration

pitz—small value coins

pleuria—a bitter herb with strong healing properties; rare

Primar—Haegan's planet

Primerians—enormous horses bred for warriors of old; small numbers exist in the Northlands

Raeng—ruthless assassins from Iteveria

raqine—winged creatures widely believed extinct or myth

Ruadh, Manido, and Unduhar—mythical people from a legend about wrongful use of wielding

Sanctuary—a self-contained city controlled by the Ignatieri; each capital of the Nine has one

sangeen—herb that disrupts an accelerant's ability to wield

scoriae—remnant of wood once it's burned at a very high temperature

searage—wood scorched and glazed

sentinel—Ignatieri police who patrol Sanctuaries

Seultrie—capital city and seat of power for the nine allied kingdoms

Shadows, the—beyond the grave; dead

shielders—cuffs that prevent accelerants from wielding

Shriekers—feral birds that are vicious, attacking anything that moves; a vulture

Siannes—formidable mountain range along the Way of the Throne

Sikir—Aselan's female icehound

singewood—coveted trunks of trees growing near the Lakes of Fire; core burns without being consumed; an epithet for someone speaking in ignorance or stupidity

Sirdarian—one of Sirdar

sowaoli petals—flower petals

Tahsca/Tahscan—from House Tahsca off the coast of Iteveria; fiercest sea-faring warriors

Tri-Tipped Flame—a constellation; symbol of House Celahar

Unauri—a race of Drigo; served the Supreme King; driven mad by the abuse suffered at the hands of those they served; slaughtered thousands in the Great Siege, betraying the Fire Kingdom and Abiassa

Umelyria/ Umelyrians—the original city of the Supreme King, set in power by Abiassa Herself; Her people

Unelithia—Combined realm of Nydessa and Iteveria; ruled by Sirdar of Tharqnis

Void Walker—Deliverer or one of the evil counterparts; one who walks between worlds

Watchman—man of the Violet Sea Watch

Yaopthui lands—lands beyond the sea out from Iteveria

Ybienn—sovereign kingdom, separate from the Nine; seat of Thurig and his family

ACKNOWLEDGMENTS

To my amazing editor—Reagen Reed. You got crazy-mad skills, and I'm so honored to work with you. Thank you for enduring my questions and panic-driven emails. Ha! It's a beautiful thing to trust an editor so implicitly with my stories!

Bethany Kaczmarek—You have been such a saving grace and god-send. I'm so glad to count you among my friends, and my editors!

Kara Peck—For reading a raw, awful first draft of this and saying it was amazing. Haha! To Starbucks and book-buddy reading!

ABOUT THE AUTHOR

Ronie Kendig is an award-winning, best-selling author. She lives in beautiful Northern Virginia with her hunky hero, their children, and a retired military working dog, Vvolt N629. The author of Rapid-Fire Fiction, Ronie and her action-packed stories transcend genres and engage readers with an exciting, clean read. She speaks to various groups, teaches at national conferences, and mentors new writers.

Ronie can be found online:

WEBSITE: *www.roniekendig.com*
FACEBOOK: *www.facebook.com/rapidfirefiction*
TWITTER: *@roniekendig*
GOODREADS: *www.goodreads.com/RonieK*
PINTEREST: *www.pinterest.com/roniek*
INSTAGRAM: *@kendigronie*

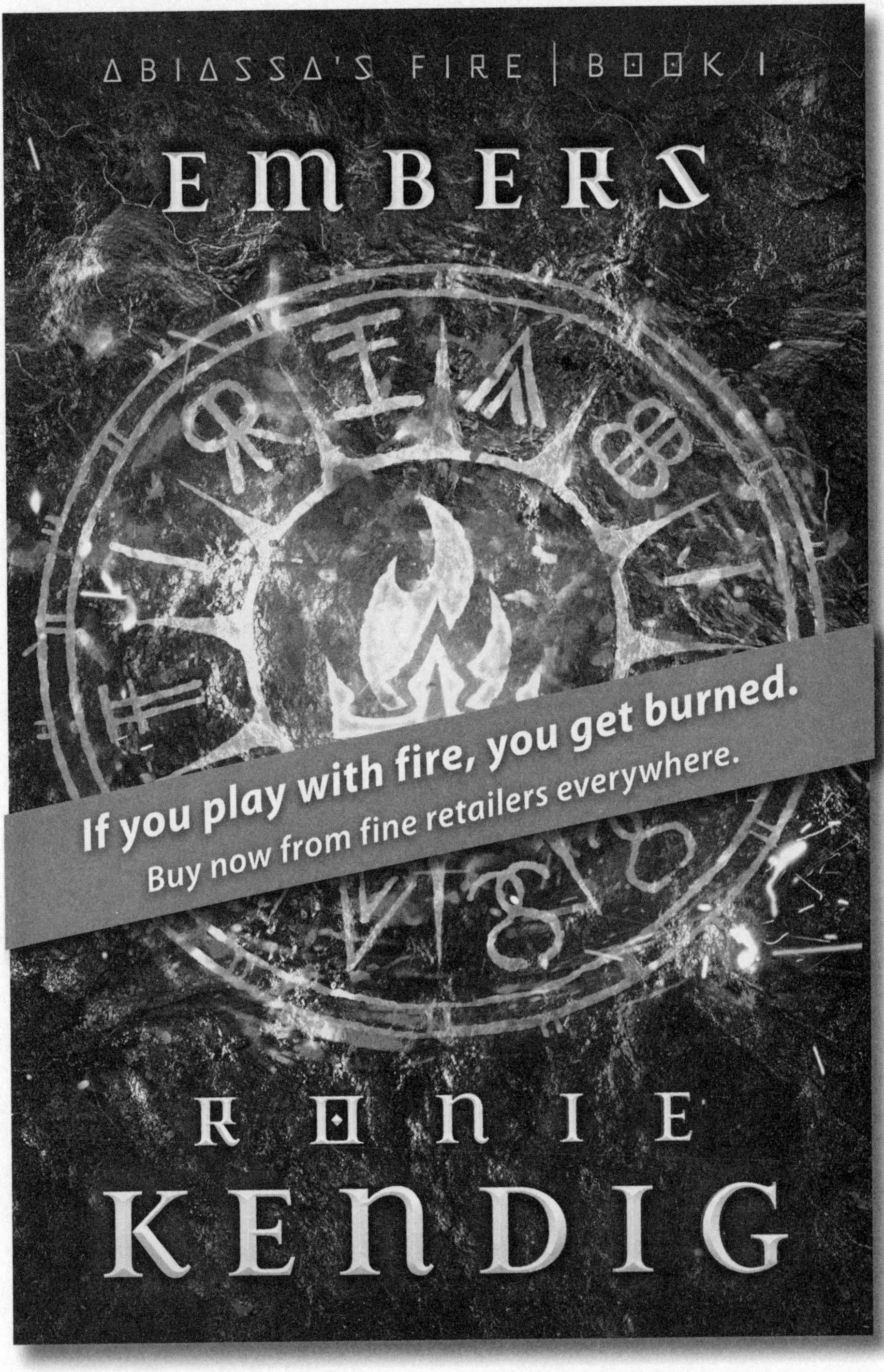
ABIASSA'S FIRE | BOOK I
EMBERS
If you play with fire, you get burned.
Buy now from fine retailers everywhere.
RONIE
KENDIG